TYGER BURNING

TYGER BURNING

T.C. McCARTHY

BAEN

TYGER BURNING

This is a work of fiction. All the characters and events portrayed in this book are fictional, and any resemblance to real people or incidents is purely coincidental.

A Baen Books Original

Baen Publishing Enterprises
P.O. Box 1403
Riverdale, NY 10471
www.baen.com

ISBN: 978-1-4814-8410-7

Cover art by Dominic Harman

First Baen printing, July 2019

Distributed by Simon & Schuster
1230 Avenue of the Americas
New York, NY 10020

Library of Congress Cataloging-in-Publication Data

Names: McCarthy, T.C., author.
Title: Tyger burning / T.C. McCarthy.
Description: Riverdale, NY : Baen, 2019.
Identifiers: LCCN 2019008809 | ISBN 9781481484107 (paperback)
Subjects: | BISAC: FICTION / Science Fiction / Adventure. | FICTION / Science Fiction / General. | GSAFD: Science fiction.
Classification: LCC PS3613.C3563 T94 2019 | DDC 813/.6--dc23 LC record available at https://lccn.loc.gov/2019008809

Printed in the United States of America

10 9 8 7 6 5 4 3 2 1

BOOK ONE

"Tyger, tyger, burning bright . . ." —William Blake

When the Sommen Came

Lev reminded himself to keep his head bowed and to avoid staring. An entire mob passed, all of them wearing combat suits, many patched to the point where he wondered if the garments had any chance of protecting their wearers but protection wasn't really the point—not for the Sommen. The more patched, the greater the warrior. That was the point.

One of the soldiers kicked as it walked by, sending Lev into a drift of ammonia snow, fine and dry. "No-name, keep your head lower."

No-name.

"Don't let it get to you," said Michael, helping Lev back to his feet. "And I know your name." They glanced down the road, in both directions, to confirm that no more Sommen were in sight before resuming their commute.

"How many more resupplies?" Michael asked.

Lev sighed. "One."

"One? *Imagine.* Soon you'll be like that old Lupan Merchant. I forget his name, but you know the one: barking orders as though born to the Merchant class, more Sommen than the Sommen themselves. It's good that you're so lucky because you're the only other human in our group and we're both from Zaporozhye, so that has to mean something—like we wound up together and we're both still alive. Luck is with us."

Lev didn't feel lucky; he felt old—old enough to remember what it had been like on ten different worlds, his pressure suit replaced three times, twice barely repaired in time to seal in the oxygen. He

3

flexed the right gauntlet and winced. His knuckles had gotten worse in the last few months, the suit's wrist joints were too tight and a slight whiff of ammonia tainted his oxygen with maybe some methane, and Lev forgot if the contamination caused arthritis but that's what he blamed; old age often had an accomplice. Everything blurred now. It was better to not think, better to forget that at the end of this run he'd have what he came for: Sommen Merchant status, and with it? *A name.* Lev banished the dream as soon as it materialized. Too many things could happen in no man's land, so many opportunities for the misfortunes of age, and he hadn't seen Earth since he was twenty-five and had trouble remembering what it was that he missed; it bothered him, the lack of memories an infected splinter that he had to excise. Better to think of things lost—or better still, things lost *and* forgotten—than what could be gained in the future. The already lost never brought new disappointments.

Vushka. The name triggered memories, the door to his past kicked in. These were his mother and father, crying, just before waving good-bye to watch Lev march across the steppes toward the waiting Sommen merchant fleet. This was his grandmother. Grinning, toothless, she poked the logs in her Lviv fireplace and wheezed in a hoarse laugh that made him smile and cringe at the same time, made him wonder if maybe she'd die on the spot and fall into the fire to be consumed and forgotten. Vushka. It was all his parents ate, all they fed him as a child, but then that wasn't true because there were plenty of other foods but vushka was the only thing that Lev remembered these days, the only thing that ever came to him. And it was enough. Enough to invite other memories so he could recall his family just one more time, to accept the fact that by now they were dead.

"Are you blind?" Michael hissed.

Lev blinked. They had arrived at the outpost and a line of no-names gathered to wait, all of them showing their respect, all staring at him until Lev dropped to his knees.

"Idiot," said Michael, "you won't make Merchant if you keep acting the fool."

"Misha, why did you do it?"

"What do you mean?"

"I mean why. Why didn't you stay on Earth, at home?"

Michael waited a moment before answering. "It wasn't a hard decision, Lev. You left years ago and things got worse, not better. When I left we had finally exhausted metals in the asteroid belt and still the Sommen trapped our ships within the solar system. The Americans sent an entire fleet against them—to try and get beyond, out into the galaxy."

"And?"

"No survivors."

Lev chuckled at the thought of dead Americans, trying to figure out why it should seem so funny until he gave up; it wasn't *funny;* he had become perverse. The temperature indicator crept downward and he imagined the planet's always-there clouds thickening, pregnant with a snow that would come whether anyone wanted it or not. It began as a sprinkle—as if someone flew overhead scattering salt to patter against his helmet. Within minutes a new layer coated the road and surrounding hills, muffling everything, and Lev suspected that should he remove his helmet it would be difficult to hear anything beyond a few meters away, anything less than a scream. The snow would be dry. Squeaky and slick. Once his exhaust melted the ammonia-water mix he could slide down a gentle slope to get lost in a mile-deep drift or sail off a bottomless cliff and maybe both were a fine way to go—better than a slow death on Earth . . .

"Misha," said Lev, "they hadn't invaded by the time you left Earth? The Sommen still hadn't taken her?"

"No. Just quarantined the entire system."

Lev was about to ask another question when he doubled over coughing, one blending into the others in a continuous roar until blackness took everything, forcing the suit lights to fade. He wasn't gone for long. The chronometer indicated that barely a minute had passed by the time he came around, watching as the mules danced in the snow around him, their engines whining and blowing cones of exhaust into the air to crystallize and drift downward in sparkling veils, making him grin. *Warsaw.* The frost reminded him of the city's winter just before he left, when Marina had dragged him from the club and into the snow on one of those mornings so cold it made his nose hurt, made his fingers numb in seconds except for where they touched her. She had smiled at him, called him crazy. For wanting to leave Earth he was eccentric, but for wanting to leave her he was a true nut case, someone to be pitied except that neither of them felt sad about the parting because they had both been in it for the sex anyway, too self-absorbed for anything approaching love and so . . . she gave him one last kiss and headed into town, calling over her shoulder a kind of good-bye: "Don't forget what my ass looks like, Lev."

The mules were as old now as Marina had been then. Twenty. And Lev cared for them in spite of everything because his life depended on the things, because facing the laughter from the named Merchants who never bothered to hide contempt for humans was easy; it was their curiosity that was difficult. The first Sommen warrior who had seen the mules approached Lev with amusement and it had been early in the game so that Lev hadn't yet learned the protocol: When speaking with a warrior you never looked it in the eye. He lost three teeth and part of his tongue when the Sommen had kicked in the side of his face, dragging one claw through his right cheek and then out the left. A lesson—to mind one's manners.

Yet even the Sommen got the point of mules, knew what Lev was thinking, because after the blow the warrior had tossed Lev a suit-sealer. "Robots so primitive they have almost no signatures. Nothing. You will live a long time, a breather of oxygen and poison and a true coward whom death cannot find."

But that was almost as old as his memories of Marina. Today the alien steppes stretched out to the horizon and blended into the sky, white and gray so that he had a moment of difficulty in telling up from down and had to sit again, the coughing threatening to resume.

Michael helped him to his feet. "It's good this is your last trip, Lev. The ammonia. It's taking to your lungs, eroding your tissues."

"And someday, Misha, all this will be yours."

Michael's voice sounded raspy over his headset, and Lev wondered if the ammonia had already started its work on him. "Mules. Everyone else uses grav carts and high-speed auto-tractors, but old Lev Sandakchiev? *He* uses ancient robotic mules that need oxygen tanks to even *function.*"

"And grav carts leave an electromagnetic trail that can be spotted for thousands of kilometers, from space. I've seen entire resupplies wiped out before the Merchants ever heard a sound or knew what was coming."

"It's all about planning, old man," said Michael. "You plan your runs to go between satellite passes, shut down at the tiniest sign of remote detection or scanning. Planning, Lev, and by now you'd have moved more than enough cargo to afford a thousand mules."

Lev pushed past him toward the general direction of the front lines, not bothering to check the guidance system, trusting instinct to get them through the snow. Angry.

"I *have* a thousand mules, Misha. And while other humans died for the sake of speed, I live. Slow and steady, like the tortoise, so I don't have to shut down for overhead surveillance and don't have to worry about dark angels above because nobody ever thinks to look for old Earth technologies. You are *of* Earth, Misha. Have some pride."

A sea of headless mules kept pace with them, bouncing up and down through the snow on four legs, cutting a path for the two men as they followed. Lev enjoyed controlling the things with his keypad, watching them turn in unison when he commanded it—like having control over a flock of grounded sparrows. Each one carried five hundred kilos of cargo. He grinned with joy when fifty of them slammed into a massive ammonia drift, sending a spray of snow into the air as if the planet itself had just vomited ice.

"My mules are magnificent!" Lev shouted, almost missing the alarm indicator on his display.

"Lev?" Michael asked, his voice a whisper. "A nano-mine just activated."

"I see it. You know the procedure, Misha. Run. It's your only chance." Lev refused to look at him now, fought the urge to scream and keep on screaming, the twin sensations of futility and despair so familiar that he almost failed to recognize them. Michael was young—too young to deserve this, and it wasn't fair and he hated the Sommen for it, for forcing the boy to leave Earth because staying home had become just as dangerous as serving them on resupply. Just as dangerous as war.

"Lev, they've locked on, *help me!*"

"I can't help you, Misha," Lev explained. The tears flowed freely now, his knowing that he had no help for Michael—that nobody could have helped—making it worse. "Once nanos zero on a signature, there's nothing I can do but go on; supplies have priority, Misha, I'm sorry. We'll both die if I stay. You must have had a suit defect that went unnoticed during inspection, something that caused a characteristic emission, one that triggered an old minefield geared toward organic life. That must be it. We just wandered into an old nano-minefield, one that's not even charted. I'm so sorry."

Lev closed his eyes. He imagined. It didn't take much to imagine anything so horrible, not since he had seen it all happen before, and especially not since Michael screamed until the last second before being consumed.

Better to forget, Lev reminded himself. Better to pretend that boys such as Misha never existed and instead focus on the beauty of the mules as they bounded through the drifts, their engines whining and screaming with perfect effort, oblivious to the threat of nanos because no nanos would have been calibrated to target anything so simple and so harmless. So terrestrial.

And the front was close now. Vibrations shook the ground under his feet.

Lev had just finished offloading cargo into the nearest storage unit when he felt his gut twist in fear, plasma artillery ripping open the air to send him flying against the entrance to a bunker. He slid down the stairs. But before he could collect himself—hand in his invoice and confirm the final shipment—the door opened and one of them snatched Lev by the helmet, lifting him off the ground and several feet into the air where his feet kicked like a child's. The thing tossed him inside and shut the door.

An isba. The term was old, so old that Lev shouldn't have even remembered it but he did, recalling the time he had gone skiing near Almaty during a cold spell that kept them from setting foot outside the cabin: an isba, half earth and half log with a blaze that allowed his friends to lounge in underwear, made them all sweat while the wind howled outside at forty below. The bunker reminded him of that time, but in nightmare. More than thirty Sommen had arranged themselves in a circle and were half naked, their skin covered with scars and mottled with the signs of deep plasma burns, so horrific that Lev forgot himself and stared until he appreciated his mistake and flinched to close his eyes. He waited for the blow.

"You are the Apprentice, the human on its final run," one said, Lev's suit translating its voice into a sterile Ukrainian, coaxing his eyes open again. "I uploaded coordinates into your computer, so that you can navigate alone to one last supply point, your mission incomplete until then. None of your robots will accompany you. In an hour we attack and you will prepare the way by supplying our forward post, after which you are to report here. To complete your service and receive your name."

The Sommen handed Lev a packet, which, as soon as he took it, felt so heavy that he thought it would pull him to the floor. He pushed it into a pouch and bowed. "I will deliver it immediately, as you wish."

Once he had shut the door behind him, he breathed again and then gasped. The plasma shells, when they burst, sublimed ammonia ice into incandescent gas that floated through the air so Lev imagined he was crawling through some kind of fairyland, where the ammonia wasn't ammonia, it was cotton candy in pale green, weightless. Misha would have liked this, he thought. But the memory of Michael scuttled in to make Lev scream, and he buried his helmet in the snow and pounded the ground until his friend's face disappeared and even then Lev stayed motionless, wanted to ensure his thoughts traversed a path just as safe as his body so he lay there as the detonations vibrated everything, including his teeth; Lev studied the map display, staring at the blinking light. His legs shook. They refused at first to propel him forward, as if the nerves had suddenly split and gone dead but then he noticed the ground shift below him, the snow parting in front of his faceplate as he slid closer to the front.

Plasma flashed overhead and Lev thought about the funhouse outside Zaporozhye, in the summertime, where the gypsies strung colored lights and kept wolves in steel cages. He believed in cages. Cages kept bad things in, trapped, but they also kept bad things out if you crawled inside. Lev's thoughts spiraled down into his memories as if they were a feathered cage, soft and warm to keep him free from plasma and snow, a Gypsy charm against the wolves that waited for him out there, robotic wolves which hid amongst an alien forest of ice and boulders on the far banks. When he passed onto the frozen river, solid ammonia and water, he didn't notice. The artillery barrage had heated it to create puddles, over which he slid, not even recognizing that the dots representing his body and destination had almost merged. Lev smiled when the old Gypsy woman tried to distract him (so her son could pick his pocket) because he had come forewarned—no money except the bills he kept in a secret belt. Her wolves growled. But caged wolves, Lev knew, were fine, their fur a mixture of gray and black that swirled with each movement, the creatures barely alive on a diet of squirrel, anything found dead on the road. His memories faded then as if a switch had flipped. Lev rested in the middle of the river, a tiny beige figure just a shade off from the surrounding white of ice and snow, terrified now that he realized what the problem was.

There was no outpost. They had lied to him, but the Sommen *never* lied. He imagined Michael then, somewhere nearby, a ghost that refused to materialize but who stared along with the ghosts of everyone else, all the humans who had come into space to die alone.

"I am not of you yet," Lev said to them, "and it doesn't matter that there is no outpost; these are the coordinates and there is a delivery to be made." He pulled out the package and unwrapped it.

Nanos. Lev rested a box on the ice and watched it open so that a wave of dark material spilled out to form a puddle, its edges spreading in a perfect circle, quickly enough that Lev had trouble scrambling out of its way. His spine went rigid. Nanos would attract attention, would call the robotic wolves, and he stumbled to his feet oblivious to the new plasma barrage that had begun, sending massive chunks of the river skyward like car-sized shards of glass. The wolves howled as he fled. Lev had never seen one of the enemies; resupply meant going to the front but never staying there, never actually observing what the Sommen fought, what could be so important to them that it formed the focal point of Sommen consciousness. And besides, the wolves changed. Each system held something different so that even if he had seen a Sommen enemy before, it mattered for nothing, didn't apply to whatever chased him now.

He reached the bank and turned. What the nanos had attracted had nothing to do with flesh and Lev cried at the sight of metal creatures, mechanical and lifeless at the same time their sensors glowed with at least a hint of consciousness. One of them clicked its legs over the river directly toward him and fired, a pulsing cannon that caused puffs of snow to erupt but the shifting ice must have prevented the thing from getting a good lock, must have made its targeting system lapse because it kept missing. Lev closed his eyes. He embraced Michael now, smiled at the memory of the man's face and lost all sense of time, floating in conversations that had taken place only the day before or two years prior, the words clear and fresh regardless of their age so that minutes congealed into an hour.

"And still it lives," said Michael.

But it wasn't Michael and Lev opened his eyes to find the Sommen in front of him, the same one who had given him the package to deliver. Hundreds of robots smoldered on the ice, burning and melting through. Already forgotten.

"You lied," said Lev. He saw the Sommen tense and half-expected the thing to reach out and crush his helmet, but this time Lev wasn't afraid and stood his ground. "There was no outpost."

"I lied. It is part of the ritual, a last test to determine if the Gods want you to live in combat, and we are permitted to lie for it. Now you must choose."

Behind the thing Lev noticed hundreds more Sommen gather, a plasma burst occasionally sending one or ten into the air, charred. Even so, the rest watched and listened—ignoring the danger.

"Choose what?"

"Your name. You may stay with us, a full Merchant with title rights, the right to live on any of our worlds and to hire your own no-names. Or you may go home. Back to Earth."

Lev had trouble concentrating and laughed at the irony: It had ended but the prize was decrepitude. Age and ammonia, he thought, and a little methane, the smell of the Sommen, the legacy of having lived with them a road map of scar tissue on his lungs, a map he'd never see but followed with each inhalation. Oxygen was expensive and N_2 a waste of good nitrogen potential, and so no-names made do with what they could afford, the cheap gases, impure, the same ones he used for his mules' engines. These had robbed him of youth. And he'd been gone too long. The memories that had kept him alive or at least provided a refuge for the moments in which the main part of his mind melted and rebuilt itself, screamed at him now—that they were tired. They wanted rest too. If Lev dusted off the thought of vushka one more time it might crumble into nothing. Real vushka, in Zaporozhye, *that* was the thing.

"I want to go home. To Earth," he said.

Lev stepped back. The Sommen shouted, a war cry that he had heard only in the distance from the rear, and never directed *at* him so that he almost turned and ran until he understood they had knelt. All except the one, who grinned to reveal the black fangs of the Sommen, a sharp horror.

"You honor us. To be a Merchant is to accept a life of shame, but to refuse is something else. When we found you Earth was not ready for war; we had to test it."

Lev let his mind slip further into haze, the day's events having hit harder than he realized so that he wondered if he'd pass out. "I don't understand."

"This race, the mechanical one dying here today, is unworthy of being even Merchant filth because they exchanged flesh for metal. So we destroy them. Most of Earth has so far retained its flesh and you, among all the Merchants from Earth, have proven that your kind has worth; you delivered the final supply. And now, because of your decision to reject Merchant, your race will be given time to prepare and when ready we will war against each other. Eternal in glory and honor for all."

"Eternal in glory and honor for all," the rest of them chanted.

Lev dropped where he stood. Before passing out he noticed that the air mix had gone out of whack and he wondered why the alarms hadn't warned him, until he glanced down and saw that portions of his suit had been blackened by plasma. He smiled. With a flick of a finger, he corrected the mix and began to fade, knowing that he'd wake up with a headache. It was OK. The Sommen lifted him, throwing his body over its shoulder to begin the trek to the rear, when the rest of them rose and screamed again, the noise of their shouts fading as the one carrying him rammed through snow drifts at the same time inhaling the ammonia atmosphere with a deep hiss.

His suit translated the fading Sommen screams. "*Honor for all!*"

Lev woke some time later in the snow. The Sommen knelt beside him, one of the thing's hands on his shoulders, pressing him into a deep drift as it used the other to work on his chest plate, and he waited for the thing to say something but words never came and both speakers only crackled in his ears. The Sommen finished whatever it had been doing, and must have seen that Lev was awake because it pulled him to his feet.

"Keep your head up," the Sommen said. "Your back straight. If we pass my kind, look them in the eye and do not turn away, no matter what happens."

"What?"

"Raise your head. You are not a Merchant, not a no-name; you are a thing with promise. I fixed your suit and uploaded into it all of our plans, weapons data, and thought. In this way, your people can prepare for our coming. Tell them. Tell them that we will allow space outside your system to gather resources and they have only a short time to become our equal, a century before war finds all of you and my killers come to collect."

"That's what you were saying at the river. I'm going home, to Earth?"

"Home. And keep your head raised, no matter what."

"What if I had chosen to stay—picked the Merchant path?"

The Sommen spat, the stuff freezing before it hit the snow. "We would have harvested more of your people for our supply ranks, destroyed Earth because it had no value, and moved on. Not much farther now, to the port."

Lev looked up and recognized the path. They stepped from the empty plains and onto a road, the same one he and Misha had traveled earlier and the outpost was close now, beyond that the Sommen transit area, their beachhead onto this world. Did *they* know of Brodyaga—the song or any of Siberia's rivers? Did Lev anymore? It took a moment for the words to come, much longer than it had ever taken for vushka, and he sang so the melody echoed in his helmet, and he had to pause at the end of each line to breathe, to force more air into damaged lungs, lungs that just wanted it to stop, screamed that they'd had enough. But he sang anyway and at the end the Sommen growled; Lev's translator changed the sound into artificial laughter.

"This is a song about convicts. Prisoners."

"Yes," said Lev.

"You are no convict. Ten times our enemies aimed for your breath, for your exhaust, and you stood on the ice, never moving and showing no sign of fear. You are no convict." The thing pointed then, down the road toward the transit port but stopped Lev so it could use a device to mark the front of his suit, draw a symbol that he had seen many times on Sommen armor and ships. "A warrior's symbol," the thing continued. "They should not touch you as long as you bear the mark, and by now word will have spread so all will expect your arrival and meet you as a hero. Act like a hero; keep your head raised no matter how tired or wounded you are."

Lev thought of something to say but nothing came, and so he walked away, shuffling through the snow and not even noticing when more fell from the sky, not even recognizing that, out of habit, he had shifted his attention to the navigation screens because now the snow came so heavily that the road disappeared.

His head pounded. It pounded like a hangover, and made him thirsty for vodka, the sensation that Earth was so close bringing a wave of exhaustion when it should have kept the energy up, the energy that he had gathered just moments ago. But it was OK. Even if he woke up every day with a headache it was more than OK, because he'd already decided on the first thing he'd do when he got back, the thing that scared him the most and almost made him choose a name.

Lev lost all interest in the Sommen. Others could take the information he'd been given, decide if man would go to war someday. To him there were more important things, the kinds of things that mattered only to old men like the fact that Misha had been young. His parents might still be alive. Lev would have to find them, to explain why the mules hadn't saved their son and he missed his mules but he'd miss Misha even more, and just before arriving at the spaceport he laughed, finally seeing their mistake: The Sommen thought men had spirit—that Lev had chosen to go home because he wanted to fight.

But the Sommen had never kissed Marina Boroshenko.

CHAPTER ONE

Maung reminded himself: He was a Dream Warrior, and when it was his turn at the desk he stepped up like a soldier, with his back straight.

"First name?"

The man was an American and asked it without looking at Maung, without noticing that this one was different from the ones who came before or who were still in line behind him. Americans cared about nothing. And why should they? *They won.*

"Maung."

"Let's see . . ." The man asked Maung to spell his first name and nodded while tapping on the green plastic. "And your last name."

"I don't have one. My full name is Maung Kyarr, but where I come from we don't name our children the same way Americans do. Kyarr means tiger."

"You're Burmese."

When Maung nodded, the man showed him the scars on his hand and Maung's heart sank. Of all the people manning the jobs desk, he got a veteran, an ex-soldier who—from the pattern on his right hand—had spent time in a Myanmar prison camp. The guards often used razor blades to carve identifiers into their captives. That way, the cuts were so deep that infections failed to heal and jungle disease would infest them with rot; the prisoner would often decompose before reaching the grave.

"I am from *Myanmar*," said Maung. "From Yangon. But I was no prison guard."

The man deleted Maung's name from his plastic pad and waved him off. "We don't need you today. Or tomorrow. *Next.*"

Maung moved away. He had been through this so many times that he questioned why he bothered with the Jobs Bureau at all, why he didn't just stick with the labor lines down at the port where work was cheap but plentiful. People stared at him as he left. They all heard the conversation and a Korean man spat on him as he passed, then lunged, but his companions held him back.

The street smelled like chemicals. A stretch of houses along North Charleston's Burton Lane all looked the same, stacked next to each other in a tight grid, tiny huts in blue fiberboard one after another. Children played in the street. When Maung first arrived he had enjoyed Charleston; the heat and the poverty reminded him of his old neighborhood in Yangon but here there were no metals or concrete or wood; cheap synthetic panels formed the walls, creating a sagging mess. Now he missed Yangon and the pagodas with their gold-leaf domes, and the jungle summers when everyone wore thanaka even though getting the wood was more difficult each year. Maung remembered the sound of stone scraping on stone at night. It always made him smile; his mother ground thanaka wood in the mortar and pestle that her mother had given her fifty years before, and the smell filled the hut in seconds with a fragrance that meant safety.

Today the lack of these things seemed almost normal because after a year of living in America, Maung recognized that all materials were precious, and anything with even a trace amount of metal or calcium or cellulose was recycled and sent to one of a thousand postwar reclamation sites. Americans stripped all they could from Myanmar; nothing went to waste. They even recycled Maung and his people, pardoning them for war crimes and relocating them to what Maung's friends called *Ngway Myoh*, "Money City"; when the fiberboard got wet it smelled like the old paper currency—money that older Burmese people stored with mothballs to prevent bugs from eating it. Maung held his nose and opened a door.

His six-year-old son, Win, tackled him. "Daddy!"

"What?" Maung pretended to be angry. "Why are you not in school? Did you burn it down?"

"No!" Win rubbed his hand across his nose. "I'm sick."

Maung's mother stood in the kitchen, which was also the living room, and frowned. "Nothing today? No work?"

"The man at the desk was a veteran. From the Myanmar campaign, an ex-prisoner."

"What now?"

Before he could answer, his son asked "What's a Dream Warrior?"

Maung stepped back. It was an instinctive move, born from terror that they'd at last been discovered and he glanced out the front window to make certain nobody was nearby.

"Who told you that name, Win?" Maung's mother asked.

"Tun Ba Kaung."

She looked at Maung, furious. "One of your friends. *He can't keep his mouth shut, not even in front of his children!*"

"I will tell him to be quiet," said Maung, relieved to find that it wasn't so bad, that it came from one of their own. "But he is a general, and still thinks he's at war. I cannot tell him what to do."

"*Was* a general. Now we are *all* nothing and he will get you killed."

She turned back to the kitchen and cooked, throwing pans to demonstrate she was angry. The boy wasn't smiling anymore. He looked at his father and shrugged, and the child's perfect English amazed Maung. The accent was American.

"So what is it?"

Maung squatted and pulled the boy in. "It is something very special, very secret. And if I tell you, you must never speak of it. Agreed?"

"*Maung,*" his mother said from the kitchen, her tone disapproving. But Maung had already made up his mind.

"OK," said Win. "I promise."

"What do they teach you of super-awares in school? Anything?"

His son shrugged again. "That they killed a lot of people—that they're bad."

"That's right," said Maung. The grandmother was quiet now, watching, and a warmth grew as if his ancestors enveloped him with a blanket of calmness. "They were very bad, but they weren't made that way originally. Smart men, scientists like you'll be someday, twisted *good* artificial intelligence, semi-awares, into a tool of war by combining them with men like me; when you combine a semi-aware with a person's brain, you make a super-aware. We fought a war against

America, and were friends with another country, one called China. The Chinese are very powerful warriors but aren't like you and me—not anymore. They are vicious, and many are super-awares."

"Are *you* Chinese?" the boy asked.

"No. I am from Myanmar, like you. The Chinese took the most talented university students and changed us. They put things into my body and replaced some of my bones with metal and . . . things. In order to fight we had to lie down and plug into computers—to concentrate on our jobs. So if you were to see me in battle, it would look to you like I was asleep. Dreaming. That's why they called us Dream Warriors and there were entire dormitories of us at one time. *Hundreds.* Dream Warriors are super-awares; but I'm a good one, not bad."

Maung's mother shook her finger. "So if Tun Ba Kaung ever speaks of it again, call him a liar. And *you* must not say anything about this, Win. Ever."

"Why?"

"Because," said Maung, "I am the only one left. The Americans took everyone from Myanmar and spared the soldiers' lives, but not the Dream Warriors'. They hunted us; it is how your mother died, soon after you were born. All of us are gone now except me, and if the Americans find out one is alive I don't know what they'd do."

"Would you go to prison?" his son asked.

"Maybe." Maung grabbed a cigarette, lit it, then glanced out the window one more time—to be sure there were no drone scanners. "Maybe worse. Or maybe nothing would happen. These Americans are funny; they get so angry sometimes, but then forget everything and forgive, so they're not at all like the Chinese. I don't trust Americans, but there are things to like."

The boy nodded and crossed his arms, trying so hard to look serious that Maung almost laughed.

"I like them," he said. "We have American kids in our class. A few. I will keep the secret."

"Good," said Maung, messing up his son's hair. "I'm off to find work; do what your grandmother says."

The walk from his home to the spaceport took almost an hour, so that by the time he got there, sweat soaked Maung's shirt. Charleston

Spaceport dwarfed everything; it rose from the shore in a forest of steel and carbon buildings that, Maung suspected, went farther underground than they did above, and the aboveground portions were at least a thousand meters high. The tallest one was also the broadest. It reminded him of the deep jungles in Myanmar, of banyans and leza trees so old they towered for miles and with bases so thick it took forever to walk around. But the jungle wasn't ugly. Banyans didn't use up half the nation's alloys and impossible-to-get metals when they grew.

Anchored within their base structures were the elevator strips and Maung looked at them the same way he always did, with his mouth open at the fact that the carbon nanotube "strips"—more like girders, three meters thick—stretched all the way into space, disappearing into the clouds where somewhere miles away they linked with the main orbital station. He had only seen the station in pictures. Someday maybe his son would go there, would have the chance to get away from the Earth and into space where Maung imagined everything was clean and new, unspoiled by war.

An alarm horn startled Maung. He reached for homemade earplugs of candle wax and stuffed them in just before the massive elevator fired braking rockets to land at the main terminal; even with plugs the noise made him wince. Maung covered both ears with his hands and closed his eyes, not opening them again until the elevator banged into its mooring locks and the hydraulic shock absorbers stopped hissing.

Away from the main complex was another facility. The Americans were dismantling it, so as Maung walked toward the temporary worker zone he saw that much had already disappeared but that some remained, spiky and broad, made from a glossy green material that could only be alien because it was—the remnants of the Sommen, who had arrived on Earth before Maung was even born. He said a silent prayer of thanks; as soon as the Sommen left, the Burmese surrendered and the Americans drafted people from all over Southeast Asia for construction projects. Maung's family would be starving or dead had the things not disappeared, because they had been losing to the Americans and their allies.

But nobody, least of all Maung, knew why the Sommen left—or why they'd come in the first place.

❋   ❋   ❋

Maung tossed his cigarette to the gutter. There was a small bodega in a trailer, just outside the main construction and cargo support area, and passing trucks filled the air with the smell of ozone and alcohol, their engines and turbines whining. Only Joseph was there, sitting on a bench outside the trailer. Maung crossed the street and sat next to him.

"I smell the stink of Yangon gutter trash," Joseph said.

"That's the smell a dead Filipino," Maung responded. "It's a good smell."

Joseph glared at Maung for a moment and then both men smiled.

"Strange," said Joseph.

Maung shrugged and rolled the dice. It was a slow day and he and Joseph were both late so the main hiring had already taken place; now those who stopped at their bench had only small jobs. So far the pair were paid to move a few wheelbarrows of rubble, barely enough to cover lunch, so they played backgammon while waiting for more work and while the day got hotter and hotter.

"What is strange?" Maung asked.

"The Sommen site. It's gone quiet. Usually there is the noise of demolition and trucks moving in and out but not now; there hasn't been any movement or jackhammering for the last ten minutes."

Another elevator screeched down and Maung barely got his earplugs in; he yelled over the noise. "Are you sure?"

"I'm sure. I hate that site; it gives me the creeps and reminds me of an abandoned church from the jungle near my home in the islands. My brother convinced me that church was haunted when we were kids."

"Bah," said Maung. He thought maybe Filipinos were prone to superstition but now that his attention was drawn to it, the facility *did* seem off. He rolled the dice again and moved his pieces. "I'm sure it's fine; just ignore it."

"Have you ever seen a Sommen?" Joseph asked.

"Nobody has."

"Exactly," Joseph said.

"Exactly, what?"

"You and I grew up knowing that other things existed out there, in space. But we've never seen them. And I remember when the news used to warn us about having to go to war if the Sommen attacked, but then one day it all ends. No war. No nothing. They just leave and magically the war between China and America ends."

Maung closed his eyes and let the breeze cool him as it flowed across his forehead; his hair dripped with sweat. The humidity in Charleston reminded him once more of Yangon and he liked the sensation at the same time he wished for air conditioning.

He moved his pieces and handed the dice to Joseph. "It is weird, and I think about that a lot; we all do. But there aren't any answers. Your turn."

Maung's stomach tightened in fear. It was after lunch and despite all the cargo carriers and trucks, nobody had work; he rubbed his eyes to pretend he was tired because it shamed him to think Joseph might see that he was almost crying and Maung couldn't remember where the instinct to mask his moods came from.

The pair were about to start their tenth game of backgammon when multiple armored personnel carriers motored past with silent electric engines, surprising them with stealth; Maung nearly dropped his cigarette.

"What are *they* doing here?" he asked.

"I told you something was wrong," said Joseph.

"We don't know yet. Maybe there is trouble in the terminal or maybe they are running an exercise."

"If something was wrong with the elevators the Army would use the main terminal or one of the support entrances." Joseph shook his head and snapped the backgammon board shut. He stood. "And they would not schedule an exercise on one of the busiest cargo upload days I've ever seen. This is trouble."

"Where are you going?" asked Maung.

"Let's get closer so we can watch. We were both soldiers once; aren't you even curious?"

"I am never curious about the American Army!" he shouted at Joseph, who sprinted after the APCs. "You don't care because they *like* Filipinos!"

Finally Maung sighed and followed.

✹ ✹ ✹

Temporary work badges provided some access, but eventually one of the automated security fences whined when they approached and Maung and Joseph backed away until the alarm silenced. They looked for a good vantage point. Beyond the security fence was a massive wall topped with barbed wire that made it difficult to see, but they eventually found a dumpster to climb, high enough to get a view of the Sommen structure, which now was only about a hundred meters away. This close, Maung spotted details. The green structure consisted of thousands of interlocked leaves, and he glimpsed different shades of green like a forest of emerald rods and the longer he stared the more he thought that the colors changed, shifting with winds that blew from the river. The view mesmerized him until movement caught his eye, forcing his attention back to the American vehicles.

The APCs formed a semicircle around the structure's main entrance. Maung watched as the soldiers spilled from underneath the vehicles, ducking between the massive wheels and then sprinting forward. Maung and Joseph were so close that he heard the turrets whine as they turned.

"What the hell is going on?" Joseph asked.

Maung's instincts told him to run. "How the hell should I know? Where are the usual boys—the general and the rest of his work crew? Did you hear anything when you showed up this morning—anything about who picked them up for a job?"

"No. I got there just before you did; everyone was already gone."

"You don't . . ." Maung started. He paused to light a cigarette. "You don't think they'd get work in there, do you? I mean that's never happened before."

"No way. Look at the security. We wouldn't be cleared to—"

An explosion stopped him in midsentence. Maung flinched when the APCs opened fire, their coaxial auto-Maxwells spitting streamers of explosive shells that left bright streaks of light from tracer phosphorus, brilliant red lines that disappeared somewhere inside the green structure's main entrance. Joseph yanked him down onto his knees; a ricocheting shell tumbled through the air and thudded into the ground beside the dumpster before it detonated, sending hot metal pinging through the container's sides and up into Maung's shin.

"*Damn!*" he hissed, almost falling off.

"Are you hit?"

Maung nodded and looked down, but the penetration was nothing and he picked two hot pieces of metal from his skin. "It's not bad. Just bad luck. I wonder if—"

A shriek interrupted him. The noise came from inside the Sommen compound, from an animal of some kind but Maung was sure it wasn't any animal from Earth; this was the sound of something unnatural, a simultaneous choking, gurgling and screaming and Maung thought that whatever made the noise, it was a thing capable of speaking the language of horror and decay, the language of demons. He *had* to look again. Several APCs inched backward, firing as they went.

"We should go," Joseph said, tugging at Maung's shirt.

"Now *I* want to see."

"See what? Your own death? Fine—I'll *see* you tomorrow at the bodega."

Maung, his attention fixed on the Sommen site, was only vaguely aware that Joseph had gone. Still the APCs moved backward. Men emerged from the Sommen structure in small groups while the vehicles' autocannons fired over their heads, and some of the soldiers dragged wounded comrades whose armor was torn and split, while workers sprinted as fast as they could. Maung recognized one and held his breath: the general. The man was dressed like he was, in a t-shirt and work pants, and hauled himself along the ground using both arms; the general's legs were twisted, broken almost into right angles.

Without thinking, Maung jumped from the dumpster. He sprinted toward the security fence and ignored the alarm as he leaped onto it, dragging himself up and then swinging over to the ground below. The next obstacle, the wall, was another matter. On his first attempt he missed; Maung couldn't jump as high as he needed and his fingers missed the top by only a few centimeters, so he cursed while looking up at an impossible height. The general screamed, calling for help in Burmese. Maung tried again and this time his right hand held, tightly enough that he could swing his left up and then scramble to the top, where he tangled himself in barbed wire.

"General!" he shouted. "*Keep moving!*"

The general was on his back now, just outside the Sommen entrance; if he heard Maung, he gave no indication. Whatever had his attention was still inside the compound's green walls, at first not visible until, finally, it appeared at the gate.

Maung went limp in the wire; his mouth had opened to scream again at the general, to tell him to keep moving, but now nothing came out as he stared at a creature that should only have existed in children's nightmares. The thing stood twice the height of a man and three times as wide, on two legs. Armor encased it from head to toe. The plates looked to Maung as though they were made of the same green material as the complex itself, so he couldn't see the thing's body, but its wide faceplate was clear and Maung was close enough that he looked into the creature's eyes—four, huge round globes, all of them jet black, a darker shade than its black and gray skin, and the creature's mouth opened to reveal what looked like multiple rows of dark, needlelike teeth. The thing screamed again. This time Maung figured the sound must be amplified by speakers on its armor.

It lifted a foot, preparing to crush the general when Maung yelled, "*Touch him and die!*"

The creature paused. Autocannon rounds sparked when they bounced off its armor and now the troops loaded back into their APCs—probably, Maung thought, so they could use plasma rounds without cooking their own troops. Then the creature looked at him. Maung's body tensed and what happened next was automatic: His internal systems activated. Maung tried shutting them down but couldn't; these were programmed defenses, which activated because the creature was scanning him and passive receivers in his wetware detected a threat. Once active, they *couldn't* be turned off, not until he was safe.

"*Enemy scan. Threat active,*" a voice said. The voice came from inside his head as though from a dream and now Maung "saw" two worlds, one in the visual spectrum, the other flicking through radio, long-wave IR, and every other part of the spectrum until settling on microwave; he flinched when the thing directed a beam of energy at him, one which caused a sharp pain in the rear of his skull so that he screamed. It took Maung a moment to recover. He gripped his head and formulated a thought, ordering his systems to begin jamming by sending his own beam of electromagnetic energy back.

The creature stumbled. It cocked its head and bellowed, then took a running start toward Maung, lifting what looked like an odd-shaped rifle at the same time it stepped on the general's head with a crunch.

"*No!*" Maung shouted.

He barely thought; it was instinctive, like breathing, and Maung's consciousness swam through the thing's electromagnetic emissions so that within milliseconds he was inside the creature's armor. It was a world so alien that Maung had to pause, confused. He viewed himself through alien sensors, trapped in barbed wire atop the site's security wall, where his own shape appeared in a mixture of light and color, and Maung made note of the fact that most of the creature's internal frequencies were geared toward ultraviolet; its natural vision probably functioned within that spectrum. Everything was calm. Despite the fact that the thing roared, bearing down on him like an unstoppable tank, Maung also "saw" the alien suit's power nodes and couldn't shake a sensation that this had to be a Sommen design. He flipped the power nodes off as fast as he could, having to adjust for the system's alien configuration. One by one they shut down. In less than a second he found the armor's servo nodes and flicked them off too, which stopped the thing in its tracks—freezing it. And when Maung flipped another node the creature vented dense white gas, and the smell of ammonia drifted over everything, making Maung's consciousness return to his own body, which now choked as he gasped for air.

Ammonia detected, his system warned. *Don chemical protection and find higher ground.*

The creature's face contorted; it opened and closed its mouth, over and over, reminding Maung of a beached fish until the thing's eyes and face went blank.

By the time Maung realized it was over, the ammonia had blown away and the thing stopped emitting on any frequency, leaving nothing upon which Maung could piggyback; his systems deactivated. Maung sagged with exhaustion. But at the same time, the thrill of having returned to the old ways, of flexing muscles that hadn't been used in years, invigorated him and he grinned until a stabbing pain reminded him of his injuries. The barbed wire was razor sharp. Several points dug into his skin and warm blood dripped through his shirt as he tried to pull himself free. The soldiers kept firing at the creature. Maung hoped stray autocannon rounds wouldn't ricochet into him, but soon the men in the APCs recognized that the thing had gone motionless and someone ordered them to cease fire.

A soldier exited the closest vehicle and walked toward Maung, but stopped at the creature, which was only a few meters away. He yanked his helmet off. "Is it dead?" the man asked.

Maung gave up trying to free himself. "I believe so." Then he thought of a lie. "I think the cannons hit its life-support systems because I nearly choked on a cloud of ammonia gas; it must breathe the stuff."

The man nodded. "You're going to need help getting down. And an ambulance. That's razor wire and some of those points are probably down to your bone. Stay put and try not to move." He turned and walked back to his APC and in the distance Maung heard sirens getting louder.

"What was that thing?"

"Forget about it, pal." The man said it over his shoulder, without turning around. "And there will be some people here to talk with you in a bit—to tell you what you can and can't say."

By the time they treated Maung and the authorities finished interviewing him, it was 3 a.m. They offered to drive him home. But spending even one more minute with the men in dark blue suits, men from the capital who were dead-faced either from being tired by the trip south or just because that was their real complexion, would be too dangerous. They asked too many questions. Maung had seen security types before—in Myanmar. They acted friendly until it was time to shoot into the back of your head, which they always did after offering you a smoke.

"No," Maung said. "I'll walk."

They nodded, and the taller one slapped him on the shoulder; Maung winced. It was where he had been given seven stitches to sew up razor-wire gashes.

"Just remember, Mr. Burma; you play ball and we can make life much easier for you—maybe take care of the whole employment thing. You don't play ball, and . . ."

"It's in everyone's best interest," the other one said.

Maung stopped at the hospital door to ask one last question. "That thing. What was it, really?"

"That thing never existed."

It existed, thought Maung. He heard the general's wife, wailing with her family because they lived only a few doors down, and many in his neighborhood lost someone today. Only two men in the work crew survived. Their families were permitted to visit the hospital but neither man was coming home soon and one lost an eye and both legs. The other broke his back. Maung's mother made tea while his son slept on a small mattress in the living room, one they rolled up and stashed during the day, and Maung sat on the couch in the dim light, watching the boy's chest rise and fall. There was a knock at the door. Maung stood and hesitated before opening it, hoping it wasn't the men from DC again.

It was Joseph. He smiled and shook Maung's hand. "You made it!"

"Barely."

"Look at the stitches on your arms," said Joseph. "That thing got you?"

Maung had forgotten he was wearing a tank top. He shrugged. "That was from the razor wire on that security wall, not the monster."

"And the general?" Joseph asked. When Maung shrugged again, he nodded. "This was a horrible day, Maung. Horrible."

Joseph sat on the couch and looked at Maung's mother to check if she was listening, and then at Maung's son. He seemed nervous. Finally the man said, "I'm sorry I left you there, Maung, I didn't know what would happen."

"It's not a problem; you were smarter than me, I should have left too."

"Maung," Joseph whispered. "I spoke to John Ngyuen, in the hospital. There were security men from the capital all over the place but I told them I was his brother so I could get in. Filipino, Vietnamese, Burmese; we all look the same to them."

"What happened to the work crew?"

"He said that our bunch was all hired by the same man: a defense contractor who was shorthanded that day and needed laborers to help with a demolition project. When they noticed where they were headed the general explained that the group lacked authority to enter the Sommen zone. The contractors said not to worry—that it was fine because all the sensitive material had been removed; the government had lowered the security clearance required to enter."

Joseph cleared his throat, and then spoke more quietly. "The inside of that place is like a maze—at least that's what John said. And there was a group of men trying to break a floor slab of that green material, in a chamber underground where John was assigned to clean up. They succeeded. But as soon as they cracked it, they choked on ammonia gas, and John barely escaped from a massive cloud that billowed out. A few minutes later that monster emerged; like it had been asleep all these years, waiting, already armored and ready for them."

"That makes no sense," said Maung.

Joseph opened a pack of cigarettes and the two men stepped outside into the street to smoke. Usually it was filled with music. But tonight everyone hid inside as if the danger hadn't yet passed and Maung shrugged as he took a drag.

"Are you going to the bodega tomorrow?" he asked.

Joseph nodded. "I have to work. I gave up looking for a permanent job a long time ago. Path to citizenship my ass. Only if you have a PhD in engineering and come from Korea can the Jobs Bureau find you permanent work."

"I'll come with you. I want to see what they're doing with that place now that this happened."

"Maung," said Joseph. "John said one more thing."

"What?"

"He said before that creature killed them all, some of the defense contractors were screaming that it was a *Sommen*."

Maung got a chill. He remembered the signals that emanated from the thing's armor and the black eyes, a spider's eyes. "That can't be true. They're gone."

"Most of them, I guess," said Joseph. He let out a long breath of smoke. "But not this one."

"Tell nobody what you just told me, Joseph; we talk about this with each other and that's it."

The next morning was hotter. Humidity clung to Maung's skin, tempting him to smear thanaka on his cheeks but it would draw attention from the whites and anyone else who thought it a quaint tradition, one that proved how backward Myanmar was. He yanked on a t-shirt and baseball cap, hoping to blend in but knowing that the deep brown of his skin prevented this when it came to Americans. He and Joseph took a back way to the spaceport to avoid as many people as possible; but who cared? It was clear nobody could access the day laborers' area and the pair of them encountered large crowds at every gate. Joseph waved someone over, then asked what was going on.

"They've shut the spaceport down so that a team from the capital can come and inspect."

"Inspect what?" Joseph asked.

The man shrugged. "Whatever. I don't know. I just heard—"

A transport horn interrupted him. The crowd parted, pushing sweaty bodies against Maung so that he had to back against a fiber wall, and less than ten feet away a convoy passed. The vehicles were all black—government electric vans and trucks with windows tinted so nobody could see in. Three of them had antennas on the roof. Some of the antennas looked like long whips, strapped into place so they wouldn't rock back and forth, whereas others were so bizarre that Maung couldn't begin to assign them shapes. But he recognized them. Maung fought the urge to run, recalling similar vehicles he'd witnessed long ago in the jungle trails of Myanmar when he and his wife tried to escape over mountains into Thailand. That was the day she had died. Somehow the Americans had climbed impossible mountain trails in small two-man transports, an army of them, each with antennas that Maung and his wife knew were designed for tracking Dream Warriors. Maung had screamed at what happened next. His wife activated her systems and ran down the mountain to draw the Americans away, sending one last message: *Run. Take care of Win.*

"They are bringing in electronics specialists," he said.

Joseph asked, "For what?"

But Maung ignored him. Instead he pressed his way through the crowd, trying to move away from the spaceport. A wave of panic choked him, tightening his chest and stomach into knots. Maung fell. When he picked himself up he heard Joseph calling after him, but

Maung no longer grasped the words; he couldn't understand what the man said, only that he said *something*. Maung guessed what the specialists were looking for and why the vehicles were here: They had detected a semi-aware yesterday, one used during the fight with the Sommen.

Me.

"You are a dream warrior," his mother whispered. "I was proud the day the generals called your name. You can get out of this, Maung. They will never catch you. On the day you were born a tiger came to Yangon, out of the jungle. It attacked and killed a boy and it was out of respect for this that we gave you your name, Maung Kyarr, '*Brother Tiger.*' Do not forget that the tiger made room for you and that you have a greater purpose."

"I am subnormal," Maung said. His voice was barely a whisper since he rarely spoke of it, but now everything came out. "I was smarter before the Chinese drafted me. Father carved wood, and you made thanaka, and I remember being able to do math in an instant because you both let me handle the money at the marketplace. I pawned our linens in the morning and bought them back at night. But after the Chinese finished operating on my head I was a genius, a million times smarter than before—but only when I could activate my systems. Without them, without my semi-aware, I am only half a person. An idiot."

Win was at school. Maung wanted to activate the system again, to merge with his semi-aware and sink into data and facts, a cold logic that made him feel invincible, a merging that created a *super-aware*. But he remembered how the Americans tracked them in Myanmar. As soon as he activated it, sensors throughout the city—sensors the Americans installed across their entire country—would register the signature. They'd sniff out the tiny leakages that were inevitable, and would match the waveforms against their database so that somewhere in DC an alarm would go off. *That* was what had happened at the Sommen compound.

His mother wiped tears away. "You are *still* my child. And I am proud of what you did. Proud that you risked everything."

"They will find me," Maung said. "Now they have my name, along with a list of everyone at the complex yesterday. They have *all* our addresses. Later today they will drive through the streets of North Charleston and broadcast pulsed attack signals, ones my system can't ignore no matter how hard I try to keep it dormant. It was a design flaw, mother. *A design flaw.* And as soon as my semi-aware activates, they'll have my location. I will be caught."

"Then you have to run," she said. "Now. I will pack some things and will take care of Win, the same way I took care of you."

"I will not leave my son!"

His mother shushed with her hands, looking around as though there might be someone else in the hut and then hugged him, whispering into Maung's ear. "You have no choice. If you stay, you will lose him forever after they kill you."

"You will make sure he becomes American?" Maung whispered. Tears dripped from his eyes and onto the dusty floor, and he shut them but it made it worse because now he saw his son in his thoughts.

"You know who to go to," his mother said. "He does this all the time."

"I'll send money as soon as I can. You will not suffer for food, I promise. Open an account with one of the local lenders under your name—one of the ones in the neighborhood so I can find it."

He left without saying another word. Talking made it worse; the more he prolonged this the harder it would be and even now, each step from his hut felt as though it would rip Maung's insides apart. He cried openly at first, but then forced himself to stop.

Maung made his way south, into the old city where an antique, horse-drawn trolley nearly ran over his foot. The encounter brought him back to reality and he kept looking for the place, the shop every Myanmarese knew—the stall owned by the only person who could give him a new identity.

CHAPTER TWO

Maung avoided staring at the Old Man's wrinkled skin, which formed a labyrinth so complex it reminded him of a human brain, but he also couldn't bring himself to look at the man's eyes, which were almost like the Sommen's—deep and black. He wheezed whenever he inhaled. The man wore an oxygen amplifier on his belt so that a plastic hose ran under his shirt, where it entered a port in his chest, pumping nearly pure oxygen to the lungs. Maung imagined the cost. Even the general, who had smuggled a small fortune in gold from Myanmar, couldn't afford such a procedure for his mother, who the entire neighborhood mourned; her death had involved months of suffocation.

"You look troubled, Maung," the Old Man said.

"I am, Grandfather. Deeply troubled. I may lose everything, including my mother and my son."

This was not Maung's grandfather and to use the honorific made him a liar. They were in the old slave market. It was an ancient structure that until now Maung had only read about, and he imagined how difficult it would have been for the men to stand in these stalls for hours, waiting while the air refused to move for anything, least of all the heat. Even now, Maung wished he had thanaka.

"There is nothing that cannot be solved," the Old Man said. "I've lived in this country since I was a boy—far longer than you. I was glad when they decided to bring all of you in. Glad that so many of my countrymen were joining me. And in all these years as an

American, I've learned one thing that you may not have picked up yet."

"What, Grandfather?"

The Old Man smiled. "Money. It makes everything go away. I imagine even the Sommen had a price, but for the life of me I never found it."

"Wait," said Maung, curious. "You *knew* the Sommen? Met with them?"

"I never met with them, exactly. I met with their go-betweens. One of the things we first learned was that the Sommen value only one thing: war. So they didn't bother with money or business or supplies. They have subjugated races who handle these things, creatures collected off thousands of conquered planets. There was a rumor that one man from Russia or Ukraine went to serve the Sommen and was the only one to ever return. But my men never confirmed it."

"And what did the go-between tell you?" asked Maung.

"Nothing about his masters. I asked if they had a cure for lung cancer but it was a stupid question; what would the Sommen care of human disease after all? I was foolish."

Maung recalled the thing he killed at the spaceport and shivered. "I think I ran into one at the spaceport the other day. I was there when something happened at the Sommen complex, the one they dismantled."

"Ah?" The Old Man's eyes flickered with interest. "And you're alive! That *is* a story to tell."

"What do they look like? The Sommen. Some say that is what I saw but nobody knows for sure."

The Old Man sat up. He reached for a cup of iced tea and sipped, then placed it carefully on the table again before wiping his forehead with his handkerchief. "Is that why you're here?" he asked. "Because I can answer your Sommen question, but this is valuable information and perhaps I even have pictures; but it will cost you."

"No," said Maung. "I came for something else."

"Yes. Of course you did. So let's get down to business and why don't you tell me what you *really* need, Maung."

The man used a remote. Servos drew an electrified curtain across his stall and then a soft static sound filled the space.

"White noise and electromagnetics to make sure we can talk safely," the Old Man explained. "Old, but still effective."

Maung squatted on the floor. By the time he finished telling his story—a web of lies, one that avoided the fact that he was a Dream Warrior—his knees ached and his body craved a cigarette.

"So you need to disappear," the Old Man said, "but you can't really tell me why. And you have no money?"

Maung nodded. "I know. And I need to support my mother and son. It is impossible."

"Difficult, yes, impossible, no. If you were a young girl I would give you a new identity and you could work it off in one of my brothels—maybe five years of service. But you aren't." The Old Man paused and tapped a finger against his chin. "Still, I have an idea but it will take time to research. Can you go home or is that now a dangerous place?"

"It is too dangerous, Grandfather."

The Old Man nodded and picked up a notepad and pen. He scribbled something down, ripped a sheet off, and handed it over. "That is the address of a hotel outside the city. Take a bus. Wait outside and one of my boys will come get you in a few minutes to drive you there."

Maung stood and clapped his hands together, pressing them tightly as he bowed, over and over. "Thank you, Grandfather, thank you."

"Don't thank. What I have planned will not be easy and you may never make it through, but for someone in your position it's the only option. And I don't do this out of charity. You will be performing a valuable service. *For me.*"

The hotel was attached to a strip club. Maung could barely take three steps in his room and the bed folded down from the wall, which thumped and vibrated from the music on the other side, and there was a small shower and toilet cubicle. Maung headed to a tiny window. The room was air-conditioned so he hated to open it, but he had to smoke and the driver's instructions were clear: stay inside or the deal was off. So he let the humidity in, feeling it wash over his arms and chest as he blew smoke rings.

⌘   ⌘   ⌘

By the third day claustrophobia almost forced Maung's mind to the breaking point, where he considered giving up on the Old Man. The room smelled dank—a mixture of sweat and cigarettes—and Maung kept the window open all the time now, so he could sit by it and breathe fresh air to imagine that hot breezes carried thoughts to his son. A girl opened his door. Maung barely noticed when she placed a tray of food on the floor and then shut the door behind her. The smell of curry filled the room and Maung's eyes watered with the memory it brought: his mother cooking dinner, his son banging a fork on the table.

On the fourth day the driver returned and took him to the Old Man's home; Maung had never seen such a place, and he thought that not even the general's house in Yangon was as beautiful. Four stories of historical mansion in downtown Charleston met him when the driver let him out, and a battery of servants ushered Maung through the door and onto the piazza, a huge columned porch that led to mahogany double doors. They strolled through a living room paneled with deep purple wood, and finally into the Old Man's study. The servants were all women. Young girls with thanaka patterned on their faces took him gently by the arm and brought him iced tea. Maung marveled at their beauty and the smell once again made him think of home. He sat in a huge leather chair; it was not long before a girl wheeled the Old Man in, then shut the door to give them privacy.

"How do you like it?" the Old Man asked, gesturing to the rest of the room.

"It is a beautiful home, Grandfather."

The man nodded. "America. This is where it's all possible, Maung. Anything."

Maung listened to the ticktock of the massive grandfather clock that sat in the corner and he was so exhausted from not getting sleep that the sound almost made him pass out. Finally he shrugged.

"What is the news, Grandfather? Do I have a way out?"

"Yes," the Old Man said. "I found a way out. But that way is for a normal human, and you aren't exactly normal are you? That doesn't mean it's impossible, only that the price goes up since now we're talking about hiding a super-aware. You're a Dream Warrior. Funny how you failed to mention that."

Maung stared at the man. He wasn't surprised, not anymore, because the arrival of the government men already prepared him for eventually being discovered and the only surprise came from the fact that it was *this* man who found him and not the Americans.

Maung shrugged. "Yes. I couldn't tell you, Grandfather."

"Did you think I wouldn't figure it out? A Sommen appears out of nowhere and American soldiers believe they've killed it with autocannons but upon closer inspection nobody can figure out how it died; there is no damage to the thing's armor. None. But you were there and government sensors detected a super-aware. Then the feds sweep in from DC with all their surveillance gear and you come to me with a crazy story about how you can't go home—that you need to hide." He paused and smiled. "It wasn't hard, Maung. Now your name is all over the net, all over the news, your biometrics fed into every police system out there. Because when they came to speak with you at home, you'd already disappeared."

"So it *was* a Sommen? That day at the complex?"

The Old Man smiled. "Of course it was. And it's important that you appreciate something, Maung: I can still get you out. It's all been arranged but you must understand that if you take this gift from me, *I own you*. If you ever act out of line, I can just turn you over to them and sell the information I have for the reward. Or I can go after your family. You will be my tool in an operation that could kill you, until I decide you've paid your debt."

Maung nodded but his mind worked overtime, processing everything the man said before he understood. "These girls. Your servants. You own them too."

"The ones I like best serve here, the rest I send to the brothels. They are sold to me, usually by their parents or grandparents who need money for all sorts of things, Maung. Things that only I can give them. The more *appreciative* the girls are, Maung, the shorter their service."

The Old Man handed Maung a stack of papers. He took it but felt as though he should be taking a shower instead, and Maung imagined there were germs in the air, scum particles that detached from the man and floated alongside the dust to infect anyone who got too close.

"You will learn to be appreciative, too, Maung. These papers are your new life. It turns out that the only biometrics they have on you are the basics—height, weight, eye color—nothing that really matters. They haven't had time to go through all the refugees yet and do retinal scans, fingerprints, and the rest. So getting you into the system will be easy." He handed Maung a card. "That will be your new identity card. The papers provide the back story so read it all—memorize the details. Then destroy them; we did this on paper so there will be no digital trail whatsoever of the changes we'll make."

"How?" Maung asked. "You can't just create a new person."

"No. But someone couldn't pay his debts and when that happens there's no reason to let them keep breathing, and why shouldn't you take his place? He had no family." The Old Man handed him one more sheet. "You have one hour to memorize your identity and then report to this address near the warehouses; tell them I sent you. The rest is up to you, Maung. Once you arrive at your new destination, your new life, I will contact you with additional instructions. Things are happening all around us, things you know nothing about but that I'm sure you feel. Why bring all of Southeast Asia into America? Why, after all these years, does a single Sommen rise from the depths and attack? Why did the someone kill all the Dream Warriors but let one get away?"

Maung's mind wandered and drowned among all the questions and the best he mustered was a shrug; it was too much. All he remembered was saying "thank you" after the Old Man agreed to give his mother a weekly allowance, and an overwhelming urge to run flooded over him. It vaulted Maung back into the humidity before the Old Man's cold and dry breath made him vomit. In war, Maung had killed. But it had been a long time since he met real evil and if the Old Man was American, no longer a Myanmarese, then this was another reason Maung would never trust this country, another motive to day dream of the jungle near Yangon where human parasites got slaughtered.

All afternoon he studied. The wind blew off the water and onto Charleston's Battery, and pink and brown Americans surrounded him as they walked their children and dogs. Maung ignored them.

He read the information he'd been ordered to memorize and immediately smiled at the Resident Identity Card's name: Maung Mi Tun—from Mandalay, the city where Maung first trained at the Chinese-built Academy. He didn't even have to change the most important part of his name because he'd already *lived* the geography. If Maung never said anything good about the Old Man he could say this: He picked the right identity, which couldn't have been more perfect. Maung said a prayer for the real Maung Mi Tun, and begged for forgiveness, asking the man's ancestors to allow him peace for the sake of his mother and son.

The address on the last sheet of paper from the Old Man was in Summerville, a surgeon's office in a white neighborhood. Maung opened his wallet. He figured he had enough paper money to pay for a few fares, and on his way to the bus stop he dropped his bank card in a mailbox. He said another prayer—that whatever money was left found its way to his mother. Maung pocketed his cash and new ID card, and threw everything else into the bay. He hoped, once he got there, he could make it from the bus stop to the doctor without anyone asking why a refugee had wandered into all-American territory.

"I'm Doctor Lawrence," a man in a white lab coat said, "and I'm told you need me to input some biometrics and then prepare your employment physical."

Maung sat on the table and shrugged. "I don't know. They just told me to come here."

"That sounds about right." The doctor reached for a green flexi-pad, snapping it open so that glowing lines appeared. He tapped at them, moving them in a pattern that meant nothing to Maung. The doctor noticed something and stopped.

"This is odd; the Old Man stopped sending people there two years ago but you're the second person he's sent to me today."

Maung sat up straight. "What? Where am I being sent?"

"It says you've been assigned to Karin 2. A prison. As a guard."

Maung smiled at the name. *Karen.* It had to be a sign, he thought, and he thanked the memory of his great grandmother, a Karen herself, her family part of a movement that once sought to overthrow the government of Myanmar.

"Karen with an *e*?" Maung asked.

The doctor shook his head. "With an *i*."

"It's still a good name," Maung said. "Where is it? In Charleston?"

He laughed and then shook his head again. "Are you serious?" When Maung folded his arms, silent, the doctor's grin disappeared. "Karin is a maximum security prison in the Kuiper belt, on an S-type asteroid with the same name of one that used to exist near Mars; Karin 2 was the former site of an American base for interplanetary operations. Our forces retreated there when the Sommen came. One of the major corporations bought it a while back and converted it into a penitentiary."

Maung forgot how to breathe. The realization that by going to space he wouldn't be able to get back to his son made him hyperventilate, and he clawed at the doctor's jacket, pulling him in closer so he could get a better look at the flexi-pad.

"Are you sure?" he asked. "I've never been off-planet. *How can they spend me to space?*"

The doctor pried himself loose. "I'm sure it will be fine, Maung. Look, there's only a narrow window for this particular job because they need you on the next transport out; we have to get going. I have to input all your biometrics including retinal and DNA data and then give you a physical but the Old Man specifically *forbade* me from actually *conducting* a physical on you so basically I'll be making up most of my data. This is going to take about forty-five minutes, only after which will you be a fully integrated identity. Do you want the job or not? I cancelled appointments for three paying Americans just so you could be taken care of, so make a decision."

Maung clenched the table to keep his hands from trembling. He couldn't speak. He'd never considered going to space and had no idea what would happen to his family while he was gone, how they would be taken care of or if the Old Man would even keep his promise. But there were no other options. He nodded, and prayed that this was the right path and that he had the strength to fulfill his part of the bargain.

"Why?" he asked. "Why does the Old Man want me on Karin, so far away?"

"I have no idea. He doesn't give me any details other than what he wants done, Maung. You know as much as I do. And there will be no training for the Karin job; you show up as is. Have you had any military experience?"

"Yes. I was in the Tatmawdaw—the Myanmar Army—and fought in the last war, against the Americans."

"I figured," the doctor said. "Combat experience should help because from what I hear, it's a violent place."

By the time Doctor Lawrence finished, it was after five and Maung got on a bus heading back into the city. His mind raced. The day had turned into a mix of horror and uncertainty that he wanted to forget and tears welled in his eyes, then slid down his cheeks as he looked out the window. It was impossible to know when he'd see his son again, and now it would be almost impossible to send money. And the thought of going up the spaceport elevator terrified him. For a moment he raged against his ancestors: *How could you let this happen to your family?*

His bus ride passed in a blur. Eventually Maung arrived at the address the doctor gave him, at a partially demolished warehouse on the river just as vapor lights flickered on, after which someone told him to stay out of the way until they were ready. Maung held his nose; the warehouse must have been used to store fish and it smelled like all of them were still there, rotting. He watched while a group of men struggled with fiberboard crates; they wrestled them off a forklift and into the back of an enclosed semitrailer, and once they finished with these they lifted what—to Maung—looked like a huge birdcage. A fine silver mesh covered its sides. In the dying sun the stuff shimmered and Maung stared at it, thinking it was beautiful, when another man waved him over and then helped Maung into the back of the trailer.

"Where do I go?" Maung asked.

The man pointed. "Into the cage."

"Why can't I just sit on a crate?"

"Look." The man climbed into the trailer and opened a flap on one side of the wire mesh, leaving just enough room for Maung to sneak through and inside. "I'm just doing my job. For some reason, our boss wants you inside this; it's a Faraday cage and will block any incoming or outgoing electromagnetic emissions. You're to stay there until arrival at Orbital Station One, Cargo Section Seven-Seven-B, at which point someone will come get you."

This bothered Maung, who until then had been dreading the ride upward on the elevator. He stepped into the cage and sat on a foam cushion. "You mean I won't get to look out a window on the way up? I won't see *anything?*"

"I make a good salary," the man said. "I mean I work here, loading and unloading and I'm not in a union, because here I make more than those boys do. You know why?"

Maung shook his head. The man's accent was southern and thick, and he had to concentrate to understand it.

"Because I don't ask questions. For some reason, they want you on the space station, in a Faraday cage, with the rest of the cargo. To me this says, 'You really don't want to know anything about this one because someone is going to an awful lot of trouble to sneak this scumbag refugee off planet.'"

The man jumped off the trailer before Maung could ask anything else, and then they loaded the rest of their crates, sandwiching his cage between walls of fiberboard boxes. Soon it was pitch black. Maung considered lighting a cigarette but then realized he'd already smoked them all and it hit him: He might not ever smoke again. If it was forbidden on the space station and in flight, things were about to get *truly* horrific.

Maung woke up. It was still pitch black and he heard a distant banging. Then things went silent again, leaving him to his thoughts and the darkness, which played tricks on him. He imagined shapes, black figures slightly darker than the darkness itself and Maung reached out to confirm they existed only in his imagination before he began praying, asking for help with the journey.

The cushion beneath him vibrated. Soon after there was a loud clanking and he heard the sounds of rockets, this time from the perspective of a passenger—not a laborer looking up from the street—and the feeling of acceleration made him smile as he got heavier and heavier, until finally the rockets cut off. Maung had seen this from the outside, hundreds of times; rockets helped the elevator start its journey upward. Now it climbed on fusion-powered servos, massive engines that turned a series of cogs, which in turn pivoted the gripper wheels and made the elevator rise. Maung yawned. For once he felt safe and the letdown made him tired, a kind of sleepiness that he hadn't experienced since the war and as he drifted off everything seemed a bit lighter.

CHAPTER THREE

Maung was falling. He screamed and reached out until his hands found one of the cage bars and he dragged the rest of him over to grip the metal tightly but still he fell. *The cage*, he thought; the cage itself must have been falling with the entire elevator because there'd been an accident, and Maung screamed again.

"*Shut up, for Christ's sake!*" someone hissed. A woman. Her voice sounded muffled as if coming from another room. "*We'll get caught!*"

"We are falling!"

"We're not falling. We're at the orbital spaceport and our containers are in customs awaiting inspection. What you're feeling is weightlessness because you are now in orbit around the Earth. *God* you're dumb."

Maung relaxed a little but the sensation still disturbed him. He maintained his grip on the bar.

"Won't we get caught during inspection?" he asked.

She laughed. "They only inspect about one container in a hundred; there are too many these days. And if they inspect *yours*, I hope your skin is made of lead."

"Why?"

"Because," the woman said, "it's done automatically, by bots, using powerful x-rays and you're sure to be cooked alive."

The words terrified Maung. This time, instead of screaming, he vomited.

To Maung it seemed as though days had passed and the tight

space smelled so awful that he was sure someone would come to inspect. Had he known what would happen upon throwing up he would have tried harder not to; his last meal coated much of his body.

"So where are you from?" the woman in the next container asked.

"Myanmar. You?"

"You're *Burmese*." She said it in a way that made Maung glad he couldn't see her, glad there were walls between them. "That makes sense. A backward country filled with stupid jungle people. No wonder you threw up."

"Myanmar is as modern as any other country."

For a few seconds she went quiet. Then the woman said, "Without the Chinese, Myanmar's greatest export would still be carved statues and Buddha trinkets. You smear mud on your faces. Jesus. What's that even about?"

"Where are *you* from?" Maung asked.

"Laos. I'm Laotian, but born in America. I fought in the war."

Maung sneered. "Yes. *This* backward jungle man killed thousands of Laotians and without the Americans your kind would still be massacring hill people with machetes." He was not sorry about saying it and ignored the regrets that usually haunted him; it was war.

"*Asshole*," she said.

Finally there was light. Maung tried to open his eyes but the brightness hurt and rough hands seized him by the ankles; *the Americans found me,* he thought. He swung at one of the figures snatching at his legs and it connected, but the impact sent Maung spinning in weightlessness so that his head banged against the bars; he took hold of one, gripping it as hard as he could.

"*Goddammit!*" a voice said. "I'm not customs, we're here to get you out. Give us a break so we can get you onto the ship."

Someone else sounded angry, punching at Maung's arms in an effort to coax him loose. "This idiot puked his guts out. We should make him clean up the whole friggin' container."

"What ship?" asked Maung. "Who are you?"

"*We're here to get you on the transport to Karin, you little bastard!*" Maung was too weak and too tired to hang on much longer. He let go. Before he knew it, someone had wrapped him in their arms, but Maung could tell from the man's cursing that something was wrong.

"Watch out for the bulkhead!" someone shouted.

Maung's head struck something and he winced, shutting his eyes from the pain but also because he was too scared to look at where they took him.

Fingers forced his eyes open and Maung's vision adjusted to a dimly lit room, tight and cramped, and everything looked as though it'd been strapped or bolted down. He'd never seen anything so modern. Someone shone a brilliant light into his left eye. Then the light hit his right eye and he said, "Stop," trying to wave his hand at it.

"How many fingers?" a man asked.

"Two."

"Good. You'll make it. Those idiot cargo handlers gave you a bit of a bruise, but not a concussion. I'd say you'll have a headache for a while but nothing major. Nothing we need to use the Medsys for." The man took Maung's hand and shook it, introducing himself as the ship's doctor but Maung was too tired to hear the name. "Anything to do with Karin is on a budget so we have to trust on X-rays and finger tests when we can. Now you're going to feel a sting on your right arm." Maung did, and the man continued. "That's just a little cocktail to help maintain your DNA structure and bone density. You'll need one of those each week on Karin to stay healthy."

"I want to sleep," he said.

"No problem." The doctor floated away toward the door. "We'll wake you up for the trip briefing. Three hours. And I suggest you clean up." He tossed a damp towel, which floated across and wrapped around Maung's face. "You're covered in puke."

Someone grabbed Maung, shaking him by the shoulders, and he cursed in Burmese, jerking his eyes open and instinctively reacting by trying to throw a punch. But he was strapped in. Maung forgot where he was until his eyes adjusted and a boy—no more than nineteen—held a flexi-pad as if it were a shield, floating at the hatchway in case he needed to exit quickly.

"Maung Mi Tun?" the boy asked.

"What? No," said Maung, before he remembered. "I mean yes, that's me."

"Captain said that the company wants the new Karin guards in the wardroom in ten minutes. Come with me?"

It took Maung a minute to disentangle from what looked like a vertical bed, narrow and gray. When he was free, he reached for the nearest handhold. "I've never been in space," he said.

"That's OK. A lot of the new hires are like that. All you need to do is follow me and try to do what I do; I'll move slow. Oh, and here." The boy handed Maung a plastic bag. "If you get sick, throw up into this. There's a plastic seal to tie it off, and since you have a head injury the doc insisted. Just shove it in your pocket for now. Once your head is good, he can give you some pills to take care of any motion sickness you might have from weightlessness."

Maung looked down to find that someone had dressed him in the same blue-gray jumpsuit the boy wore, and he shoved the bag into one of the pockets. He felt his ID there and a pair of plastic cards, which he drew out.

"What are these?"

"Company chow card," the boy said. "You get three meals a day, no more, and the other is company coms card. You stick that into coms terminals if you want to talk with anyone off Karin; coms are free but the card helps keep track of who uses what, I guess in case they have a jailbreak. Don't lose any of that stuff. Ready?"

Maung figured he wasn't, but he nodded anyway.

Moving became easier. Maung sweated at first and did his best to keep from looking stupid but soon he got the hang of it and kept up while the boy explained how the layout of the ship made movement simple: Each corridor had a handrail bolted to the wall. The rail for pulling yourself toward the bow was blue striped and the aft red striped. At first, gripping his rail was the only thing on which Maung concentrated. But once he got the hang of it he had time to look around and appreciated that as easy as it was to move, it was also easy to get lost; each intersection gave Maung a glance down side passages that extended into darkness and all around him humming pumps, electronics, and engines filled the cramped spaces. Not a single cubic centimeter was wasted. And, when after ten minutes they still hadn't seen another person, Maung wondered if they were the only two people on the ship.

"What kind of ship is this?" Maung asked.

"Aframax tanker. We carry almost all hydrogen so whatever you do, don't smoke." When Maung frowned, he said, "That was a joke."

"Hydrogen? A prison needs this much?"

The boy nodded. "Yeah, well it's not *just* for the prison. We all work for Carson Corp, a system-wide multinational conglomerate with its headquarters in Singapore. So this vessel services all of Carson's holdings when she's needed. Right now we have two guards headed for Karin 2 along with 300,000 liters of hydrogen, and then we'll deliver the rest to about a dozen other installations throughout the solar system."

"How many of us are onboard?" he asked.

"Including you and the other prison guard, thirteen. We have two crews of five so we can take turns on duty and one company physician. The crews and the doc are all located forward, near the bridge, and you guys are in the guest quarters, all the way aft. The rest of this ship is hydrogen storage, engines, and bots; she's mostly automated."

"That's it? Eleven humans for a craft this big?" When the boy nodded, Maung got a chill and thought that the ship could hide a lot of things. *Like ghosts.* He prayed to his ancestors and hoped he wasn't too far from them, still close enough that they heard.

Maung almost ran into a pair of tennis shoes when the boy stopped at a hatch. The door chugged upward. Once his escort was through, Maung followed into a small space about ten meters square and three meters high, with desks bolted to what must have been the floor. Only fifteen desks fit into the tight space. All of them were empty except one, and from her glare, Maung figured that this was the girl from Laos—the one who told him to shut up from the next container over.

He was sure of it when she flipped him off.

Once the boy left, Maung pulled himself into one of the desks and slipped his feet into floor straps to help him stay put.

The girl chuckled. "You won't make it at Karin, *Tatmaw.* Look at you: You're already bandaged and can barely function in zero g."

"Zero *what*?"

"My God, you *are* stupid." The girl slipped a cigarette from a pocket and Maung was startled when she inhaled without lighting it, then blew a white cloud of vapor.

"What is that?" he asked.

"Electronic cigarette. They've only had them for *centuries*, jungle boy."

"Not in Myanmar," Maung said.

The girl laughed and Maung couldn't help but notice that she was beautiful. A red band kept her black hair in a ponytail and he guessed it was about shoulder length, and her nose was thin, pointed, reminding him of his wife's so that he stared for longer than he intended to, marveling at skin that was smooth and light brown.

"*Quit looking at me*," she snapped. When he did, she continued. "Alternative nicotine delivery systems. In space some people use electronic cigarettes because they like to keep it as close to the original thing as possible. Others chew tobacco. But you can't spit; so unless you've done it long enough to swallow all that nicotine—without getting sick—forget it. Then there are microbot systems in a transdermal patch that respond to stress levels, and which give you random jolts of extra nicotine. Those are fantastic, but expensive. Of course there are people who decide to move on to other drugs altogether but I'm old-fashioned." She paused to take another drag. "You've *never* heard of these?"

Maung tried to answer but couldn't. He knew that what she said was true and it sounded familiar but the memories refused to surface, and his face went hot first with embarrassment then anger.

"I am not *stupid*," he said and pounded his fist on the desk, but the movement forced him upward and he almost floated away.

"Where we're going, Tatmaw, we'll be prisoners just like the convicts, so you better learn zero g; you'll have to fight in this shit if you want to survive."

"How do *you* know about Karin?"

"This is my second tour; I ran out of money after getting back from my first stint on Karin, and got into a bit of legal trouble. So unless I want to work in a brothel, it's the only job I know. Don't kid yourself, Tatmaw. One out of ten guards never come back and the ones who volunteer, the ones who aren't forced here like you? They usually quit in *one* month—hop the next hydrogen transport out on credit and work it off on some mining station in deep, deep space. I don't want to mine."

Maung shivered. He was about to ask her more questions when

the door opened again and a short man, fat and bald, barely fitting into his jumpsuit and sweaty with the effort of having gotten himself there, burst into the room.

The man looked them both over and then wiped his head. "I'm Captain Jacobsen. You two are guests on the *Singapore Sun* and just so we're clear, I have a few simple rules you'll follow or I'll blow you out the airlock. The fact that they sent you to me in boxes means one of three things: you're wanted, you're idiots, or you're both."

The captain's voice irritated Maung and his mind wandered; he *was* stupid. Part of him wanted to break down, right there, because he feared the girl was right and that he wouldn't make it if he had to survive at Karin as half a person. The captain described where the entertainment and fitness centers were and Maung laughed internally, thinking that if they were like the rest of this ship they were probably in the same kind of space, a tiny box into which you could barely cram one person. Finally the captain finished and before leaving said, "Carson Corp has a training video for Karin guards. You're to watch it here, and then you can pull it up in the ship's library at any time. I suggest you watch it a few more times to memorize the rules; that's all the help I can offer except for one more thing: pray. Pray all the way to Karin that you don't die on that frozen rock."

He floated to the door. Just as it closed behind him, a holo-vid began, the blue and green fields intersecting in patterns that formed a person, but which reminded Maung of *the soak*—the instant in which he bonded with the semi-aware and merged into the safety of power. He wanted to activate so badly that he almost switched on, imagining the supremacy if he once more let his organic mind join with an electronic buzz. The semi-aware would have jacked into each of Maung's neurons, almost making decisions for him and suspending his consciousness in a kind of hammock of semi-aware logic, giving his brain a chance to rest.

"Watch and learn," the girl said, ripping Maung from his daydream. "This is your first taste of company life, Tatmaw. Your killing days are about to start again."

After the holo ended Maung pulled himself back to his cubicle. He prayed. A clock stuck to the wall but Maung ignored it because time was another enemy, a kind of threat where even the thought of minutes and seconds might have prevented him from concentrating on the words that already formed in his mind; praying had never been this difficult. Several years had passed since he prayed this much, but Maung shouldn't have forgotten the words this quickly and recalling them should have been easy. Eventually he relaxed. With a long sigh, the words rolled off his tongue and he said them aloud in a whisper, carefully traversing the lines and the verses to get them right because the pattern mattered just as much as the words. His pulse slowed.

Maung ignored it when engine tests made the lights flicker on and off, and he was deep enough into thought that the meaning of the flickering was lost on him anyway; Maung cycled back to the beginning of the prayer. Before long he saw them and grinned. His dead comrades watched over everything and his wife stood next to him so he kept his eyes closed for fear of sending her away but when he finished he realized that she was crying.

Maung sensed something behind him and spun around, forgetting about the lack of gravity and sending himself into a corkscrew. But he caught a glimpse. A mass of black hair was at his hatch, which he had left open, and the Laotian girl breathed too loudly as she retreated back into the corridor.

The prayer still rotated in his mind. It was not a prayer from Myanmar but from India, and Maung didn't mind because there were two lines that resonated: *Examine your speech when with many people; examine your mind when alone.*

The Laotian later returned, half dressed, and she zipped her jumpsuit the rest of the way while his hatchway framed her. She was like a picture. For a moment, Maung thought she was the only woman who ever existed and when he opened his mouth to speak nothing came out.

"I came to see what you're up to," she said. "I'm super bored."

Maung coughed and an idea came to him. "We'll be in transit for a while and you are right; I will not survive if I can't fight. Will you teach me how to fight in zero g?"

"Do you have a brain, Tatmaw?" she asked. "I'm not here to serve you; I'm not one of the Old Man's toys."

His face went red from embarrassment. "I'm sorry. I didn't mean . . ."

The girl laughed and shut his hatch, nearly catching Maung's fingers in the sliding mechanism.

Maung floated in the mess hall. He slid his card into the reader, which pinged, and then he placed his bowl under a nozzle that exuded a brown paste reminiscent of ngapi, which made him miss the Yangon streets. Maung reminded himself most of the smells were horrible. But for now all he remembered were the good ones, the spices in the marketplace and the smoke from cooking chicken and fish, and how his mother served ngapi with everything.

The machine pinged off.

He snatched his bowl of paste and floated over to a table where he slid in, hooking his knees underneath the way he'd learned from watching others. There was no taste. The paste had the right nutrient mix and the correct amount of fiber, but was so flavorless that Maung had trouble swallowing, having to force it down with exaggerated gulps. He was almost finished when something slammed the back of his head and forced his face into the plastic bowl.

Maung jerked his head up to see a white man in an orange jumpsuit—one of the crew. He had seen the man before, one who worked with robots in the engine room, and was about to say something when someone grabbed him from behind, pinning his arms so the first could close in. The one in the orange jumpsuit clutched him by the hair and punched him with his free hand, over and over, and Maung couldn't believe how large the man's fist looked. While pounding, the man called him *a damn gook*.

There was a flash of bluish gray and the men shouted. One screamed and blood floated in the air, some of it mixing with the paste in his bowl.

"Well," the doctor said, "*this* didn't help your head injury and now you have a black eye, but you'll be OK. I injected a bolus of microbots to handle everything so that in a day or two, it'll be as good as new."

Maung blinked. He was in his quarters again and had no idea how he got there; he remembered the fight and that he'd been knocked unconscious.

"What happened?"

"Word's out that you're Burmese, Maung. A few of the guys on this ship fought in the war and aren't too happy about having you here."

Maung's face went red. "I lost friends. *My wife.* Americans took everything from me and *this* is why I'm on my way to Karin. To hell with all of you."

The doctor patted him on the shoulder and sighed. Maung felt the pain in his face, but even more intense was his need for a cigarette and his skin crawled with nervous energy and nicotine withdrawal.

"Look," the doctor said. "I'm not the kind who still lives in the war. But I can understand how they *and* you must feel. Think about altering your eating schedule so you don't run into those fellas? It's a big ship."

"How can *you* understand?" Maung asked. "You're a doctor. *Not a soldier.*"

The doctor put away his gear. "I was there, Maung. Navy surgeon stationed at the main hospital in Bangkok when it was overrun by Chinese genetics. In less than a month they killed most of us for experiments—the women and the wounded too—and if the peace agreement hadn't been signed when it was, I would have been next."

Maung closed his eyes. The pain in his head throbbed to the point where he lifted his hand to press it against his temple, but now there was an uneasiness in his chest from not having realized the doctor was a veteran.

"I didn't know."

The doctor pushed himself to the open hatch but then stopped before leaving. "Don't sweat it, Maung. And you owe Nang a big thank you."

"Who?"

"Nang. Nang Vongchanh, the girl headed with you to Karin. She nearly killed those two guys and we'd all love to know where she learned to fight."

Maung closed his eyes again and tried to remember but couldn't, only calling to mind the flash of blue-gray, which he assumed was Nang, maybe her jumpsuit. *Nang Vongchanh.* Maung hated the twangy sound of spoken Laotian—and their names—but this one slipped through his thoughts in a gentle way and the when the doctor pronounced it the word made a soft noise, barely disturbing the air. He opened his eyes to ask the doctor if he had any electronic cigarettes, but the room was empty.

Someone knocked on his hatch. Maung opened it and shoved back, preparing himself for a fight by grabbing the handhold on the far wall and getting ready to kick. When he recognized Nang's hair he relaxed; she shut the hatch and braced herself against the walls.

"You're alive," she said.

"Thank you, Nang."

"So now you know my name, *Maung*. That doctor talks too much. Don't get too grateful; I would have helped if those animals had been kicking a rabid dog."

"Well, I still thank you."

Nang looked at her feet and Maung stared. A feeling of guilt grew in his gut. Somewhere his wife rested, watching, and Maung said a quick prayer to beg for her forgiveness, but the words were confused and he started over. There was something about this girl, and it hit Maung quickly so that for the first time in years his heart raced.

"There," Nang said, "*that!*"

"What?"

Nang opened the hatch. "What you were just muttering, what is it?"

"It's a prayer."

She nodded and then said "My father used to pray like you do. He was first generation and came from a small village in the mountains near China; spent his whole life fighting Chinese border incursions and eventually lost a leg. The Americans took him and my mom from the jungle. Regrew his leg. My first memory was of him saying prayers like that at bedtime. I was always embarrassed by him—always thought he was dim witted, a mountain villager who would never fit in with the families of my white friends." She stopped talking and her face hardened again.

"Get ready," she said, pulling herself out into the passageway. "We'll start tomorrow."

Maung shrugged and the motion sent him down to bounce off the floor. "Start what?" he asked. "Where can I get one of those cigarettes?"

"Get some rest," she called out. "Tomorrow is a big day."

"You have to *learn* this," Nang said. "Otherwise, you're dead already."

It was the next "day," although Maung had no sense of time and had not been able to sleep in zero g, so his eyes squinted and haze filled his head. They floated in the corridor outside Maung's cube. Somewhere in his mind was a memory of zero-g combat training; he had *already* learned it. But no matter how hard he tried to recall the details, it remained locked away in the structure of the semi-aware along with all the things that transformed him from a village idiot into a humanlike thing.

"I'm still hurt," he said. "My head."

"It doesn't matter if you're hurt; every soldier knows this, what's wrong with you? It won't matter to your enemies on Karin, and you need to get used to the likelihood that you will always have some kind of injury. The first thing about zero g: have a good grip on something or brace yourself in a doorway, or between walls, before you strike."

"Look," said Maung. "I'm tired. I—"

He didn't get to finish. Nang launched herself by yanking on the railing and twisted so that her feet rocketed forward, impacting against his stomach. All of her momentum transferred. While he tried to catch his breath, Maung sailed down the corridor, finally stopping himself by grabbing a rail.

"*What the hell are you doing?*" he asked.

She laughed but then got serious. "Those two men were going to kill you Maung. One of them had a knife. I barely stopped him from slitting your throat *and we're not even to the prison yet!*"

Maung shook his head clear and asked, "What did you do to them? Someone was hurt worse than me?"

"I took the knife from one of them and liberated him of a finger. He can grow a new one back on Earth."

The joke made him laugh. He felt warmth in his stomach and decided that *this* was the path; for a split second Maung thought he'd heard his ancestors' agreement: Nang was good and there was a smiling nod of approval from his wife which made him smile. *Nang means well.*

"Thank you," he said again.

She launched herself before he was ready and this time her fists slammed into his solar plexus, one after another, knocking the wind from him, and then Nang hooked her feet under the wall railings, bracing herself before grabbing his shoulders and yanking downward. Maung spun in the air, somersaulting.

"*Stop being so nice; this is combat!*"

Maung sat across from her and gagged on his paste. Nang had a squeeze bottle of spicy fish sauce and she loaned it to him, watching as he squirt some on. It helped. At least now the paste had more flavor and Maung waved his hand across his mouth, smiling at her while his tongue burned.

"Hot," he said.

Nang looked away. "Did the Tatmawdaw soldiers train the same way we did in America—direct cortex loading?"

Maung stopped smiling. Unconsciously he reached up and traced the thick scars, four of them on the back of his head, and he nodded slowly, scared of where she might take the conversation. He had never been good at lying. And now, without the ability to merge, he was certain that he'd forget how to describe things in a believable way.

"Yes," he said.

"Isn't zero-g combat part of the training package? I know it was for the Chinese and assume you used the same or similar package."

Maung thought as quickly as he could. Nang must suspect something, he figured, and she stared at him so intently that Maung looked down at the table.

"Well?" she asked.

Maung picked up his bowl and stuck it into the recycling chute, and then kicked toward the hatch. He waited for it to open. "You're right, Nang. I *am* too stupid to be a soldier. If I were to sign up today, the best I could hope for is assistant ass-wiper, and you're much more intelligent than me—a better soldier. But in war people make decisions and then things happen and some people wind up defective. Subnormal. That's all I'm going to say; I can't remember my training."

Maung guided himself into the corridor and almost collided with two crewmen, who knocked him out of the way, sending him out of control and into an overhead pipe gallery; he noticed that one of them was missing a finger. Maung hooked a foot under a railing, seized on the closest one and wrenched the man's head straight down, jerking a knee upward at the same time so that the crewman's nose cracked on contact. Maung let go; the man spun backward and an arc of blood spread outward from his face.

The other looked about to throw himself forward but Maung said, "I'll kill you. Now it's just you against me. You're all alone."

Maung heard someone move in the hatchway behind him; he thought it must be Nang. She had come to see what was going on but Maung wanted nothing to do with her right now; he was ashamed of how stupid he looked to all of them.

The other man grabbed his shipmate, who was holding his face; he nodded toward Maung and said, "I think you broke his nose and he needs the doc; can I get by?"

"Sure."

The man pushed his friend down the hall. Blood had already splashed against Maung's jumpsuit and he felt sick, so he waited until the crewmen disappeared before heading back to his cube, ignoring a call from Nang to wait for her.

CHAPTER FOUR

Maung spent his time in the entertainment and exercise rooms to avoid running into Nang, but boredom threatened to split his mind into fragments. There was *nothing* green here. The walls were either sterile gray plates, scrubbed clean and polished by microbots, or galleries of white pipes, red pipes, blue conduits—all of it man made and perfect, the temperature constant. There was no balance. He knew they were still close to Earth but were about to begin the acceleration phase where, as soon as the window opened for a safe path to Karin 2, the ship would activate its main engines and all of them would be confined to their quarters until they reached target velocity. He wanted to taste his mother's soup again; Maung remembered what it was like to hold his son and to smell the boy's hair, a scent which reminded him of springtime.

Maung now doubted he could handle running from his family and a sense of solitude crushed his chest.

Instead of knocking, someone used the button outside his cube; the bell chimed. Maung shouted "come in" and the hatch slid up. When Nang entered, the sadness left because here was something that made sense, which was strange because during the war she was the enemy and there was a time he would have gladly slipped a knife across her throat. Nang was a symbol. She represented a part of his past that he hadn't recalled in years, and wasn't like the American crew; she had a round, gentle face and her skin reminded him of home—of dead friends and his wife.

"You fought all right," she said. Nang grasped the wall strap farthest from him, but this was only a meter away; she smelled clean and new. "The other day when you ran into those two crewmen who knocked you out. I haven't seen you since then."

"I wanted to kill them."

"Maybe you're ready for Karin after all," she said and then laughed. "I'm sorry I pried, Maung. Into your past."

"It's fine."

"No it's not. I was there the same as you and the war got ugly. My unit forced the Chinese out of Laos and across the mountains, through the villages like the one my father was from. I saw what the Chinese did to civilians. I guess when I look at you I see them and the Tatmawdaw, and maybe it's not fair; maybe that's *not* who you are. But it's hard to forget what happened."

Maung couldn't remember much from the war. He tried, but instead of memories a swarm of guilt and sadness overtook him, because he suspected the truth but couldn't picture it, as if trying to watch a movie through smoked glass.

"I don't remember much," he said. "but you have to know, Nang: I think I was guilty of doing things that would make you sick and perhaps it would have been better had I died. I just don't remember."

He thought she would leave. The expression on her face broke a barrier in his mind and Maung remembered something small: the horrified look of mothers and fathers when they watched as his drones and bots swept into their village and extracted DNA samples and organs from their children. As far as his superiors were concerned, the war was one of resources—mineral *and* human—and little went to waste. But instead of looking disgusted, Nang's face softened.

"I figured you had done awful things. They used to prosecute people like you and the Chinese, Maung; war criminals." She wiped a tear from her cheek. "But when we were training I noticed scars under your hair, the ones you try to hide, and I think you've been punished already. I don't hate you, OK?"

Maung looked away, embarrassed, but for some reason there was no fear. He'd told the truth about what he'd done, *without* revealing the scars' real meaning, that the Chinese replaced a part of him he could never recover, and she'd assigned a meaning of her own. For now his secret was safe.

"I was not wounded. But yes, they operated on me and I think the Chinese removed parts of my brain—without making me a vegetable. This is why I am so slow, why I can't remember."

Nang nodded. She slammed her fist against the hatch button and waited for it to open. "I won't ask again. I promise. You aren't the only one with secrets, Maung; let's agree to just leave them alone."

Maung nodded and before she left Nang said, "I'll come back for training tomorrow; you still have a lot to learn. Maybe to *relearn*."

"Why are you helping me?" he asked. "Someone who might be a war criminal?"

Nang said, "Part of me doesn't want to help you, the part that hopes you die on Karin. But I'm done acting like a soldier—a murderer—and if I can help you gain at least a fighting chance, I'll feel like for the first time I tried to save a life instead of take one. Plus, you're just like how I imagine my dad was, when he was young."

Maung couldn't breathe. Their training session had ended and Nang had tried to pull her kicks but on the last one her foot connected with his solar plexus, hard, so that it knocked the wind out. Finally he caught his breath and smiled.

"You did that on purpose—didn't try to pull your kick."

"You almost beat me," she said.

Maung nodded. "That must really make you mad."

Nang laughed and plucked a towel from one of the room's wall loops, then used it to wipe the sweat from her face. Maung watched while floating in midair; he was grateful. Time spent in the training room made him forget Earth, and for an hour or two he could stop worrying about his mother and son, and stop guessing what the Old Man would want once he reached Karin.

"How did *you* get sent out here?" he asked.

Nang wrapped the towel around her neck. "What do you mean?"

"I mean we both arrived secretly, in shipping containers and I think I've figured out why the Old Man sent me here; I was running from the police and he sent me away until he could figure out what to do. To buy time. You're going back for a second tour because you have debts; I get that. But you were in a box too. So if you went to the Old Man, why? Why not just sign up for guard duty directly?"

"First, that's not why he sent you," said Nang. She stretched, and the movement sent her into a slow spin, which to Maung seemed graceful. "I was in a similar spot. The debt I couldn't repay was a debt to *him* and the Old Man wanted me in one of his brothels; I told him I'd been to Karin before and would prefer a posting there. He agreed."

"What does that have to do with why he sent me?"

Nang laughed again. "You're not being sent here just so he can figure out what to do; he already figured out what to do. The Old Man gets a finder's fee and three quarters of your salary; the rest you can try to send home since there's nothing to spend it on out there, but he'll likely intercept that too. And all that time you're risking *your* life. So sending us here was a no-brainer, Maung; easy money for the Old Man, impossible for us. They pay an arm and a leg for guards to serve at Karin because nobody will take the job."

Maung thought for a few seconds. All he wanted was to reach out and grab her, to pull her in close and shove his nose into her hair, to smell the mountains again and be connected to home—to her. Maung perceived a kind of beauty in Nang that even his wife never had, and he must have been staring for a long time because she finally said, "Stop it, Maung."

"What?"

"Looking at me like that."

"Sorry, but I was just wondering about what you said; how long were you on Karin the first time you went?"

Nang finished her stretching. "I went there straight out of the army when the war ended. I did six months as a guard, which, I later found out, was a record for volunteers." She gestured for him to follow her out the hatch and back into the corridor. "We have one more day before they light the main engines. Let's train some more. We'll do it in the main corridor so you can get more practice in tight spaces; there won't be much room to maneuver in Karin."

"I don't hate you. At all." Even Maung was surprised he said the words; they came from nowhere and he wondered if the semi-aware somehow activated itself—but it hadn't. He went cold with embarrassment when she giggled and punched his arm, sending him against the bulkhead.

"You will when I kick your ass again."

As soon as he was through the hatch, Nang landed a punch to his ribs but Maung managed to push down from the overhead pipes and stop himself from flying away. He grinned and readied a counterattack.

"*My* turn."

By the time he climbed into bed, Maung's muscles ached and he imagined one or two might have been torn; at least one of his ribs was bruised. The ship thrummed around him and its walls vibrated at a frequency that translated into a warning of impending doom, and with every second the vessel brought them thousands of meters closer to a frozen asteroid. Soon they'd be hundreds of millions of kilometers from Earth and sun, at a place where he was sure the spirits of unrest waited. None of his ancestors died on Karin; how would they know the way if he needed help? Maung said a prayer, asking for them to join him on the trip and to show Nang's people—especially her father—the path too, so neither were alone. He repeated it, over and over, until sleep fought its way in.

Eight hours until ignition. Maung didn't know what to expect and he couldn't concentrate on training, waving Nang quiet so he could watch the news reports from Earth; soon these would be hard to get. Nang had begun telling him more about what to expect, and the captain had laid out the trip, which from here on out required them to stay strapped in.

"It's not that you can't, in theory, get the news on Karin," she continued, crammed into a corner of his living space, "it's just that they control it and keep a lot from people, including the guards."

"Who are *they*?" he asked.

"The chief guard, the guy who runs Karin."

"What about the warden?"

Nang shrugged and stabbed at a bowl of food paste, not really eating it. "The warden never showed up while I was there. Not once. He or she is a Carson Corp rep on Earth who manages remotely unless there's something really important to attend to. And the chief guard usually makes sure those kinds of things—if they happen and they're bad—don't get out. The higher-ups are such cowards they have an emergency ship stashed in a hidden dock in case there's a prison revolt and they *happen* to be there for some inspection."

"So how do I survive?" asked Maung.

"You survive," Nang said, "by not being noticed."

"I can do that."

Nang laughed into her bowl and looked up at him. "Somehow I doubt it; by now they'll already know that a Tatmaw is on his way, and most of these guys will be survivors of the war. Americans and their Asian allies."

Four hours until ignition. Maung did his best to flatten himself against the corridor bulkhead while an engineering team pulled their way past, too busy to even notice he was there. They seemed concerned about something. Maung was shaking by the time he reached the doctor's cube and he pressed the door chime. A moment later he was inside, grabbing a wall loop and terrified to the point he forgot what he came for.

"Is something wrong with the ship?" he asked.

"What do you mean?" Maung told him about the engineering team and the doctor laughed. "That's standard procedure. Before lighting the main engines these guys have to reinspect them one last time and it was a process that took at least an hour, even with the help of bots. They're under pressure, that's all."

Maung nodded but didn't say anything and the doctor squinted at him, then leaned forward against his sleeping restraints so Maung suddenly understood he'd woken him; it was too late to go back now, he decided.

"Sorry I woke you."

"Maung," the doctor said. "There is nothing to worry about. The ship is basically a massive cylinder that consists of three layers. In the outer layer we carry slush hydrogen in baffled tanks that surround us on almost all sides. Inside that is a thin layer. We fill that with a self-sealing material and dormant bots so that if small ruptures occur, bots are immediately activated to fill the break with a metallic patch. Bots are also dispatched outside to patch external damage, and these are all designed to work at super-high g-forces. Maung, a micrometeoroid struck us a few days ago; the system worked and everything is patched, and it's such a routine procedure that you never even noticed."

"Where are *we*?" asked Maung.

"In the inner core. We're in a small capillary in the center of the ship, and our engines and fuel tanks fill up the entire rear. We're completely safe—encased in layer upon layer of metal."

Maung nodded and apologized again for waking him up, twisted himself through the hatch, and made sure to thank the doctor one last time before the door closed. He began to shake again. If they'd already been hit once, what was to stop something from hitting them *again*, something so large that the entire ship was destroyed, or an object just large enough to penetrate and vaporize his head? Maung turned back to the doctor's hatch, but the *do not disturb* lamp blinked on.

One hour until ignition. All had been confined to quarters except the captain and his on-duty crew. Maung jerked the straps tight across his chest and waist, then watched the tiny holo in the middle of his cube where a woman in a Carson Corporation jumpsuit confidently described the safety features; Maung guessed that *she* had never been in space.

"One emergency vacuum suit is located in the storage space over your head, and consists of a reinforced, pressurized jumpsuit with integrated boots and gloves, a two-hour oxygen supply, and a semiflexible helmet unit. In case of depressurization, this compartment will open automatically. Place the jumpsuit on first . . ."

Maung screamed when a roar filled his ears. G-forces slammed him backward against his mattress, which hardened and shaped itself to support his body in foam—with a curved pad that cradled his head. It helped. But the pressure only increased and soon it took effort to inhale and Maung barely heard the automated voice announce that additional oxygen was being pumped into living quarters and work stations, and that crew members were to be wary of the increased fire danger. Maung closed his eyes. But he opened them right away because he was sure that the g-forces were liquefying them and he had to make sure they were fine and that his room wasn't engulfed in flames. The urge for a cigarette made him want to shout.

The ship's computer chimed onto his cubicle speakers, and Maung barely heard it over the engines. "*Administering first dose of acceleration drugs.*"

Before he could react, a needle jabbed Maung in the back of his neck and then retracted, so that now his neck burned as the drug soaked through his muscles. But the needle had come too close. After living with it for so many years, Maung could almost see exactly where his semi-aware resided; part of it stretched from his brain to his spine, and down. The injection had just missed it. In the future, he decided, he'd be ready to move out of the way and he was lucky that none of the ship's automated med sensors had found it. *Yet*.

The drugs made him sleepy and he barely recalled the video that had explained what was happening. The solution consisted of elastomer building blocks, which strengthened his connective tissues, and blood thinners that activated above one g so his heart wouldn't beat out of his chest under sustained acceleration. They also included microbots—tiny factories that scavenged spare amino acids to build temporary protein supports around vital organs—and Maung imagined he could feel them but figured this was impossible. He prayed to his ancestors that they wouldn't damage the nonorganic connections to his other half, rendering him stupid for the rest of his life.

Maung's vision blurred. He shut his eyes and tried to pray, but had trouble concentrating through the constant pressure until finally he drifted off.

When Maung was in Myanmar, even during the war, it had never occurred to him that one day he would be strapped into a miniscule cube room, hurtling through space toward a prison station that nobody wanted to see. He could barely lift his arm. Everything he needed to do—brush his teeth and eat, go to the bathroom—involved pushing himself slowly up from the pad, struggling against two gees to reach the other side of his quarters, and then functioning there for as long as it took. Days passed before he acclimated and sleep only came in increments, interrupted by his body's realization that he wasn't getting enough oxygen, forcing him awake to gasp for breath every twenty minutes.

Maung was inching his way along the bulkhead to the toilet when a deafening clang sounded behind him, followed by a whooshing noise and then silence. The air went cold. A panel overhead dropped down and the emergency suit unrolled between him and his bed while the ship's computer made a calm announcement as if everything was normal.

"Malfunction. Pressure and oxygen levels falling, please don your emergency suit."

Maung panicked. He grasped the suit and crawled back onto his acceleration pad, turning onto his back to begin sliding the legs on, one at a time while his muscles fought against gravity. There was a black spot on the opposite wall. Maung squinted. What he originally thought was a mark was actually a fist-sized hole in the steel bulkhead, an inch thick panel bowing out toward him, and when he looked at his cushion he recognized that his head rest was gone; another fist-sized hole had appeared in its place. Maung finished pulling the suit on, gently forced the helmet from its overhead slot, and then sealed it. He clipped on the oxygen unit. A few seconds later he could breathe and collapsed back onto his cushion, already exhausted, so tired that not even being terrified gave him energy.

Maung was grateful when the announcements stopped, but the next one almost made him scream with joy. *"Engine cutoff imminent; prepare for zero g."* It repeated itself three more times and then counted down, sending Maung into yet another panic while he struggled with his straps. The engines cut off and the change to zero acceleration barely sent Maung against his restraints with a return to weightlessness. Everything had gone silent.

Maung's hands refused to work while he tried to unbuckle, and he cursed before pounding on the wall in frustration.

"Get me out!" he screamed.

Maung calmed down when the survival suit's radio cut in and linked to the ship's communications network, where he heard the captain giving orders. Finally the buckle gave and Maung kicked off toward the hatch; he pounded on the panel and as soon as it opened he saw Nang in the corridor. Her face looked pale until she took Maung's hand, their environment suits preventing him from feeling her skin.

"You're alive!" she said. Her voice come over his helmet speakers.

Maung laughed. "Why wouldn't I be?"

"We've been hit by a meteoroid. As soon as I got my suit on I heard the computer list the compromised compartments and yours was on it. The doctor thinks you're injured or dead."

Maung had forgotten the holes in his bulkheads. Now he felt dizzy, and had to fight the urge to throw up since it could be potentially dangerous in the suit. "Well then where is he?" he asked. "Where's the doctor?"

Nang towed Maung from his cube and then led him down the corridor. "He's treating the crew; they're more important right now. The meteoroid sliced right through the main crew area, and almost destroyed the bridge."

"Nang," said Maung. He heard the fear in her voice and it unnerved him. "What else is wrong?"

"We're losing water. Coolant for the fusion reactors, and at least half the engineering crew is dead, maybe all four of them. The captain will need our help."

"But I heard the captain giving orders to the engineers."

Nang nodded. "He's sedated now because he has a head injury, and didn't know what he was doing. The first officer is taking command."

It took a few minutes to reach the front of the ship, and when they passed through the crew berths, droplets of floating blood adhered to Maung's suit. All the starboard cube hatches were open. It looked like the meteoroid went through the exact center of the ship, down its axis on the starboard side, and punctured the crew compartments one by one before heading out the rear and into the engine spaces.

"I don't understand," he whispered.

Nang asked, "What? What don't you understand?"

"How it missed me. I had just gotten up to use the toilet when it hit and the thing whizzed past me. It must have missed by millimeters."

Nobody on the bridge spoke. It was impossible for Maung to recognize anyone in their suits because the crew wore real ones with mirrored visors, the kind of suits capable of repair work inside and outside the ship. Including Nang and Maung, there were only seven people in the bridge. Someone sobbed. The urge to access his semi-aware hit with a force that Maung barely controlled, and he thought of it as an addiction, one that he'd never be rid of as long as the thing was attached to him. But he couldn't risk it. All they could do was wait for the first officer and hope that, in the meantime, the bots were doing their jobs.

Maung grasped that the first officer was barely conscious. After pulling himself into the bridge, the man tucked his left hand under his belt and his labored breathing echoed over Maung's speakers because it was loud enough to trigger his mic. But when the first officer spoke, it was barely in a whisper.

"I need you guys to stay focused. The bots should have the damage to the main crew section repaired within the hour and main life support will be able to repressurize this section within two. That's the good news." He paused to catch his breath before continuing. "The bad news is that we have a waterline rupture in the reactor area. The bots can't patch it. Without coolant we can't run the main engines, which means we drift until rescued."

"Or we drift forever," someone muttered.

The officer used his feet to hook under a console and punched on the touch pad with his good hand. A schematic holo popped up. Maung recognized the rear of the ship and the engine compartments, and the computer traced a red line to show the meteoroid's path.

The first officer pointed to a blinking red dot in the engine area. "The rupture is right here. It's in a spot too small for any of us to reach, and because the reactor still needs cooling the system won't allow us to deactivate pumps, which means water is shooting at high pressure; none of the bots can seal it. So somehow we have to get a manual patch on there so the microbots can do their job, in a space that the crew can't access." He shut the holo off. "I'm open to suggestions."

"Which idiot designed *that* system?" someone asked.

Nang raised her hand. "Where are we? Can we decelerate and get help?"

"Jennifer?" the officer asked.

The person who had been working at the control station was the navigator, who stopped, and Maung thought that she was looking at Nang but he couldn't be sure. "If we begin deceleration now, there is enough coolant to bring us to a stop. After that we can maneuver with gas thrusters."

"But would we be close to anything?"

"Europa," she said. "Jupiter was part of our navigational path, which included a leg to use its gravity to slingshot us and save fuel."

Maung's skin went cold. "That moon belongs to the Chinese. It's their main base in the system. Other than what they have on Earth and in orbit."

"That's right." Jennifer turned back to the panel and continued working. "But Beijing granted permission for our navigational route and asking them for help may be our only chance. That's all I can give you guys right now, but I'll try for a plan B."

One of the crew members muttered, "Chinese. I bet they *put* the meteoroid in our path. I mean, does anyone really think the peace treaty with them and Burma means anything?" He laughed then, but nobody else did, and Maung knew why: The Chinese were nothing to laugh at.

"How do I get one of those electronic cigarettes?" Maung asked.

CHAPTER FIVE

Maung couldn't allow them to stop at Europa; he remembered their bureaucracy, their systematic methods. Beijing's government representatives would demand to board and then half-human, half-machine creatures would scan every inch of the ship and when they did, it would activate Maung's systems, alerting both the Chinese and the ship's computer to his presence. There would be no hiding after that. Either the Chinese would leave him with the crew, who'd lock him away, or they'd take him off ship to their outpost. It terrified Maung to think of what would happen next—the experiments they would run. He was about to protest the idea when the first officer raised his hands.

"We're not stopping at Europa," he said. The rest of the crew began speaking at the same time, but the man spoke over them. "It's my decision not yours. This ship has been contracted out by the American and European governments, so we *can't* let the Chinese board as long as there's a chance we can handle things ourselves."

"Just what does that mean?" Nang asked.

"I know exactly what it means." Jennifer stopped working the navigation board and turned around. "It means they rented out part of the ship for spy gear. Observation equipment, sensors, and God knows what else because they predicted we'd be passing closer to Europa than anyone else in a long time. I bet Carson Corp just couldn't turn down a fat pay check like that."

The first officer broke into a fit of coughing, during which Maung sensed the tension; every second they waited, they lost more coolant.

And now they weren't just a tanker. If the ship had to ask for Chinese assistance they would *all* be labeled as spies and taken prisoner, or worse.

It took a few seconds for the first officer to finish coughing. "Just wait a minute. We don't know what the contract is for, but our instructions were clear: not to let the ship be inspected—by anyone. In the event we have to abandon ship, we're to destroy her."

Nobody said anything. Maung heard the alarms and occasionally the computer announced the status of different systems, but nobody spoke until Nang raised her hand again.

"So let's go to Europa and once we get there we all pile into the lifeboat. We send a message to Earth that we're in need of rescue, and then we self-destruct the ship."

Jennifer nodded. "I agree. A hundred and fifty percent."

"*No.*" The voice came from behind them and everyone turned to look.

The captain stood in the hatchway and behind him was the doctor, his helmet marked with a red cross, who helped the captain through the hatch and into his chair.

"There will be no abandoning ship—not as long as she can maneuver. All my engineers are dead or injured so I need a volunteer to attempt repairs, now, while we still have some water left."

Jennifer pounded her fist on the console, and then gripped it to keep from pushing off. "Sir, if you take that chance and we fail, there's no shot at decelerating for help and we end up heading off into space or run into a solid object."

The room went quiet again. "*Patching of main hydrogen storage tanks complete,*" the ship's computer announced, "*loss of approximately three point seven-eight percent by weight of hydrogen slush. Approximately twenty minutes until life-support systems reactivate.*" Maung tried to convince himself that everything was fine, mentally fighting back terror, and he wondered if the crew were thinking mutiny so he moved back and away from them, not wanting to get in anyone's way. He was about to leave the bridge when he had an idea. The thought scared him and despite the fact Maung had decided none of this was his responsibility, the idea refused to vanish and burrowed into his brain: *I may be the only chance we have.*

Before Maung knew it, he'd spoken. "I volunteer."

Nang grabbed his shoulder, spinning him to face her. "You *can't* volunteer. You don't know *anything* about ship operations."

Maung shrugged. "So tell me what to do. I'll learn. I'm also smaller than most people here and might fit into the space they described."

The captain hammered at buttons. He rattled off names and commands so fast that Maung couldn't follow, but people kicked off, one of them grabbing him by the arm and pulling. It was Jennifer, the navigator. She shoved Maung into the corridor and the two of them yanked along the railing as hard as they could, rocketing toward the aft sections and engine rooms. When they arrived at what looked like a workshop, Jennifer told him to wait in front of a massive hatch and not to move, before she disappeared into one of a dozen service shafts that lined the walls. Maung felt dazed, numb. Another crew member arrived and buckled a belt around his waist, to which the man added equipment that Maung'd never seen before, and he wondered if Nang had been right: The idea of him fixing anything was insane. His heart raced. Jennifer finally returned and detached the oxygen generator from his suit and slapped on a new one.

"This will give you another full hour of oh-two," she said. "And if you haven't succeeded by then, it really doesn't matter."

"Can't we just radio someone for help?" Maung asked.

"We have. The computer sent repeated automated distress calls as soon as we got hit and we've gotten no response; there's a good chance nobody will even hear it until it's too late—except for the Chinese. And now we all know why that won't work."

She spent five minutes explaining how to use the equipment on the maintenance belt, including the pipe patch, and Maung hoped he wouldn't forget it once she left. Jennifer punched a code in a panel beside the hatch. It split in the middle to open, the plates noiseless since there was still no atmosphere, and water sprayed out so Maung had to wipe his faceplate clear. A maze of pipes and machinery, their complexity and interconnections making him think they looked like the colorful veins of a monster, waited on the other side.

"Come on," Jennifer said, pulling him in after her. "We move forward toward the crawl space and then you just follow the water to its source; patch the pipe like I told you. I'll talk you through it on the radio if you forget anything."

⌘   ⌘   ⌘

What Jennifer called a crawl space was a barely one meter wide, forty centimeter high gap within the center of a pipe gallery, so that Maung had to squeeze into it on his back while she thrust against his feet. Now he understood why nobody else fit; his emergency helmet was cheap flexible plastic and so it conformed to the narrow space where regular helmets like Jennifer's wouldn't, and his thin frame barely scraped through with the suit, belt, and added equipment. His tools bounced against the pipes. Maung tried not to think about getting stuck while he hauled and wormed his way through the access space, doing his best not to touch one of the secondary coolant outflow conduits, a ceramic pipe that glowed red hot where insulation had chipped away.

"Section eight." Jennifer's voice crackled over the helmet speakers. "That's where you are right now. So keep going about another hundred meters and you should see the spray."

Maung didn't have to look. Water shot onto him as though he fought his way toward a fire hose, and then the droplets gently curved aft. A moment ago the captain had ordered the area semipressurized with argon. That way, along with partially opening a rear airlock, it created a gas flow and emptied the area of water to minimize potential damage to electrical components.

"Crank it up, Maung," said Jennifer. "We're running out of time."

"I know." He tried to sound calm despite the fact that he was starting to get angry; what did she think, that he was having *fun*?

Plumbers never looked at stars, thought Maung, and he thanked his ancestors for the opportunity to contribute something to life instead of killing, even though this wasn't how he envisioned it, and he asked for the willingness to continue forward with enough courage to ignore his fear. Little by little, he moved closer. The spray impacted his faceplate now with force, and the plastic pressed against his nose so it immediately fogged; Maung cursed out loud.

"What's wrong?" asked Jennifer.

"I can't see. Fog. I'm going to keep moving; maybe if I get past the break I can look at it from behind and see a little better. The rupture is in the overhead gallery, right?"

Jennifer confirmed it and he moved again. Soon the jet impacted against his chest, then his stomach, and Maung tried to block it with his arms but then gave up when he realized he needed them. He tightened his stomach muscles against the high-velocity jet and wiped his faceplate clear.

The rupture was huge. Maung watched as water shot in a wide Mohawk shape, and microbots looked like a greasy smear around its edges as they tried to adhere to the pipe.

"It looks like the bots have at least cleaned the rupture," he said. "There's no bent or twisted metal that I can see and it may be possible to get the clean seal you said we'd need."

This time when Jennifer clicked in, she sounded tense. "Abort, Maung. We just did another round of calculations and the computer is giving new numbers; it won't be long until there isn't enough water to run the engines. We're going to start deceleration and you have to get strapped in."

"How much time do I have?" he asked.

"Twenty minutes; enough time to get to your cube. Otherwise you'll take the gees down your axis and be thrown head first against a bulkhead; that helmet will split wide open along with your skull."

Maung's hands shook as he squirmed to pull the manual repair kit from his belt, but when he reached for the patch it wouldn't budge. Somehow the thing had worked its way between a set of pipes and wedged itself tight, just below the small of his back where he couldn't get leverage.

"Shit," he whispered. "*Shit!*"

"What's wrong?" she asked. "I don't understand what you're saying."

Maung had spoken in Myanmarese without realizing it, the fear like a vice around his throat. "I'm stuck. Shit, shit, *SHIT!*" He jerked himself as best he could to either side, then, without thinking, seized hold of the red-hot pipe overhead and used it to pull himself upward a centimeter and then back; the patch sprang free.

Another voice chimed in, one he'd never heard before. "*Suit integrity failure; depressurization in five minutes.*" The message repeated itself, and Maung yelled at it to be quiet.

"Maung," said Jennifer, "We're reading that your suit is splitting open in the palms of both gloves."

Maung remembered Jennifer's instructions and concentrated on a section of the pipe that wasn't broken, opened the clamp patch on its hinge, and wrapped it around. Then he inserted bolts into the patch's holes and threaded the nuts on, ratcheting them down halfway. Now, he thought, came the tricky part. Maung had to slide the partially assembled clamp sideways, over the broken section of pipe, and use the electric wrench to clamp it all the way down—while a super-pressurized jet of water fought his efforts.

"*Suit integrity failure imminent; depressurization in three minutes.*"

Maung used the other end of the ratchet as a hammer, and slammed it against the patch so that it scraped sideways, eventually seating itself over the leak. Now, instead of spraying downward, the water jetted out on both sides of the patch, turning into steam when it hit the hot pipe nearby. He was almost there. Maung attached the ratchet to first one nut, and listened to servos whine against the water pressure as the clamp tightened.

"*Suit integrity failure; depressurization in one minute.*"

He chuckled. Somewhere in the back of his mind Maung recalled a training video on basic spaceflight and hypoxia, the first sign of which was giddiness from breathing gasses like nitrogen or argon instead of oxygen, but the warmth made him chuckle again. He couldn't concentrate. Next his ears popped and the change in pressure hurt like a bad ear infection, changing his happy mood to one of anger.

The water suddenly stopped. Maung let out a whoop because the patch had finished and the smear of gray bots spread over the area, sintering the metal to the pipe and making a permanent fix. He moved back the way he came, singing as he went.

Jennifer's voice came from the speakers, but she sounded like a breeze and he had no idea what she said, only that it was hysterical. Maung wished Nang could talk to him. He giggled at the thought of her finding out what he *really* was and then he imagined that maybe she'd be OK with that. "*Suit integrity failure; depressurization complete. Seek immediate medical attention.*" That voice was annoying, Maung thought. Now the pain in his ears almost forced his eyes shut but he suspected he was almost safe, almost to the opening when he decided to hell with it. Maung's eyelids became like lead. He closed his eyes and dreamed that Jennifer and Nang were both there, screaming at him and dragging him back through the corridors of the ship as fast as they could.

"What did I do," Maung asked, still speaking in Burmese, "to piss off *both* of you? I am cold, and my fingers are freezing at the same time my joints feel on fire. I just want a cigarette."

CHAPTER SIX

The doctor leaned over him, wearing a facemask that made him look like an evil spirit and Maung struggled but grasped that he couldn't move, that he'd been sedated. The man shone bright lights in his eyes. Maung remembered. He had taken hold of a red-hot pipe to get leverage and the heat had been enough to melt through his suit and weaken its shell so that he depressurized. Soon he'd find out how much damage he'd taken to his blood vessels and brain. As if reading his mind, the doctor put drops of a gray opalescent material in the corners of Maung's eyes, administering diagnostic microbots that worked their way into his retinas, examining everything.

Everything.

Maung was strapped into a bed in the ship's small sick bay. He still couldn't move. The doctor floated nearby and held a scalpel to Maung's cheek, and the man's angry glare confused him until he remembered the doctor had administered microbots. *He knows,* Maung realized.

"You aren't human?" the doctor asked. When Maung looked away, the doctor rested the scalpel against his throat. "Answer or I'll slice you open from ear to ear."

"I'm human. Partially. I'm Dream Warrior. Parts of my brain have been replaced by a semi-aware system so I'm not sure how much of *me* is me. Not anymore."

The doctor's eyes went wide and he pushed off, floating backward and slipping the scalpel into a case. "*My god.* You guys were supposed to have all been killed."

Maung nodded, relieved; there were no secrets left and soon it would be over, one way or another. They might, he thought, even send him back to Earth but he doubted it. If it were his people, they'd torture him to death on the spot but at least he wouldn't have to maintain the lie anymore.

"So what are you here for? To spy?"

"*No*," said Maung, "I want to get away from Americans—all of you. Your government brought me and my family to Charleston to help with port duties and shipping, a slave, and now my son is in an American school where they call my people monsters. I have seen the Chinese up close. *Have you?* I want nothing to do with them *or you* anymore. I want the war to be over."

The doctor looked confused and yanked on a table, launching himself toward the hatch where he paused to say, "What to do with you is the captain's decision. But don't expect sympathy; he lost two sons in the Philippine jungles."

"How's the ship?" Maung asked. "Are we safe, did the repair work?"

But the doctor ignored him and left.

Sounds came and went and every time Maung tried to open his eyes it was as if someone had sewn them shut, an impossible weight that no amount of effort could lift, but he heard the doctor and the captain anyway. They couldn't seal his ears. Maung knew he'd been sedated and he understood why, because now more than one of them saw him exactly for what he was; he couldn't figure out why they hadn't killed him. Maung fought the urge to activate his system and promised himself he wouldn't switch on until he knew their intentions because he didn't want to go there, was sick of destruction. Besides, he might need the crew alive to reach Karin, even if he went super-aware.

Once more the engines roared and Maung came to in the sick bay when an almost unbearable pain made him scream; the room was dim, lit only by the blinking lights of dormant medbots as they rattled under the stress of high gees. The ship, he guessed, must have accelerated again. Before he reacted, one of the medbots came to life and jabbed his arm with a long needle, sending sedative into his bloodstream. Maung smiled as he fell asleep, happy to have reality erased. But before he passed out he remembered what woke him and Maung noted that both his hands were bandaged because he'd fried them while repairing the water pipe; that had *really* happened.

"Wake up."

Someone smacked Maung's face and he flinched but couldn't open his eyes. Then they shouted, "*Wake up*," punching him in the stomach so that Maung coughed and spat. The captain was there. The doctor floated in the hatchway, glanced up and down the corridor outside, and then shut the two of them inside, alone.

"They think you're in critical condition," the captain said. "The rest of my crew."

"Am I not?"

The man smiled and shook his head. "You could be and maybe should be. *Hell.* You don't know what it's like to face someone like you, a mass murderer who may have killed my sons, and yet who just saved the ship and the lives of half my crew."

"I *was* a Dream Warrior. That's not who I am anymore." Maung realized that the ship was no longer pulling gees and he looked down; the bandages were off. At first he was scared to see his palms, but then opened his fists, relieved to find there were no scars and Maung reminded himself to thank the doctor. "I am not anything anymore, Captain. Nothing except a father. I just want my son to have a chance."

The captain seemed older than he thought. Maung hadn't bothered to examine him until now and saw he had white hair, close cropped and snowy atop gray skin that looked as if it had been overworn and stretched. His neck was scarred on the left side, below the ear, down to his collar—and probably below that, Maung figured.

"You were in the war," he said.

The captain nodded and stopped himself from rotating, facing Maung again. "Twenty years ago, when the Sommen were still here. They had blockaded us, trapped us inside the solar system so we couldn't move out and look for more resources. I was part of a fleet that went after Sommen space-based assets in a joint expeditionary force. It was all classified; I guess someone in the government thinks it would have once caused a panic, and now they've forgotten. But the Sommen ordered us to stay put, all of humanity—*trapped on our home planet.* That's why the last Asian War kicked off, because we'd bled Earth's mines dry of metallics."

The captain paused and patted his pocket as though he was looking for cigarettes, which reminded Maung of his own craving. "Anyway, before going to war with them, a small group of countries, including us and China—if you can believe it—tried to break out. The Sommen slaughtered us. It wasn't even a fair fight, like a two-year-old trying to take out a fighter carrier with a squirt gun." The captain was about to say more but then cocked his head and stared at Maung. "It doesn't matter. We have a problem right now; one that you might be able to help us with."

"What?" Maung asked.

"You saved the ship. And none of the other crew know who or what you are; we can't tell them because they might kill you or mutiny, or both, despite what you've done for them."

Maung nodded. "I thought *you* were here to do that."

"No," said the captain. "I'm too old now. Soon I'll be with my sons again and that will be enough, I don't need to get even."

"Then what's the problem?"

The captain reached out and unbuckled Maung, then released his arm and leg restraints, and when he was free Maung thanked his ancestors for being in zero g. His limbs were asleep. Without asking the computer he couldn't tell how long he'd been held, but he guessed days and it would take another day or so for him to regain normal muscle control.

"We received a transmission from Earth," the captain said, "from Carson headquarters in Singapore, ordering us to send our lifeboat down to Ganymede to investigate an anomaly."

"An anomaly?" Maung asked.

"That's all they'll tell us. We're in orbit around her right now, and luckily Jupiter is between us and Europa, but you and Nang are going to be really late for your first day on the job at Karin."

Maung nodded and massaged his arms; he smiled at the fact that he was alive, that the bots must have repaired any depressurization-related damage. "So the pipe patch is holding."

"We have just enough water," the captain said, "to continue normal operations and a detour to Ganymede *would* allow us to replenish reserves. But that's not why they're sending us there."

Maung groaned from the soreness; whatever happened after he blacked out must have caused significant damage because his muscles and bones ached, and even his teeth radiated a dull pain that he couldn't ignore. "Why do you need me?"

"Ganymede is also technically within the Chinese sphere of influence, and if the company won't tell us anything except surface coordinates, it makes me nervous. I want a weapon down there. For now you're confined to sick bay, but get some rest." The captain navigated toward the hatch and kicked it twice so the doctor opened it. "We leave in twelve hours. If you do a good job down there and keep my crew and boat safe, Doc and I might keep *your* secret and let you go on to Karin."

"What do you think is down there?" Maung asked, as the hatch inched shut.

"I don't know. But whatever it is, Carson wouldn't risk a mega-tanker unless it was important, and they never do anything like this unless the government guarantees to fund the ship's replacement— in the event of catastrophic loss or capture."

"Why doesn't Maung have a weapon?" Nang asked.

Four of them floated inside the lifeboat hangar—a tight compartment in the ship's aft. To Maung, the lifeboat looked like a brick with rounded edges; he was not an expert on spacecraft, but was almost certain that this one was uglier than most.

The captain answered before Maung could. "He doesn't want one. And we have limited supplies of firearms, anyway. Get in, suit up, and then helmets on. We don't want to wait any more than we have to."

"Well then why is he coming?" she asked. Maung wondered why Nang pursued the issue, and he considered asking her to stop. "Maung is recovering from rapid depressurization and a day ago you told us he was critical. Shouldn't he stay in sick bay?"

"Miss," the captain started. Maung guessed the man was about to lie, but part of him wanted Nang to see through it; part of him *wanted* the captain to tell his secret because it dragged on his soul, an impossible weight. "Carson Corp wants me, a navigator, and two nonessential personnel to tag along on this little mission and that includes Maung. Now, that's *all* I need to know. And it's *more* than you need to know."

⁂

There was only a slight bump, but it was enough to startle him and Maung heard his own breathing accelerate with fear, his suit helmet amplifying every sound that he made. He was in a proper suit this time—a bright orange company model. Maung couldn't even begin to remember how to work its controls, but for now he decided not to worry about it and had to trust that the expedition was solidly planned and someone would help if he needed it. There was another option. But activating the semi-aware, according to the captain, was only to be done in an emergency and only if he ordered it.

"That bump," Jennifer said, her voice coming from Maung's headphone speakers, "was Ganymede's wisp of an atmosphere. I wish you guys could see this. It's beautiful. Ganymede is gray and white and blue; you'd never guess that ice could look so pretty."

Only Jennifer and the captain could see out the main window; Maung and Nang were in the rear of the small craft, facing backward and strapped into black seats.

"Quiet," the captain said. "On course. ETA ten minutes. So far there's no sign of Chinese assets. Stay low to avoid radar, just in case they have something here that didn't get picked up in scans."

Maung said, "Captain, did you scan the coordinates given to you by Carson? Did you pick up anything on the ground?"

"Affirmative," the man said. "A little over twelve thousand spherical objects arranged in a geometric pattern—a huge square. All of them solid. All of them the same density of material used by the Sommen to construct their bases and ships."

Maung turned his head to glance at Nang, but her eyes were closed, and he tried to slow his breathing by praying. Cigarettes, he thought again. Although his cravings were starting to fade, he needed to ask the doctor about that patch, the one that used microbots to deliver nicotine.

"What the hell are Sommen materials doing all the way out here?" he asked. "And how come nobody ever detected this before?"

The captain sounded amused. "I think, Mr. Maung, that those are exactly the kinds of questions Carson expects *us* to answer."

"I need a cigarette," Maung whispered and the captain chuckled. "Me too."

⁂

A part of Maung's brain swore to him that he was about to fall off the ground and sail into space. He had never seen a sky so black, so huge, or so occupied by another planet, with Jupiter filling almost all of it and close enough that he reached up. His feet slipped. Maung fell gently onto his back and he stayed there for a moment, taking it all in and breathing so hard that his suit computer chimed a warning: "*Heart and breathing rates above nominal levels; increasing CO_2.*" He thanked his ancestors. Tears formed and he began to laugh until Nang yanked him to his feet, which was easy for her since the gravity on Ganymede was so much less than Earth's.

"This is amazing," said Maung.

The captain's voice clicked in. "This isn't a vacation, Maung. Everyone stay ready. The ship is scanning this area and keeping a close eye on things but that doesn't mean the Chinese won't show."

But Maung didn't hear. To him it didn't matter if the Chinese arrived because he was lost in the endless panorama, the horizon a brilliant white line in the distance that faded into mottled gray and then hit a band of brilliant blue again before merging with light blue ice near his feet. There were mountains. Huge chunks of ice dwarfed the group, even as they skirted the cliffs to stay clear of any avalanches. Only their footing concerned Maung. Most of the surface was rough and so there was no problem with grip, but occasionally they hit a patch so smooth that it seemed like glass, and Maung wanted to lie on his stomach and slide across.

"Starting the melt now, Captain." It was Jennifer. She had stayed behind at the lifeboat to rig the water collection equipment and load the craft. First the ice had to melt. Before they set out, Maung had helped her unroll a massive metallic mat, a grid of thick wires that now carried heat from the boat's small fusion reactor to melt the ice in a perfect rectangular pattern. Over it was a tent. The rig was designed so that a pump transferred sublimated steam to the ship, where it then condensed into liquid water.

"Will it be heavy on takeoff?" Nang asked, as if reading Maung's thoughts.

"She'll be all right," said Jennifer. "The boat's designed to hold all the water we'll be collecting—plus sixteen souls. That's more than enough margin for her engines."

Nang clicked in again, and Maung judged from her breathing

that she must have been getting winded. "How much farther, Captain?"

"It should be . . ." The man stopped and tapped at the console on his forearm and Maung blinked when a map appeared on his faceplate. "We're the blue dot. These green rectangles are the objects."

"Then we should be there," Maung said. "It looks like we've passed over the lower edge of the field and are standing right on them."

Nang backed up. "*I don't see a damn thing.*" Maung thought she must be nervous because she raised her weapon, a coil gun that could fire fléchettes at an insane rate, piercing anyone's suit; if the fléchettes didn't kill you the exposure to vacuum would. "This is a crap show."

"Calm down." Maung dropped to his knees and scraped at a thin layer of ice crystals about a centimeter thick. "Someone help me with this."

Soon he and Nang had cleared a section of ice about two meters across and the captain stood over them, watching, before he whistled and motioned for the two to move away. "You're right, Maung. Whatever the things are, they put them in the ice. I have to record this." The captain typed on his forearm console again, then slapped a hand against his helmet, clearing the video aperture of ice.

"Almost looks like they tried to hide them," said Maung, standing up. "They melted a huge rectangular section, lay these in, and then filled it."

Nang stayed on her knees and backed up again. "This makes no sense. Captain, I'd like to go help with water collection if that's OK."

"Fine. Go ahead."

Maung watched as Nang left, and noticed that she ran as fast as she could, a bounding jog in light gravity that sent her sprawling more than once. He wanted to run after her. But before he could call out on the radio, the captain slapped his shoulder.

"Something's happening," he said.

Maung knelt again and leaned over so that his helmet almost touched the ice—to get a better view. Beneath them, in the patch they had cleared, he saw a green sphere and Maung's skin tingled. He recalled the story he'd heard about how the contractors broke through a slab at the Charleston spaceport and then one of the Sommen showed up, but this wasn't the size of a Sommen; it was only a meter in diameter. Now, though, the ball pulsated, alternating from a luminescent light green to a dark color, and Maung nearly jumped, startled when someone from the ship clicked in.

"Captain we're getting thermal readings right on top of your coordinates, and they're inconsistent with water collection operations. Is everything OK?"

"It's fine," he said. "Keep monitoring."

Maung shook his head. "It's *not* fine. The ice is melting all around us. We should move back."

He and the captain retreated and found a raised area, a small hill that gave them a better view of the melt. When Maung looked back at the field, he gasped; much of it had already gone, and as he watched, the ice sublimated into steam, which rose a few meters before it drifted away as ice again, a kind of artificial snowstorm that looked as spooky as it was beautiful. Soon it was over, and in front of them a massive pit had opened, inside of which rested thousands of dark spheres. Then the green faded into a crystal clear kind of glass, perfectly transparent; Maung recognized what was inside and clutched the captain's arm.

"Those are bodies. Human corpses."

The captain stepped forward and Maung advanced with him—despite the fact that he wanted to run. "I know."

"Captain . . ." Maung felt sick now. He'd seen far worse, but it dredged up memories that he never wanted to recall and as they walked the spheres disappeared, letting their curled-up contents collapse slowly onto ice. "None of them have heads. They've all been decapitated. Murdered. Why did the Sommen do that? These are *people.*"

The captain said nothing. Maung and he walked silently through the field and Maung prayed while the captain documented as much as he could, beaming the video information directly to the ship so it could be cataloged, and then he stooped every few meters to collect a tissue sample. Maung spoke for the dead. He asked his people to let their ancestors know where they were and when Jennifer called them back, announcing that the water tank had filled, he said a prayer of thanks. He and the captain bounded over the slick surface as fast as they could, neither one wanting to stay on Ganymede.

CHAPTER SEVEN

Although Maung had discarded his suit and wore only a set of corporate coveralls, being aboard ship gave him a warm feeling of security; the captain ordered them out of Ganymede's orbit so with every passing second they moved farther away from the dead, farther from the Chinese on Europa. The captain and the doctor were with him in sick bay. A holo of the ice field rotated in front of them while the computer analyzed their data and Maung began to respect the men; maybe it was his Burmese upbringing, or maybe it was because both men had the slow thoughtfulness of age, but they reminded him of his father and several times he had to remind himself to speak in English.

"Have you seen anything like this?" the doctor asked.

Maung nodded. "I've seen the green material; it looked similar to what the Sommen used to construct their facility in Charleston. And probably all their other facilities on Earth. But I've never seen them use it to encase bodies like that, and I've never seen them collect headless *human* bodies."

"How long will processing take—for both video and tissue samples, Doc?" asked the captain.

"Another hour. After that we'll beam it to Singapore but given our position relative to the sun and Earth, it will take almost an hour for them to start receiving, maybe another hour to process, and then, if they respond immediately, we'd get it an hour after that. Three hours, minimum."

The captain nodded. "Computer—navigation." When Jennifer's

face appeared on a screen he asked, "How long until we get a burn window to Karin?"

"Another day," she said.

"Notch it up, Jennifer; push maneuvering fuel consumption as close to the line as you can because I want to get away from this place. And keep scanning for vessels; if Carson's people tracked this from Earth, the Chinese picked it up too."

The captain turned back to the holo then and Maung doubted the man really understood what he'd face if the Chinese decided the *Singapore Sun* was a target worth having. The ice field looked strange in hologram, he thought. It rotated quietly and instead of corpses there were tiny green dots in neat rows, a total of 12,756 that someone on Earth would have to somehow identify so relatives could be notified. Maung tried to keep from shivering at the number. Since the Sommen had them, it was possible the bodies had been taken over a period of years, killed, and then put in storage until *now*, a time when the Sommen thought returning them was appropriate. *Why?* he asked himself for the hundredth time. Why did they go to all this trouble? Why did the Sommen depart in the first place and leave behind one of their warriors to attack at the spaceport—setting off a chain reaction that robbed Maung of his family and threw him into deep space?

Jennifer's voice clicked in again, her voice sounding stressed. "Captain, we just received a message from one of the freighters closer to Europa. A pair of Chinese warships are headed this way."

The captain stared at Maung, as if reading his thoughts. "We can't be taken."

"I know," Maung said.

"If I help you do what you do—to kill—what do you need?"

"Captain?" Jennifer broke in again.

"Message received," the captain responded. He then turned to Maung. "*Now*, son."

Maung shrugged. "For one, I need you to disarm the ship's automated defenses so your microbots and internal weaponry don't come after me once I'm active."

"*Captain*," the doctor said, his face drained of color. "That's suicide. If we—"

The captain silenced him with a raised hand. "What else?"

"I'll need someone to strap me into an acceleration couch where

I won't be bothered, after which you'll have to give me control over the ship's computer and coms arrays. I need to leverage her beaming and broadcast range."

The doctor looked even more incredulous and was about to say something when the captain cut him off. "Doc, get Maung ready. Here in sick bay. Strap him in while I take care of everything else and on second thought, get him in a full environment suit so he'd be safe in case of decompression; full linkup with ships' systems, and a backup hose link to ship's oxygen."

The captain floated through the holo to shove his face close to Maung's. "I want your word, son. If they show up, and it looks like we can't get away, I want you to swear that even if some of us elect to stay with the ship that you'll blow it to hell."

"You have my word. But I'll only do this if you promise me one thing."

"What?" the Captain asked.

"Think of a good lie," said Maung, "to explain what's going on. If we survive, and I make it to Karin, I can't have Nang or anyone else knowing what I am. Or what I can do."

The captain nodded. "Deal."

Maung wanted out of the suit. It included layer upon layer of specialized cloth and capillary nets that provided cooling, insulation, and some radiation protection, and although it included equipment so that the wearer could go to the bathroom without moving, it threatened to drive Maung crazy with the fact that he could barely move.

Jennifer clicked in. "Maung, you're doing it again."

"What?"

"Praying," she said. "I've been ordered not to disable your coms system so you've got to stay quiet, we need the system clear."

"Sorry. I didn't even know I was."

Maung struggled to understand how she and the rest of the crew did it—kept track of all the information needed to run the ship and now that he plugged into it, he heard the traffic. They were in contact with Singapore. But the messages were delayed by over an hour so the communications officer was keeping track of a conversation over an hour old, and folding into it brand-new data, while at the same time monitoring local traffic and internal coms. A note of urgency underpinned their voices; Maung figured that everyone was nervous and thinking about the same thing he was, that the Chinese would show up soon.

"Jennifer?" Maung asked.

"What?"

He was embarrassed now that he interrupted her but the thought just occurred to him and made him uneasy. "I'm listening to all the local traffic and it seems like there are freighters and private vessels that could have helped."

"Yeah," she said. "So?"

Maung heard her impatience but continued anyway. "So how come nobody answered our distress call a while ago?"

"We were too close to Europa. Before the treaty, the Chinese Fleet there would fake distress calls to lure ships into traps. Nobody's forgotten about that and it's too risky to take the chance when you're this far out."

"Oh," Maung said, and something else occurred to him. "One last thing: Is there any way to get electronic cigarettes on the ship?"

"No, Maung. None of us smoke except Cap. *Now* can I get back to trying to drive this beast?"

He detected it before the ship's systems did. It was a gentle touch, one that woke his semi-aware with a pressure no more than that given by a parent stroking their child's head or patting them on the back, and it was something that Maung had forgotten about. *A friend or foe beacon.* But it was more than that, he realized: It was a method of recognition for a people whose communications included both human and digital forms, so that it also asked one's political leanings, processing capabilities, and weapons systems *in addition* to querying about whose side one was on. Maung's semi-aware responded automatically. But he said a silent prayer of thanks that his transmission range was too short to be received; the Chinese didn't realize he was there.

Hello, his semi-aware said, interrupting Maung's thoughts. *All systems ready for merging.*

Maung hit a key on his forearm, one the captain taught him to punch for privacy.

"Go ahead, Maung."

He took a deep breath, almost giddy with the feeling of being active again; it was like standing on the edge of a cliff, looking down into a vast ocean of data and knowledge, which beckoned for Maung to dive—to link up and fuse with systems that he hadn't used in years. "They're here, Captain. Just out of your scanning range."

"Thank you. I've turned off our internal defenses so you should be safe to activate."

"I know," said Maung. "We already woke up."

He dove off the cliff, letting his semi-aware wrap him in its grasp so that Maung grinned at the realization: He was smart again.

Welcome home, Maung. The semi-aware "felt" as happy as he was. *There was no time to communicate during our last awakening, but you seem to be in good health.*

Maung whispered to the ship's systems. He imagined himself like a creeping vine, shooting tendrils and roots out to take hold in shallow ways, not yet fully infiltrating so that people like Jennifer had no clue he was there. Every new contact energized him. The ship vibrated in a different way than before because the main engine was more than just the idling of a bull with no place to charge, it was his own heartbeat that added to the totality of his thoughts and experiences and now he was part human, part supertanker. There were two places that Maung hadn't yet accessed. One was the ship's command and control system, which he planned to take last since doing so would give him control of all the ships scanning sensors and beaming equipment; for now, he wanted to avoid giving himself away to the Chinese by changing the ship's electronic signatures.

The second place was a mystery. It shouldn't have been there. To Maung it "looked" like a series of tiny black holes, and one was present in each system he'd infiltrated, a snippet of code that made copies of all traffic and dumped them into a one-way subroutine, from which nothing emanated. He created his own subroutine and wrapped it in innocuous life-support data—like candy coating on a pill. Maung sent it in and waited. Two minutes later, there was still no response and Maung had an uneasy feeling because his routine should have given him total control, no matter what was inside.

But he couldn't spend more time on it; the Chinese hailed the

Singapore Sun, and simultaneously blasted it with full-powered scans that flooded Maung's semi-aware in a wave—thousands of access attempts per millisecond, a digital sledgehammer that nearly split his brain. Maung's nostrils became warm with his blood, which now trickled out.

All of the crew spoke at once and Maung focused on the communications officer who was first to notice that the Chinese had hacked their way in but Maung already knew this; he was in combat. Maung ignored the blood and decided there was no point in hiding. He harnessed the processing capacity of every ship's component and converted them into weapons; all of them focused on wrapping the invaders' thrusts with useless code to keep them busy while he leapfrogged packets that took him outside the ship, through space, and into the Chinese command system. There he shut down the Chinese ship's communications in a way that looked like it was a malfunction; the move cut the infiltrators off from their parents and Maung jumped back to the *Singapore Sun*.

The Chinese had left something behind. Maung focused all his attention on a remaining Chinese artifact, a nonintelligent thing, an amputated limb set on autopilot and coded to mutate when contact was lost, and Maung used the ship to watch it shed parts of itself to his attacks while it simultaneously scavenged for other bits of code; it used these to mutate into a dormant bomb, an egg or seed that hid until its parents came back to save it.

Maung ripped it apart and then swept the ship's systems and smiled at how clean everything was, and he imagined the confusion onboard the Chinese vessels because only a moment ago they had been winning.

Maung no longer heard their voices but registered the words as data when Jennifer said, *Something's wrong with the ship; notify the captain that I no longer have access to navigation. All ship's systems are offline and we don't have control.* She was more confused by his answer, though, that there was nothing to worry about.

"*Everything is fine, Jennifer,*" Maung said, his voice now that of the ship's computer. "*The Chinese do not have control.*"

It's time, Maung thought. The enemy's attack had nearly

overwhelmed him and part of him shook with fear; this was his first time fighting the Chinese, his parents and creators; what he was about to do could kill people and that bothered him too because he'd hoped to never kill again, but this was different. This time it was defensive, to *protect*. He set traps in command and control. It took a few more seconds to re-rig the communications system encryption to better defend against Chinese attacks but he left one channel less secure than the rest. Maung was sure they'd detect and concentrate on it. He had already sensed the Chinese confidence during their first attack and almost sympathized because they wouldn't anticipate a counterattack by a super-aware; once he was inside *their* ships again, he'd be ready with a more complete plan—one to end it for good.

The *Singapore Sun*'s crew had one advantage. They were not integrated with their ship, weren't hardwired or radio linked to each other and to a central processing matrix used to formulate collective decisions that could be read and used to predict their moves and intentions. In cases like this, where the Chinese were blind to the fact they fought a super-aware, their hive-mind structure was a weakness and he knew exactly how to exploit it.

Nang cried. Maung's attention wavered and before he restarted the ship's communications he monitored the video feed from her compartment where she was alone in her couch and he heard the sobbing. He'd forgotten about her. The feed was grainy but Nang's hair was in a ponytail and looked so black that it shined blue, and the human part of Maung wanted to talk to her but unless he could extract them from this, that wouldn't happen.

Maung shut off the feed and refocused. He flicked the communications' power nodes simultaneously, activating all the receivers and transmitters and noted the incoming Chinese frequencies so he could interfere, blasting space with meaningless beamed transmissions at exactly the right frequencies and modulation. The Chinese compensated by hopping. Maung pretended to let it work and then waited, sensing that they'd once more entered the command and control network, but were more cautious this time, probing instead of using a frontal assault. The Chinese suspected, he thought. They appreciated that the American ship was more than it seemed and now a part of their hive got nervous, jumpy with each dead end they encountered and with each second spent decrypting his codes.

When they arrived at his trap, Maung prepared himself. He prayed to his ancestors and asked them for the speed of a spider, begged for the swiftness and ruthlessness that came from being a silent predator and he brushed off any shame in what he was about to do. This was easier than the Sommen; Maung needn't have worried. Despite the fact that his attackers were part machine, they had fundamentally human thought patterns, not like it had been with the Sommen. Plus, this time Maung was on a battlefield of his own making and witnessed his encryption failures as one by one the Chinese unwrapped a channel that led to the real ship's command and control—the node leading to Maung. He "sat" behind the code wall having already arrayed the ship's computer systems to launch their own frontal assaults against the Chinese at just the right moment. Finally the last barrier fell. Maung almost heard the joy in the Chinese because at the same instant his defenses failed, he jumped inside their beam, using one isolated ship's transmitter to send a part of his consciousness back to the Chinese vessel—just like he had done with the Sommen.

To know your enemy, you must become your enemy, Maung reminded himself.

He understood them now. There were two Chinese ships and he had their schematics, which depicted an almost random collection of cubes and rectangular modules that had been pieced together to form electronic and kinetic attack platforms—two destroyers. Each ship had a crew of forty-five half-human things, so connected to the ship that they were a part of it. The one he was inside was the lead vessel, the *Lanzhou 101*. Now the Chinese panicked. Maung's automated counterattack onboard the *Singapore Sun* had them struggling with security programs that isolated or tore apart their first elements, and their initial joy of victory shifted to surprise and fear. He read the exchange of code between the *Lanzhou* and her sister, the *Dandong 98*; both ignited their main engines to close the distance and get within kinetic attack range because they already concluded something horrific: They might lose.

Maung slipped behind a deeper set of security screens. Someone sensed his presence, one of their most talented, and where there was a clear path a millisecond before, now there was a wall. A checkpoint. Maung could hit it with a decryption effort but then they would detect him and he cursed his bad luck, wondering what he had done to give his presence away. He backed up to the less secure outer shell and took another look at his options.

They have control of our navigational systems, Jennifer said, breaking Maung's concentration. *We're now braking and will be within their weapons range in ten seconds. The Chinese never asked to board,* thought Maung. This shocked him because of the treaty, because they immediately attacked without wasting time on friendly overtures, as if they had already calculated it would take force to get what they wanted. Maung refocused. He'd already wasted seconds thinking and now a stream of communications that hadn't been there before pulsed brightly so he probed it with a query. The security response was almost immediate. Maung smiled and dove into it, assaulting with decryption algorithms and leaping upstream to its origin so that within milliseconds he had control of the *Lanzhou*'s forward missile magazines. The Chinese panic went into high gear. Someone tried to cut communications but a portion of the ship's targeting system was already locked onto the *Singapore Sun* and Maung kept it there, using a small dish to maintain his link. They probed him again. Maung guessed from its pattern that this was the same one that threw up a code wall earlier but now he was ready, and when the next probe hit, he absorbed the data and returned nonsense in order to buy time. All he *needed* was time. A few more milliseconds to finish aiming and locking the *Lanzhou*'s missiles at its sister ship.

Maung fired. He tried not to think about what the crew of the *Dandong* experienced just before the *Lanzhou*'s missiles struck her, a hundred of them piercing amidships and splitting the organo-synthetic core into pieces. They all died alone—disconnected. He reeled at the horror among the crew of the *Lanzhou*, overcome by the shock of having just killed their sister, and then there were a few milliseconds of anger from the one trying to stop him, just before Maung self-destructed the Chinese ship's remaining missiles. *This was an act of mercy,* he figured; Maung had never forgotten what it was like to live with the guilt of killing and now he'd put the Chinese abominations out of their misery.

Before the *Lanzhou* died it ejected a capsule. The tiny dot rocketed toward Europa and Maung couldn't see what it contained because he never had control of the entire ship, but he feared it may have held data about him—that the smart one escaped to warn its masters that one of their creations was back: a Dream Warrior turned traitor.

Maung returned to the *Sun*. He opened his eyes and realized that his mouth was parched and he could barely speak, as if his throat had been coated with sand. The battle had lasted only one hundred and thirteen seconds. But Maung had bled and sweat enough that when he croaked "*I need help*" into the mic he wasn't kidding, and almost couldn't punch up the captain's coms code. The captain and the doctor ripped Maung's helmet off.

"You did it. We're on course again for a window to Karin, and the crew don't know what the hell just happened."

Maung said, "I got lucky; their weapons systems weren't secured as well as they should have been; they weren't expecting one of their own. Is Nang OK?"

"Of course she is," the doctor said. "Why wouldn't she be?"

The captain handed him a water bottle, and after Maung took a long drink he coughed and then said, "Someone onboard their ship recognized what I am, Captain—evaluated my signature. He got away. We need to leave as quickly as possible before they try again. Now that they know I'm here, what we found on Ganymede won't be their primary interest."

"Why?" the doctor asked. "Why would they risk starting another war just to get *you*?"

But Maung passed out; he couldn't have given an answer anyway, not one that didn't boil down to *You wouldn't understand.*

CHAPTER EIGHT

In ten minutes they would accelerate. The captain held a hasty burial ceremony for crew members killed in the meteoroid strike before ejecting them out an airlock, and even though he wasn't friends with them, Maung knew the ship was emptier now in a bad way—a vast empty tube of steel and ceramic ruled by spirits. He helped Nang cinch up her restraints and spotted red marks on her cheeks.

"Why were you crying?" he asked. "We escaped the Chinese. In ten minutes we accelerate beyond Jupiter and their reach. The dead are with their ancestors."

Nang smiled and looked down, then at the wall. "I'm not crying about them or Beijing. It's about you."

"Why?"

"Because. I'm not who you think I am and when we get to Karin, you and I will be on different sides of a fight. Again."

Maung shrugged. "It can't be that bad. I'm sure working as a prison guard is not easy, but a *fight*?"

"You're so silly." Nang laughed, wiping a new tear from her eye. "Always the Burmese villager. This is not the kind of heat that thanaka will relieve, and ancestors have nothing to do with anything, Maung. I hate Karin. I don't want to go back and wouldn't if I didn't have to."

"I will not fight you, Nang." A pressure grew in Maung's chest and he wanted to brush the hair from her face, but he couldn't bring himself to move.

Nang shook her head. "You don't get it. But you will."

❆ ❆ ❆

Maung grunted under the two gees of acceleration; his breathing was ragged. The captain clicked into his cubicle and Maung vaguely heard him say that there was a sudden power drain that they couldn't explain, and he asked Maung to check it out, which made him sigh with relief. Maung activated his semi-aware and merged; almost immediately it stimulated portions of his autonomic system and numbed others with weak current, and although the acceleration continued, his body now compensated in ways it couldn't before, relieving at least some of the pain. Once that finished he relaxed, and his eyelids drooped as he readied to merge with the ship.

Maung reached out. In milliseconds he was within the ship's systems and before he closed his eyes, the semi-aware superimposed its interpretation of signals onto Maung's normal vision so that he smiled and became dizzy from the mixture of separate worlds. He homed in on the power logger. The thing resembled a fire hose spitting streams of data into storage bins but some streams only flickered while two were strong, their lines like brilliant white beams in a sea of black. Maung probed one and traced it to the engine systems; he sent a query list to the ship's computer, which responded that engine function was normal.

But *something* wasn't right. He linked with the second stream, just long enough to read its metadata, just long enough to see that the ships communications systems were sucking in power, and that for some reason the backup transmitter was active. Maung chuckled at the fact that his semi-aware urged him onward, sending waves of encouragement; he followed its lead and rocketed through the data, feeling a different kind of acceleration, one that didn't really exist because it was an illusion born from interpretations fed to the organic portions of his brain. Within a fraction of a second he was there. Maung caught a glimpse of the backup coms system, which resembled a web of light connecting the transmitter and receiver to data streams that, in turn, connected to the millions of ship's systems. His semi-aware couldn't focus at first. Then Maung saw a pearl—a huge pulsating sphere of data that something constructed within the transmitter's storage unit—and he reached out to form a link.

Before touching it, the transmitter fired. The pearl vanished and Maung mentally blinked, seeing nothing but an empty space where the thing's bright light used to reside. He checked the transmitter's most recent settings, then backed out of the ship's systems to find himself shaking under the acceleration.

"Captain," he called out. "Did you just send a message to Earth?"

"Negative. I haven't sent anything in over three hours. Nobody did."

Maung couldn't shake a feeling of unease. "*Someone* did—with the backup transmitter. And because of the size of the data pack and the fact that they wanted to form it in a short time and burst transmit, the system sucked power at detectable levels. But there was no sign that it was the Chinese, and transmitter settings suggested the burst went to the US."

"Any ideas?" the captain asked.

"A guess only," said Maung. But he ran the data through his semi-aware now for the third time, grateful for the fact he was more than an idiot, at least for a few minutes. "It looks like someone or something on Earth is keeping tabs on us."

"Let them," the captain said. "A short acceleration, then we begin deceleration for our approach to Karin. Not much farther, Maung, and you'll be at your new home."

BOOK TWO

BOOK TWO

CHAPTER NINE

Days later, when they finally docked at Karin and the airlock opened, a smell washed into the ship and Maung dry heaved. It was the smell of death. He was never on the battlefield and so had never experienced that aspect of killing, but Maung heard it described by others and assumed it couldn't be anything else. The odor of human decay corrupted the air itself, converted it into a fume that wound its way down through his windpipe and into his stomach. Maung dry heaved again. He expected the prison to be filthy but never imagined *this* kind of smell and when he looked beyond the airlock door, he raised his eyebrows in surprise.

Instead of filth, the prison walls were pristine. A glossy black tunnel stretched away and through the asteroid's rock until, about fifty meters away, a solid wall of bluish glass blocked it.

"Good luck," the captain said, "We're dropping you off here and then locking down until the hydrogen transfer is complete. I never like to stay long at this place. The smell gets in your clothes, even in your pores; it takes days to get rid of."

"I don't blame you," Nang said.

"Keep your head down, Maung." The captain slapped his shoulder. "Choose your friends carefully and you might make it through."

But Maung thought otherwise; the odor was a portent. He pictured the smell soaking into *his* jumpsuit and penetrating *his* pores so that before long, he wouldn't be able to smell death at all; death would be a part of him. And then his ancestors wouldn't be

105

able to find him, not as long as he was trapped in clouds of decay because even spirits avoided burial grounds.

"Do you think they'll sell electronic cigarettes here?" he asked.

"Shut up, Maung," Nang said.

Nang led him toward the glass and then stopped. The wall, Maung understood, wasn't just a wall but a huge chamber that blocked the tube, and inside a man in a vacuum suit sat at a desk and stared through his helmet faceplate. Nang said, "We're the new guards," and he flicked a few switches. The entire thing, cube and all, rose and disappeared into the ceiling, stopping overhead with a loud clunk and Nang waved him forward. There was barely gravity, Maung noted. They pulled themselves along using pockets carved into the rock, handholds that were only visible as blacker patches against the already dark rock. Strings of tiny lights—set into stone— lit the way.

"We head into receiving, just up this corridor, and fill out forms. Then they give us our suits and gear and assign us to our different stations."

"Different stations?" Maung asked.

Nang looked away and nodded. "I told you; I might not see you that much, Maung. The main guard force is located here near the docking station and with the main prison population—low and medium security."

"Where will I be?"

"On Karin's dark side. All I know is that it's a massive metals reclamation and recycling operation manned by high-security male prisoners. It's an old outpost or something; I'm not really sure. None of the guards assigned there talked to us during my last assignment."

Maung's legs and arms trembled as they moved forward, and behind him he heard the cubicle assembly lower from the ceiling and lock into the floor, sealing them off from the *Singapore Sun*. He shivered. "Why will I be assigned there? How can you be so sure?"

"Because." Nang stopped him before they reached a solid metal door. "Maung, listen to me. Anyone from a Chinese sympathizer nation gets the hardest duty—the most dangerous. It doesn't matter how long you've lived in America. The guards probably already know you're coming and have prepared your assignment. But the danger on Karin isn't just the guards who hate the Burmese; there's also Karin itself. Be careful. Pay attention to everything and learn."

"I thought you hated me," said Maung. "When did you become so nice?"

Nang paused. "Not hate, Maung. Just instinct. I'm not that easy to get to know and sometimes it takes a long time for me to decide if I trust someone. I don't know. After seeing what you did on the ship, by patching that pipe? You're OK."

Maung smiled back but not broadly; he wondered what she would say if she ever learned what he did after that, to the Chinese vessels, as well as *how* he did it.

The guards wore unsealed vacuum suits with soft armor plates, and carried emergency helmets for use in case of decompression. Maung had never been on an asteroid. Despite the low gravity, it was like being inside the caves he used to play in as a child, long before the war—wide mountain caverns, into which Maung made sure never to go too far because the darkness threatened to swallow him. Maung couldn't imagine how far they'd gone and soon lost track of time, passing intersection after intersection. They reached another intersection and someone called out. Nang laughed and then hugged a guard who sailed toward them, and Maung still marveled at how graceful she was, able to counteract the man's inertia at the last second by pushing off his shoulders with a nudge.

She has friends; it hadn't occurred to him before. Maung clenched his fists with the realization that not only would they be separated, but that Nang would be too far away for him to keep her interest— an interest that this one had somehow already earned. The man hugged Nang again. Maung was about to say *Come on, Nang, let's keep going* when two more guards arrived, both of them white. They stared at him and from the looks on their faces he decided Nang was probably right, that everyone already knew who he was, and he nodded at the pair with a smile. Finally the man said good-bye and the three guards continued on their way, pulling into a side tunnel and out of sight.

Nang stopped and looked at Maung. "What's wrong?"

"Nothing. Let's just get our gear."

�֍ ✶ ✶

A bald guard stood next to him, and a small bot hummed near Maung, who was now naked; the room was cramped and cold, and the rock nearly froze Maung's feet so that he barely stayed in one spot, having to grab ceiling straps to keep from bouncing away.

"Stay still, dammit," the guard said. His face looked Korean but Maung couldn't be sure. "If you move you'll have to do it all over again."

Now the bot raised a limb and scanned, playing a cold laser over Maung's body as it spit air from maneuvering jets to move around him in a perfect circle. Its measurements were critical. His dimensions would be used to fit a vacuum suit and to provide proper weapon sizes, neither of which he could survive without, so Maung fought the urge to shiver and did his best to stay still. He sighed with relief when it ended.

The guard handed Maung a roll of something and Maung asked, "What's this?"

"Undersuits. They're made from superconducting fibers that will link to your suit's environmental controls, to keep you warm or to cool you off. There are flaps for where you need to connect waste tubes."

"Waste tubes? Like the ones in vacuum suits on spacecraft?"

The guard laughed. "Where you're going, Tatmaw, there aren't going to be many toilets and drifters won't hold your willy for you. Your suit will be your home, your kitchen, and your bathroom." Maung was about to ask *What are drifters?* when the man continued. "Get one of those on and then come outside; I'll take you to get your vacuum suit and weapon."

Maung slipped on an undersuit. The synthetic fabric scratched, and he wanted it off even before he got it all the way on, and the clinginess made it hard to adjust so that by the time he finished, Maung spun in midair from contorting in low g. The other undersuit was a spare; he rolled it up, tucked it under an arm, and palmed the door panel, scooting through as soon as there was enough room to exit.

The bald guard moved out as soon as the door shut, and Maung struggled to keep up. Here, corridors were barely wide enough for one. Maung and his escort elbowed through crowds of officers moving in the opposite direction. In crowded spaces, the lighting made it hard to see. Tiny LEDs set in the rock provided just enough brightness to see the handholds, but Maung couldn't make out any of the faces he passed and he worried he'd never see Nang again and would never get to the point of knowing his way around. *And the smell.* In places it got worse but sometimes it almost went away before returning unexpectedly, forcing Maung's eyes to water.

"What's that stink?" he asked.

"I don't know. It was bad when I first got here and every once in a while we try to figure it out but we never have. It's like it comes from the asteroid itself. You get used to it, though; I don't even smell it anymore, Tatmaw." The man stopped in front of a beaten metal door, bits of yellow paint still clinging to it in spots next to faded white letters that spelled *supply*. "Go on in. Once you're outfitted someone else will escort you to the transport, which takes you to the other side."

"There is no training?" Maung asked. "No briefings?"

The guard chuckled. "Training? You must think you're on Earth; we don't have a training budget out here. I don't know how they handle it where you're headed but here on Sunny Side we usually assign a mentor; you tag along until someone higher up decides you can work alone. Or until you screw up and go to the big resting place. See you around, Tatmaw."

The door rumbled open. Maung stepped through into a tight space, a narrow slot that faced a counter and over it a wire grate, beyond which was another tunnel—a wide cylinder filled with rows and rows of vacuum suits and racks of coil guns. One man bounced there, behind the grate, smiling. He glanced at Maung and then gestured.

"Your suit is right there. Beside you, near the floor."

Maung glanced to his left. An old suit drifted against the wall and at first he thought the man must be joking, that it must be the source of his grin, because the suit should be white like the new ones on racks but instead was gray—red in the places where it had been patched. He tried to hand the suit back.

"I don't know much about suits but this one looks like it won't last for long. What about one of the new ones?" He pointed behind the man. "One of the white ones?"

"No. I got your measurements from the system. That's the one that fits, Tatmaw—that one right there. The white ones are for

Americans and allies only." The man must have seen his expression, Maung guessed. "Don't worry. It's vacuum-tested, prison-approved gear, better than the ones we give the drifters."

"What's a drifter?" Maung asked.

The ventilation system rattled overhead and a cold breeze pressed against Maung's neck, hard enough that he grabbed the grate to keep from moving. The suit rubbed against his face. Maung bristled at the humiliation, but the focus needed to put on the suit helped him forget and he tried to remember what he learned about gearing up, going over the procedure for making proper seals and connecting the waste hoses.

"Drifters work hard, Tatmaw. You'll like them, almost as much as you'll grow to like that suit."

Maung pulled the thick fabric over his stomach when he noticed something. "You spelled my name wrong, here on the ID patch."

The man shook his head again and slipped a coil gun with two magazines of needles and a utility belt through a slot. "It's close enough and nobody needs your name anyway. Take your weapon and have fun over there but I'm telling you now: It's nothing like the jungle."

Maung finished suiting up. He took the gun and strapped it over a shoulder before buckling the belt and shoving the magazines into a pouch. He was about to leave when the man stopped him.

"One last thing," he said, sticking a fat hand through the grate and handing a data chit to Maung. "This is for you. A message from Earth. When you get on the transport they'll provide you with a helmet and you can review it then, in private."

Maung nodded, took it, and slid it into his belt. "Thanks."

"Don't thank me, Tatmaw. I hope you freaking die."

A Korean guard waited outside, talking to Nang. Maung froze. He was happy that she had found him again, before he had to depart, and was about interrupt them when Nang glanced over, covering her mouth with a hand to laugh.

"What are you wearing?" she asked.

The Korean guard laughed too and tugged at a strap on Maung's suit. "It's so old that the fabric is turning to dust—a good suit for a Burmese."

Maung stared at Nang. Slowly, she stopped smiling and he stared for a moment longer.

"Sorry, Maung, I didn't mean—"

He cut her off. "It's OK. I know what you're thinking: the perfect suit for the idiot from Myanmar." Maung couldn't hide his anger and his face turned red from embarrassment. His gut and chest tightened with shame but also with sadness—that he was about to leave Nang and the good-bye had been ruined. All he managed was "Good luck with your friends, Nang."

Nang said, "Maung, wait a second," but he ignored her.

"You must be my escort," he said to the Korean guard. "I hear there's a transport waiting for me. Let's get going."

"You got it, Tatmaw."

Maung followed the guard into dark tunnels amid the crowds; behind him Nang shouted, "*Wait!*" but he kept going. Maung did his best to ignore a realization that Nang meant more to him than he had appreciated. *Feel nothing*, he thought, repeating the phrase until she left his thoughts.

Maung considered the data chit from Earth; he couldn't wait to be alone. The chit probably contained a message from the Old Man but might also contain news of his son—maybe even a message from his mother. He hadn't heard any news from Charleston in so long that Maung didn't care what it was or who it came from.

CHAPTER TEN

Maung's heart raced when he spotted the "transport," a tiny carbon-fiber elevator cage into which the Korean shoved Maung before handing him his helmet; it took a minute to get the thing sealed. Then a minor leak formed in Maung's forearm under a flexible plate, and the Korean fixed it with a tube that shot sticky fibers into the gap, a kind of plastic that hardened in a second. Maung mentally corrected himself: There was no real up or down in the tunnels so calling it an elevator meant almost nothing. On the other hand, there was no time to figure out a new name for the thing. Without warning it moved. The elevator accelerated at half a g so that Maung struggled against slight gravity and he checked his suit systems, which indicated that his surroundings were pressurized. He linked his suit with station communications and almost immediately an automated voice clicked onto his headset.

"*Welcome to Karin Prison,*" it said. "*Time to destination is fifteen hours, thirty-seven minutes.*"

"Is this the only way to the other side of Karin?" he asked.

The computer took a moment to answer. "*No. The main transport runs parallel to the shaft you currently occupy.*"

"I'm not in the main transport?" Maung asked. "What transport am I in and what's the difference?"

"*You are in the prisoner transport pod. The main transport is a larger vessel, which seats eight and has reclining seats so the occupants can sleep on the way.*"

Maung promised to get the Korean guard, too. He slapped the

chit into his suit computer and snapped, *"Play,"* hoping to hear the voices of his family. But a second later the Old Man's voice disappointed him: "Meet with a guard named Nam Su Thant and follow his orders as if they were mine." The message ended with a hiss and Maung cracked the chit in half and then slipped it between the bars—careful not to catch his fingers on the rock as it screamed past.

He was alone. The urge to again merge with the semi-aware assaulted his consciousness and although there was a chance the activation would go undetected he couldn't be sure, so he abandoned the thought. Instead Maung counted the lights as they blinked past his bars, hoping that it would put him to sleep—a sleep that evaded him because he had to stand in the small cage, trapped upright for fifteen hours.

"Can I get electronic cigarettes?" he asked the computer.

"Electronic cigarettes are prohibited on Karin; see corporate policy manual one-A section five point two."

"That figures."

By the time he reached the other side, Maung's legs had gone numb and he gritted his teeth at the stabbing pain that came from trying to move. The door slid open. A man helped him exit the cage and Maung heaved into the tunnel where he floated for a moment, which relieved the pain in his limbs; soon, though, muscles in both legs cramped and refused to relax. It took Maung a moment to work the pain out, after which he grasped that the man waiting for him was another guard and had been asking questions Maung hadn't heard. The language—Burmese—brought a grin to his face.

"You awake?" he asked. *"Are you Maung?"*

Maung's throat was parched. He bit the plastic tube inside his helmet, drawing on it to drink water for so long that he stopped, gasping for air.

"Anyone home?" the guard asked. He knocked on Maung's helmet. "You there?"

"I'm here. Can you show me to my quarters so I can get some rest? That was a long trip."

"Nah, kala. Sorry. Someone hates you already on Sunny Side; it was cruel to send you here in that cage. It made you late and now

Nam is pissed off. So you can't go to your cube until your shift is over." The man held out his hand. "I'm Than. You'll be shadowing me until Nam is convinced that you got it."

Maung blinked rapidly, trying to keep his eyes open. "Just Than?"

"Just Than." The man beckoned for Maung to follow. "Come on, kala. We have work to do, this isn't Sunny Side, we earn our pay here." When Maung unslung his coil gun Than waved his hand. "Nah, kala. Keep that on your shoulder for now. You won't need it and I don't want to end up dead."

Kala. Maung noticed the word for the first time and it surprised him that he'd been speaking English for so long that he had to search for its meaning. *Outsider.* Here, just like in Charleston, he was an outsider and Maung kicked off the wall, reaching for handhold after handhold in an effort to catch up with Than, who now yanked himself down a narrow tunnel so quickly that he threatened to disappear into the dim light ahead. Maung was too sleepy. He missed one handhold, which sent his back scraping against the tunnel wall, and in order to prevent himself from spinning he tried for another but missed. Maung remembered what Nang taught him. He put his hands and feet out, spread eagled, to stop himself with friction, stopping just in time so he didn't barrel into Than at an intersection.

"I thought I'd lost you," the guard said.

Maung asked, "Where are we going?"

"To the spaceport."

"Spaceport?" Maung tried to remember all he'd learned from Karin and he couldn't recall any details about the dark side. Than pushed off again and Maung kept up. "What spaceport?"

"You'll see, *kala.* They only allow Burmese to work there, only us. The Americans don't want word to get out about how badly we got our asses kicked."

"Who?" Maung asked. "Whose asses—the Burmese and Chinese?"

"No. The human race's ass. You got a lot to learn so shut up. We're almost there. Once we go through the airlock I want you to do exactly like I do, and keep your mouth shut because nothing you've been told up until now is even close to being true. Understand?"

Maung shook his head. "No. I don't understand. I—"

"Good. Because you're right, you don't understand anything; not yet. Set your visor for starfield dimming so the stars don't mess with your head because you don't want to go all dizzy, not where we're headed, and make sure you clip in your suit exactly the same way I do mine." Maung figured Than must have seen his mouth start to move because he held up a hand. "Just watch. Since you're late, there's no time to explain anything but I'll try to go slow and maybe you'll live. Day one is always when we lose guards. Drifters, though? The damn things seem immune to this crap; who would have thought?"

There was *nothing* but space. Maung almost somersaulted when they vaulted through an airlock exit and onto a steel platform set in a cliff, far above the bottom of a crater, and overhead the sky was black. It was not really a sky, Maung told himself. His helmet faceplate turned everything luminous into a black dot so that the darkness almost enveloped him, pressing down from above and forcing him to look away because he understood there were stars there, millions of them that tried to shine through with a reminder that he was insignificant. Maung didn't need the reminder; he believed it already, figured that until he turned on his systems and *kept* them on, he'd always be slow. Stupid. Someone who Nang would never take seriously.

The bottom of the crater seemed almost a mile below them and Maung whistled.

"How far is that?"

Than was trying to secure a pouch that came loose on his belt. "Fifteen hundred meters, give or take."

Maung saw it—a spaceport completely unlike the one in Charleston. Missile pods encircled the crater rim and most of them looked charred and blackened, the remnants of their frameworks the only thing telling him what they once were. And there were towers— at least what remained of them. Massive tubes ran up the center of what remained of the towers' framework, tubes that once carried plasma from fusion reactors for a point-defense network that no longer existed. The tubes now looked like segmented earthworms— frozen in a position of raising their heads to the sky. Maung got dizzy again and looked down.

Below lay more wreckage, a sea of bent steel and titanium, and Maung recognized the remains of ruined warships, cradled in what was left of the port's docks so that they looked as though they slept;

he imagined that someday the ships could wake up and move again, but Maung knew it would never happen because of the black holes along their sides, where Sommen weaponry had punched through and melted their guts.

"*This is the Fleet*," he whispered.

Than shuffled toward an opening in the railing and turned. "What?"

"The Fleet that went out to fight the Sommen. This is it."

"What's left of it," said Than. "I'm surprised you even know about that; the Americans and their allies still keep this secret."

"Why us?" Maung asked. "If it's so secret, why show it to people who once fought the Allies? We were enemies so why give us a job in such a secret place?"

Than laughed. "You are one stupid kala, kala. We're not *ever* leaving. Who are we going to tell? You have a radio that can reach Earth or access to some coms pod we don't know about? You may as well throw away the coms card they gave you. You think you're going to do some time here and then move on like it's a normal job, working the docks for a while? Nah-no, kala. You just became a prisoner here; just like the drifters."

Than turned away again; he jumped off the platform and fell, then laughed on the way down as he got smaller in Maung's view screen; he called out, his voice full of static. "I've been a prisoner here for five years so come on kala; you get used to everything. And there's little gravity; we only use the ladders to slow us down a bit on the way down; just grab onto the side railings until you slow, then let go again. It saves time."

Maung leaned over the edge—making sure his grip on the railing was tight. It was like being on the roof of the highest building he'd ever seen, one of the skyscrapers in Charleston, but ten times higher. His heart almost beat out of his chest. Maung closed his eyes, prayed for help, and stepped off. When he opened his eyes, he screamed.

"*Speed exceeding safe limits.*" The suit computer sounded soothing. Maung reached out and took hold of the railings, squeezing until his descent speed slowed to almost nothing, then he let go again.

Than was already at the bottom. "*Woohoo!* I'll tell you, kala, that never gets old. Keep a gentle grip on the railing now and don't let go so you stay at a reasonable speed; you don't want to break your ankles."

Maung hit the rocky bottom to send up a cloud of gray dust, and the blow caused his knees to buckle so he rolled on the ground before bouncing to his feet. He waited for his head to clear. The partial gravity was so different that it made him grin to think that outside of the tunnels he was light—not weightless, but lighter as if now he was made of feathers and if he tried hard enough, he could jump, sending himself up and into space and away from everything. For the moment he forgot what Than said, that he wouldn't ever make it back to Earth; he could travel to Sunny Side and jump as hard as he could, launching himself into space and toward home. Of course, he'd die long before he ever got there.

Than ran a kind of wand over Maung's suit. "This is to make sure those assholes on Sunny Side coated it properly."

"Properly with what?" Maung asked.

The pair stood on the crater floor and Maung stared up at the steel and carbon fiber buildings, which stretched toward the blackness above and reached higher than anything he'd seen on Earth. Yellow dots moved on them, near their tops. Maung watched as the dots danced across the faces of the buildings and they occasionally sparked, sending searing white flames to jet outward and form something like a plasma flower.

"Null fibers," said Than. "They mask electronic emissions from your suit so that other than your radio, there's nothing coming from you, no emissions that would give you away."

"I'm not following—you mean hide me from the prisoners?"

Than laughed and finished his sweep. He tucked the wand into his belt. "I mean hide you from *the Sommen*. They left all sorts of neat toys for us to find, including nano-mines that activate when they detect the presence of living organics and then before you know it, they're all over you and the prisoners, eating at your suit and then finally your flesh, at the same time decompression makes your saliva boil. But the coating of null fibers messes with their targeting. Keeps you safe, kala. Invisible."

Maung was about to respond when something flashed past and hit the ground next to them, silently, and then bounced up until it reached its apex and fell again. Maung fought against nausea. It took less than a second for him to understand that this was a person and the environment suit was yellow; the yellow dots that he had been watching were prisoners, Maung realized. And one was here now, having fallen quietly to his death. Whoever it was, his body was still bouncing and the fact that it all occurred without any sound made Maung shiver.

"That's why you need to be careful," Than said. "Looks like the drifter wasn't wearing his harness. You might think that the lighter gravity means you can't die, but you can reach speeds of over a hundred kilometers per hour in this place—if you go high enough. And you don't want to break *their* fall either, kala; so look up every once in a while."

"What *is* a drifter?" asked Maung. "I've asked two other people and nobody will tell me."

Than knelt beside the body and waved the floating dust away before wiping off the faceplate and looking inside. "This is—a *dead* drifter. They're prisoners. Drifters wear yellow so we can see them more easily and they've been subjected to a medical procedure called *trammeling*. A tiny chip goes into their brain and deactivates any portion that made them violent. It also makes them obedient. They'll do anything you tell them and that might seem cool at first, but really it's strange. Drifters are totally out of it—like zombies, kala. You'll see. They just kind of drift through their sentence. Forever." Than paused and held up a finger to keep Maung quiet. A few moments later he clicked back in.

"Come on, kala, we have to go. The boss is pissed because we're so late."

Maung bounced over the body and followed Than into a narrow alley between two structures. He felt it again—the same kind of danger he had experienced during war when the Americans hunted him in Burma. The jungle itself had been alive, watching. But this time what searched for him wasn't human or even alive, it was the creation of an alien race that Maung had trouble fathoming and it made him nervous to think that creatures like the one he killed in Charleston had laced the area with automated killers—things that he couldn't even see and that could activate at any moment. Every time he took a step, he expected to die.

"Where are we going?" he asked.

Than pointed upward, toward the yellow dots. "Eventually up there. We're supposed to be watching those guys and making sure the job is done right. But first we have to do something."

"To hell with this place," Maung whispered, but Than overheard. "This *place* is already there, kala. This *is* hell."

"I can't do this," Maung said.

Than crossed a thin steel girder at the top of a hangar, the roof of which had been almost totally destroyed; flaps of torn metal sheeting on either side reminded him of sawteeth. Maung waited by the edge; he did his best to keep his balance, imagining that the hole in the roof was the mouth of a demon and although he'd been praying since his arrival, he still doubted that his ancestors could get near Karin. Too many ghosts. This place lured the unaware and the desperate, the forgotten who nobody cared about, even when they died. Maung shook the thoughts off. When Than reached the middle of the girder he turned, waving for Maung to follow and Maung looked down at the impossibly thin line that linked to his belt by a single metal carabiner. The other end attached to Than.

"It's safe," Than said. "The girder was placed by us and welded in. Besides, I've done this before, alone, and you have me to catch you. If you fall, Maung, I promise the line will hold."

"I can't!" Maung shouted. Now his hands shook, and he backed away, but the safety cable kept him from moving too far.

"I thought you were army—thought you were some kind of war hero or something. Fearless. Killed lots of Cans and Pinos."

"Who told you that?" he asked. *Cans and Pinos*—slang for Americans and Filipinos. Maung hated the words, not because they were derogatory but because they were mutated forms of English not Myanmarese, suggesting his people couldn't even come up with their own slang.

"Nam told me. He knows a lot about you, kala, and he told me some but the old man keeps his mouth tight. Even tighter than the Old Man in Charleston, same one sent me here as you. Before we start our shift you have a meeting with him, with Nam. And I always deliver, kala."

The line went taut and Maung screamed upon realizing what was about to happen; Than heaved him over the edge. Maung fell toward the blackness below, between the demon's lips and past jagged sheets of fang-like twisted metal. Maung closed his eyes. Then the cord tightened again, and he had a sensation of butterflies while accelerating, swinging across and underneath the hangar roof like a pendulum, toward some height based on the physics at play—physics he couldn't understand without awaking his semi-aware.

Quiet. Than spoke and Burmese floated through Maung's speakers but he wasn't there, he was under a blanket of thoughts as he inched toward the hangar roof. Than must be tired, he thought. In this gravity Maung weighed next to nothing, but it still couldn't be easy to reel in that much carbon-fiber cable, going hand over hand for hundreds of meters of line and there was still a long way to go. Maung stayed silent out of respect. Far below him the hangar's contents rested: A semi-intact ship that looked split in two so that Maung imagined a massive beetle, burst open from a weapon that no insect could have imagined. A mixture of bodies surrounded it; some were in vacuum suits, which appeared pristine and untouched, while others were only in jumpsuits. *Frozen.* Maung was close enough that he saw expressions of horror and pain in those ones, captured forever in faces whose eyes stared upward.

"*You fucker!*" Maung screamed and launched himself at Than, who was laughing, making Maung even angrier. He missed and sailed off the roof until Than yanked on the line, pulling him back onto an unbroken section of metal sheeting with enough force to knock the wind from him.

"You don't get it, kala. We're on a budget and a schedule. Our drifters have to process so much metal every period and collect a certain number of bodies. Without guards to guide them they won't reach quota. You're holding me back, kala."

Maung got to his knees. "What happens if we don't get to quota?"

"Then *you* get to work alongside the walking dead because every pair of hands helps. And then you stay outside until you reach quota, and then you and your team lose sleep so the next period you can't perform and you wind up missing quota again, but worse this time; it's a spiral."

"Nobody told me about the dead," said Maung; now they were on the downward slope of the roof, carefully picking their way through wreckage. "Nobody said that we would be their keepers or that they would be frozen like that, like they're still alive. What do we do with them?"

Than changed direction. Maung turned to follow so the two moved parallel with the hangar axis, bouncing toward a black tower, the top of which had already been partially disassembled. Maung ignored his vertigo. He barely kept his eyes open for having gone so long without sleep, and the experience of moving across the face of an asteroid was beginning to weigh on him, now that all his adrenaline had vanished.

"What do we do with the dead?" Than asked. "We recycle them, the same way we recycle everything here. Our business is reclamation. Now shut the hell up so we can concentrate on where we're going; one wrong step here and you fall through."

For a while they said nothing. Maung heard only his breath and was almost too exhausted to pay attention to his footing, and even if he wasn't, he had no idea what to look for or where to step. He had no business being there. Even through his exhaustion he factored it, understood how stupid he'd been to think Karin was a better route than facing federal agents, because it was possible that his chances for survival were lower on the asteroid. He wished he'd said more to Nang before they parted. Maung conjured her in his mind and if he thought hard enough recalled the smell of her hair, which had wafted over him whenever the two had been together on the *Singapore Sun*.

"Wake up!" Than shouted.

Maung's head jerked up; he was less than a few centimeters from the hangar's edge and Than was to his right, moving across a narrow bridge connecting the roof to the tower structure. Maung edged toward him and shivered, realizing he'd come close to falling again, floating downward to land among the bodies.

"Thanks," he said and pointed toward the tall building. "Where are we?"

They'd reached an airlock door and Than opened a panel to punch in a code. "Electronic warfare center and listening post. This entire tower was filled with transmitters, supercomputers, and storage. Its foundations go into the asteroid for a kilometer, where the personnel bunkers were."

"Did *everyone* here die?" Maung asked.

"Almost, I'm sure. You'll see. From what I've seen, it looks like the Sommen hit their defenses and any ships in port, then took the time to invade with ground troops and make sure nothing was left alive. Later, after the Sommen left here, some of the Fleet limped back after attacking the blockade and as far as I know they were the only survivors. Just a few crew members."

The airlock opened silently and Maung and Than entered. A screen showed that the facility was trying to cycle air but Maung knew there was no air to cycle, and Than wasn't waiting for it to finish anyway; he punched at the screen and overrode everything, forcing the inner door to open. The entire port, Maung recognized, was a crypt—*vacuum sealed and preserved*. It was an empty shell, slowly being reclaimed not by rot and decay but by humanity, who wanted each atom of carbon, titanium, and iron it could get, each atom of nitrogen squeezed from the corpses.

"That's the smell," he said.

Than waved him out of the airlock. "What smell?"

"The smell on Sunny Side. Death."

"Yeah," said Than. "The reclamation process gets nasty and some of the off-gases travel through the transport tunnels; they have no idea what it is on Sunny Side, though. And we can't say anything to them about what's going on over here; every two months the Allied military sends a rep to monitor our progress and we get the same warning: a shit storm on anyone who doesn't keep their secrets. You know. Bodies are just as important as metals."

Maung laughed. "Talk to the Koreans? Back on Earth, as soon as other Korean workers find out you're Myanmarese and not Filipino, conversation stops anyway."

"Exactly. Like we'd even *want* to talk to those bastards on Sunny Side, so who *we* gonna tell?"

Than stopped. They were inside the structure now and it shocked Maung to see gleaming white walls, plastic panels that covered everything with graceful curves and perfect joints. Except for the blood. Before freezing in vacuum it pooled on the corridor floor to form a small river, locked in a solid state until some time in the future when someone threw the entire thing into a furnace for reclamation.

"We're heading for the control area now. Guard teams are usually three to four of us, so someone is already there but are you OK with the concept of a drifter?"

"Sure," said Maung, "why would you even ask?"

Than poked him gently in the chest. "Your accent, kala. You aren't exactly a city boy. Where you from? Mandalay district? You Karen from the mountains or something?"

"Outside Mandalay. Way north of the city, a small village in the foothills but we moved to Yangon eventually."

"See, kala?" Than slapped Maung's shoulder. "You're from the jungle and I've seen guys like you before: getting used to living and working on an asteroid isn't exactly easy for someone who smears on thanaka. You guys freak out about ancestors and working with the dead and when the drifters show up it's the last straw because then it becomes something about demons. So I need to know now: Are you good so far?"

Maung shook his head. "No. I need a cigarette."

Only one man stood in the control room, a steel box that barely held the three of them, but which was airlocked and connected to the prison's main life-support system. Maung rushed to take his helmet off. The room smelled of sweat and staleness but he was grateful to have his head free and no longer had an urge to vomit. It was the first time he'd seen all of Than's face, and Maung was shocked to see a four-inch-wide scar, which ran down the left side of his forehead and cheek, and ended just under his jaw.

"Torture," said Than; Maung was embarrassed for having stared. "Cambodians held me head against a motorcycle tire and then throttled up the engine. They did it four times until an American patrol came by and took me from them. The Americans saved my life and sent me *here*."

The other man looked old to Maung, and his skin was a deep brown with hollow cheeks, a skull with just a thin layer of skin separating it from the air. He looked at Maung, up and down and then sneered at Than.

"Old Man Charleston said he was coming earlier," he said.

Maung nodded. "Nam Su Thant?"

"Yeah. You do everything I tell you, kala, and we'll be fine." He used his thumb to point to the airlock. "Than. Go wait outside until I tell you to come back in."

Than looked dumbstruck. "Nam?"

"Get out. There are things the kala and I need to discuss. Go check on a drifter or two and by then we'll be set."

"Nam," said Than, "this one is nothing, a country idiot whose accent makes me laugh; what the hell could *he* have to say that's important?"

But Nam didn't answer and just looked at Than until the man bowed and picked up his helmet. Maung noticed his face had gone red. Than glared at him as he sealed his suit, and he kicked Maung's feet out of the way when he headed to the airlock, sending Maung into a spin. Once he was gone, Nam sighed.

"He has no idea, does he?"

Maung shrugged. "No idea about what?"

"Don't play dumb with me, kala; *Dream Warrior*. Old man told me everything and we need you here, especially now because you can just tell that something is in the air. Not just death. The end of the game, death of us all—of the species. I'll tell you something: Burmese used to rule Dark Side. Nothing happened over here that I didn't know about and the military never showed their faces because they were happy with the amount of materials we sent them from our reclamation outfit.

"But not anymore. Not since the Sommen packed up and left Earth. Now things go down that none of us understand and if I didn't know any better I'd say those stories about demons and ghosts were true. Drifters don't just die anymore; they disappear without a trace and I have to conjure up some excuse for the chief on Sunny Side. We lost three more today and if we keep going at this rate, the incoming supply of prisoners won't make up for the ones we lose. So I don't have the time to play games with you; I know you're no country idiot."

"I'm not *playing*." Maung was angry and relieved at the same time—angry at being thought a liar, relieved that he finally didn't have to hide. "Half of me is artificial and so I lost part of my brain. I *am* dumb, Nam. I'm the country idiot until I can switch on my semi-aware, which holds half my memories in its storage units—memories of my wife and child that I can't even access."

Nam gripped a nearby table. "Bullshit. That's a load of crap." He looked at Maung for a few seconds. Finally he shook his head and said, "You're *serious?* My God, the Chinese did that to our people—stripped pieces of their brains?"

"They had to," said Maung. "The original goal was to create super-awares that looked human so we could move freely and avoid Allied targeting. But there's only so much room in a human skull and Chinese specialists needed space to place their equipment. They picked out small parts of our brains—along with the top half of our spines. They also replaced most of my upper skeleton with some kind of metal, to store information and make an antenna. The good news is that I'm superhuman. The bad news is that I'm alone, and most people want me dead so I have to let the *super* part of me sleep. I can't ever get back to being *just* human."

"I'm sorry, kala. It must be hard—harder than I can imagine because most of us can't even begin to think what it's like. And to have to hide it for as long as you did."

A holo floated over the main control panel and Maung stared at it, a three-dimensional map with yellow dots showing the locations of all the drifters, and he tried to find his dot but the information jammed in his head, making him want to slam his fist into the wall. His eyes teared. If he were somewhere on Earth, he would get up and run, ignoring the consequences.

"I can't see my family," he said. "My son."

"They're supposed to allow you some video contact. But with who we are and why we're here, you can forget it; be patient, Maung. Here, at a prison, you're safe—at least from the police. Though I don't know which is worse."

Maung nodded. He wasn't looking at Nam, but figured the man stared at him. "What does the Old Man in Charleston want from me?"

"You're a hero." Nam put a hand on his shoulder and turned Maung to face him. "To those of us who know the truth, you're a spark of hope, that maybe we can be more than spoil from yet another lost war."

"I'm no hero. All I want is to see my son become something. The sooner I repay my debt, maybe the sooner I can go home."

Nam laughed and grabbed him by the other shoulder, shaking

Maung gently. "That's good. Because what the Old Man in Charleston wants is what I want: to figure out what's happening to my drifters. But I'm sure Than told you not to get your hopes up about going back. Finding the lost drifters though . . . It will give you something to do. Maybe forget Earth for a while."

"So I merge." Maung shrugged and pointed at the holo. "I scour the prison computer systems for information and figure out if it has anything to do with the military or Sunny Side."

Nam held up one hand. "Not yet. We can't have you merge for now."

"Why?"

Nam pointed to the holo map and mumbled something into his throat mic, so that blinking red dots appeared. Now that Maung saw them he noticed how many there were, thousands sprinkled evenly over the complex and nonmoving. "What are they?" he asked.

"Sommen mines. Traps. The ones we know of and have no clue how to disarm. If you activate your semi-aware, they'd detect your signal and you'd be dead within minutes. Null fibers won't mask your signal once you broadcast outside your suit."

"Do you have a surgeon on site?"

Nam frowned. "He is Japanese. On Sunny Side, and more corrupt than a gutter plum. Why?"

"Because," said Maung. "I know of another way—an access port that I haven't used since training, after which they sealed it inside my skull. You'll have to cut me open. If we do it that way we can use shielding to prevent my signal from going far, because I can insert directly using a cable. But the last thing I want is infection; best if a surgeon does it."

Nam called Than back and while they waited he said, "We will not cut you open. Not yet. The risk of having our doctor reveal your secret to others is too great, and I must weigh those risks against what can be gained."

"Can I trust the other guards?" Maung asked. "The ones here, under you?"

The airlock opened and Than entered. While he removed his helmet Nam nodded and pointed at Than. "You can tell them what you are, Maung. All of them are loyal to me and to you—to any Burmese. *This* one most of all." Nam laughed then.

"What is so funny?" Than asked.

"Put your helmet back on," said Nam. "I need you to take Maung outside and show him the ropes. Start with our high ground, he may as well get used to it and you should know, Than: this is no simple country Burmese. Have *respect*."

"So who are you?" Than asked.

They'd been walking in silence for ten minutes, and Maung still had trouble getting accustomed to light gravity; he had to move in a way that combined bouncing off the floor and then pushing off walls and ceilings so that more than once he flipped over and had to regain control. Holes in the wall suggested there were once hand rails, long since removed for their metals.

"Nobody," said Maung.

They reached a dead end and Than cracked open a panel, then punched on the tiny keys inside. A wall opened to reveal an elevator shaft.

"I doubt you're nobody, kala. Nam just gave you the respect he'd give to one of his equals or to an elder. That *never* happens."

Maung hesitated. Than waited at the elevator doorway, and beyond him was a vertical shaft for a service lift, its walls disappearing into darkness. Maung's stomach went cold when he imagined how many ghosts might live in such a black place.

"We're going in there?" he asked.

Than leaped. He floated across the shaft and gently landed on the opposite side where he looped his hands around a ladder rung. "Of course. It's easy. Look, kala, there's no other way so you may as well go free and easy, just embrace the lifestyle. You won't even get tired."

Than disappeared then without saying another word, pulling himself upward into the shaft. Maung hesitated. He hated heights and knew they were already hundreds of meters from the crater floor, and that if he looked downward it would either be pitch black or there would be lights—going so far down that even lit, he wouldn't see bottom.

"Jump like it's a puddle," Than said over the radio. "No more force than that or you risk bouncing off and falling."

"Why can't we use the safety line?" Maung asked.

"You gotta learn to live *without* the line, kala."

Maung inched to the edge. The prayer he said was admittedly self-serving, but this was a terror that rivaled his experience patching the *Singapore Sun*, and he would rather crawl back into the ship's guts to fix another leaking pipe than take this leap. Finally, he jumped. Within seconds he crossed and Maung panicked because he moved too fast and hit the far wall with such force that the inside of his helmet rang and both hands slipped from the rungs. He bounced off. Now the ladder was out of reach and Maung watched, horrified, because the rungs moved past as he fell and his speed increased by the second. He had almost reached the smooth, opposite wall. Maung tried kicking off it gently, which was the wrong thing to do because his boot made contact for too long, sending him into a violent head-over-foot spin, and although he succeeded in re-traversing the shaft toward the ladder, his helmet hit a rung and sent his head smacking against the hard plastic with a crack. He passed out before getting a chance to scream.

"*Wake up, kala.*"

At first Maung thought it was Nang speaking, and he smiled but couldn't grasp why she called him *kala*—or where a Laotian had learned the word. His eyes fluttered open. Someone shone a light through his faceplate and the suit computer was pinging, its computer voice repeating, "*Oxygen levels low.*"

"Come on, kala," Than said, "You OK?"

Maung shook his head. His back screamed with pain until he understood that his legs were pinned beneath him, twisting into an odd shape, and once he succeeded in freeing them, the pain became more manageable; he'd sprained something, but nothing worse. Maung was still in the shaft, but now sat on a springy web that someone had stretched across and fastened to the walls with bolts.

"Safety net?" he asked.

"It saved *your* ass, kala," Than said. "They put them in all the shafts when the project first kicked off, so that dumb shits like you wouldn't kill themselves."

Maung stood and tested his legs then moved his arms, relieved to learn that everything was fine; he had a headache and his back muscles were sprained, but he'd live. The shaft was almost pitch black. Except for Than's helmet lamp, there were no light sources and

Maung wanted to get out because he couldn't shake the feeling that he was in some sort of tomb. He flicked on his helmet lamp.

"We're below ground, aren't we?" he asked.

"*Way* down. I've never even thought of coming this far down and we're not even at the bottom." Than pointed to the ladder. "Let's get the hell out of here."

Something caught Maung's eye. Behind Than was the elevator doorway for this level and it looked out of shape, as if the thing had been made of candy and someone took a blowtorch to it, melting the frame and turning a rectangular opening into a misshaped oval, the top of which was crusted with plastic—frozen in the form of a bubbling and dripping mass.

"What happened here?" he asked.

"Sommen," Than said. "I've seen this before but had no idea they attacked down this far. Usually they just rolled a bunch of their nano-weapons into the shafts and let *them* take care of everyone who was hiding in the sub levels."

"How do you know they didn't do that here?"

"Because." Than bounced toward the exit and reached up, breaking off a teardrop of plastic. "They used their personal weapons. None of their nano tech melted like this that I know of, so why? What was so far down here that they wanted to send their troops?"

Maung moved toward the ladder. "I want out of here."

"We have time, kala." He was already moving through the molten entrance. "I checked the drifters when you and Nam were talking so we may as well explore. Come on and keep up this time."

"What about my oxygen?" Maung asked.

"I clipped an extra tank to your belt."

Maung fumbled with the tank but after a few seconds managed to activate it, switching the feed to the new one so the computer stopped complaining. When he looked up, Than was gone. Now Maung drifted alone in the shaft and although it was perfectly silent in the asteroid's vacuum, what remained of his mind played tricks, forcing Maung to imagine that it was not safe and that someone whispered in the darkness. He kicked away, diving into the corridor after Than.

CHAPTER ELEVEN

Steel beams and shards of plastic hung from the ceiling and Maung had to be careful so his suit wouldn't snag or puncture on jagged edges. He prayed again. Amid the wreckage lay bodies of men and he recognized the uniform of Allied forces, the frost on which made him realize that decompression caught many of them by surprise. Their faces also showed the splotchy red marks of burst blood vessels; some had only made it half way into their suits.

But there were also bodies of those who fought; coil guns lay scattered amid the wreckage along with grenade launchers, left and forgotten so that while Maung heard his own breath through his speakers he couldn't shake the sensation that this battle had just ended. He kept turning around, sure that a Sommen warrior hid nearby. The dead hands of men and women locked onto their weapons still, faceless people whose suit helmets frosted over from moisture that once came from breath, and their frozen blood covered the hallway—so much of it that Maung had to look away.

"A slaughter," he said.

Than picked his way through the wreckage. "There are only humans here; I don't understand."

"What?"

"Why there are none of *them*," said Than, "no Sommen bodies. Nothing at all."

Maung remembered the battle in Charleston—how the American weapons had no effect. "It's because they have armor like none you've seen. Green. Maybe a similar material to what they use for building, and nothing these troops had would have penetrated."

"How do *you* know what Sommen armor is like?"

"Because," Maung said. "I fought one. It's why I wound up here, I had to run from American forces or risk being thrown in prison. Or worse. I fried its armor systems with a transmission."

Than laughed. He stopped and grasped the barrel to a coil gun, one that stuck up from the frozen hands of a dead soldier so it reminded Maung of a sapling, and the man used it to make sure he stayed grounded. Then Than reached out and gripped Maung's shoulder.

"That was a good joke. You may be a lousy prison guard but you *are* funny. A transmission, *right.*"

Maung laughed too. "Remember what Nam said and how he treated me with respect?"

"Yeah, I remember. You fell before you could tell me why."

"I'm a Dream Warrior—the last one alive."

Than said nothing. Maung saw his face through the helmet glass and the man's eyes were wide, his mouth open now that he'd stopped laughing. "Bull."

"I'm not kidding," Maung said. "Why else would Nam treat me the way he did?"

It took a moment for Than to speak again; when he did it was a whisper. "You're telling the truth. Then you're *invincible.*"

"Not invincible. The Americans found a flaw in our system and exploited it to track and kill us. Including my wife. In order to keep from getting caught, and to keep from activating the Sommen mines in the area, I have to keep my semi-aware portion shut down. If I don't, the signal can be detected."

Maung took the lead, unsure of what they were doing or what Than hoped to find. He couldn't stand another minute among the corpses and prayed there was less blood in the hallway ahead.

"A Dream Warrior?" Than hissed over his speakers. "Are you freaking serious? Now *I* need a cigarette."

There was a hole in the wall to his right. It looked as though something melted its way through the plastic, insulation, and supports, until gaining access to a room beyond. Maung increased the illumination from his helmet light. The area was small, and looked as though it housed computer equipment. A thin column or tower vanished through a hole in the floor and also continued upward through an open ceiling so that he couldn't see where it started or stopped. Then Maung saw the corpse. A man in a vacuum suit faced them, suspended by a Sommen spear-like thing that spiked him to the tower so his feet hung frozen in midair. The corpse had no helmet; Maung shivered when he realized that a dead man stared at him, a smile frozen on his mouth as if amused.

His new oxygen supply was halfway gone. "We should return," Maung said, "my oxygen is at fifty. And this place is cursed."

"A little farther," said Than. "I at least want to find something to justify what we've done so Nam doesn't give me crap for wasting time. And you have got to give up that country superstition crap, Maung; this place isn't cursed. It's just filled with dead people."

Maung was about to answer when he stopped. The hallway ahead opened into a huge chamber filled with desks and monitors, some kind of control room, he thought, but a portion of the floor was missing in front of them and had he taken another step he would have fallen through. Than whistled and unslung his coil gun, which he held with one hand, using the other to grab onto a molten lump of plastic.

"What's wrong?" Maung asked. He whispered it before realizing that he could have shouted and it wouldn't have mattered, not in a vacuum.

"*There*. In the center of the room."

Maung looked. It took a second for him to see what Than was pointing at but he made out a shape, a hulking form slumped over one of the tables on a lower level; the room was tiered, with wide platforms that stepped down into the center like a circular amphitheater. Maung squeezed inside.

"Where the hell are you going?" Than asked. His voice sounded high pitched and Maung heard him breathing rapidly. "That's a Sommen, Maung. Are you crazy? What if it's still alive? *We don't know anything about these things!*"

Maung ignored him. He floated over the floor gap and bounced down slowly, drifting closer until his helmet lamp hit the Sommen with its beam. Like everything else, it was frozen. Maung saw the green armor and supposed it was the same material he'd witnessed in Charleston, but which here was masked by a thin coating of frost or dust, and the material pulsated under his light—as if reacting to it. He reached out. Maung's gloves scraped the dust away and he noticed the armor plates were soft, semirigid, as if constructed of plastic and filled with gel. He pressed harder. Maung raised a fist then and slammed it down onto the thing's thigh plate and it went rigid, at the same time glowing so he had the strange sensation that his fist stopped before making contact; something repulsed it even before his hand actually hit.

"Come on, Maung," Than said.

Maung shook his head, too engrossed to realize Than couldn't see it. "This is amazing. And it can't hurt us." He gestured at the Sommen corpse, which was at least three times larger than him, and so massive that in Earth's gravity it would've crushed the computer underneath. "And the only reason it's dead is because it looks like someone blew up the doorway at the same time it floated in. They must have used a massive, massive charge."

"Maung, I'm telling you; we need to—" but Than went silent before he finished.

Maung saw something out of the corner of his eye. At first what was happening wasn't obvious and he watched while a rubble pile near the door shifted, sending small pieces of plastic to float before they settled. Whatever it was, the thing had blinking lights. Finally it worked its way free and Than hissed into his microphone.

"Shit! That's a security bot. *They were supposed to have all been deactivated!*"

Maung froze. The bot shot jets of mist from its base, using gas propulsion to float along, swinging multiple coil guns and grenade launchers along a wide arc as it scanned. It hovered away, toward the door.

"What do we do?" he asked. "Will it come after us?"

Than didn't answer. The robot floated closer to him and shot a blue laser, which rastered back and forth over Than's helmet, inching its way down until it stopped, shutting off once it reached his waist. A flashing light cut on. "We're going to have to run, Maung. It's using shape detection to see if I'm human and from what I know of these things, it's pinging me now to see if I'm friendly; military units have auto-transmitters—both radio and light based—that respond with the correct code. We don't have them."

Maung thought for a second. He knew that what Than said was important and the words reminded him of something else but he couldn't remember. He was about to curse the fact that his semi-aware was off when it hit him.

"The nano-mines and the traps," he said.

Than whispered. "What about them?"

"If that thing is pinging or sending any kind of signal other than radio, has it activated the Sommen traps nearby?"

As soon as Maung said it Than jumped, first kicking off a nearby desk and then placing his boots against the robot itself, pushing off hard so he rocketed toward the exit; the robot smashed into a table, then spun at the same time it careened toward Maung.

"*Run!*" Than screamed.

The robot knocked into Maung and sent him sprawling on top of the Sommen corpse, pushing him forward so that his faceplate slid against the green armor. He closed his eyes. Maung almost switched on his semi-aware but the robot jetted away, sending a hissing sound through Maung's helmet from control gas that slapped against it. By the time he lifted himself up, the robot had already steered itself after Than and was picking up speed before it disappeared through the exit.

Maung slipped, floating toward the floor. Whatever he'd held onto had broken free from the Sommen and he looked down to see it tumble next to him, a long rifle-like object, jet black except for a silver end that narrowed to a point. This was important, Maung thought—not like anything the one in Charleston had carried. He was about to reach for it when his headlamp illuminated what looked like a cloud of mosquitoes and a pattering against his helmet sounded like a sandstorm, just before his suit computer chimed. A red light blinked on his heads-up display.

"Than," he whispered. "Nano and microbots. Thousands of them."

"*I have my own problems, Maung!*"

Maung went rigid. Within a few seconds the sounds on his helmet ceased and the air cleared so he lifted an arm and tried to see them, telling his suit to magnify the view. Nothing. Maung did his best to recall what he could about microbots but the data wasn't there, only the information that he already knew: They could be deadly, but his suit made him invisible as long as its coating remained intact.

"Circle back," he said, "bring the security bot to me, the way you came." Maung pushed off through the room's exit and down the hallway, following after Than and hoping he still had contact.

"What? Why?"

The signal was weak, and Maung breathed harder, using every muscle to pull himself through the dark corridor and wreckage. "The nanos. You'll be safe in your suit but the bot won't. If you lead it back this way the cloud of nanos may attack it."

Than didn't answer. After a minute Maung stopped himself, shoving his hand into a hole in the wall and grabbing hold of its edge when he recalled this was the spot where the man had been staked to the tower of computer equipment; ahead of him was the tail end of the nano cloud. It looked wispy. Portions of it stuck to the hallway's wreckage and white plastic and then let go, leaving Maung with the impression that the cloud was a single organism, an amoeba-like thing that crept forward according to wants and needs that he couldn't comprehend. It was gray, but where his helmet lamp shone, the cloud sparkled.

"Come back this way," Maung said. "I'm at the cloud, all you have to do is float through it!"

Than's voice sounded strong in his speakers, and Maung thought he perceived a light in the distance, making the cloud of nanos look like fog. Without warning, sparks pierced the cloud and flashed past him, some bouncing off the walls and forcing Maung to duck through the hole; he tried not to think about the corpse, which now stared directly over his shoulder.

"It's shooting at me!" Than shouted.

"You're almost to me. Once you're through the cloud, there is a hole in the wall on your right; I'm there. We can go up to get away."

"*This better work.*"

Maung stared at the hole leading to the corridor where the nano cloud floated, and noticed the light from Than's helmet lamp got closer. He looked up to check if they could escape that way by launching upward, above the staked corpse and out. The tower passed through the ceiling above where a meter-wide gap opened between the ceiling and the computer equipment so he sighed with relief after mentally gauging the gaps—plenty of room for them to pass. He was about to push off and investigate further when a flash of light blinded him; Maung raised an arm to shield his face, making him spin slowly until his head pointed toward the floor.

"Concussion grenades," said Than, chuckling for a reason Maung failed to grasp. "At least they weren't fragmentation. Stupid bot must be half broken already; it thinks there's an atmosphere here."

Than was beside Maung now, pressed against the corpse so that his helmet scraped against the man's frozen face. There was no time for a prayer. Both men were upside down and the bot tried to navigate its way through the hole so that it could take another clear shot at Than, but there was something wrong. The cloud thickened and swarmed around the bot, dimming its blinking lights, and the machine fired a jet to send itself smashing against the wreckage in the corridor. It fired again, blindly. Fléchettes ricocheted everywhere, sending sparks each time they contacted metal.

"*Screw this!*" Than shouted; he kicked at a section of electronics, forcing himself down into the gap between the computer tower and the floor.

"We need to go up," said Maung, too late.

Maung followed him. Now there was time for prayer; he begged his ancestors to stay at his side, to help him not to fear the deep into which Than took them and for them to keep demons at bay.

"We are almost out of oxygen," Maung said.

Than sounded out of breath. "I know. But we'll make it, Maung; if there are still bodies, wreckage, and weapons on these levels, there are still oxygen bottles. Somewhere. Reclamation crews and drifters haven't touched this stuff yet and leakage on oxygen would have been minimal."

Maung lost his sense of time as he followed Than, who kept going downward, and the wreckage and death became a blur since it only got worse as they continued. Finally they reached a level where the equipment tower stopped, blending and broadening into a massive conical base or foundation that looked as though it was anchored to the asteroid itself. Maung's headlamp couldn't shine far enough to see any walls and he thought to himself that the chamber they'd landed in must be huge.

"What is this place?" Than asked.

Maung touched the base of the tower, which had been partially molten. "I don't know. The Sommen melted parts of this, though, for some reason. So it must have been important." His headlamp lit up a line of chairs, their backs to the tower and reclined as if they were acceleration couches that circled the tower base, disappearing on either side in darkness. A distant, unreachable part of his brain recognized them and Maung got goose bumps. "I've seen this before. *Or something like it.*"

"Come on," Than said. "Let's see if they have an emergency supply station around here. I need air."

But Maung waited; he was half there, half in his memories where he dug to reach the source of his unease and recollections. Than's light dimmed. It looked to Maung as though he watched a firefly at night, its tiny glow insignificant and small compared to the infinite darkness and he was about to ask Than to wait when the man clicked in.

"Maung, come here! You have to see *this.*"

Maung's knees were stiff, his legs exhausted. He thrust into the darkness toward Than and gently floated down to the floor where he jumped off again, advancing in lazy bounding arcs through the huge space, until finally his headlamp illuminated something green. Than was close now. But Maung still couldn't tell what was giving off the green tinge until he got closer, where his exhaustion evaporated as soon as he pulled focus.

"Sommen." he said.

Than nodded. "Dead. And more than one."

"How many?"

"I don't know. Hundreds. Thousands? I guess that whatever reason they came down here for, it was important. Why else would they sacrifice this many?"

Something else clicked in Maung's mind, aligning itself with his experience in Charleston, with the computer tower, all the couch chairs and now this. He pushed off.

"Where are you going?" asked Than.

"I have to know. This means something, Than; it's important."

"Know *what*? *What's* important?"

But Maung couldn't answer. The Sommen dead lay thick so they obscured the rock floor and he guessed the creatures had frozen on massive stomachs, face down as if they expired while crawling forward with their last strength; all of them carried the same weapons that Maung had seen previously. But there were no marks—no indications that any of them had been shot or damaged. His light played over them and its limited range made it impossible to see everything in the pitch blackness, so that he had to mentally piece the images together in a mosaic, a scene where thousands of Sommen corpses formed a gruesome carpet of green.

"We need oxygen, Maung." Than bumped into his shoulder and Maung sighed with relief, glad that he wasn't alone.

"I know."

"I mean soon, I'm on my last ten minutes."

"We need to find dead soldiers," said Maung. "Human ones. It's possible they carry spares. I don't think—"

Than grabbed his shoulder and stopped Maung, then pointed in the direction of his headlamp. "There. In the direction the Sommen were heading."

They hauled themselves along the floor, using the Sommen corpses as if they were handholds and Maung remembered snorkeling as a kid where his father told him not to swim but to pull himself along the reef instead. He smiled at the memory. The Sommen formed a long green reef and Maung wished he were back there now, back in Myanmar where every winter his father took him to the beach for a week.

They reached the far wall. Black rock sloped upward into the darkness and where it met the floor Maung saw orderly arrays of equipment and workstations, with massive couches like the ones they saw earlier, but these had been ripped apart and Maung thought he traced claw marks on the metal desks. The Sommen must have been furious upon reaching this point, he figured, because the alien corpses stopped in an almost straight border, past which there were only humans. Parts of them. The dead soldiers wore vacuum suits like Maung hadn't seen—ones that were skin tight except where the creatures had clawed their way through, allowing human insides to spill out before freezing. None of them had heads and Maung dry heaved.

"Take it easy, Maung," said Than. "Breathe."

Maung kept searching. Some humans must have been hit by the Sommen weapons, which blew holes through them and then through the equipment, melting everything in its path and leaving deep pits in the rock. Than scavenged for oxygen while Maung reached down for one of the soldiers' helmets; they looked strange. An external air line attached to the side instead of the back, and from the rear protruded a cylindrical socket that looked familiar; when he ran his fingers over it Maung saw the gold contacts inside. He dropped the helmet and backed away.

"We have to go, Than."

Than lifted a pair of small black tanks. "I found two. They're awkward to carry but thankfully have universal valve fittings and are half full."

"*Now,*" Maung said. "We have to go. I know what these are."

Than took them on a different route back to the control center, and soon Maung went dizzy from navigating through crawlspaces and access ports. He understood why the helmets had sockets. There was no need to crack one open and see the dead face of a frozen warrior, his or her last expression stuck in one position, and he remembered the Sommen's reaction back in Charleston even *before* he took over its armor systems. It had charged. Just like these Sommen had swarmed and charged, ignoring the danger to personally address the threat of human Dream Warriors instead of using nanos, and he imagined how they must have been frenzied by the time they reached the wall— enough to tear their human targets to pieces.

The Allied dead in this place; *they were all Dream Warriors.*

If the Allies had Dream Warriors too, *so many*, this must have been how they won against the Chinese; but why hadn't they slaughtered Maung and his unit?

Nam yelled at them over the radio before they could return but Maung was too deep in thought to hear and he barely kept his eyes open for having been through so much in such a short period of time. His muscles weakened. The low gravity took longer to get used to than he'd anticipated and now that he'd seen the deepest part of the rock he wondered how he arrived at this place, asking his ancestors to certify this was the path, to send him a sign. Maung guessed that it had to be; only someone like *him* recognized the corpses for what they were, which meant he was here for a reason.

They squeezed into the control room airlock and Than motioned for Maung to raise his arms.

"Why?" he asked.

Than pointed at the spray nozzles, which popped out of the walls and ceiling. "Dielectric mist. Followed by a shock that kills any nanos remaining on our suit. You can't get rid of them all without it."

Maung watched as Than transformed; blue electricity arced along the creases of his suit and over his helmet, and he looked down at a forearm to see the same. A few moments later they finished and opened the inner door, which was when Nam propelled forward and poked Than's chest with a finger, shouting, and Maung smiled because he was glad to finally remove his helmet and not have to hear his own breathing. He hooked into a seat and closed his eyes.

Maung woke up and thought that his mother was there, and that his son sat on his lap, and he swore he smelled thanaka. But it must have been a dream; his family was on the other side of the solar system and for a moment he'd forgotten. He forgot what he just learned about the Sommen and human corpses and forgot that death was the smell that seeped through Karin and into sunny side until he recalled a version of a game he used to play in school as a teenager— when he and his friends put a dead fish in the ceiling over their teacher's desk. Within a day or two, it stunk up the whole school. Nam stared at him from a chair on the other side of the room and between them was the prison-port hologram, the dots slowly moving across it in a way that showed Maung nothing, a meaningless dance impossible to understand.

"Than is off duty," Nam said. "You and I will be too, as soon as our relief arrives. They're late."

"What was this place?" Maung asked.

"What do you mean?"

Maung rubbed the sleep from his eyes. The day seemed like it couldn't have happened, but he smelled the rankness of his suit; he reeked like a garbage dump.

"I mean besides a port. Like the building we're in right now. What went on here?"

Nam shrugged. "A communications facility. That's what we've always been told, Maung. Than said you ran into nanos and found a sea of Sommen corpses, was there something else that makes you think there's more to this place?"

"That many Sommen corpses . . ." said Maung. But the idea was lost, and he cursed himself when he couldn't pick up his original train of thought. "I'm tired, Nam. I don't want to ever have to clean up what we saw today. Not that much blood. At least in the war the blood would run off, soak into the soil; here it just stays. Frozen forever."

Nam nodded. "You don't have to worry. I already notified the chief and he's going to tell the Americans that they have a problem with one of their bases—a cache of Sommen dead and their technology that somehow got overlooked."

It took a moment for Maung to realize what Nam had said, and he gathered his thoughts. "If they come," he said, "what if they find me?"

"Then the Americans will find the new Maung, the Maung who volunteered for guard duty because it paid so much, not Maung the Dream Warrior, running from capture."

Maung considered telling everything. His thoughts traced a path that made him feel cautious, but they hit the same dead end as always—without revealing why he should worry, without allowing him to reconnect the dots, ones which he had seen so clearly before falling asleep. He sighed and, despite the low gravity, never felt so heavy. Maung was about to give up when he saw the hose leading into the back of Nam's helmet.

"The Americans," he said, trying to get the words out before he forgot again. "They were researching their own Dream Warrior program."

Nam had been about to leave because the replacements were now opening the outer airlock door; instead he slammed his fist against the emergency locks, engaging them with a hiss and setting off the alarm.

"What?"

"They were researching their own program, Nam. The evidence is still there. An entire army of Sommen hit this place because of them and I know that because the same thing happened to me when I activated in Charleston; the Sommen there was attacking

Americans but as soon as his defensive systems identified me, he
turned and charged. They had multiple APCs and soldiers with coil
guns and grenade launchers, and instead of focusing on them, it
swerved and charged *me*. Someone without weapons. That's the same
thing Than and I saw today. The Sommen went into a frenzy."

Nam shouted into his throat mic at the replacements who were
now pounding on the inner door, and he told them to wait before
looking back up at Maung. "You are sure of this?"

"I've never been more sure," said Maung. "You didn't know this?
It's right there—out in the open."

"*Of course I didn't know it!*" Maung flinched at the anger he heard
in Nam's voice, but the man was looking at the floor, thinking. "*You*
don't know it either. Forget about it. Give me time to think and we'll
talk on our next shift. Do you remember how the Sommen would
let anyone just walk up to their bases and ships—to join their
merchant ranks?"

"Yeah," Maung said.

"I'm starting to wonder if things would've been better if I'd had
the guts to do *that*."

Nam opened the inner airlock door and apologized to the
replacement guards, who stared at Maung but said nothing. When
the door closed behind them he gripped Maung's wrist before he
could get his helmet on, then whispered. "I mean it. Don't talk to
Than about this at all, and I'll go straight to his quarters to make sure
he keeps his mouth shut."

"Why?" Maung asked. "Why should we be so secret?"

"Because we may be able to use this to our advantage. But now
thanks to that idiot, Than—who had no idea what those dead
humans represented—we have no time to think; if I had known, I
never would have reported this to Sunny Side. You should have
spoken up as soon as you got back, Maung. Make a mistake like that
again and Old Man Charleston will have you killed."

CHAPTER TWELVE

Maung stared at the guards' "barracks"—a narrow vertical slot, ten meters wide and carved into the rock so it extended a hundred meters away from him and fifty meters above. Each side of it contained dormitory cubicles. Maung slipped into the slot, and climbed. His space was near the top and he squeezed into a three-meter cube, the open side of which was covered by wire mesh and a thin curtain to form a private cage. Maung closed the cage door. He drew the curtain, shut off the single light over his bed, and then tried to sleep while fending off nightmares of the Sommen. It was nice to hear Burmese voices, he thought. While drifting off, Maung listened to the other guards talk and gamble, and for the first time since the war he forgot he wasn't in Myanmar.

Maung woke when someone pressed his shoulder. Without thinking he clutched at the air and made contact with a forearm so he wrapped his fingers around it and twisted before a voice hissed into his ear.

"Stop, Maung; it's Than!"

Maung let go and yawned, grabbing a handhold to prevent himself from floating upward and bumping his head. "What time is it?"

"Come." Than tugged on Maung's suit. "Time is meaningless here, except in terms of when your next duty shift is. And we're on duty in eight hours."

Maung floated after him and saw the bluish-white LEDs outside his cube, gleaming in reflection off Than's helmet, which hung from a strap over his shoulder. Wherever they were going, he thought, it was vacuum or Than wouldn't have bothered carrying it. They made it all the way out of the barracks before Maung realized his mistake.

"I forgot my suit helmet," he said.

Than kept going. "It doesn't matter. We got you an entire new suit, a proper one this time. Nam is waiting for us so we have to hurry; try and keep up."

"Where are we headed?" asked Maung.

"Just a second." Than popped a panel off the wall outside the barracks and checked to ensure nobody watched; he then dove into a tiny access shaft. The panel floated downward to land at Maung's feet.

"Get in and shut it behind us. Once we meet Nam, we're heading back to that place we found yesterday—with all the dead Sommen—because Nam wants to grab as much stuff as he can before the Fleet makes it off limits. We may be too late already."

Maung squeezed in behind Than; once he sealed the access panel, darkness swallowed them both.

"We want you to access the dead," Nam said.

At first Maung thought he'd heard it wrong because of interference from the humming conduits that touched his new suit and helmet so he shrugged. "Access *what*?"

"The dead," Nam repeated. "You have to try and plug in—access whatever's been frozen for all these years in the computer portion of their brains."

"I don't know if that will work," Maung said. The thought itself induced a sense of dread. "From what we saw when we were down there, it looks like the Sommen specifically went after the wiring on these guys. *None* of them had heads."

They were deep within the station now. Nam said that he had a map display on his heads-up so they wouldn't get lost, and Maung picked up the sounds of the station, vibrating through the gauntlets and into the air inside. The structure moaned. He imagined that the towering buildings above were like banyan trees, their limbs and massive trunks shifting in the winds of a monsoon and he and the others crawled through the roots, protected. He squeezed through a tight hole. Nam had forced open a metal, sphincter-like valve that looked razor sharp and Maung took care to make certain the edges didn't slice his suit. He looked back; Maung hoped nobody was following, but couldn't shake the feeling that the place was haunted and since he was last he shone his headlamp behind them into the darkness—relieved to see nothing.

"Not much farther," said Nam. "We're almost there."

"Why is this so important to you?" Maung asked.

Nam chuckled. "It's not—not to me. It is to the Old Man and you know the rules: We do anything he says."

"No questions?" Maung said. "Don't you ever wonder why he cares about things—like this?"

"No questions." Nam grunted and the sounds of clanking metal came over Maung's helmet speakers. "We're here. I'll clip off and drop the line down, but we're coming in from above and it's a long drop so be careful."

The second time was no easier. Maung wrapped his arms around his chest and surveyed the pile of headless bodies, watching while Than and Nam dug, breaking through the thin layer of ice that held the corpses together and looking for one that might still be whole. He refused to get close and neither Than nor Nam insisted. Maung said a silent prayer for protection from evil, for protection from the souls that had lived here for so long, frozen in place only to face a form of grave robbery. After an hour he sat on the floor. He hadn't been on Karin that long and suspected that low gravity and stress were getting to him, and he fought the urge to pound his own helmet with a futile rage.

"We should let them rest," he said.

Nam straightened and turned. "Not out here, Maung. These are American devils who got what they deserve and there's no room here for superstition. We're millions of miles from Mandalay."

Maung smiled at the slang, reminded of home. The phrase, *miles and miles from Mandalay,* was used to describe things that were too far to reach and it felt good to talk in Burmese.

"They are dead, though, Nam," he said. "Their dead, our dead, spirits are the same all over. We should leave them be. And don't call them American devils; you never faced them in war and don't know what they're like. They're not devils."

"I think Maung's right," Than said. "Even if we find one that looks intact, the chances of this working after they've been frozen for so long—"

"What do you know about semi-awares?" Nam interrupted. "What do you know about anything? You're half as smart as Maung is without his semi-aware and that's pretty dumb. So keep working and don't say another word, either of you."

But Maung was glad to see that he'd had an effect. Instead of treating the American dead as if they were wood, tossing them here and there in the light gravity, Nam and Than worked together and lifted the bodies carefully, stacking them neatly wherever there was room. After fifteen more minutes Nam held his hand up. He reached down and motioned for Than to help.

"I think we found one," he said.

Than grabbed the feet. "It's a girl."

They placed the body in front of Maung, who scraped the ice from its faceplate to reveal the pale face of what to him looked like a young woman, maybe in her twenties, and she stared up into the blackness with an expression of surprise, her lips coated with frost. The preservation was perfect. Her skin was soft and white, matte with a layer of ice crystals that formed long ago on her cheeks, but the layer was barely there. Even covered by ice she was beautiful.

"It reminded me of the old kids' story from the twentieth century," said Nam. "The one they've made like a trillion versions of." He thought for a second. "Sleeping Beauty."

"This is wrong," Than said.

Nam smacked the side of his helmet. "Shut up or I'll send you back alone; let's see if you can find the way back again, this time without a map."

"He's right, though," said Maung. His stomach was uneasy, nervous with the anticipation of what was about to happen. Nam wrenched off his back pack and opened it, yanking out bundles of different cable loops so that Maung imagined the man was gutting a wild animal. "If I connect, it will be for a moment and will be with the last thoughts of a dead woman. What about this seems *right* to you? This is bad luck, Nam—something a kala would do."

Nam sorted the cables and laid them across the floor. "You said that you have the ability to link directly with computers and from what Old Man Charleston said, you may be able to power one of their semi-awares with yours. So pick a cable and do it."

"What if the sunny-side detail shows up in the middle of my link? Who's going to deal with any nanos that lock in, like they did the last time we activated unshielded tech down here?"

"We'll worry about that if and when it happens," said Nam. "You're to power her up and gather as much data as you can, as quickly as you can, and then we go back the way we came; there wasn't time to work out the proper shielding. Also, as far as we can tell, this area is clear of nano-mines." He cracked the seal on the dead woman's helmet and carefully pulled it off; the helmet split down the middle, clamshell, and a bundle of small golden rods slid out from the back of her head. "How can you stand this, Maung. How could anyone stand having metal inserted into their skulls?"

Maung ignored the question. "I don't see how this will work, Nam. How can I get the cable into my helmet? Do you expect me to do this in vacuum?"

"I'll show you, but first find a cable that works on the woman; all of these will work on you, I guarantee it. And we don't need to operate or tell the surgeon."

Maung leaned over and turned the woman onto her face, where he could look more closely at the back of her head. Then he scanned the cables. Once he found one that looked like a good fit, he pointed and Nam nodded, lifting the cable before shuffling behind Maung; he fumbled with Maung's hoses before snapping the cable into place. A whirring sound filled his helmet. Maung panicked for a second, thinking that microbots had gotten inside his suit; a slight pressure pushed against the back of his head where his port was, then a sharp pain when something cut through his skin, and finally a click when his port locked. There was no connection to anything yet so his semi-aware remained inactive.

"Where did you find this helmet?" he asked. "These cables?"

"The Old Man," said Nam. "He already thought something like this might be needed. This suit and gear got here at the same time you did and microbots are integrated into the helmet port, on the inside; they tunnel through your skin to form the linkage."

The faster this was done the faster he could be out of her mind, Maung thought, and he reached behind the woman's head to lift it gently, holding the connector steady. He prepared the other end of the cable before activating his system.

In less than a second he understood what to do. He estimated the proper amount of juice to send down the connector, assuming the woman was designed in a manner similar to himself, and set up shields and traps to prevent her semi-aware from going on the offensive and taking him over. She may be dead, but now that he was fully aware, Maung realized there was a chance her system stored some power and could try to force through his defenses; there was no telling what the Americans were up to. Just before sliding the connector into the woman's port he thought that cold air had entered his suit, but then his system reminded him that the cold came from suit sensors, linked directly to his brain, and the thought of it made him smile; he'd never *touched* absolute zero before—or however close to it they were on Karin. It was a cold beyond cold, an extreme that his semi-aware monitored almost at the individual fiber level, making sure the strands could still flex despite the environment and that they didn't snap to create micro leaks. He was aware at a level that made his existence blend seamlessly into that of Karin. But at the same time Maung imagined he was like a ghost and that his soul expanded beyond the flesh of his body and into a thin layer that bled outside the asteroid to contact space itself.

He slid the connector into her neck port and waited. At first there was nothing. Then time itself seemed to melt, sending Maung into a universe of slow motion as data streamed first in one direction and then in both when the woman's basic systems booted. Maung had to close his eyes. The stream of visual information confused him because Nam and Than looked as though they were frozen compared to the speed at which Maung absorbed the data, a kind of golden light that made him warm, just at the thought of being alive again. If only he made it to the main communications center, Maung could reach out to American commanders and let them know of the Sommen. The Sommen were unstoppable. All of his comrades were dead already and it was up to him to . . .

He shut off incoming traffic and opened his eyes. "That is *way* messed up, man."

"What's wrong?" Nam asked. "You just started a second ago."

"She's trying to take me. I set defenses and it's like they aren't even there, like her semi-aware can detect traps and break through the firewalls instantaneously. If I didn't know any better I'd say it could predict my every move. And she's sending me her thoughts; the last ones she ever had. It's like I'm *her*."

Than jumped to his feet and Maung guessed he was looking at something on his heads-up. The man's voice sounded panicked.

"Nanos. They're still far off and the structure is giving me a lot of interference, but they're headed this way, moving slowly. We have time."

"Get back in there," Nam said.

"What if it takes me over?" asked Maung. "I've never experienced anything like this, like the semi-aware has a real personality, and all of her is contained within it."

"You have five minutes. Then I'm pulling the plug and we're heading out."

"What happens if we pull the plug while he's still hooked up?" Than asked. Both he and Nam looked at Maung.

"Don't. I get a really bad headache and it takes me a week to walk again."

"Five minutes," Nam repeated.

But five minutes, Maung recognized, may as well have been five hours. Communication down the cable was blocked and the woman's semi-aware bombarded the optical fibers with its will, a kind of energy stream, strong enough to disturb his systems and at first he was too frustrated to even open the connection again until his semi-aware finished analyzing the pattern, identifying it as something that diminished. A moment later the signal weakened to almost nothing. He'd given some juice to the woman's semi-aware but not enough so it could run for any great length of time and now her energy cycled down.

The memory of his wife popped into his thoughts without warning. Maung hesitated before flicking open the line because as soon as he saw her, sadness made him fight the urge to cry and it took almost thirty seconds to regain control of his emotions. When it passed, he opened the line to the dead American.

Almost at once the woman's system flooded in. The signal attenuation had been a ruse and Maung drowned among wave after wave of multiple frequencies, too much for him to handle so that he almost gave up until he had an idea. His semi-aware pulsed a code, one that hadn't been used in years but then again it had been a long time since the war ended and Maung noted that the *last* time he used it the code had been old. But it had worked. The main Chinese target had been a massive parallel setup of American semi-awares in Thailand, one of their main centers for strategic planning, and Maung was still shocked to find even more powerful capabilities in such a small package—an American human. In less than a second her attack stopped. He couldn't believe the code worked, but one moment his brain and semi-aware were flooded with electrons and now it was empty, a kind of computational wasteland. Maung probed deeper into the woman's semi-aware, wary of the possibility that other traps waited.

The outer structure was gone. Maung had to send out more feelers than normal to trace a path and he wondered what could have caused such destruction, not spending the computational power to figure it out now, but saving the data for later. When he reached the core he found the last bits of activity. A decompression bomb—the thing that nearly overwhelmed his systems—looked like a spinning drum, its outward section spinning so fast around a horizontal axis that it hurt Maung to just scan it; the rest of the area had been converted into a capacitor, designed to supply a burst of energy to power the bomb as soon as a target appeared. Maung examined what remained. All of the woman's memory was gone and if this were a city it was one that had been blown out, the spires of skyscrapers the only thing left, with shattered windows occasionally letting a piece go with a distant crash. But there was something else; one of his feelers sent back a ping, like a fishing bob that just disappeared under the water and then popped back into sight, and he was about to send a query down its length when his alarms tripped. He backed out. Like so many times before, Maung sank back into his training and relaxed his mind, getting out of the way of his reflexes and letting them do what they'd been taught, at speeds so fast that his body temperature instantly slid upward.

Something pinged *all* of his feelers now. His semi-aware threw up walls and traps as fast as it could while a portion of it examined the decompression bomb to see if it was of any use. Maung powered up the capacitor again. Now he watched a visualization of what approached, a black mist that slipped in from every side, like nothing he'd seen before and he barely had time to activate the bomb before making his final escape. The bomb wrapped the mist in streams of energy, making much of it disappear.

Maung's system calculated that the mist was probably a creeper. A fragment of it—so small that it must represent only a few lines of code—grew nearby and Maung considered something that he never would have under different circumstances. A millisecond later he had the creeper fragment, stored in his wetware, in a sector isolated from the rest of his brain to keep it trapped. In such a small space it could only grow so much.

Maung cut loose. He shut down and jerked the cable from her head before pausing, listening to his breathing as he went over every inch of his semi-aware, then did it again before he was satisfied that nothing followed him down the cable and that his captive, the creeper, was well contained.

Nam shone a light in his eyes. "You OK?"

"Yeah. A little thirsty. How much time do we have?"

"Not much," said Than. "We're reading about ten minutes until the outermost nanos reach us."

"That means you have three minutes," said Nam. "What did you learn?"

"A creeper. The Sommen used a creeper that hit these people internally at the same time the Sommen attacked them physically. I can't think of a worse way to go."

"What's a creeper?"

"It's like a virus," said Maung, "but instead of hitting programs immediately, it exists alone on the first network it infects and takes its time to analyze the environment. It's a complex code, almost semi-aware. Once it gets a handle on the host it makes changes slowly, so the infected don't know they're infected and the thing doesn't replicate. It sends subroutines out to other users who access the main system, and in that way it infects them with backdoor access points, viruses, whatever it needs to collect a host of slave computers and then convert the entire thing into one big super-aware, spread out over a wide geographic area and ready to do the bidding of whoever owns the creeper. If it had succeeded, these people would have been made virtual slaves."

Nam backed away from the bodies. "The Sommen are beyond evil."

"I don't know," said Maung. "I don't think the Sommen thought it was evil. This was . . . different. In examining it quickly I got the sense from its code that the creeper is just something they do to anyone who merges with machines."

"Can we just go?" Than asked. "I don't even know what this all means but it scares the crap out of me; let's get the hell out of here."

Before they could leave, Nam reached behind Maung's helmet and deactivated the microbots, waiting a moment before pulling the cable off and stuffing it with the others in his bag. Maung stood. At first he almost fell, the exhaustion from linking up more than he expected, but he found his balance and bounced toward the wall stations.

"Not yet," said Maung. "Now we know the Americans had their own Dream Warrior project going, maybe *before* the Chinese, and yet we never saw them use it on the battlefield. But they must have; otherwise how could they have defeated us, and how did we never see signs of it? And we still don't know what this place was, Nam, or where the creeper came from; that must be information the Old Man can use. Five more minutes?"

"You're crazy." Nam said nothing for a moment, then reached for Maung's shoulder. "I can let you have two; that's it. We really have to go soon; I'm not messing around—Old Man or not."

It took Maung over a minute to find a wall port that worked. By the time Nam plugged him in he estimated he had less than twenty seconds and Maung told them to pull the plug if they had to, then closed his eyes and submerged into the darkness of a mainframe, one long dead and whose fibers and superconductors were so compromised that it seemed like every path was a dead end. Maung wrote a routine to automate the search. He created copies of programs that ran feelers down every route until they found one he had a chance of following, but the process was risky. If he hit a creeper with one, these wouldn't be able to alert him to the weapon's presence so he needed to move fast. All but one reported back negative; Maung pinged it and waited, but still nothing came back.

The lack of any signal puzzled Maung. His systems operated so that even a dead line created a detectable echo but then he kicked himself for forgetting: The only power came from him. So it was possible that on a good line his signal weakened to the point where it couldn't report back, meaning that path was still open and intact for a long distance, but too far to receive a response. He followed it eagerly, almost forgetting to lay traps and alarms at each branch off the main trunk so he wouldn't get stuck.

Something took shape ahead. In the electronic darkness, a visualization of the lifeless system in gray upon gray, one line faintly glowed pink. It was barely there. At first Maung thought his system had made a mistake, created an artifact, but he moved off the main line and after branching a few times stumbled onto a live conduit— this one propagating its waves at almost half the normal speed, a fact that puzzled him for a moment until he grasped they'd used coaxial cable. Maung almost laughed. From the spectra it was clearly copper and the speed of propagation was spot-on for coax but he'd never encountered the stuff in his entire life and he could only imagine what Nam must have thought now that a smile crossed his face. He stifled his amusement and edged into the line, probing the electron flow and wave traffic simultaneously.

Who are you? something asked.

Maung almost withdrew. But the question was a challenge and he tracked American feelers on every side of him, their wave patterns barely overlapping with his but moving at the speed of light—on superconductors. They weren't there a moment ago. His semi-aware warned him in a whisper: *This is a threat.*

Maung almost froze in terror when he realized he'd stepped right into a trap: *His* main wave patterns had moved onto an ancient coaxial zone that moved at half the speed of his adversary. If he needed to retreat, there would be a moment of agonizing slowness as if trying to flee through quicksand, making him vulnerable.

Maung responded, his message flowing outward in bands of color along with the old code he used earlier. "Someone with the proper credentials."

You aren't authorized.

"Wait. Before you act you need to know; your system is dead. The facility inside which you were constructed is destroyed and the Sommen slaughtered all authorized to use it; check your chronometer. You know it's been a long time and you know that something catastrophic occurred. I'm part of the salvage team sent here to investigate what happened."

There was a flurry of wave motion, but it soon settled back into its original pattern. *I know of the Sommen attack. They came soon after we were hit with a creeper and I was assigned the task of backing up key data in an area they or the infection would never look—*

"Maintenance and waste handling," he interrupted. Maung knew that it was setting up a wall behind him and he winced when his timer went off—the two minute mark. With what he was about to try, he hoped Nam was ready to pull the plug in case he failed. "You disguised yourself as waste handling and had microbots set the entry line as coax with air-gapped superconductor channels you can bridge with mechanical actuators. What was this place? What were the American Dream—what were the humans assigned here for?"

Maung wanted to wait for the answer but couldn't; the thing's trap was almost ready. He launched himself at the exit but before Maung got halfway there the strange system had almost an infinite number of cycles to attack and his electron stream disintegrated, picked apart by bursts of focused magnetic fields, each one ripping through to the point where he had trouble keeping track of who and where he was. Once he reached the trap, Maung almost stopped to examine it; he had forgotten his purpose. The bursts became more intense, forcing his electrons to merge with the greater environment but before the trap closed a portion of his consciousness reassembled. Maung leapt back onto the superconductor and reconnected with his main signal to tear off, retreating so fast he couldn't drop feelers behind him. He mentally screamed at Nam, *Unplug me now!*

"*Damn it!*" Maung shouted. It was as if a saw cut through his head and he clapped both hands to the sides of his helmet.

"Two minutes," said Nam. "I said two minutes. I had to unplug you, the nanos are almost here and could cut off our escape."

"I'm not complaining, Nam; you may have saved my life."

Than picked Maung up and the three of them started bounding toward the line, the one leading upward toward the air-handling system through which they had entered. Maung resisted the urge to pass out. His head pounded and he ran a full diagnostic before shutting down, just to make sure that there was nothing permanently damaged, but he couldn't feel his extremities and guessed he was on the verge of losing consciousness.

"What did you learn?" Nam asked.

He was about to tell everything when he stopped; holding onto the information about a backup storage site for the entire dataset for the American project might be useful one day, and he was tired of Nam holding all the cards.

"Nothing," Maung lied. "I didn't learn a damn thing, but almost got caught by an American trap. It was useless."

CHAPTER THIRTEEN

They reached the line and climbed. Halfway to the top Maung looked down and had the sensation of being in the middle of a black world, with darkness on every side and in which he was the only thing that existed other than the cord, which was the only thing that promised him a reconnection with civilization. And his semi-aware was still active; he was on the verge of switching off when it alerted him about an incoming transmission, tight-beam, coded for his reception only. The abnormality of it made him shiver. Nobody except the Sommen nanos should have known his position and to transmit on these codes was impossible for anyone except other Dream Warriors, and he admitted the message only after setting up his defenses; the structural interference filled it with static but he understood the words, just before he shut down his entire system.

"*Hello brother.*"

Maung relaxed when they reached the access panel. He looked back. Nam brought up the rear this time and the man paused to fumble with something that he then dropped into the chamber below.

"What is that?" Maung asked.

"A transmitter that mimics your emission pattern for one hour— to give the nanos a target—and if you haven't switched off, now would be a good time."

"I did. Nam, I just received a transmission; it was from the Chinese. They must have a ship nearby for the signal to have had the strength to pass through all this crap."

"Great," Nam said. "This is turning into an awful day."

"Why the Chinese?" Than asked.

"We had a run in with them at Europa. One of them got away and must have told its superiors about me."

Nam pushed him upward. "Move, Maung. Hurry."

The return trip lasted forever. By the end of it, Maung could barely move his arms from the effort of dragging himself through the tight passages, and he was so tired he almost failed to notice the bright lights that hit when Than popped the exit hatch. Maung's visor dimmed to compensate, and he pulled himself out, wobbling on cramped legs and angry because he just wanted to go to bed but now couldn't. The Sunny Side team had arrived and gathered outside the access port, waiting for Nam to extract himself before one of them spoke.

"Are you the last one, Nam?"

Maung recognized the man; it was the Korean guard who insulted him in front of Nang on Sunny Side. Nam chuckled. "Yeah. Last one."

"I told you to stay put in your barracks; that Sommen area, the site, is restricted until the Americans show."

"You're not on Sunny, kala." Nam popped his helmet and stepped closer to the Korean guard. "I go where I want on Dark Side. My side."

"We'll see what the Americans say, dumb ass."

Maung had a flash of admiration for Nam. He seemed undaunted by the Korean or his guards, and Maung popped his helmet, about to give Nam support when one caught his attention—a guard at the rear of the Korean group. A woman stepped to the side so Maung could see more clearly and he held his breath. It was Nang. He couldn't see much of her through the bulk of her environment suit, but her hair was in a ponytail and her smile made him warm.

"Hi, Maung," she said.

Maung nodded. "Nang. If the Americans won't be here for a while, what are you guys doing here?"

"Hey, it's the new Burmese," the Korean guard said, holding up his hand to keep Nang from speaking. He stepped between them and poked a finger at Maung. "We're here for security—to prevent you from messing things up."

Maung clenched his fists and was about to grab for the man when Nam stepped forward again and snatched the Korean's finger, snapping it like a twig. The man screamed. The Sunny Side guards lifted weapons and Maung's rage disappeared to be replaced with fear until other Myanmar guards arrived, gathering and pointing their weapons at the Koreans.

Maung nodded at the injured one. "That must hurt, *kala.*"

"Screw you!"

Nam, Maung and Than joined with the other Burmese and filtered back through the passageways, heading for the barracks. Maung could barely hold his helmet. His eyes closed and his head ached so badly that he wore a constant grimace. Once they arrived he said good-bye to the others and made the climb to his cubicle, not bothering to de-suit before crashing into a deep sleep.

CHAPTER FOURTEEN

There is no way to get anywhere near the site, Than said.

Maung's eyes snapped all the way open. He'd fallen asleep on watch and waited for Nam to scold him, but the old man just nodded.

"Welcome back," Nam said,

"What day is this?" asked Maung. "How long has it been since I linked up with the dead woman?"

Than lounged in a couch, watching the holo-display of his drifters, and flicking through the camera selections to make sure they worked. He glanced up and asked "What?" so Maung had to repeat himself.

"A few days, Earth time," said Than. "Long time. And congratulations; we thought you'd never wake up."

Maung shook his head. "I feel like a truck ran over me. I never had it this bad, just because someone unplugged me."

"Nah, it's probably not just that, Pa; the bone-density drugs are hell. You get hammered at first, even though you've been at zero g for however long it takes for your ship to get here. The meds, the transition from Earth g, to zero g, to low g—it's way too much for people to handle. Then you went and did all that Dream Warrior stuff, Pa."

Nam nodded. "We've been dragging you here during your watches and let you sleep through."

But Maung ignored the old man and looked at Than. "You called me *Pa*." he said.

"Yeah." Than shrugged. "Guess I did."

163

Pa. It was a term of respect and Maung noticed that Than's head bowed when he spoke and that his eyes focused on the floor, not on him. Pa was for holy men, for the pure, and Maung shuddered to think that some viewed him this way; they wouldn't, he suspected, if they knew how many people he'd slaughtered in the war.

"Everyone calls you that, Maung. Pa-Maung."

Maung sat up at the implication. "Do they know? Does everyone know what I am?"

Than waved him away. "Nah, Pa. Relax. They just see the way that Nam treats you and they see something—like you're special. But nobody knows the real deal. We're Burmese, dude. Take it easy, you're with your own people and it's safe."

Maung settled back into his seat, slowly bouncing up and down with every movement of his arms or legs. The red dots looked like a disease. Measles. It was hard to focus on the faint blue lines of the structures, massive buildings that probably took only a few years to erect but which would take decades to disassemble, and which consumed so many valuable resources—resources that people had killed for on Earth. It was a monument to military power, now disintegrating, but even in decline the enormity of it filled him with awe.

There was no order in the data. Maung couldn't make heads or tails of all that had happened and he closed his eyes to concentrate on the creeper, the Chinese, the Sommen and American Dream Warriors and most of all the structure, within which the Americans fought one last battle against a Sommen onslaught. Tears formed in his eyes. Maung struggled to contain his emotion because he wanted to keep from fogging his visor but without his semi-aware his mind threatened to give in, unable to interpret the complexity.

"Why is the control room in vacuum?" he asked.

Than propelled himself off his seat and grabbed a ceiling handhold. "Power constraints. The American team got here fast and are already working on the site; they need all the power they can get so we have to cycle down. No environment controls except for critical areas." He motioned for Maung to get up. "Come on, it's time, Pa."

"Where are we going?"

"Outside." Than kicked off a table and headed toward the airlock, the doors of which was open. "Nam wants me to keep your mind off the Americans and what happened in the deep—to the American Dream Warriors. Besides: It's time you did some closeup work with drifters."

Maung took hold of his shoulder, stopping Than. "Why closeup?"

"It's OK, Maung. Just don't get near the ones with yellow helmets. The treatment makes most of them passive but those ones are still aggressive—the worst of the murderers and rapists. If you have to kill one it's no big deal but try not to because we need the workers; killing one creates a lot of database work."

"This is wrong," said Maung. "We can't do this to people, no matter what they've done."

He and Than watched from above, perched on a platform that overlooked the work area, a narrow alley between two massive structures, each of which was covered with hundreds of prisoners dangling in space. The prisoners' plasma torches flickered; their work created a random pulsating blue glow across one entire face of the closest building, and it reminded Maung of arc welders in the Yangon shipyards, who worked even at night during the war. Harnesses and safety lines secured the drifters to the walls while tiny droplets fell from their work, hot particles of steel or other material that melted under the assault and which filled the area with orange stars that quickly solidified and went dark while they plummeted.

Maung looked into the faceplate of a man just a few feet below him; streamers of saliva and mucous hung from his nose and thin tubes ran across his bare scalp until they disappeared into a main inlet at the right temple. It made Maung shiver. The man's eyes were vacant and while he cut the drifter's arms moved slowly with a tremor.

"How many cut themselves or have accidents?"

Than kicked a piece of debris off the side, watching it float downward into darkness. "Not many. The treatment makes them methodical and we upload their duties before every shift so they can't deviate from a very specific program—unless they're a special kind of person."

"The dangerous ones with yellow helmets?"

"Yep," said Than. He bounded toward the far side of the

overwatch. "Come on. I'll show you one. Most of the time they can't override the program, but occasionally their mind gets tweaked—to the point where we lose control and they go off the deep end. Then you have to put them down."

"Did I already ask what happens when these people are released?" Maung asked, following carefully as he reached the edge. "How they live again? Does the treatment damage their minds?"

Than laughed. He slid down a makeshift construction ladder bolted to the building's side, and Maung waited a moment before following. The sensation of floating in midair still made him dizzy and he gripped the ladder sides, slowing his descent until he followed Than into an upper floor of their building.

"Drifters don't get out," said Than. "If you do something bad enough to wind up here, you're a lifer, just like us. Only way to leave the dark side is when you die and you oughta know, Maung: Materials are worth more than people."

Maung was about to say something but stopped. He looked up and turned off the light filter, saw the millions of stars in a narrow band defined by the buildings that now surrounded him and he imagined that Karin was a monster; it had swallowed him whole. Now all he could do was look out from its stomach.

"There's one you *definitely* have to see," said Than. "He's real special, Pa."

He pointed downward and Maung leaned outside the window, doing his best not to slip and fall.

"That's Walther." Than leaned out from the inside of the structure too, pushing his suit helmet through a shower of sparks that rained from above in orange and pink.

Maung ignored the feeling of vertigo. He reached for a steel girder and clamped his fingers around it, aware that they were at an insanely high level and could almost see across the entire port crater—into the darkness of space. Below him a drifter worked, moving his plasma torch slowly across the wall to his right, cutting through the building's ceramic sheathing. To Maung, he looked just like the others, maybe a little smaller.

"What's so special about him?"

"Wait," said Than. He punched something on his forearm keypad and Walther's torch extinguished. The drifter then hooked it onto his belt and climbed his line toward them. "Get ready, Pa, here he comes."

"Ready for what?"

"Walther doesn't like Burmese, Maung. Or Filipinos or Koreans. Anyone Asian pretty much. He got a life sentence for being a serial killer up in New York, where he used to work the immigrant neighborhoods and use our people for target practice."

Maung stepped back from the edge. "At least they got him."

"Yeah. After he wiped out a couple hundred women and children. And now he's here but the treatment didn't take so well; Nam said it must be something to do with the fact that he isn't wired right to begin with."

When the drifter climbed over the edge, Maung was surprised. He was short. Even in an environment suit, Walther's helmet was below Maung's chin and he briefly thought maybe Walther was a child until his internal helmet light flickered on, showing Walther's face. Other drifters had no facial hair; the treatment was supposed to prevent hair growth so that the prisoners didn't need grooming, but on Walther it hadn't worked. A thick beard hid his cheeks and above it the man's eyes stared with an intensity suggesting he wasn't a drifter at all. Maung squinted to look more closely; the tubes and wires were there, and dried saliva matted the prisoner's beard to make it look greasy and tangled. Maung flinched when Walther stepped forward.

"Stand down, Walther," said Than, "Rest," but either Walther had gone deaf or he ignored the command, instead continuing toward Maung.

Maung backed up. The room was empty, having already been stripped of everything except the ceramic flooring, but a thick layer of dust and rubble made it slippery. "What's he doing?"

Than punched at his forearm again. Maung saw it out of the corner of his vision, which was focused on Walther, who yanked the plasma torch from his belt again and ignited it with a flick. Plasma flashed so brightly it almost blinded Maung; he tripped over a piece of steel, drifting slowly onto his back.

"*Stand down!*" Than shouted. He grabbed the carbine off his shoulder but the barrel snagged on his belt and Than struggled to free it. "Kill him, Maung. He's off the grid and not responding."

Maung couldn't reach his carbine. He'd fallen on it and Walther bounded from side to side—to keep from bouncing upward and to maximize speed—closing the distance and gripping his torch with both hands. Maung remembered what Nang taught him on the ship. When Walther leaped, he took advantage of the fact that his opponent couldn't change direction while in midair, and Maung pushed off the ground, moving to the side so Walther drifted to the ground where he used to be, his torch cutting a black gouge into the floor. Maung reached for his carbine. But before he swung it around Walther leaped again and smashed into his chest so the pair of them slid through the dust and past Than, who raised his weapon and fired, sending a stream of fléchettes through Walther's chest. The firing cut through the man's torch. It flickered out before he could use it to burn through Maung's faceplate but despite being hit, Walther was still awake, swinging the torch with a force great enough ring Maung's ears when it impacted at the base of his helmet, through a soft section in the suit. The last thing Maung remembered was a sharp pain in his neck.

Maung woke up to find Walther collapsed on top of him and Than was only beginning to drag the corpse clear. Finally he was free. The drifter's suit was shredded from where Than's fléchettes ripped through his chest, leaving behind a kind of perforated pattern marked with hundreds of tiny holes, clotted with frozen blood. He was glad Walther's faceplate was fogged; a memory of the drifter's face had already burned into Maung's brain and the last thing he wanted was an image of Walther's death expression to accompany it. Maung tried to sit. A sharp pain in the back of his neck made him wince, forcing him to roll over on his stomach and kneel, pulling his arms into his chest in an attempt to control or ride out the agony.

"Are you hit?" Than asked. "Did I hit you by accident?"

Maung waved him off. "No, I'm fine. Something is wrong with my neck."

"Maybe you sprained it in the fight."

"I don't think so." Maung suspected it was a serious injury and wished he could crank up the semi-aware for a diagnostics run. "Help me up. I think it's gone now."

When Than helped him to his feet, the back of Maung's neck burned with a dull kind of pain that screamed infection. *It could be anything,* he thought. Maybe the blow delivered by Walther shattered his data ports, or maybe when the data cable's microbots opened his flesh down in the American super-aware's chamber, microbes were introduced along with them. Whatever the reason, something was out of place. He barely noticed when Than waved him onward.

"We have to get moving, Pa. When it rains, it pours."

"What happened now?" asked Maung.

"We have to get back and report this—what happened with Walther—to Nam. But first we've got a drifter wandering offsite and need to pull him back."

"How does this happen?" Maung asked.

"How does what happen?"

Maung pointed to Walther and then the other drifters, who continued cutting off pieces of the building, unaware of anything that just happened above them. "Walther. Them. How do any of them overcome the chip to attack us, or to just randomly wander off? I still don't get it."

"Nothing in this hole is normal, Maung. But since you got here, things are getting more abnormal—by the minute. I already sent a preliminary message to Nam and he's running a trace to see if anyone messed with our drifter codes. There's also a team coming to inspect the corpse."

"You think someone set us up?" Maung asked.

Than headed deeper into the building, into a corridor and toward an empty elevator shaft where Maung followed him, doing his best to ignore the searing pain.

"I think it's possible. We've had problems with Walther but nothing like this, and it's too much of a coincidence: You, then the American and Sunny Siders show up, and then Walther loses it completely? And he targets *you*—of all people?"

Than stepped off into darkness, one hand loosely gripping the rail of a ladder, and disappeared. Maung hesitated. A thought popped into his head and froze him with a realization: What difference was there between him and the drifters? *Neither of us will ever see our families again.* For the first time since waking up he remembered his son and mother and their images appeared in his mind for only a second before dissolving into afterthought, memories that refused to surface again. *We do what we're told and wander through a dead city, like automatons with no future—no memories of those who matter.*

Maung followed Than, crying on his way down; he had to get off Karin no matter what—had to find his way back to Earth.

"That's the one," Than said. He had his coil gun out, aimed at the drifter, but Maung caught his shoulder to pull him back.

"Not yet. Let's see where he's going. Have you ever been this far out?"

Than lowered his gun and then slung it over a shoulder. "No. But from the looks of it, this place got hit just as hard as the rest of the port."

They'd been following the drifter for over an hour, sometimes losing its signal only to find that it moved incredibly fast, the dot appearing hundreds of meters away as if the thing was sprinting from them. Maung almost laughed. Where was there to run on this rock? Even if the drifter managed to evade the signal detection hardware, and even if it found extra oxygen cannisters, there was no way to escape Karin and no place to get food except from the prison itself. It was possible, Maung figured, that some drifters broke control like Walther did, and some went insane like this one: running to nowhere because to die running was better than to die as a drifter.

The area was a part of the port that Maung hadn't bothered to examine on the maps, and the buildings yielded no clues to their function, but now that he was close to them he reached out and touched one; they were soft. The towering structures had been coated with a layer of a kind of rubber that also looked metallic, with trillions of gold and silver fibers running up and across the face in an infinite web. The view almost dizzied him. They were on the far side of the port, halfway up the other side of the crater, where these buildings had been constructed into the side of a cliff so that even though he and Than were between buildings, the alley entrance behind them looked as though it dropped into space.

"He's gone inside," said Than, pointing. "That one."

"How is your oxygen?" Maung asked.

"I'm on my last reserve, but it's three quarters full. You?"

"The same," said Maung. They were close to the portal through which the drifter had passed, and the darkness beyond made him nervous; he unslung his coil gun and flicked the safety off. "May as well get this done."

Maung motioned for Than to hide. The corridor was long and identical to the white ones they'd seen in their initial exploration when Maung first arrived, and the dead covered every inch of it. These ones died from microbots, he realized. Most of their flesh was gone so that partially eaten corpses lay frozen in poses of agony, their hands clawing at themselves in attempts to scrape the bots away. But this wasn't what frightened Maung. Ahead of them, at least a hundred meters away, the corridor's lighting system was active, casting a brilliant blue glow that reflected off the white walls. He and Than squeezed into doorways on opposite sides of the corridor.

"This section is active," Maung said.

"It can't be," said Than, "none of the port is active, none of it except where we're conducting demolition. We would notice a power drain coming from this area, and there's nothing on my screens; check for yourself."

Maung punched on his forearm computer and waited for the fine web of green data to appear on his faceplate. It took a minute for him to figure out the patterns but Than was right; the dark side's power distribution grid didn't run to this area. He cursed himself for not being able to think clearly and wished he could numb the pain in his neck. It throbbed with each heartbeat, making him dizzy.

"Then it must have its own power."

"Yeah," said Than, "but why? Who is stationed here and what are they doing?"

Maung was about to answer when Nam cut into their frequency. "Get the hell out of that area, you two. *Now.*"

"But what do we know about this area?" Than asked. "We tracked one of our drifters here."

"I told you to get out. It's none of your business what that place is and I don't care about another drifter; we'll hit our quota somehow. Return to your section, *now.*"

Maung cut Nam's frequency off and switched to another to ping Than. "I'm not going until I find out what this place is."

"You're crazy. Nam will have us ejected—back to Earth—and what happens to you then, Pa? Think about it."

"I have thought about it; we're already drifters. There's no difference between us and them except that we get to carry a gun."

Than was silent for a moment, but then Maung heard him sigh. "Screw it," he said, waving his barrel down the corridor. "After you, Pa. But be careful; I'm surprised we haven't been caught yet by motion or shape sensors, given that this place has to be some kind of secret site. Nam's message said it all."

"You think he knows what this place is?" Maung asked. He moved into the corridor cautiously, trying to keep his footing among the frozen bodies.

"I think he knows that it's off limits and that it exists; someone told him as much. But I doubt he knows why it's off limits."

A red light flashed on Maung's heads-up and he knew it was Nam—signaling on the frequency they'd just cut. He ignored it. Ahead was the lit section of corridor and Maung shouldered his coil gun then lowered himself to his stomach, close to the dead so he could pull himself along slowly. It took him at least a minute to remember his training and he wanted to pummel his brain, to punish it for having given up so many memories: If they moved slowly enough, motion sensors couldn't trip. And, he hoped, if they stayed close enough to the bodies, the jumble would defeat shape detection. Maung said a quick prayer, just in case.

Since it was not safe for radio, he turned off his transmitter and motioned for Than to stay behind; Maung pointed to one of the side rooms, assuming Than got the message and hid.

Maung was exposed. These were not the LEDs of the prison, but were fully lit halogens so bright that he had to dim his visor to see. And the silence made his skin crawl; it left only his own thoughts and the sound of his breathing for company. Without air there would be no warning. He couldn't hear anyone approaching and there was little doubt that someone passing would notice a brand new, white prison suit amidst all the half-eaten dead.

He hesitated at the sight of a door. The corridor curved so that Maung hadn't seen it until now, when he was less than ten meters away. *Think.* His heart beat faster and Maung had no idea what to do except go forward, no other ideas except that what was the point of taking this risk in the first place if he turned back now? Everything in his body told him not to go on. He barely noticed the suit against his skin and his systems registered the increased heart rate and breathing, warning him of potential hyperventilation.

The area immediately before the door was clear of corpses. Maung moved a centimeter each second, closing his eyes for the last meter and praying that there was no shape detection, no cameras pointed at the hallway. His left hand touched it. Maung was about to reach for the door's controls when he stopped, noticing a gentle vibration that translated to his suit glove and into his fingers, registering somewhere in his mind that this was an important observation. He drew his hand away. The fact that the door vibrated should've told him something—should've given him an idea—but for now his mind was *still* blank. When he rested his faceplate against the door in frustration, Maung almost laughed. There had to be air on the other side; the vibration was from machinery and air handling that now echoed faintly inside his helmet and it occurred to him that if the air carried those sounds it might carry others.

Maung worked his forearm pad at the same time he whispered orders to his suit computer. When he was ready, he sat up and adjusted himself, making sure that one of the suit's audio pickups pressed against the door, feeding sound into his headphones. There were voices. They sounded garbled, but he deciphered most of it and the computer assisted by transcribing the conversation onto his heads-up.

"You know this is a one-way deal. You take this option and you're giving yourself a death sentence." The accent was different from the American ones. Maybe British.

The man who responded sounded tired. "I get my mind back for a few days. And you take care of my family."

"That's the deal. You enter our test program on Mars and your family gets a free ride. Your kids can go to any school for free, and the government moves them into a nice place where they'll be safe. They never have to worry again."

"I want it," the American said. "Send me to Phobos."

Maung heard a shuffling near the door; someone was close by on the other side. The sound of approaching footsteps alerted him and Maung drifted backward and toward the bodies, picking several of the closest corpses and dragging them over his suit, not knowing if his movements triggered an alarm, but there had to be an inner airlock door that would close and then the air had to cycle, giving him time to bury himself. By the time the door opened, a blanket of corpses hid him. Maung prayed, closing his eyes and then opening them just a slit to see the shadows of men floating overhead, one of them in the yellow suit of a drifter.

Their shift was almost over and Maung and Than sped back to the control room as fast as they could, taking chances at every elevator shaft and climbing with leaps. Nam pinged them the whole way. But Maung told Than not to answer because giving details wouldn't help them get out of trouble and the signal could be intercepted by anyone within range. It took twenty minutes. By the time they arrived, Maung's suit had filled with moisture and his faceplate fogged from the exertion, so that it was a genuine relief to get there—despite Nam's rage—just so he could rest.

"You don't know what you've done," said Nam.

Maung gestured for Nam to wait. "We found something, Nam. We need your help."

"Listen to him," Than said. "I don't even believe what he heard, but maybe you know more."

"I don't need to listen to Maung. I don't need to listen to you. You went someplace that's off limits and refused to listen and I bet that by now the American security team is on its way here to arrest you both. I don't know how you made it *this* far back after bootlegging it into a restricted zone."

"First Walther attacks and now they're taking our drifters?" Than shouted. "Something is going on, Nam. That's why we've been losing so many. The Americans and their allies have some kind of a program where the drifters can volunteer in exchange for their families being taken care of."

Nam looked at Maung and then back at Than. *He didn't know,* thought Maung. He wasn't sure if Nam was in on it until then but the man's face slackened and he let go of the handhold so that Nam floated upward without realizing it, then banged his head on the ceiling.

"Walther was an accident; my team found nothing except a faulty brain connection that made him less controllable, so stop creating conspiracy where none exists."

"Fine," said Maung. "But Than's not inventing the Allied unit; we watched them take the drifter. I heard the conversation and recorded it." Maung hit a few buttons on his forearm and direct transmitted the recording to Nam's suit. It took less than a second. A minute later, Nam sat in his seat with both knees tucked under the desk, and his face in his hands.

"I have no idea what this means," he said. "Old Man Charleston told me to stay out of that area because of one of his side projects but if what you're saying is true . . ."

Maung finished his sentence. "Then Old Man Charleston might be *with* the government—with the Allies. At least for some of his projects."

"And has been forever," Than said. "I don't know why this upsets you so much, Nam. It's common knowledge the Old Man has his own side deals—that he makes money however he can."

Nam launched himself from the desk and seized Than by the front of his suit, sending both of them to slam into the far wall. "You idiot. Do you know how many of those drifters were Burmese? Do you know how many Burmese guards died trying to keep quotas up when we were short on drifters?"

"So?" Than asked. His voice shook with fear and he looked at Maung with a confused expression.

"So they're our people. Old Man Charleston's people. I thought even scum like him had its limits. We took our own chances coming here and knew the risks. But he'd been making the risks worse, stacking the deck against us to earn a little extra on the side, and we have to go out there and take up the slack to make sure we meet quota every time he steals one of our drifters."

Maung gasped with pain. He yanked a glove off and snatched at his neck to feel the hot skin puffed around his port. He touched it and hissed.

"What's wrong?" Nam asked.

Maung caught his breath and blinked the tears from his eyes. "You want to get back at the Old Man?"

"Now I do. If they don't come to arrest you and me, I do. Yes."

Than shook his head. "You two are crazy."

"Nam," said Maung, "we need to do three things: The skin around my data port is infected; when Walther slammed me with the torch it worsened something that had already been stewing. The doctor has to see me. Now. Then you need to get me coms with Old Man Charleston. But before that, we need to find out what's going on at Phobos. That's what this is all about. I have a feeling that if we look there, we'll find out what's going on out here and on Earth."

Nam nodded. He pulled himself over and motioned for Maung to lean forward, then took out a flashlight to look at his neck.

"They're going to have to amputate your head, Tatmaw," he said. "That looks bad. Why didn't you say something sooner?"

"I didn't feel really bad until today. Next time you give me a data cable, make sure the damn bots are clean."

Maung heard voices. He assumed he was in the dark side sick bay, but Nam gave him a narcotic to ease the pain and he floated in and out of consciousness, doing his best to remember everything that happened. Sometimes Nang spoke. She stood next to his bed and stroked his hair, which made him sad because it had to be a dream; she would never touch a Tatmawdaw. Other times his family came— all of them. His mother looked stern and upset, like getting sick was his fault, and Maung guessed he was a kid again. His mother held his hand. She led him through the crowded streets of Mandalay, taking him to a monk, the one that everyone said could see through you and into the future. The sun beat on his forehead and mosquitoes clouded around them until finally they reached the steps of a temple where his mother smiled down at him, motioning for him to go forward. She couldn't go in. Maung had to do this alone . . .

"He is *what*?" someone asked.

The other voice was Nam's. "He is a Dream Warrior, Doctor. A killer. And if you don't fix him, he'll die, but we need him for a project that the Americans are running on Dark Side. So this has to be a secret; if you tell anyone, *you* die."

"I need to see the orders on this one, Nam. This can't be true. There's no way I'm going near him and I'll be damned if I'm keeping this a secret."

Maung heard movement around him; he opened his eyes.

Burmese guards streamed into sickbay, surrounding the doctor, and a few of them grinned in a way that suggested they *wanted* the Japanese doctor to keep refusing so they could "convince" him.

"Your people killed a lot of ours, Doctor," said Nam. "Tokyo was almost as ruthless in their orders as Beijing."

"I had nothing to do with that!"

Nam gestured at his men. "I'm pretty sure they don't care whether you did or not."

The doctor had a moustache. It surprised Maung because it looked so odd on an Asian and in the bluish lights, the man's skin looked pale. He leaned over Maung and whispered something in Japanese.

Finally he straightened. "It's bad. This may be staph or something else so I'll try microbots but he may need to be taken off Karin; if that's the case, there's nothing I can do. You can't blame me for something that's out of my control."

"Of course not," said Nam, grinning. "That would be unreasonable."

Maung cringed when they began cutting. The bots removed sections of his neck but he was immobilized on an operating table and felt nothing except a slight pressure—the sensation of millions of tiny creatures nibbling on rotting skin. He smelled the rot now. It reminded him of the decay permeating the entire asteroid, but since this time the odor came from him, Maung couldn't shake his fear and wondered what would happen if it didn't work. The doctor stepped into view, interrupting his thoughts; he lowered his face toward Maung's and then spit on him.

"You're dead, Tatmaw. As soon as I get back to Sunny Side, you're as good as dead. I'll report your ass and there's nothing Nam can do to stop it."

The smell of incense made Maung smile. He was a child and when he looked back, the temple exit framed his mother, the Myanmar sun silhouetting her on an early morning. He turned and looked forward at the monk who waited for him. The man's youth surprised Maung. The way his mother had talked, with respect only reserved for old people, Maung had assumed the holy man would be ancient like the ones in the local village temple. This one looked like a teenager; his robes almost were too big for the monk's small frame and dragged on the floor.

The monk smiled and took Maung's hand, leading him deeper into the temple. "I already see why your mother brought you here," he said.

"What do you mean?"

The monk led him through a long, narrow passage, the walls constructed by clay bricks, which tinged the air with a red color, and which deepened the orange of the monk's robe. The colors made everything warm. Unconsciously, Maung swung his and the monk's hand back and forth, the way he did with his mother.

"You glow. We will look at you more closely and give you a message for your parents."

Maung was about to ask another question when someone shook him, forcing the dream to evaporate at the same instant he opened his eyes. Even the dim light of Karin's LEDs made him blink and Maung had no idea how long he'd been unconscious. He wanted to remember. Maung tried to return to sleep, to follow the monk into his temple and recall what happened that day but now someone shouted at him and shone a bright light into his eyes.

"It's OK, Pa," said Than. "It's me—not that scumbag of a doctor."

Nam was there too. They both grinned and Maung could barely speak; he motioned toward a squeeze-pouch of water and when he finished taking a sip he whispered.

"The doctor. He spat on me and said he was going to report me anyway—when he got back to Sunny Side."

"Don't worry," said Nam. "It's not a problem anymore."

Than looked away. Maung sensed the tension and looked back at Nam. "What? What happened?"

"The elevator had a catastrophic decompression event on the way back to Sunny Side, just after it left here. Vented all its air. And it turns out the doctor's suit, and all the emergency ones onboard, were defective. And by the way." Nam paused to flick his finger against Than's shoulder. "*You* two got lucky; nobody detected your little trip to the classified area—as far as I can tell."

Maung grinned. He saw that the murder bothered Than and wished he had that kind of conscience, but the doctor's expression and words erased any kind of sympathy he might otherwise have mustered. This was a killing that needed to happen. As far as he was concerned, there was no need to pray except to say thanks that Nam's assassination plan succeeded.

"I don't think what the Japanese did was so bad," said Than. "So they used nukes. So what? It was war."

"Yeah, but have you seen *any* North Koreans lately?" Nam asked. "Any survivors?"

"No."

"Exactly."

Maung's eyes almost closed again. He glanced at the clock but time was meaningless without knowing how long he was out, and he struggled to sit up before Nam motioned for him to relax.

"How long was I out?"

"A week. We thought we'd killed the doctor too soon because I swear that you almost died from fever twice. But we managed with the drugs we stole from him before he got on the transport elevator."

Nam grinned from ear to ear; so did Than.

"What are you two smiling at?" Maung asked.

"You have a visitor," said Than; he glanced at Nam. "Should we let this villain in?"

Nam's expression went serious again. "Maung. We've bandaged your neck, but from now on your data port is exposed; unless you're in a suit, everyone can see it. The Sunny Siders think we called the doctor for someone with meningitis. That's what you'll tell anyone who asks; you don't know how you got it, it just happened."

"Got it," said Maung. "Who's the visitor?"

But Nam and Than drifted noiselessly out of sick bay and sealed the door, leaving Maung's question unanswered.

Nang was more beautiful than he remembered. She held onto the bed railing and smiled, and for a moment he believed that he hallucinated again and that this wasn't really Nang but a vision like the many he'd had so recently. But he smelled her hair. It was in a ponytail and Maung noticed that she'd put on makeup—something she hadn't done before—and somehow she managed to make the bulky environmental suit look good. He couldn't talk.

"You're alive, Tatmaw?"

Maung took a sip of water. "Barely. Apparently I nearly died. Or maybe I did and you're talking to a phantom."

Nang touched his arm and then his forehead. "Nope. You're real. I was worried about you. When I heard that the doctor had come over here for someone with meningitis, and then saw your name on the sick roster, I asked a friend to assign me to the American detail again."

"The Korean guy."

"Yeah," said Nang. "At first he didn't want to but I was able to persuade him."

"Are you two? You know . . ." Maung tried not to get angry at the mentioning of the Korean guard, the one who originally put him on the prisoner's elevator when he first arrived. *The one who gets to spend so much time with her.*

"Are we what?" she asked.

"Seeing each other."

Nang punched him in the arm. "No. Why would I be with him? Sure, he tried but his face is too American. It's puffy." She smiled and when she looked at Maung the rest of the room vanished.

"Look," said Nang, "I wanted to apologize for the way I was when we said good-bye on Sunny Side. Those guys are jerks. I shouldn't have laughed at you."

Maung smiled. "It's OK. I was a jerk too."

"Why did you want to know if I was seeing the Korean guy?" she asked. When Maung shrugged and looked away, embarrassed, she grabbed his chin and turned it to face her. "You really *are* stupid, but in a cute way, Tatmaw."

Maung almost choked when she kissed him. Nang leaned forward and now the smell of her hair sank down, soaked through his face and drowned him while her tongue met his. Before he knew it, both his arms wrapped around her. He tried pulling her into the bed, but she backed off and laughed.

"No way, Tatmaw. Not while we're in sick bay and not while I'm in this awful suit."

Maung hadn't smiled like this in years. Part of him reached out to the dead and to his wife, looking for forgiveness, but the sight of Nang erased any doubts; his wife would like her. "It's been a while; I'm not too good at this, Nang."

"Me neither. I have to go but we'll figure this out, OK? Maybe your assignment won't be like all the other Tatmaws; maybe you'll get a chance to leave someday, with me."

She kissed him again. Maung held her for as long as he could but finally she broke free, laughing, and headed for the door; before it slid shut she looked over her shoulder and grinned.

"You're also kind of sexy, Maung. For a jungle-village idiot."

CHAPTER FIFTEEN

"Everyone talked about how Karin is a living hell," said Maung. When he moved, the stiffness of his neck made him wince, as if all his muscles and bone had frozen into a solid block of steel. "It sucks, but it's not as bad as everyone said."

At first Nam laughed. "People exaggerate. Tell stories." Then his face went serious and he shook his head. "But it's not easy, either, Maung, and you've seen some of it already. People die here. And I hate to do this but we need you back on duty; it's been a week. How are you feeling?"

"Like we need to find out about Phobos."

"How?" asked Nam. "How can we hope to find out anything on the dark side of Karin, where there is no civilization and no tie to it except for a few optical connections, all of which are heavily guarded and shielded?"

"Exactly. *Those* are what I need to access."

"The American teams are still here," said Than. "The risk is too great. They patrol in our areas now, checking on us and asking questions. You can't risk connecting, Pa, not right now."

"We don't have a choice!" Maung slammed his hand on the desk and bounced upward, catching himself with his knees. "The Old Man will get us, eventually; he'll do it as soon as he figures out a way to get more money from our dying than from our living. How long will that take? Ten days or ten years? All that time you rot here."

Than glared; his voice was quiet but Maung heard in it a trembling anger. "Your family is on Earth, Maung. So is mine and so is Nam's. The second you cross the Old Man, he'll go after them; how can you protect them while stuck on this pile of crap?"

"I know," said Maung; he softened his tone and tried to sound calm. "You're right; there is a risk to our families. But right now we'd just gather data. If I do it right, and if I don't trigger any alarms, there's no way he'll *ever find out.*"

"If, if," said Nam who rubbed a hand through his hair and sighed. "I know I said we'd do it, but now I'm having second thoughts. Than is right. The Americans aren't just here for the Sommen attack site— although that's probably of great interest to them. They're looking for something else. Some of them are asking about the Chinese attack on the *Singapore Sun* and if any of us heard anything from the captain or crew—about how they escaped Chinese capture."

The news made Maung numb. *The hunters are gathering*, he thought, and there was no way to estimate how much time remained before they closed the ring. "Then that's even more reason to act. *Now.* You two won't have any chance of getting out of here without me—without my semi-aware—and the longer we wait, the more opportunity they have to capture me."

"They have to know you were on the *Sun*," said Than. "Why don't they just bring you in for an interrogation and get it over with?"

"Because they're scared."

Nobody said anything for a while. The thrum of air handling throbbed against Maung's eardrums, and he gently touched the wound on the back of his neck, feeling the tenderness but relieved that his flesh was healing. Both his friends stared at the floor and Maung felt guilty; he had put them in this position, just by coming here. Neither man had planned on doing something so dangerous as leaving Karin and if he hadn't come, they would have continued their lives, safe from the Americans and oblivious to the depths of the Old Man's depravity.

Finally Nam nodded. "Maung's reasoning is sound. The Americans are scared. They know there's a Dream Warrior on Karin, they must suspect it's Maung, but they also know what he did to the Sommen warrior in Charleston and what he did to the Chinese vessels off Europa. They won't move until they're absolutely ready."

"Great. What do *we* do?" Than asked.

Nam shrugged, and smiled at the same time he gave Maung the

middle finger. "You son of a bitch. You're going to get us all killed but what the hell; I've lived a long time. Let's get you to a main axis data port."

They'd been squeezing and crawling through pipe galleries for hours, so long that Maung's vision blurred and he could barely read the chrono on his heads-up. He pretended to be a cockroach. The darkness enveloped him outside the range of their helmet lamps and to Maung it appeared as though a sea of black velvet trapped him, Nang and Than, with only a tiny sphere of light to give some hint of what the universe contained: pipes and conduits, most of it frozen inside years of condensate that had formed after the Sommen attacked. At one time, there were microbots to maintain these areas and clean them of water and gases, to patch the leaks, but those times seemed ancient. Maung couldn't imagine Karin ever having been alive. To him, this kind of decay and stagnation was the natural state for the place, proper for a rock that orbited far enough from the sun that it barely received any light.

"It's another few hundred meters to the area," Nam said; they couldn't risk radio so each of them was connected by a fiber-optic coms cable, long enough to give them space from each other, but short enough that nobody wandered too far away. "We're almost to the pipes that Than will have to cut."

Than chuckled. "Sure. Give the dirty job to me."

"Not dirty," said Nam. "Just . . . lousy. And work slowly; the vibrations will travel through the pipes, and we don't know if the Americans will have sniffers deployed. At least one of these pipe galleries goes close to their work zone."

Sparks burst from the metal when Than started cutting and they bounced off Maung's suit and into the blackness below, winking out almost immediately in the vacuum of Karin, but staying lit long enough to give a show. It was silent. There should be noise, Maung thought, but he reminded himself that outside his suit was the nothingness of space, despite the fact that they were inside a rock. A moment of disorientation gave him a new perspective: They were earth creatures thrust into an alien world, and would never acclimatize.

Once Than finished, Nam helped Maung through the narrow gap; it looked jagged, forcing him to move slowly because Than had already used sealer to mend his suit fabric, twice. Maung forgot to breathe; although the gap was narrow, they had to cut through multiple layers of metal and now the edges of pipes gleamed in his helmet lamp, almost blinding him. When he was through, Maung almost shouted with joy; finally he could do something other than wait.

"Where is the axis cable?" he asked.

Nam pointed to a thick plastic conduit to their left. "That's it. In there. Than is almost finished cutting through and we think it's at a point that has a data port."

"Why put a port all the way out here?"

"Who knows?" Nam asked. "Probably for the times when people had to come here to inspect."

The three of them drifted inside a large square chamber, which reminded Maung of an elevator shaft as it disappeared into darkness both above and below. Everyone clipped into the pipes to prevent drifting too far away. In the middle of the shaft, Than used a small circular saw to cut test holes in a plastic conduit about a meter square; the conduit extended as far as they could see in either direction. Finally Than gave the thumbs up.

"Found it. And it looks like we have the right cable."

"You sterilized this one, right?" Maung asked.

"Look," said Nam. "Now that your port is exposed, it's not a concern. We didn't know that cable was so filthy or that the micros hadn't been sterilized. I'm sorry."

But Maung waved a hand at him. "I was just teasing. Let's see what kind of secrets we can find."

"As soon as you activate, they may sense you. There aren't any Sommen mines we know of here, but I can't speak for American sensors."

"I know," said Maung. "We have to take that chance."

Nam nodded. "Than and I will wait outside in the access space. You won't be connected to us, so come out and let us know when you're done. If you sense any trouble, don't take any chances; get out of here."

Maung reached up and disconnected from the coms cable and watched the pair of them drift out, wincing as they squeezed back through the tiny hole with sharp edges. When they were gone he turned back to the conduit and plucked a black cable from his pouch. It took a second to jack it into the back of his helmet; the microbot linkage hooked in at the same instant, inducing the sensation of an imaginary colony of ants that moved over the skin of Maung's neck, tickling and pricking him at the same time.

"Let's get this over with," he whispered.

The amount of data surprised him. Maung had expected the line to be dead since the Burmese guards never used the fibers, but the traffic was American. Millions of sniffer programs scoured the fiber for signs of infiltration and Maung had to encapsulate his stream in layers of data to make it look like he was just another set of American packets. The sniffers gave him the sensation of being touched. Maung knew he imagined it, but his skin crawled again, this time as if a million spiders streamed over his face and eyelids, looking into every crevice to make certain nothing hid there. Once they were finished, they left a marker—something to show the others that a scan had already been done. Maung breathed easier. The American sniffers labeled him a legitimate presence and he rocketed outward, moving with the stream and careful to track every side route and branch until soon he noticed something.

One of the branches was different. He stopped midstream and created an excuse to inspect the node, quickly wrapping himself in a new routing code before probing the branch's firewall. This was a secure site. With a quick query he retrieved the fiber schematics and located the branch, excited when it showed this one leading directly to the classified area—the place where they tracked the drifter, where Nam had forbidden them to go.

Maung dove in. First he created an additional cloud of packets around him, portions of code that acted as his own sniffers, and which blocked the American packets by mimicking them so they looked as if they've been assigned to work the area. It took a few seconds to complete. Maung's clock counted the minutes but at these speeds it felt like weeks of probing ports one at a time, of testing access pathways and finding that they were dead ends or traps, then carefully backing out without getting caught. At last he found a firewall. Maung stumbled upon it in one of the farthest nodes of the fiber network and watched as packets popped out every once in a while. Nothing went in. As time ticked by, Maung faded into this world where legitimate American packets streamed over him like a river of white light, pulses that he analyzed in microseconds but that required so much concentration he was oblivious to the fact that an hour passed.

The monks gave a message to you, his semi-aware said. *For your parents.*

A chill went through Maung; he wanted to recall the message but there wasn't time. "Not now. Why are you even spending the processor time to look at my thoughts?"

Because it makes us more efficient. And you are wasting thought energy on that memory, even now while we work; it impedes your performance.

"Fine. What message did the monk give me?"

The semi-aware showed him an image from his memory, one that must have been buried so deep that it was almost lost, but now Maung remembered it and smiled. The young monk, and twelve others, surrounded him in a circle where they all sat facing him in front of a massive white-marble Buddha. Hundreds of candles lit the room. The young monk looked serious when he lifted his head and spoke.

"Tell your mother to sacrifice everything for your education in science and math. You will be great, but your daughter, Maung; she and her children can save the world."

That's all of it, the semi-aware said. *I'll make sure to save the information so you can be sure to recall it.*

"But I don't have a daughter," Maung said. Part of him wanted to disconnect from the data stream; he wanted to concentrate on the message and figure out what the monk could have meant, or if maybe he actually said "son" but the memory had somehow corrupted.

The semi-aware dragged him back. *If you don't stop with this line of processing, Maung, there is a greater than fifty percent chance we will be detected.*

"Fine. But make sure you log *everything*."

It is already done.

Maung concentrated on finding a way through the firewall and his semi-aware adjusted its efforts; a vague awareness that in the real world, someone changed his oxygen source, floated into his consciousness but the realization faded at the same instant it came. All his concentration focused on the data, and both he and his semi-aware suspected something: that they were failing. There was no way to break the firewall without an obvious brute force attack and he was about to give up when something happened. A burst of electrons raced past his sniffers and Maung almost missed it when several streams of data flashed into the firewall, all of them converging on a single port that appeared out of nowhere; he fired a string of packets at them. These were programs designed to unpeel the layers of encryption on the American traffic, to expose the code and information within, and in less than a second they shot data back to Maung who could barely contain the excitement from having won: Now he had at least a hundred different codes and handshakes.

Maung picked one. A few seconds later, a path through the firewall snapped open.

Maung recognized the alarm. It wasn't from anything he'd done by penetrating their security, it was a simple beacon—so simple he had no chance of seeing it—from magnetic systems set up to look for his signature, the weak electromagnetic waves that his semi-aware emanated. Somewhere within the asteroid, the Americans were on the move. They were reaching out from their project in the Sommen attack site and trying to pin down his location.

Maung refocused. Project status, assignments, a massive list of drifters that had transferred off Karin, and loads of other data streamed through his semi-aware for analysis and he imagined that he was standing in front of a fire hydrant, swallowing all the water that shot out and then processing it for consumption. Within less than a minute he completed a review of what they were doing on Karin, but the picture was fuzzy. Not all the data were there. He was about to pull out and return to Nam when something else caught his attention: an assignment server for transferring Allied personnel.

We could use this, his semi-aware broke in. *We can insert a false profile to transfer you to Mars; the Chinese would likely follow. As things stand now, if one of their Dream Warriors tracked you here,*

there is a greater than forty-six percent chance that they will assault the
asteroid. I know you don't want more Myanmarese to be killed.

Maung saw the logic, but his chest tightened with the thought of
leaving her behind. *And Nang*, he said. *If I'm going to Mars I will still*
need help. Put her, Nam and Than in the database for transfer with
me. If they don't want to go, can they refuse?

They can appeal, a process that takes so long the error would likely
be detected and none would be forced to leave Karin. And we have to
hurry. The American patrol will be here within twenty minutes. They
are using the same route you used to insert into the conduits.

Maung spent over a minute loading false data into the server and
then backed out, one node at a time, one handshake at a time, until
he merged with the main stream again—this time moving back to
the real world.

When he unplugged, he nearly fainted; Maung's belt bit into his
stomach where he'd been dangling in the conduit space for over an
hour, and he took a moment to drink before unclipping and moving
back toward the hole, careful not to rip his suit.

Outside, he plugged back in with Nam and Than.

"Well?" Nam asked.

"I found it. What information I could, anyway."

Than moved closer, making sure his cable was firmly connected.
"What did it say?"

"I'll have to explain later. Right now we have to find another way
out. We can't go back the way we came."

"Why?" asked Nam.

"Because the Americans sensed my EM leakage; two patrols are
on their way now. I intercepted some of their coms packets and they
dove in through the same access panel we used."

Than cut as fast as he could. Maung prayed for his success
because even though there was no sign of the Americans, they'd be
there soon; if they pinged him his systems would light up. Than was
cutting a hole so they could access an adjacent but separate pipe
gallery, one they could climb into and use to disappear, dropping
deeper into the station than any of them wanted to go.

"Hurry!" Maung said.

"I'm going as fast as I can. I have to be careful because if we're going to weld these back into place so they can't tell where we went it has to be done just right. You can't—"

Nam broke in, his voice sounding irritated. "This route is no good, Maung. If we go this way we'll head into more unmapped territory, where there will almost certainly be nano-mines and God knows what else."

"What other choice do we have?"

"I know," said Nam. "But what if we face the Americans instead? What if you turn on your systems and hit them here, hit them now?"

Maung sighed. Part of him wanted to do it, the old feeling of power drawing him into the thought of flicking on and hitting back. But he couldn't; not since he'd done the things he did when linked into the main axis cable—the entries he made into their personnel assignment data server. If they figured out that Maung penetrated their firewall . . .

"We can't, Nam; I found a server when I linked in," he said.

"So?"

"It was a personnel-assignments and security-clearance semi-aware logistics suite; I cracked it. We now have four fake profiles for personnel transfers to Phobos and then to Mars, with midlevel clearances so we don't raise any flags: you, me, Than, and her. Nang can come with us. And I changed our nationalities to Laotian."

Than stopped cutting. "You're kidding? You're getting us off this shithole? As *Laotians*? I *hate* Laotians—no offense, Maung; Nang is pretty."

Both Maung and Nam shouted at the same time. "*Keep cutting!*"

A few moments later, Than finished and the group of them dove through. Maung then held the section of steel they'd just cut in place while Than welded the hole shut, after which the three of them dropped into darkness, holding onto icy pipes to control their descent speed. Nam took them away from the Burmese area—deeper into the spaceport's guts. The last time he tried this, Maung recalled, he and Than nearly got killed by a security bot and nano-mines, and now his skin tingled with fear. It was like falling through clouds at night. But somewhere below them, in the black spaces, lay monsters who hadn't seen humans in decades and Maung figured that even if the three of them managed to evade American patrols, that didn't guarantee they'd make it out alive.

※ ※ ※

"This wasn't decompression," Nam said. "And it wasn't a nano attack; the bodies have all their flesh."

They hauled themselves through a barracks, which was now a mausoleum, a massive warehouse-like space with row after row of bunk beds that each contained a corpse. The bodies were twisted. Whatever killed them had been painful, he figured, because the vacuum froze the expressions on their faces along with streams of mucous that ran from their noses and glittered in his headlamp.

"A poison?" asked Than. "Maybe a gas or biological? None of them had time to go for emergency suits, which they would have— even if it was explosive decompression."

"What kind of gas works so fast?" Maung asked.

"Nothing we have," said Nam. "Nothing I want to ever encounter. And some biologicals can survive in a vacuum when frozen, so make sure we don't get any suit rips."

The thought of yet another invisible enemy made Maung cringe. So many ghosts. The dead surrounded them on all sides and he prayed again for his ancestors to protect them from the spirits, ghosts of those who died so quickly that they had no chance of preparing for the next life—the pain so great that their spirits must be furious with having had their lives cut short.

They reached the barracks entrance—a series of sliding portals adjacent to each other, doors which had long since lost power connections; one was open. A thin layer of ice sealed the other two shut. Nam was about to move to the open one when Maung noticed something on the floor.

"Freeze!"

Nam stopped, barely catching himself on the last bunk.

"Look at those things," said Maung. "What are they?"

Small green objects littered the floor. When they focused their headlamps on them, the green material pulsated and Maung stepped back with the realization that whatever they were, they came from the Sommen. One end looked like a drill bit embedded in the rock and the other end like a pod, the leaves of which had blossomed open to release what they once held. Than pointed to the ceiling. Above them were a row of holes, as if something had bored through from above.

"These things killed them. They drilled through the rock and landed here, then discharged something."

"Yeah," said Nam. "So let's get out of here."

Maung was about to move when Than's headlamp flashed on one of the objects; it moved. The drill tip rotated silently in the vacuum and Maung watched in horror when its petals slowly opened, followed by a puff of dust that jetted out and continued to grow, enveloping all of them in a pink mist. Maung's suit alarm went off.

"Holy shit," Than said. He launched toward the door and their coms chord went taught, which yanked Nam's hand off the bunk and sent him skidding through the Sommen devices. He kicked one; the thing sprang to life and shot thin spikes from its sides, latching onto Nam's boot.

"Than, stop! This damn thing is climbing up my leg; if it gets to the suit fabric, it's going to puncture!"

Maung moved. "Stay still." He drifted toward Nam, kicking up off the floor gently so he could hover over the things, unslinging his coil gun at the same time. Now he understood what Nam was talking about. The Sommen device had transformed its drill bit into thin spiky legs to claw its way upward, and in a moment it would be close enough to the top of Nam's boots to pierce his suit with its legs. Maung swung. The butt of his rifle slammed into the thing, which clung to it, and Maung let go, sending both into the darkness, out of range of their headlamps.

Nam sounded out of breath. "Thanks, Maung."

"Let's just keep moving. There's no sign the pink stuff can get through our suits, so we can decontaminate later."

Maung figured they must have been at the very bottom of one of the dark side's structures. In places the floor changed from the white materials he'd seen in so many places, to bare rock that glistened in their lamplight despite the fact that it was almost totally black. Tiny minerals sparkled. If it weren't for all the dead, he figured, it would have been an interesting place to explore.

Ahead they found an elevator shaft and Nam motioned for everyone to stop while he checked schematics. "Maybe this one. We take this all the way up and it might land us somewhere in section seven, one the drifters finished clearing last year. From there it's a quick walk."

Maung stopped at the entrance. Than peered over his shoulder, down into the shaft, and then inhaled sharply. He whispered something that Maung couldn't make out, but he turned and looked down to see the body of a Sommen, impaled on a sharp metal girder at the bottom.

"It's dead," Maung said.

Nam pushed past to look. "It must have fallen far to have gained this much momentum—enough to pierce its armor. From what you said, nothing can get through that stuff."

"Or maybe its armor was defective or weakened."

Maung ignored the chill he got from seeing the creature. He reached for the nearest ladder rung, pulling himself upward a short distance where he waited for the others to ensure their coms chord stayed untangled.

"You still haven't told us what you found out about the Phobos stuff, Maung," Than said. "What did you learn?"

Nam came next, following close behind Maung. "Yeah. Come on."

"Not much about the program. It looks like all drifters are coded with knowing that they have a choice on how to serve out their life term and can switch to this second option any time. Whatever the program on Phobos is, it's a death sentence.

"But they also have a need for guards with security clearances. Lots of them. And from what I could gather there's a separate guard unit that is highly trained—more like special forces than prison guards. So whatever is there, it must be something dangerous, and it has national security written all over it."

Now they had a steady rhythm. Maung worked his way upward, ignoring the ache in his arms since he was fully accustomed to navigating the prison and wreckage, an old hand at climbing Karin's elevator shafts.

"When do we leave?" asked Nam.

"Tomorrow. I found out there's a bunch of drifters heading out on a transport that's due to arrive tomorrow, and our assignments should come through tonight."

"That doesn't leave us any time!" Nam said. "I don't even know if I want to go. And how the hell do we even make our way to Sunny Side and to the port? Even with fake identification, most people over there *know me*."

Maung sighed. "I know. We have to plan. I'll risk turning on my semi-aware soon to try and figure it out, but trust me: It's the only chance we've got. If you don't want to go you can appeal the transfer and stay. Listen. The Chinese want me, so as long as I stay here, I'm putting all Myanmarese at risk; I have to go."

They passed the rest of the time in silence, moving steadily up the elevator shaft. His family was one of two things that concerned Maung—the other was Nang. He had no idea how she'd react and there was no telling if she'd go. But what other option was there? It wasn't like he could stay there, on Karin, since he was the one putting everyone in danger and Maung guessed she'd understand; she *had* to say yes.

An hour later they reached the surface, exhausted. By the time they finished decontamination and made it to their racks, Maung was already half asleep.

He almost missed his signal to wake up but Maung was ready because all he needed was his suit, which he slept in, and he raced through the tunnels. It made him dizzy. Maung barely remembered making the decision to place their identities in the transfer system and normally he wouldn't have dared make that kind of decision, but for his semi-aware the calculus had been simple; there was little risk in the short term. Eventually someone would discover the error but there was no way for them to attribute it to Maung without first discovering that he was a Dream Warrior, in which case breaking into the system and forging a transfer would be the least of his problems. Mars, he thought. For the first time since his arrival, he allowed himself a feeling of hope—that maybe someday he'd see his son again.

Maung arrived with only a few minutes to spare; Nam and Than were already waiting.

Nam poked Maung in the chest. "Old Man sent a message to me while I was asleep; I just got it. He's mad, Pa. Got word already that we've been gobbled up by some super-secret outfit to be sent to Mars."

"What'd he say?"

"He's going to find the bastard that made this decision and make him or her pay."

"He can't find out," said Maung. "And if he does, he'll go after me, not you."

Than smiled. "I'm more curious to know what you're going to tell that girl of yours; how do you explain all this?"

"For now I don't. And you two stay quiet about it since I don't know how she'll take it either."

Nam was crying. At first Maung didn't notice because he looked in the other direction, but when the old man turned back he saw wet tracks on his cheeks.

"What's wrong?" he asked.

"You don't get it," said Nam. "Nothing is wrong. I never thought I'd leave this place. This is the best day of my life, Pa. Thank you. Maybe I won't make it to Earth, but it's a lot closer than Karin; it'll be nice to see the sun again."

By the time the elevator arrived to take them to the Sunny Side port and then to their escape, Nam smiled. Then all of them grinned.

CHAPTER SIXTEEN

Halfway to Sunny Side an alarm went off. Maung grabbed his helmet; within moments of donning it the reports streamed across his heads-up display and Maung almost stopped upon seeing the news—wondering if at any moment they could be arrested. Everyone was being called to their duty stations and all prisoners were to be returned to their cells so that Karin could lock down. He looked at Nam and Than, who were white faced, and Nam shrugged and smiled as if to say *It was a nice dream but this is our home, and it will never let us go.*

"Are you getting any news that's different from what I see?" Maung asked.

Nam tapped his head. "Same as you, Pa. Lockdown. Nothing more than that."

"And do lockdowns happen all the time?"

"I've never seen one since I've been working here. Twenty years."

Maung yanked his helmet off and threw it across the transport, wishing it could punch a hole in the thing and decompress them out of their misery.

Maung and the others debarked and barely found handholds when a team of American soldiers barreled through and into the transport, shutting the doors behind them. Than looked stunned. Maung waited for someone to arrest them and expected another group of Americans to appear at any minute when someone tapped his shoulder from behind. He recognized the smell of her perfume.

"Hi Maung," Nang said.

Maung wrapped her in his arms and kissed her, ignoring the fact that men streamed by on either side, pushing them against the wall and ceiling.

"Pa," Than said. "Maybe this isn't the place?"

Maung let go of her. "I missed you."

"Me too," Nang said. "I'm surprised to see you here because I have bad news. There wasn't any time to come in person."

"You're leaving for Mars. For Phobos."

Nang's jaw dropped. She was about to say something when Nam cut in. "We're heading there too. We only got the orders this morning and we're supposed to hook up with a hydrogen ship in the next couple of hours."

"Why?" she asked. "Where did this come from?"

Maung hated lying. He tried not to talk and wished that he could have told her sooner, but decided he couldn't—not yet. "We don't know. Maybe the Old Man in Charleston. But I don't think we're going anywhere if Karin is in lockdown. Do you know what happened?"

Nang put a finger to her lips and motioned for them to follow. She led them through the tunnels where the four did their best to dodge hordes of personnel moving quickly in the other direction, until finally they entered the female guards' unit; she led them into her cube where they squeezed in as best they could, their legs dangling out into the hall.

"They're coming, Maung. It must be because of Europa."

"Who's coming and what happened on Europa?" Nam asked.

"The Chinese," she said. "Four of their destroyers just appeared out of nowhere and must have been making their way to us for weeks under minimal power. None of our sensors picked them up."

Maung was about to respond—relieved that the uproar wasn't about his hacking into the data networks—when the lights flickered. A deep rumble followed.

"I think they're already here," Than whispered.

"Where can we get weapons?" Maung asked. They were moving out of the barracks now and into the confused throng of prison guards. He fumbled to seal his helmet. The rock vibrated again and the suit's audio pickups relayed the sound of a distant boom, one that Maung knew had to be big since it filled the tube with a cloud of dust shortly afterward.

Nang slung her coil gun across her back and said, "I'll take you to the armory; why didn't you bring yours?"

"Because we were supposed to get off this rock!"

She led them through the maze of tunnels until they reached the armory, where a long line of guards waited for body armor. Every instinct in Maung said to get out. He guessed by the looks on their faces that even though most of them had seen at least some combat, none were ready for what they were about to experience—a Chinese assault involving everything from attack ships to their own, *newer* versions of Maung. He *knew* it; the one who sent the message when he'd first arrived, the one who'd called Maung *brother*, was out there.

When it was their turn Nang explained everything to one of the girls manning the armory desk. "They need coil guns at least. Armor if you've got it."

"We can give them guns but no armor—that's not for Burmese."

Maung saw that Nang was about to argue; he put his hand on hers and squeezed. "No need, Nang; riot armor won't help anyway. The coil guns are enough." He turned to the girl then. "Do you know what's going on? Are we under attack?"

She passed three coil guns over the desk; Maung took one and handed the others to Than and Nam. "The Chinese took out an incoming hydrogen ship and now they're hitting Dark Side. The main transport elevator is gone too. They overran the site where the Americans were working and an Allied fleet is on the way but we're talking at least a week out."

"Any casualty reports for Burmese guards?" Nam asked. His hands gripped the coil gun so hard that it shook.

"Sorry, no. All coms with Dark Side are gone."

Maung made his decision in an instant and kicked toward the exit portal. "Let's go."

"Where?" Nang asked.

"The prisoner transport elevator; we're going back to Dark Side."

"Maung, you can't do that! Only one person at a time can fit in that thing and it's probably locked down anyway."

Nang sounded scared and he wanted to hide her somewhere, but even without his semi-aware he'd concluded there was no point in hiding; eventually the Chinese would make their way in and track down each living thing. He couldn't just let them die. Those were men from Myanmar dying on Dark Side, he decided, and they'd do the same thing for him.

"We have to go, Nang. And we won't be using the elevator—just the shaft."

"We're Myanmarese," Than added. "We're used to getting the shaft."

Nang clung to his hand. They were at the prisoner transport portal and Maung inspected the panel to read its status, but then he reached out to touch her faceplate; the suit made it almost impossible to feel anything. He let go, worked to pry the panel off the wall, and wedged part of his gun between it and the rock. Nam helped. A few minutes later, it dangled from the wall, hanging off a forest of wires and cables.

"Nam, there's a data port right here," Maung said, pointing. "I can get a read on everything that's going on, lock down the elevator so they can't activate it while we're in the shaft, and maybe probe the Chinese."

"What do *you* know about data feeds?" Nang asked.

Nam gestured for her to be quiet. "Do it, Pa. Link up and get us to Dark Side."

"Nang . . ." Maung said, but the words wouldn't come. Part of him hurt from the way she looked at him, incredulous that a villager thought he could access Karin's data feeds, and then there was another part—terrified by the thought of how she'd react when she found out he could. He should have told her before, Maung thought. In sick bay or maybe on the *Singapore Sun*. Now there was no time to explain everything and he wanted to do it when she wasn't in a suit so he could hold and smell her one last time before she left.

"I'm not what you think I am," he said, and then activated his semi-aware, handing the cable to Nam. "Link me."

Brother . . .

The data feed shocked him into awareness. As soon as Nam connected him, Maung's semi-aware heated with its effort to ward off thousands of simultaneous attacks. Copies and copies, Maung thought. He sensed in the code his adversary from the *Singapore Sun* and at the same time understood it *wasn't* him, but rather cloned versions, shadows of the Chinese super-aware's intellect that now orchestrated a coordinated assault using an almost infinite number of methods. It had been waiting for him. Maung shunted part of his effort—the fraction of a percent of his semi-aware that wasn't engaged in active defense—into building his plan. He used the attacks to learn; with each probe Maung gathered fragments that gave clues as to how his adversary thought, his weaknesses, and, most importantly, where he hid and how his forces had been arrayed. Finally he gathered all he needed. The old Maung would have been stunned to find that the Chinese Dream Warrior was off planet, in a small craft that hid itself by appearing like a fragment of rock drifting along with Karin, but the new one wasn't. Maung's mind was infinite; the power of his semi-aware and the resources he conscripted from Karin's servers allowed him to rule with logic and he calculated that the Chinese moves made sense, even if flawed. It was a subtle strategy—one that relied on surprise. Now Maung assessed they'd been there for weeks. Studying. Sending out probes. And he wondered how the Americans could have been so stupid that they never detected the Chinese landing party infiltrate Dark Side near the Sommen site days ago, in preparation for this moment. All of the Americans over there, Maung judged, were already dead.

When he was ready, Maung launched the attack. It wasn't designed to destroy his enemy, just distract—to give him enough time to permanently deactivate the elevator while skimming Chinese tactical data from any communications picked up by Dark Side relays. It was like he stomped on an anthill. Bursts of colored packet traffic shot toward him and Maung mentally chuckled while distributing his programs like seeding a field, taking only milliseconds to gather the information he needed before blowing the elevator power supply with a surge. After finishing, he withdrew.

Nang's face went pale. "You're a Dream Warrior," she said.

"Yes." Maung reached up to unplug. His arm was tired and his heads-up clock showed that only a few minutes had passed, but the level of exertion had been so intense that he barely found the strength to grab the data cable and yank. Nam helped him.

"I'm a Dream Warrior. The last one. The Americans killed all my friends and my wife, but somehow I got away. They've been chasing me ever since the war, and ever since the *Singapore Sun*."

"That's not—" she said, but Maung interrupted her.

"I destroyed those ships off Ganymede. The captain gave me control of his ship and I used it to take the over one of the Chinese vessels."

"He's our best," Nam said, nodding. "Pa, I don't mean to be rude. I know you two have a lot to talk about, but our people are dying and we have a long way to go."

Than folded his arms. "A long way? *It's hundreds of klicks, Nam!* All hand over hand and you two are freakin' nuts. Like a couple of kala."

"Wait," said Nang. She stopped staring at Maung and kicked off toward the barracks. "Stay here and don't move. I know something that could make this a faster trip. *Much* faster."

"I hope they have cigarettes on Mars," said Maung. "Because I could really use one now."

Maung had to practically hold Nam back. "We can't go yet. Give her a few more minutes."

"We've already given her *ten*. They're dying over there, Maung!"

He was about to answer when Nang returned. Maung couldn't stop smiling since there had always been the possibility that she had gone to report him or that she simply would never come back, but there she was. She dragged a bulky object—something like a combination between a backpack and tanker ship. Before he even pinged his semi-aware, it gave him the data.

"It's a maneuvering pod," Maung said. "Why didn't I think of that?"

"Think of what?" Than asked.

Nang grinned and held up the pack. "It's for work outside the asteroid when we need to suit up and replace hardware at the docking port, or wherever. There are control jets and it has enough fuel for one hour of continuous acceleration. It's designed to fit in tight spaces."

"How nice," said Than, his voice thick with sarcasm. "Such equipment doesn't exist on Dark Side; we just get safety harnesses and handholds. What a luxury it must be to work over here; what bravery it must take."

"Shut up," said Nam.

Maung grabbed the pack. "I'll take the lead. The first half we'll be falling so we can tie into each other to keep from drifting too far apart. We can't get going too fast or someone could get hurt just by touching the wall. So use your hands and feet to decelerate; we'll keep our speed reasonable. Then, once we pass the asteroid's core I'll use the pack to accelerate so we can keep our speed up. We'll see you when we get back, Nang."

"No you won't," said Nang.

"What?"

"I'm coming too. The pack was my idea. I may not be as smart as a Dream Warrior, but I know how bad things would get if the Chinese take Karin's dark side. There is no safe place, Maung."

Nam pulled nylon cords from his pouch and the four tied off to each other. Maung took Nang's hands. He looked through her faceplate and at first she didn't look back at him, but when she did she smiled.

"I wanted to tell you on the *Sun*," he said. "About me."

"You should have. I don't know what to say to you right now."

"I'm not who I used to be." Maung paused. Even with all the data and processing power he had, trying to express feelings left him frustrated. "I'm not a killer anymore. I just want to find someplace to live without being hunted."

Nang nodded and pointed to the elevator portal. "I know. We can talk later. Right now it's time to get moving."

"I'm serious; you don't have to go with us."

"The hell I don't," said Nang. "I don't know what I think about you right now, but I'm still not letting the Chinese kill you before I do."

She drove Maung forward, helping him squeeze the backpack unit through the narrow hatchway where it dangled from a strip of webbing, and then he popped through, sliding down the narrow shaft to make room for the next person. It was dark ahead. Maung used friction to slow his descent and thanked his ancestors that the tube was ultra slick, because its diameter was barely wider than he was, and Maung knew that he'd be bouncing off the walls once he accelerated; the trick was to keep everyone sliding at the same rate—something that would be difficult—so the group stayed evenly spaced. Finally Nang radioed that she was in.

"Here we go," Maung said. He let the semi-aware take over, feeling like a spectator as the computer guided his hands and knees against the walls. The acceleration was instantaneous. In less than a minute they reached one hundred kilometers per hour and Maung smiled at the minute pressure changes his system made, keeping his hands pressed against the tube walls. Maybe, he thought, this would work.

There is a thirteen percent chance that friction could disrupt suit integrity at your gloves and knees, the semi-aware informed him, but Maung shrugged; it was too late now.

"The fighters launched," Nang said over the radio.

Maung almost lost focus, but then corrected speed using his feet. "What?"

"Fighters. We had three fighters and pilots, just in case we had to defend against something minor—not something this big. I just got a transmission that they took off to try and intercept the destroyers."

Maung said a silent prayer, asking his parents to guide the craft even if their pilots weren't worthy. *Especially* if they weren't worthy.

Despite having the maneuvering pack, they still had to claw their way through the tube for the final kilometer since there wasn't enough fuel to carry all four of them to the exit portal. The going was difficult—despite low gravity. Without handholds and with walls that were as slick as glass, the group had to press their backs against one side and then used their feet and hands to press against the other, sliding "upward" while moving away from the asteroid's core and closer to Dark Side. Maung's shoulders screamed in agony by the time he saw light in the tunnel; he'd had to push the maneuvering pod the whole way up, using only his head.

He stopped and held position. "We're almost there. I can see light."

"I'm not getting any radio traffic," said Nam. "Are you, Than?"

"Negative."

Maung made sure his semi-aware stayed in passive collection mode, minimizing any signal leakage that could give away their position. "They must be jamming. Where would you defend, Nam, if you were the guards?"

"The control center. It's adjacent to the armory and the mess hall, so you'd have ready access to ammunition and food—maybe long enough to hold out for rescue."

Without warning, Maung's defense system activated, and his concentration broke so that he slipped and collided with Nam, below. It almost caused a chain reaction. Than braced against the walls and supported both the men above until Maung gathered his wits and regained position. His mind raced. The Chinese controlled data feeds on this side of Karin and ran constant random pings designed to overwhelm any logic platforms in range, and the assaults lasted anywhere from one second to a full minute before dying off. Maung relaxed. There was no way to tell when the next would come, but there was also no point in staying inside the elevator shaft. He pushed upward for the last hundred meters, threw the maneuvering pack out the exit, and rolled into the corridor at the same time he unslung his coil gun. Nam followed close behind, cutting the webbing for him. When Than and Nang emerged, Maung had already compared their position to the data he gathered back on Sunny Side and decided there were probably no immediate Chinese threats.

"The tunnels are still pressurized," he said. "We can talk via speaker, not radio."

"Where are they?" Nam asked.

"The biggest concentration was at the Sommen attack site, with a small group hitting the control center to keep our guards pinned down. They want to consolidate the place where the American Dream Warriors fell; it's important to them for some reason."

Than moved closer and Maung heard the nervousness in his voice. "Probably for the same reason it's important to the Americans. Whatever reason *that* was."

Now that his semi-aware was active, Maung took a second to analyze the data. He was surprised at the answer. "I think some Americans were as shocked to learn of it as we were."

"Wait," said Nang. "The Sommen attack site was part of an old American Dream Warrior program If that's true how could our people not know about it?"

"The Sommen. They attack super-awares almost without reason, and then wipe all connections to them that ever existed. I encountered one of their programs; a creeper that was still working after all these years and designed to wipe Karin's data systems clean—to destroy any super-aware that survived. We saw their bodies. The Sommen kept attacking in waves, oblivious to losses. And this was obviously a secret program. So if the Sommen succeeded in destroying all data centers and personnel associated with it . . ."

"Then if there wasn't any record on Earth . . . If it were so secret that this was the only place where records of it existed, most Americans had no idea," Nang finished, her face pale. "Except for the ones with the highest clearances."

The rock shook, knocking out some of the LEDs and then a deep boom followed, rattling Maung's teeth. He moved forward. His thoughts focused on what needed to happen first and with the adrenaline spike that came from being fully aware, fully activated, he became almost invincible.

"Where are we going?" Than asked.

"The Sommen attack site. We're going to retake it before the Chinese can get any useful data. That site, and me, are the reasons they're here."

Nang moved up behind them and he heard her safety click off. "Are you insane? Four of us? Against all of them and their destroyers?"

"I was hoping you could send a message," said Maung.

"Send one to who? Asking for what?"

"To your Korean friend. Explain to him what's going on and convince him to send a team of his best fighters here, to meet us at the site and help with a counterattack. But we can't let him know what I am. And you can't tell him exactly what we have planned because the lines are monitored now."

Nang sighed. "He doesn't like you, Maung. It'll take some convincing and a minor miracle. And you *better* hope he doesn't find out who you are; he and all the other guards from the Allied nations will skewer you on the spot."

"Fine." Maung laughed. "There's a coms port nearby. We'll make our way there so you can hook in, then book it; the Chinese will surely send a patrol once they zero in on your location."

Maung was fully aware. Not just his active sensors worked overtime, but the metallic portions of his skeleton acted like a compact passive receiver and his semi-aware fed data via his retina so that Maung read thermal variations. It was as if he were born with the ability to see across the spectrum; with a flicker of thought he could switch to ultraviolet or infrared vision. And now his aural implants amplified sounds. *He was superhuman.* Maung judged that the thought wasn't necessarily organic and that his semi-aware must have detected depression, compensating for it by feeding him flashes of inspiration via adrenaline and neurotransmitters. The compounds bolstered his confidence. The semi-aware was reacclimating to old neural pathways, ones that it hadn't used even during the more recent episodes where Maung had linked into the data feeds. Those were just a tease. Now it took control without concern for signal leakage, just like it did in the war when Maung slaughtered everything that moved.

Maung caught himself smiling. Grinning at the memory of so much killing. He shut his eyes and sent a stream of conscious thought to the inorganic portion of his brain, reminding it that his long-term survival prospects improved if he showed some remorse for what happened in the war.

The semi-aware gave no response.

"Which route, Pa?" Nam asked.

Maung scanned the data he'd collected on Sunny Side again. "They have a defensive perimeter one hundred meters out in every direction from where I linked up with the dead American girl at the Sommen site. Sensors fifty meters beyond that. It's best if we come in from below; we'll start through the pipe galleries and down the data-feed conduit like we did earlier."

"That'll take a long time," said Than. "You sure?"

"How's it going with coms, Nang?" Maung asked.

Nang put a hand up to tell him to wait, then lowered it a few moments later. "I think I convinced him. He said he'd put together a group and send them within the hour; they'll get here about fifteen hours after that, using the prisoner transport shaft."

"Yes," Maung said, turning back to Than, "*now* I'm sure. The Chinese will focus most of their attention on the incoming from Sunny Side because those guys transmit like crazy. We move now, so that we can be in position to attack as soon as possible."

"You're using the guards as a diversion?" asked Nang. "They'll get slaughtered if we don't protect the tunnel!"

"Not if we get to our positions in time, early enough to attack before the Allied guards make it too far."

Maung cracked open an access panel that Nam had pointed out earlier and slithered through; he moved forward so the others could get in, reminded them to keep their helmet lamps off, and slid downward into the pipe gallery as soon as they all connected a fiber cable for communication. With his vision set to infrared, he felt as though he slid through the intestines of a cold dragon, dead for centuries.

"I'm getting a reading on nanos," Nam said. "Maybe half a klick to our right."

Maung nodded; his semi-aware already posted the data, dots and numbers that represented potential nano activations, probabilities of danger and exposure.

"The Chinese activated Sommen mines but they have decoys like ours to attract the nanos and then fry them. It'll help us."

Maung slid downward head first. They passed the place where only a while ago they cut into the data feed and now he hugged the plastic conduit with arms and legs, barely feeling the tug at his foot where Nang had a grip. Than was gripping her foot, and then Nam had Than's. He knew it must be nerve-racking for them not to be able to see but this was the safest way since they couldn't risk giving off too many signatures, and even waves from their helmet lamps could bounce through the structures and trip Chinese sensors.

In places, the shielding was faulty. Maung broke through EM waves as if falling through a layer of water, and his systems soaked up the data, sifting it for anything of import, anything that gave a clue to Chinese activity. It was during one of these intersections that he stopped; he told the others to hold in place.

"Nam," said Maung, "the Chinese broke into the control center a while ago. All the Burmese guards are either dead or captured."

"Jesus," said Nang.

"Maung, get us down," said Nam. "Now."

Maung moved faster, loosening his grip a bit on the conduit and letting gravity do the work, pulling them deeper into the complex.

According to Nam's schematics, they'd popped out of the conduit and into a service section, where old American corpses littered the floor. All of them were suited. Maung figured the men put up some kind of final defense, a last stand against the Sommen where empty rocket tubes and a plasma conduit suggested they risked using heavy weapons in an area where the effects could have been deadly to both sides. Their suits were clawed open. Maung's semi-aware processed the images and concluded that unlike the corpses he recalled from other locations, these ones were different.

"Nam," he said, "look at their suits."

"What about them?"

"They're clawed open in the same way. All of them. Like the Sommen ripped a pattern in them—a word or letter. A symbol."

"Maung, we don't have our lamps on so I can't *see* anything. And anyway, I want the Chinese; who cares about the Sommen?"

Maung guided him closer and leaned down next to a body. He took Nam's finger to trace the pattern. Then he moved to the next one and did it again so that Nam whistled.

"OK. They're the same."

"And," said Maung, "all the corpses are positioned the same way, with their weapons next to them."

"So what?" asked Nang.

"So I'd say the Sommen respected these men. Enough to perform some kind of ritual."

Nang laughed. "Or you're looking at some kind of Sommen magical ceremony meant to curse their souls to eternal damnation."

But Maung couldn't shake the feeling—that it was important, like the message from the young monk, something that would one day matter. He stood and moved on, taking the lead and creeping forward toward the spot Nam showed him on the map, where a service elevator shaft led upward and into the massive chamber. All of them crawled on their stomachs. They inched over the dead in an attempt to evade Chinese sensors.

Maung's alarms went off. He hissed into his mic, the signal for everyone to freeze, and in less than a second his eyes portrayed the scene in multiple colors, each one coded to different threat levels. Everything was green except for a single sphere. It hung from the ceiling, adjacent to the service elevator entry, and once the semi-aware finished its work, it labeled the thing in red: *sentrybot, Chinese origin—active threat.*

"We're there," said Maung. "But there's a sentrybot at the access shaft we need to use."

"Did it see us?" Nang asked.

"Doubtful. If that had happened, it would have opened fire since it probably has weaponry that can kill all of us in a second."

Maung clicked for the map again. He focused on their section. Assuming nothing had changed since he'd constructed it, there should have been a defensive position halfway up the shaft and then the bulk of Chinese forces concentrated in the chamber. Almost an hour had passed. If Nang's Sunny Side contact wasn't lying, then the Korean guards should now be inside the transport shaft, where the Chinese would hit them.

Maung said, "Stay put. I'm disconnecting the coms cable and seeing if there are any workable heavy weapons back with those dead Americans. If there are, maybe we can use them."

Maung disconnected and backed away. He moved through his team slowly, sliding over them until his sensors showed the threat was out of range, and then he kicked off to move as fast as possible—back to the strangely marked bodies. His semi-aware was already plotting probabilities in terms of the history of rocket launchers, temperature, materials properties and elapsed time; the odds were horrible. Even if he found a workable heavy weapon, the ammunition would likely fail. If it weren't for the half-life of tritium, he figured, the reactor and plasma conduit would have made a better weapon and given them something capable of frying their way up and into the main chamber.

Maung scoured the area. After an hour he found a couple of launchers that appeared serviceable but no ammunition, and the battle that had raged there spread out over a vast area—too vast for him to search completely. He was about to give up when the semi-aware stopped him. In an open area ringed with ventilation pumps two bodies lay on the floor. One of them was human, the other Sommen. What struck Maung was that this time the Sommen was unarmored, its bare skin a deep black that was perfectly smooth except for what looked like long ridges and pockmarks near its shoulders and on both arms in asymmetric patterns.

Scars, he realized. So many scars covered the thing that he marveled at the damage it had sustained in its lifetime, almost missing the fact that what finally killed it was still there—a spear, hand fashioned from wiring conduit, one end sharpened. The metal stuck out of the thing's chest, pointing directly upward.

His human opponent had done no better. The man must have been impressive in life since in death he looked at least six and a half feet tall, with muscles frozen solid at their peak—the body of a weightlifter or linebacker. Maung couldn't tell what had lodged in the man's neck. He tried to remove it but the thing was frozen in place and, he guessed, it was probably only a Sommen knife, which wasn't of much use anyway. But there was something else. The Sommen had removed its armor and stacked it on the floor near the circle, where it now sat, frozen and ice covered; a rifle rested next to it. It was the same kind of Sommen rifle Maung examined so long ago, when he first arrived and went exploring with Than.

Maung lifted it carefully, breaking the thin layer of ice that held it in place. His semi-aware churned. Details that weren't visible at first now leaped out in infrared and as he flipped through the spectrum his mind mapped the rifle's features, comparing them with how he and Than had seen the weapon held in the dead Sommen's hands. Maung worried he might activate it; he needed more time. But a small part of his brain reminded him that Nang and the others must be in agony, and he couldn't imagine having to stay in one position this long, but the weapon was important; evidence of the Sommen rifle's damage potential was all around—molten ceramics and steel as if the sun itself had attacked the station.

Then he got it. There were aspects of the rifle that his system couldn't fathom but Maung had enough observations to a least help determine a probable way to fire the gun, and he had to decide: test it now and alert the Chinese, or try it in battle and risk having a weapon that failed.

Once Maung returned, he plugged back into the coms cable.

"*Where the hell have you been?*" Nam hissed.

"I was busy."

"Busy? I've taken so many leaks now that my suit smells like a urinal, Maung. I don't give a damn what we do as long as we *move*."

Maung told him to be quiet and slid the rifle into place one centimeter at a time, making sure that he didn't trip the sentrybot's motion detectors. Both hands shook. It was only a slight tremor, arising from the fact that neither he nor his companions had seen the weapon fire, and Maung had no idea how to aim or what kind of damage it caused. And there was no way to reload. A million questions barreled through his thoughts in a matter of only a few seconds, but one kept repeating: What if it ran out of ammunition?

"Nobody move," he said. "When I open fire, disconnect from the coms cable and move to the shaft as fast as you can. I'll spray fire upward and take the lead, you all follow. From here on we'll risk the radios. But remember our coms are being monitored and analyzed by living super-awares—like me. So don't say too much, only what's urgent."

"What is that thing?" Nang asked. "Some kind of rifle?"

Maung took a deep breath. He guessed as to where the barrel was pointed because of its odd shape and because his faceplate made it difficult to aim down the gun's long axis. But the sentrybot was close. When he thought he had it, he let his semi-aware take over to squeeze three fingers against a pressure membrane on the rifle's underside. Nothing happened. His mind cycled through the various possibilities and while his fingers moved on autopilot, Maung did his best to keep the weapon aimed. One after another, he tried different combinations—none of them effective. Finally he wondered if you needed to wear the Sommen armor for the thing to work. He was about to ask Nam for an idea when the rifle erupted with fire, sending a searing bolt of energy in the sentrybot's direction.

At first Maung couldn't see. The burst automatically triggered his faceplate to frost over as if he'd been looking into the sun, but it cleared within a second. He punched wildly on his forearm computer, disabling the faceplate and reminding himself to close his eyes every time he fired.

"Move!" he shouted.

The sentry was gone, along with portions of the rock to which it had clung. Maung glanced around for pieces but there was nothing. Once he got close enough Maung saw that the rock itself melted away, forming a perfect circle where the blast hit—a crater three centimeters deep.

Movement, his semi-aware warned. Something was coming down the shaft, not bothering with stealth since it was broadcasting data in a wide enough beam that his body picked it up. Maung fired upward; he looked away so it wouldn't blind him and a moment later something slammed into the rock floor to cast a slow moving puff of dust and ice crystals into the air. It looked like a spider. Maung's semi-aware labeled it Chinese from the radio emissions, but it was a design that the wetware couldn't identify and Maung stared in horrified fascination. He'd blasted away part of the thing's steel shell. Inside something vaguely human squirmed at the same time a hint of vapor leaked from the massive hole, until finally the squirming stopped in a puff of ice.

He blasted three more shots up the shaft and dove toward the ladder with Than on his heels.

"Get on my shoulders," Than shouted over the radio. "*You* keep firing upward and I'll carry the both of us."

Spider-things covered the top of the shaft. Maung took aim and blasted them before they fired back, and noted that when they shot, the Chinese aimed wildly as if they couldn't see, and his semi-aware concluded that the rifle fire was overloading their sensors. He jumped up and then drifted down onto Than's shoulders.

"They're blinded," he said. "When I fire it overloads their sensors so they can't take aim."

"How do you know?" Than asked. Maung had trouble aiming while he swayed on Than's shoulders, but it didn't matter; the top was clear.

"They're chattering like crazy now—in the open. I hear everything."

Maung settled in. He divided his processing into two streams— one that operated the rifle and kept the rim clear while they climbed, and the other that prepared to dive into Chinese communications. Once ready, he broadcast. The closest signal was well above them, beyond the rim of the shaft, but the Chinese unit was piping signal almost continuously and Maung inserted without interrupting it, sliding through and into the waves until he was first inside the Chinese transmitter, then beyond and inside the enemy network. A few moments later, he owned one—a Chinese soldier. Part of Maung almost gave in to an urge to vomit at what this one had become, a thing barely human locked inside a robotic shell and wired into systems devoid of sympathy or empathy. It was all practical. The thing's weaponry was part of it, as if Maung's arms were rifles. Six robotic legs moved jerkily, but with practice Maung got the hang of moving and soon his mind encountered its memories, which leaked into his own consciousness no matter how hard he tried to block them. Images flashed of sharp legs piercing American and Myanmarese guards. The thing laughed when it killed. Maung realized almost nothing human remained in the creatures; these were as alien as the Sommen, machine-animals the Chinese created and bred for killing.

Maung forced it to fire. It shot dual guns into its own kind and he mentally recoiled at the sensations the Chinese shared with him, the fact that now it drooled with joy at the sight of death and the pure glee inspired by the slaughter of its fellow soldiers. Killing fulfilled it. When another unit knocked out the one Maung occupied, he took another, and then another until finally the chamber was clear. There were no more transmissions in the area. Maung stepped off Than's shoulders and climbed for himself, until finally they reached the top and dragged themselves over the edge of the shaft's square hole. Maung dove behind the cover of a dead Chinese unit, exhausted.

Nang joined him. "You did all this?"

"Yeah." Maung was crying. The visions shared by dozens of hijacked Chinese soldiers rattled around his brain, taunting him with their insanity. "But they deserved it."

"I thought this would be impossible; how do you do this?"

"It *should* have been impossible. But this rifle messed with their systems and they dropped their guard for a second to try and deal with it; their super-awares never considered the possibility that we'd have this kind of firepower."

"Don't cry, Maung," she said, touching his shoulder. "You just saved a lot of people—the Sunny Side guards."

Nam settled in nearby. He scanned the area and then clicked in. "Maung, what now? Do you know where the rest of them went and where the Americans and Burmese are? Are any of them still alive?"

"A drop ship." Maung sifted through all the data collected during his occupation of the Chinese units, which to him seemed like an eternity ago but was only a few seconds. "They retreated to their drop ship—the landing zone just outside the port on the face of Karin. They have Burmese prisoners with them and some Sommen tech."

"We can't let them off Karin," Nam said.

"I know."

✹ ✹ ✹

"How are they moving so fast?" Than asked.

The four of them kicked off walls and pulled themselves along a white corridor; it was once covered with bodies and frozen blood but now was empty, the corpses taken by the Chinese.

"They fold their legs back," he said, "and use gas jets to propel themselves. When that runs out they use their legs; with eight of them, they're better in microgravity than we are."

Maung again took the lead. He moved as fast as he dared; around each curve there could be a trap, and he told Nam to bring up the rear, and watch for any doors that might open behind them. The movement was hypnotizing. He had to remind himself to focus, to pull his mind back into the present instead of memories of the Myanmar city, Pagan. Funny, he thought. Maung hadn't thought of the place since he left his family and now memories of Pagan, with hundreds of royal monasteries that shone pink in the setting sun and reflected heat in shimmering waves off their spires, wouldn't leave. Most of the monasteries were gone now, destroyed by the war. But he remembered them as they once were, the way he wanted them to be again and even on Karin the thought made him smile.

Your daughter Maung; she and her children will save the world . . .

An alarm blared in his mind at the same time his semi-aware sent the message *multiple sentrybots*. He shouted for the others to take cover. It was too late for him to maneuver into a doorway, and a field of bots coated every free surface in the corridor ahead. He fired. The rifle had no kick but the searing bolt, when released in a confined space with white reflective surfaces, forced Maung's temperature sensors to spike and he smelled the melting plastic of his helmet; part of its circuitry sparked out, but the way ahead was clear.

"I fried the right side of my helmet but nothing major is out."

Than said, "Hold on, Maung, you're venting. Aren't you getting a warning?"

Maung checked his system again; there was no warning at first but when he banged his forearm computer against the wall, the red alarm flashed onto his heads-up. "Now I am. Shit."

"It'll just take a second." Than slid over and yanked out his sealant, working his way up the right side of Maung's suit; a minute later, he finished.

"How much farther to the crater wall?" Maung asked.

"One more klick," said Nam. "Then a climb to the top, and their landing site is just a few hundred meters beyond the rim—if the data you fed me is right."

"It's right. I just don't know if we'll get there in time."

Nang clicked in. "Maung, I just hooked into a coms port. All remaining Sunny Side guards have been ordered to evacuate and move to Dark Side and arrange a defensive perimeter around the Sommen chamber we just cleared. Two of the three fighters that attacked the destroyers are gone. The third changed course and is now going after the same Chinese drop ship we're headed for; the fighter has orders to destroy it before it launches, despite the presence of friendlies. We have to get there. Fast."

Maung scanned for signs of Chinese communications but found nothing. Whatever panic the new weapon had created was gone, he figured. Now an urgency took hold and he kicked off, hard, bouncing dangerously off the walls in an effort to propel himself faster down the corridor, keeping his receivers open for the smallest indication of Chinese EM leakage.

"Faster," Nam said, "If we don't get there before the fighter does, all our brothers die."

Better than being taken alive, Maung thought.

Five times they stopped to battle sentrybots or waiting soldiers, and Maung wondered where the Chinese semi-aware had gone. Something wasn't right. By now there should have been some signature of his presence or work, and Maung figured it was still nearby in its craft. His mind calculated the different probabilities. With the destroyers still incoming, there was almost no chance that the Chinese super-aware gave up and left; since its forces failed to hold the Sommen site, the thing was likely regrouping—waiting and watching, gathering more data before it acted again.

"That's what I would do," Maung whispered.

Maung told the group to spread out as they climbed the outside of a building, one at the very edge of the port's crater; it was the least probable route for them. Had they taken the same path the Chinese had, up the building's elevator shaft, Maung projected that they would have had to fight their way through—a waste of time that would guarantee they'd arrive at the drop ship too late. He was about to reach the roof's edge when Than screamed.

Maung held on to a ledge with one hand and leaned out to look down. A Chinese unit pinned Than to the building with one leg, its sharp point driven through his shoulder and into the concrete wall so Than's face pressed against the edifice.

"Close your eyes, Than!" Maung said.

"Don't shoot that thing; you'll fry my suit!"

The Chinese raised another leg, this one slowly, pointing it at Than's head as if to show Maung that he needed to watch what he did. Now Nang screamed. Three more spiders had emerged from empty windows below and scrambled up the face toward them.

"We'll patch it as soon as we can, Than. Hold on!"

Maung fired. The spider holding Than vaporized and now instead of chasing Nang and Nam, the remaining four paused and zeroed on Maung, firing. He watched in horror. The fléchettes were virtually invisible until they struck something and he flinched when they tossed up pieces of concrete next to his head, and then several went through both Nam and Nang. She screamed. Now Maung's system practically steamed as it tried to calculate shot angles and every targeting solution was the same: fire through his friends. Instead, Maung dove off the building. While he sailed into space, he twisted around, facing the building upside down until he passed Nang. Maung fried the four spiders once he was clear of her. The beam passed through them and into the building itself, leaving the things stuck to the concrete, their metallic legs motionless.

"My suit's venting," Than said. "You melted the crap out of it!"

Maung's shoulders slumped with relief when Nang gave him a thumbs up, and she was already patching her suit; she must not be hurt badly. But he couldn't tell what was happening with Nam. The old man had held on, but wasn't moving upward.

"I have my own problems, Than," he said. "I'm not sure what to do next. Plug your suit and help Nam and Nang, then head for the Chinese drop ship."

"What are you going to do?"

"Fall."

At first it was a gentle drop but soon he moved faster. Maung estimated he only had seconds before it got out of hand, but there was almost two meters between him and the nearest building—too much space for him to grab at a window.

"I should have run the numbers on this *before* I did it," he whispered.

Maung unslung his coil gun. The Sommen rifle was in one hand, which meant he had only the other to use, and he tried to work as quickly as possible. He squeezed the trigger. Maung kept firing until the last fléchette streaked out and then he flung the gun away from himself as hard as possible before looking to see if it worked—hoping that he discarded enough mass to propel him back toward the structure from which he'd jumped. The windows moved quickly now. He slowly drifted toward them until finally he was close enough to reach out and grab a ledge, instead clamping onto the edge of a broken window.

The window rim was sharp; its seal had been designed to hold thick slabs of clear plastic and the rim provided enough of a sharp angle to give Maung a place to grip, but a loud hiss came at the same time the rim bit through his glove. He winced at the sensation of freezing metal cutting into his skin. A few seconds later Maung climbed through and into an empty room, where he paused to seal his glove while ignoring the agony. His hand had to wait. Already the blood pooled around his fingers, the warmth and stickiness letting him know the injury was severe.

"Than, are Nam and Nang OK?" he asked.

"Nang is fine; her suit is sealed and a few fléchette nicks is all. Nam's hurt, though, Pa."

"I'm on my way back up now."

Maung tucked the Sommen rifle into his suit straps and leaped back out onto the building face, jumping from window to window, his semi-aware stimulating the production of biochemicals to counteract the searing pain from his fingers.

"Let me find my way back to the control room, you Tatmaw idiot," Nam said.

Maung smiled; if he was arguing, it couldn't be that bad. "I thought you were dead," he said.

"So did this fool." Nam lay on the rooftop, the front of his suit covered with blotches of sealer. He pointed a finger at Than. "He wants me to wait here. Not with those spiders running around."

Than clicked onto a separate frequency so Nam couldn't hear. "Maung, he has five fléchettes in his chest and abdomen. His suit's med unit is saying he's lost a lot of blood."

"Is he going to live?"

"Maybe. It's fifty-fifty either way. If he moves he could make it worse, but if he stays here he could go into shock and bleed out."

"We don't even have a doc anymore," Maung said.

"No, but there's an old medbot there. It should be able to do at least the basics."

Maung helped Nam to his feet and walked him to the edge. "Think you can make it?"

"I'm sorry, Maung. I wanted to get my boys back."

"I know." Maung nudged him gently off and watched to make sure Nam descended normally, dropping from one window to the next. Then he turned back. The other two were already pushing off side to side, building up speed and heading for the drop ship landing site. He caught up and passed them. The building's roof was almost even with the crater rim, and Maung leaped upward, rising at least ten meters into the air so he clipped the rim with his feet and rolled against the black rock before coming to a stop. He raised his Sommen rifle. From this distance the huge spherical drop ship was dime sized, resting on a cage-like structure and Maung observed a long line of figures moving underneath it. Even though those might be the guards, he had to take the chance; the fighter might be close and if he failed to immobilize the vehicle now, they'd be lost forever.

His first shot missed. The figures scattered from the craft and Maung saw the glow of engines, four of them warming on the ship's underside, about to touch off. He settled his breathing and willed himself to calm down. The gun fired again. This time it hit the tip of the craft, blowing off metal plates that scattered and turned, floating gently down toward the rock and landing at the same time the engines stopped. Maung fired three more times to guarantee the ship stayed put and by the time Nang and Than caught up to him, he knelt behind cover.

"It's decided to stick around," he said.

"Now what?"

"Now we go get our guards back and kill the rest of the Chinese."

But before they could move the ship exploded. At first Maung thought the fighter might have arrived and fired on the Chinese drop ship without warning, but Nang assured him that it couldn't have arrived yet. They bounded toward the ship as quickly as they could. Several Myanmar guards hid in nearby cracks and craters, and after gathering all of them together he counted only about twenty. Motionless Chinese figures dotted the landscape, with their spider-like carapaces blown open from the inside. There was no sign of any Americans.

Nam asked, "Did these Chinese blow up because of your hits?"

"No. They all blew themselves up because they'd rather die than be caught. We'd better get back; I just changed out my last oxygen."

CHAPTER SEVENTEEN

Nam and Nang slept, recovering in a corner of the chamber while strapped loosely into beds where Maung watched Nang's chest rise and fall; a pressure disappeared from his chest. She had been wounded in the shoulder and would recover. He smiled through a tear and closed his eyes to mumble a prayer for them both, and when he looked up he saw all the remaining Burmese kneeling at his feet. There were so few now; Maung could tell they expected something from him. The men were quiet and as soon as he turned to face them they bowed deeply, touching their foreheads to the floor at the same time they tried not to bounce into the air.

Maung stepped back, a feeling of shock numbing everything. So many of his countrymen were in sick bay, waiting their turn for the overworked medical bot, but the Sunny Side guards still hadn't shown up so the only non-Burmese in the room was Nang, who woke up and gripped his wrist—startling him.

"They want to pray with you," she said. "I didn't really understand you were capable of these things, Maung—what you did out there just now. You saved all of us."

"I'm sorry, Nang." His memories—of villages and massacres—swamped his thoughts. "I'm so sorry if I hurt your people and for not telling you sooner about what I really am. What I *was*, I mean."

"We can talk about that later. It's not like I don't have secrets either. But right now I think these guys expect you to lead them, and a good place to start would be in prayers for the dead. You're more than a Dream Warrior to them. And soon the Chinese will attack in force so I have to admit: It's nice to have someone like you on our side."

Maung closed his eyes and searched for the right prayer. When he decided, he swept his chair aside and knelt beside Nang's bed, bowing to the floor so his forehead pressed against the cold plastic.

"*I bow down to the youthful Arya Manjushri,*" Maung said, continuing the prayer to its end and repeating it ten times until his back screamed in pain. When he finished, he stood. One by one the Burmese came and hugged him, bowing and pressing their foreheads against his hand and each one said the same thing, "—Pa-Maung."

When it was Nang's turn she leaned in and kissed him, pulling Maung in tightly so she could whisper, "I'm fine. Come lie next to me, *Pa*-Maung."

Maung, Nang, and Than recovered in the control room. The holo-map spun in front of them and Maung studied it so carefully that he soon dropped into a trance, oblivious of the conversations around him and energized by the calculations that ripped through his consciousness; he overrode a warning indicator that he needed sleep and additional medical attention; eight of his fingers had been stitched back together. Something else tugged at him, though. Maung waved his hand, annoyed at the distraction, until he eventually grasped that Than was pushing on his shoulder, trying to get his attention.

"*Maung!*" He shouted.

"What?"

"We patched the control room's airlock doors and found four of the Chinese nano-traps but they're not activated; we can use them," said Than. "After those are gone, it's just coil guns and your Sommen rifle."

"And my Sunny Side guards are arriving any minute," Nang said. "That Korean is leading them, Kim Su Michael. They call him Mike."

"He's American?" Maung asked.

"As American as cheeseburgers," she said. "Doesn't speak a word of Korean or anything that isn't English."

Maung nodded. He dreaded the arrival of the 127 Sunny Side guards even though he needed their help, to be followed soon by the rest. They may as well have been Chinese. Koreans were arrogant—wouldn't follow his orders—and so the addition of their numbers meant little in the sense that when the fighting started, chaos could result from their refusal to act on his commands. Maung knew the fastest way to fix this: break their leader. Maung would do it in front of his men to show who was in charge, but it would damage the man and could create thousands of less probable, but *potential* unwanted results. He shook his head at the insanity of what was about to happen and then glanced over at Nam when the old man entered, taking his usual seat at the desk.

"Well, Pa?" he asked. "What next?"

"You should be in bed, old man. And I wish you wouldn't call me that."

Nang grinned and poked Maung's side. "Why? I think it's cute. *Pa.*"

"Our guys are all resting, Than, right?"

He nodded. "All in their bunk, sleeping like babies."

"Fine," said Maung. "Nang and I have to go; you and Nam start coding the drifters. When the Chinese attack again I want all the able-bodied prisoners out in the port, spread out everywhere, with whatever they can use as weapons. Plasma torches, demolition equipment, the works. And turn off their beacons so the Chinese can't track them too."

"What should we code them to do?"

"To kill anything moving that isn't human." A red light flashed on his heads-up, which meant a motion detector at the prisoner transport had activated. He caught Nang's hand. "Our Korean friend has arrived."

"Maung!" Nang said, so that Maung paused until she caught up at the door. "Your suit ring hides your wetware port, but be careful. They don't know what you are, and you want to make sure they *never* find out."

Maung and Nang bounced in the corridor, watching the guards approach. Their gear made Maung angry. All of them wore clean white environment suits covered with a layer of ballistic nylon riot plates that protected their arms, torsos and thighs, and their coil guns were the latest models—shorter and lighter than the ones the

Burmese carried, with integrated sight packages that linked to their heads-ups. The Burmese guns used ancient, down the axis green-dot sights.

"Hey, look," said one; Maung recognized his voice—the Korean, Mike. "It's Tatmaw and his little Laotian."

"You're on Dark Side now," said Maung. He ignored the insult, trying to keep his voice calm. "This area belongs to me but I'll gladly take you under my wing."

Mike's smile disappeared; he drifted closer to Maung and stopped himself with a handhold. "We own Karin, by order of the warden. There's nothing about my taking orders from you, and to be honest, I don't know why it's so important to defend Dark Side anyway; only the shit gets assigned here."

"That's because you're an idiot."

"You Burmese piece of—"

Maung seized Mike's helmet ring and yanked down as hard as he could while holding himself in place with a free hand. He jerked his knee upward—the same way he'd done to the *Singapore Sun* crewman. A loud crack echoed through the rock corridor when his knee impacted against Mike's downward moving face, and droplets of blood drifted down onto the man's white suit, dotting its surface with scarlet.

"I'm *Myanmarese,* asshole," said Maung. "And now your suit is finally broken in. You should be wearing your helmet, not carrying it."

He let go of Mike to let him flip end over end, then forced his semi-aware to take over, following its anticipation of hundreds of possible defenses and reactions for the guards while it simultaneously plotted attack vectors. Mike righted himself with an outstretched hand and faced Maung again, pulling himself forward and closing the distance.

"You don't even know who you are," Maung continued. "A Korean *pretending* to be American."

"I'm going to kill you, Tatmaw."

As soon as he was within range, Maung kicked at the Korean's arm, his semi-aware pinpointing the area where it was weakest; the bone cracked. Mike screamed and clutched it with his free hand, which sent him tumbling again and when Maung looked at the other guards he recognized their anger; in a moment they'd attack.

"And since you don't know what a drifter is or what we found that the Americans thought was so important . . ." He took hold of Mike's hair and twisted, turning him so that he faced away, then jerked back to expose his neck; Maung yanked out a knife and placed it against the man's exposed throat. "I don't really think you'll be of any use to us."

"Maung, *no!*" Nang yelled.

Mike's nose was broken, and blood continued to flow from it, settling slowly onto the front of his suit. "Please," he said.

"Please, what?"

"Please," said Mike. "Don't kill me. We'll take orders."

"You and your men will do as you're told?" Maung asked.

"Yes."

"And you understand that the second you don't, or the second I catch wind of any plans to shoot me in the back, you're a dead man?"

"Fine," Mike said, his breathing ragged. "Just let me go to sick bay. Where'd you learn to fight like that? I can feel the bone sticking out."

Maung scanned the group. He glared at the other guards, trying to guess their nationalities; there were some Japanese and some Filipinos—maybe a few more Koreans—and all of them glared but none of them looked brave enough to do anything now that their leader had surrendered. Maung let go. He and Nang moved to the side, letting the group file deeper into the dark side and toward sick bay.

"We'll meet in one hour," Maung called after them. "I'll give your orders and an orientation briefing from my men, the Burmese. Welcome to Dark Side."

"Why did you do that?" Nang asked.

"He never would have respected me if I didn't. He's a coward and they need to be expunged or brought in line. How much longer until the Chinese ships arrive?"

Nang shifted her helmet to rest under the opposite arm while they made their way back to the control room. "I don't have any new data and the last time I tried linking to Sunny Side systems, something was blocking all the readings. But I'd say a day, given their last location and heading."

Maung figured there was time to spare. He towed Nang into a storage facility and sealed the door, peeling off her suit; he'd never felt skin this soft. Nang was lean—almost bony. Maung imagined he could snap her in his arms so he was gentle when he slid her against the wall and heard her breathing stop for a moment.

She smiled and said, "Maung, don't be so gentle. I won't break."

"What took you two so long?" Nam asked.

Nang's face turned red and Maung shook his head and muttered for Nam to never mind. "Is the drifter coding done?" he asked.

"All set. As soon as you give the word, we can have them in position within an hour; it will take time for them to work their way out into the port."

"Good," Maung said. "And make sure they have enough oxygen to stay out for hours, just in case."

"What happens to the prisoners on Sunny Side?" Than asked.

They all looked at Nang.

"With nobody there to watch them," she said, "I would guess they stay locked up."

Maung's eyes went wide. "What about food? Won't they starve to death?"

"If we don't get back to them in a few weeks," she said, shrugging, "then . . . yeah. But first they'll turn to cannibalism."

Maung shook the thought from his mind. There was nothing they could do about it, so he focused his thoughts to finalize a plan his semi-aware had been analyzing since the moment they destroyed the Chinese drop ship. Part of him heard Nang talking. But her voice disappeared when all his resources shifted into calculation mode, billions per second, and he imagined that it looked odd to the others—him staring into space with a dead expression, in a trance that resembled a coma. Finally he finished.

"Where's the closest place I can link to Sunny Side systems?" Maung asked.

Nam pointed to his console. "Right here. But look around, Maung. The Chinese cracked this place more easily than anyone thought, even with all the security features of a prison. We might want to move to a better location soon."

Chinese fléchettes had chewed up the walls and spent ones still drifted on the floor in the dust. And Maung knew it took the Burmese hours to repair both airlock doors, which had been cut down the middle as if someone took a blowtorch to them. The corridor outside was the same. Defensive positions that the Burmese had rigged in their last stand lay shattered and disintegrated, blown to bits by Chinese rockets and grenades, weapons that none of the guards had. They couldn't defend against that kind of firepower. This was why Maung's plan was perfect, he figured, except for the fact that he couldn't use the Sommen weapon—one of the only two strategic advantages they had.

"Nang," he said. "Come here." When she did, he handed her the Sommen rifle.

"What am I going to do with this?" she asked.

"Pay attention so I can show you how it works. You're going prevent anybody from getting in here because when the fighting starts, I'll be deep in the system and unable to help. You have to prevent them from getting to me—no matter what."

Maung plugged into the console and edged carefully through Dark Side's network. There was almost no traffic. All the drifters were in holding cells and none of the guards were working so the fibers *felt* empty, as if he strolled on a desert road. But every once in a while a packet flew past. He concluded from leakage that some of these were Chinese weapons, waiting for a new system to activate so they could go on the offensive and carry out whatever mission was assigned to them, but overall Maung was grateful for his fortune; the Sommen rifle had made all the difference when it surprised them. Otherwise the Chinese would have had time to destroy the network. Since Maung and the others overpowered them quickly, Chinese forces only had time to lay a few traps that he now deactivated.

Maung finished and closed all nodes, including the one leading to the classified zone in which he and Than first found the Phobos data. The port to this area looked dark. Its firewall was gone and he calculated from the lack of energy that whatever happened in there was over, and that the lines were probably destroyed from some defensive countermeasures that literally melted the cables or hardware—or both—before the Chinese could get in. Just in case, he coded an alarm to trip if any traffic flowed out, and then moved on.

Maung paused at the node leading to Sunny Side. Cycles and cycles passed as he wrote tiny algorithms and then shot them out, millions per second, bouncing them throughout Dark Side's network where some of them tested for Chinese logic and others ordered nonessential systems to shut down. Eventually, Maung decided he was safe. From afar, Sunny Side looked dead, and the entire Dark Side system was under his control and littered with traps and weapons that should stall any Chinese efforts to regain control, at the very least giving him enough warning to counterattack. He was about to move in for a closer look at Sunny Side when something nudged him.

A code fragment—one that somehow managed to sneak through the firewall from Sunny Side—pinged against his output stream and Maung was analyzing it when another emerged. Then another. Soon he realized that had he not been there to quarantine each one, they would have self-assembled on his side of the wall to form a larger entity, maybe a weapon designed to corrupt their networks or something worse. It was Chinese; the encryption had a whiff of the kind he'd used during the war. Maung watched the quarantined fragments join with each other to form a kind of snake, after which the thing copied itself until every bit of quarantine storage filled with squirming programs eager to grow larger and move out. Maung guessed but couldn't be sure: It was a self-replicating copy of a Chinese super-aware's wetware. It was *him*.

The realization alarmed Maung. Every simulation he'd run had indicated a clear Chinese advantage and there was no call for such a move because of exactly what was happening now: potential detection, quarantine and decryption. The snakes were useless without pass codes and other data that a Dream Warrior could turn against the Chinese, so to insert itself like this was a great risk—so great that Maung concluded he'd missed something. Maybe there was a fragment of data in his storage that seemed insignificant, one he'd missed and which would have shown the true nature of things on Sunny Side or outside Karin; something that had the Chinese terrified. But there was no time to reanalyze everything that had happened since the Charleston Spaceport. Maung needed access to Sunny Side and its planetary coms systems so he could gather new data, information from Earth and Allied monitoring of Chinese activity that he thought might clarify the tactical situation.

He removed one of the "snakes," putting it into its own new

quarantine space where he began probing. Maung dedicated almost every resource to decryption. His semi-aware scanned the first layer and pinged it with a code he scavenged from Chinese warriors at the Sommen site and the snake went rigid. Then a tail segment slid open. It reminded Maung of a puzzle box, where the opening now gave access to a second encryption layer, which he "moved" toward with the care of someone traversing a minefield.

The second stage looked relatively simple compared to the first and he used a combined library of standard codes from the war and new ones from earlier in the day. Within a picosecond of hitting it with his first code, the snake dissolved before Maung's eyes and transformed into a meaningless collection of characters as if it had done the digital equivalent of dousing itself in acid. He mentally sighed; this would take longer than he thought, and Maung selected another to try again.

You are showing signs of organic fatigue and buildup of toxins, his semi-aware warned. *Rest; I can perform the decryption and wake you when it's finished.*

Maung was a child again. He sat in the center of the ring of monks, who chanted in a low tone that reverberated in his ears and made him sleepy. He lay on his back and red clay bricks formed a high dome overhead, and with the candles and incense he wondered, just before falling asleep, if the color red was special for some reason.

When he woke, the young monk was handing him to his mother who asked, "What did you learn?"

"Much," the monk said. "But only part of it is for you. A great suffering is coming and this child is highly intelligent; he must learn science and math so he can leave Myanmar to be part of something greater and carry our people forward. He will be a warrior who fights with dreams. He will have a son, who will be a great danger to all. But his daughter and her children will save the world."

The semi-aware pinged Maung awake, ripping him from his dream. *I've finished. We now have a potentially complete list of codes. I suggest we move to Sunny Side now because we don't know how frequently these codes are changed.*

"You got it wrong," said Maung.

What did I get wrong?

"The memory of what the monk told me and my mother. There was a message about my son and about carrying the Myanmar people."

I don't know where you got this "data," the semi-aware said. But I assure you I recounted all that was transferred to storage. Perhaps your incessant desire for nicotine has corrupted your mind.

Maung penetrated Sunny Side's firewall, where thousands of copies of the semi-aware assaulted him with challenges, asking for pass codes and identifiers, but to them Maung looked like another Chinese program and within less than a second the queries stopped. He passed them a data packet, one that said most of the Dark Side network was fried. The others ingested the data and then moved off to conduct other operations for which they've previously been tasked. Before any of them queried further, Maung shot off toward the coms center.

Its node was firewalled too. Maung's expectations of this being an easy mission dissolved when the self-assembling code he had analyzed on Dark Side turned out to be one without clearance for full access, and he figured that a real copy of the Chinese semi-aware—or at least a truer copy—was running things from somewhere on this side, maybe beyond the coms center firewall. First he'd have to break through. Then there would be a fight like none they'd experienced so far and Maung doubted that he was in shape for that kind of mental battle. Already he'd been operating for hours; despite the rest his semi-aware gave him, his performance had slowed and his body was exhausted. He pulled away from the node and shot back toward Dark Side, squeezing through the firewall after making sure that he hadn't been tagged or followed.

Both eyelids rubbed like sandpaper and his tongue was dry, and when he tried to sit up Maung found his muscles so sore that he could barely move. New blood seeped from between the sutures in his hand.

"You're back," Than said.

"Where are Nang and Nam?"

"They went to get some sleep. We sent a bunch of the new guards out for acclimatization to Dark Side; to train them how to move and watch out for nano-mines. You know. The stuff you had to learn when you got here."

"How are they handling it?" Maung asked.

Than grinned and shook his head. "Like a bunch of seven-year-old kids who want their mommy. Two dead already because they knew better than us Myanmar idiots. And when we showed them the drifters? Terrified."

Than laughed and it made Maung smile. He understood the guards' reactions; when Maung first arrived it seemed crazy to convert human beings into zombies, no matter what they'd done to deserve it.

"I need rack time and to get my sutures checked. I'll be back in a few hours but I've set up a bunch of trip alarms on the network; wake me up if any go off."

Sleep refused to come at first. Maung slid in beside Nang and scooped her into his arms so that she melted into him and then halfway awakened. She grinned. Then Nang slid on top of him and whispered to hold still until she finished. He did, and after Nang took what she wanted, he kissed her neck.

Maung forgot where he was when Than's voice broke over the coms panel and he jumped up, bumping his head on the ceiling of his barracks cubicle. He pounded the panel to shut it off. Maung squeezed as quickly as he could into a pressure suit, grabbed his helmet and coil gun, and then jumped off the ledge, floating headfirst through passages and shouting for people to make way. A few minutes later he reached the control center.

"There you are," Than said, "I thought we'd lost you."

Nam was at the desk and pointed to the flashing signal that hovered within the holo readout. "That's one of your warnings, right?"

Maung nodded. "This is it, Nam; they'll come soon. I'm going to attack Sunny Side systems. Remember: If the Chinese arrive early, do what you can to keep them away from me. Wake up Nang and get her down here to help with defense."

"Got it," said Nam. "Anything else?"

"Get me a cigarette."

Nam laughed and handed Maung his helmet, which he put on in case the area decompressed while he was inside the net. Nam plugged him in. Once Maung dove into the network he saw that his traps and defenses had held off an attack but that the enemy had gained ground where the Dark Side firewall had been destroyed. While his defense codes kept the Chinese super-aware busy, he got to work. This time it was his turn to generate copies of himself but they were copies coated with the shell that he used earlier, the one with all the Chinese passcodes, and when he finished there were thousands, each one producing another thousand until finally he gave the order to attack.

Maung grinned as he slaughtered. His programs ripped through the attackers, shredding their codes and rocketing up the cable toward Sunny Side so quickly that they couldn't organize a defense. Now millions of copies of Maung branched out and scoured the networks to destroy every enemy they found and recover control of the nodes and systems, while Maung himself headed to the coms center. This time he attacked. Not bothering with finesse, Maung threw trillions of packets at the wall in an attempt to brute force his way through, but after several minutes of failure, one of Maung's copies reported back: They'd taken control of the main Sunny Side reactor and backup power supply systems.

The Chinese super-aware's codes exist on network systems that draw power from Karin's reactor, his system said. *We shut down all power transmission then wait. When we restore power, the firewall will be gone. It will also destroy all our copies and codes.*

"We'll reconstruct all that," Maung said. "Do it. Now."

A second later all power to the communications center was cut, and the node went black. Maung waited ten minutes. Then he ordered power restored and as soon as the node flickered to life he assaulted again but it wasn't necessary; he encountered a new firewall—one that was a barely existing screen of default code—and broke through, with millions of copies of himself following. The Chinese super-aware was gone and Maung sighed with relief that the battle had been delayed; he was still exhausted.

We now have control of all of Karin, his semi-aware announced. *I estimate that the main Chinese battle group will attack us within an hour.*

Almost immediately, communications flooded in. Maung staggered under the amount of data and routed it to storage while he scanned messages for anything important, soon focusing on one report from Earth. Once processed, he set up his copies to defend Sunny Side, and returned to the control room.

"That was fast," Nam said when Maung sat up.

"Chinese forces will land here within the hour."

Than whistled. "*Great.*"

"Wait." Maung caught his breath, waving for Than to be quiet. "That's not all. I got a transmission from Earth. Because of the Chinese incursion on Karin, the Allied Nations organized a second fleet—this one for going after Europa. The first fleet is still headed here and has accelerated so they'll arrive tomorrow. China just declared war. Again."

Everyone stared wide-eyed at Maung and for a time he stared back in silence. Finally Nam nodded. "Maybe now our people can redeem themselves, Maung. You can show them we're not all bad."

"So what?" said Than. "Earth is hosed."

"Maybe," Maung said. "But I still don't understand what's happening. All this centers on the Sommen attack site, forgotten American Dream Warriors, and a secret program on Phobos. And I still can't see any connections."

"Maybe there aren't any," Than said.

"There *have* to be. It's all interconnected and without the proper data, I'll never figure it out."

Nang slid through the airlock and removed her helmet before Than told her the latest news; she looked at Maung. "Maybe you can show the Americans that you're not a bad guy anymore; that you're on the right team this time."

"That's what *I* said!" said Nam.

Maung ordered Nam to release the drifters. After that they called a meeting of the guards—everyone, including the Sunny Side ones— and Maung grinned at the sight of Mike's arm in a sling. The medbot had fixed it. But Nam whispered that the humerus still had a day or two of healing and for now he'd have a hard time firing a coil gun. Maung had to stop himself from feeling sorry for the man; he deserved it.

Maung ordered the men to settle in so he could brief them on the situation, and at the end turned from the holo, shocked at the expressions of horror on their faces.

"We can't hold out for a day," Mike said. "The Chinese will be here in a matter of hours—four destroyers and whatever landing forces they carry, not to mention bombardment capabilities. We have to wall off a section of the asteroid—a deep one. Hide out until Fleet arrives."

The other Sunny Side guards nodded, despite grumblings from the Burmese; Maung held his hand up, quieting them all.

"Nam. What do you think?"

Nam smiled and looked at his countrymen. "I think that not only is your plan going to work, Pa, but that we'll kick the Chinese asses off this rock."

"Wait a second." One of the Sunny Side guards stood, trying to be heard over the Myanmar guards' laughter. "Wait! So you guys managed to fight off one drop ship. Great. Those destroyers will carry several drop ships. Each. Do you really think we can win? How?"

Maung nodded and flicked the holo-viewer so it backed up to a data image; he pointed to the columns, one at a time. "These are the numbers of drifters we have; we didn't even have time to use them in the first attack, so the Chinese won't be expecting it. I'm not sure they have any plans to deal with them."

"And we have you—an additional force of 128. This will help. But the most important thing . . ." Maung motioned for Nang, who ducked out into the hallway. When she returned, she carried the Sommen rifle and Maung continued. "We have a secret weapon—a Sommen weapon, against which they have no defense."

"It's just one rifle," Mike said.

"This rifle is a destroyer of worlds," said Nang, "and is so powerful that I dare not fire it here, for risk of melting your suits and causing eye damage."

"Laser?" someone asked.

Maung shook his head; he reminded himself that even his wetware had trouble with the answer. "I think it's plasma."

"Plasma. That's impossible," said Mike. "Where's the reactor? Where's the—" He stopped when Maung glared.

"It shoots plasma. Tiny amounts at the temperature of a blue star, over ten thousand Kelvin. But we still have to have the weapon tested somewhere, and have no idea how it creates the stuff without a reactor. As you say: There's no way to create a reactor so small and even if we did, those temperatures are unattainable. But with this we could destroy even their ships if they get within line of sight."

Some of the Sunny Side guards began to smile and Mike shrugged. "OK," he said. "But you'll have to go over your plan one more time; I want to make sure we know *everything*."

Maung resisted a wave of guilt. He wasn't going to be on the line with his friends and when Nang left the control room to position herself in the ruins with the Burmese, he wanted to grab her and change his mind, to ignore the numbers and probabilities that now chugged through his consciousness because this was just like it was the last time. When he lost his wife. A part of his brain that the Chinese surgeons hadn't excised, a primal chunk of gray matter in the back, now screamed at him that he needed to protect Nang and pull her back from the line because Nam or Than could easily fire the rifle too. But these thoughts dissipated. The wetware fired bursts of logic that made his instinct look silly and Maung winced at the mental upbraiding he'd just given himself. He watched until her figure disappeared into the airlock.

"Maung," Nam said.

"What?"

"We're getting an alarm. The Chinese Fleet is now on radar."

Maung turned back from watching the airlock and focused, leaning back while Nam carefully inserted the cable. When it snapped in, he gritted his teeth.

"Let's do it," Maung said. "Good luck, Nam."

"Don't worry. We won't let them get in. Just promise me."

"What?" asked Maung.

Nam pushed back toward his station, where he and Than controlled the drifters and made sure everyone was in position; they'd take care of communications. But Nam would also be able to electronically "tap" Maung's consciousness in the event that they needed help from him, sending messages from his control station.

"That you'll kill them all."

Maung nodded. Then he closed his eyes and dove in.

He hummed across the cables connecting Karin's sunny and dark sides as data slipped past, packets that to him resembled tiny fireflies vibrating at a frequency that made it difficult for his mind to process and represent as specks of light. He pulsed one with a query. To his surprise, it returned its own query, and Maung disassembled the fragment to find multiple layers of security, all of them stamped with Allied official transmission verification codes. Someone on Earth or from Fleet was trying to hail Karin with a constant stream of data—somehow breaking through any jamming curtain the Chinese threw up. Maung wished he could move faster than the speed of light, urged on by a sense that something was wrong.

In less than a second he arrived in the coms system, where he analyzed the communications architecture then coded madly to tie everything into his wetware at the same time he threw up defenses. A part of Maung's wetware spun up when it appreciated what was happening, and it reminded him of the danger; Maung paused when a mountain of statistics erupted before him to outline the chances, the odds that his defenses would be breached by more than a trillion different attacks. It couldn't force him to stop. But the safety program had never spun up before, and now that it cautioned him against tying into so many disparate systems with different functions and hardware, Maung worried it was right. He paused to run his own set of scenarios and probabilities. When the results showed that a failure to execute his plan would result in almost zero chance of survival, he quieted the safety program and kept going.

He finished and tried to brush away the excitement—the power. Maung *was* Karin. He controlled the antiship missile batteries scattered on all sides of the rock. Karin's tactical semi-aware linked with his, taking much of the load off his wetware, and several blisters of communications domes fed such an enormous and steady stream of electrons through his brain that he had to ignore much of it, casting a net that only picked up messages related to the Chinese and Allied Fleets. It wasn't long before one popped up. Maung churned through and nearly withdrew from Sunny Side when he absorbed what it said, and in the control room his hands clenched into fists; he scanned it a second time to ensure his wetware hadn't made a mistake.

TO NANG VONGCHANH, EYES ONLY
FROM JCS J2 LIAISON

NO TRANSMISSIONS RECEIVED FROM YOU SINCE LAST
CHECK. REPORT ON OP TYGER BURN IMMEDIATELY
END TRANSMISSION

It took a moment for Maung to cycle the data and another for
him to actually believe it, and he fought reality until his semi-aware
forced the concept to sink in: *Nang was an agent of the Allied Fleet.*
She had been assigned to work on him—to follow him and keep
track of what Maung did. And she probably knew who and *what* he
was, the whole time.

Maung ignored the pain. Even in this mode, where his wetware
limited most sensory perceptions to what he experienced in the
cables, he realized it would hurt badly when the full effect of it hit
him on Dark Side, after he unplugged. Maung was about to pulse
Nam with a message about Nang when another arrived. This time it
was different; it didn't filter through the coms system, but instead
pounded Maung's brain with a direct beam that must have been
close.

Hello, Brother.

At the same instant, the Chinese destroyers attacked; Maung
almost froze at a ping from the Karin tactical-defense semi-aware
feed, which alerted him that it was tracking over three hundred
incoming missiles.

Maung sent a data pulse to Nam, warning him of the incoming
fire. Once it was delivered, he linked with the Karin semi-aware and
scanned for destroyers, his frustration making him want to scream
once he discovered that all of them were outside missile range.
Maung's semi-aware decided on a tactic: use his batteries to act as
point defense for the station and destroy the incoming Chinese
missiles. But Karin was a prison—no longer a military post and
couldn't defend against missile waves forever; his semi-aware made
it clear that the destroyers could stay out of range and continue
attacks like this, softening up their targets, waiting until the Karin
missile batteries were empty. Maung fired. There was no point in
waiting since the analysis was the same no matter how many
different scenarios he tried: The Chinese wouldn't risk landing until
they'd taken out Karin's defenses.

One by one the incoming missiles blinked out. To Maung the process took forever, the seconds feeling like hours as he tracked the progress of each target and each of his defensive missiles on radar, his wetware simultaneously plotting trajectories to determine the Chinese targeting strategy. To his surprise, most of the incoming missiles were aimed at a single location: Karin's communications domes.

Maung's alarms tripped and before he reacted his wetware alerted him to hundreds of infiltrations; it was *him*. The enemy super-aware probed at each of the vulnerabilities that his safeties had warned against and now Maung had to dedicate every resource—including Karin's tactical semi-aware—to fending off the attacks. It must be bad, he thought. Maung's wetware now generated enough heat that his head burned and the real-world pain distracted him, forcing his thoughts toward hot Yangon days and the smell of thanaka. And then, at the moment he began beating back the attacks, the Chinese pulsed him with new energy. Maung screamed. The Chinese Dream Warrior's ship must have slipped in on the dark side of Karin, close to the control room where it beamed an attack directly, through the rock, and his defenses crumbled. Maung retreated from Sunny Side, unable to keep up with both the missile defense and this new threat.

The safeties activated again and Maung's system warned that the risks were too great but he quickly shut the message down, telling his semi-aware there was no choice; in a few seconds, the Chinese Dream Warrior would own him. He created a kind of capsule, a cage of code that he hoped would hold for at least a few seconds—long enough for the Chinese to find it and long enough for him to shut down all receivers in the station. When it was ready, he injected the creeper, filled the packet with his captured weapon and then shut it tightly, scouring his own systems for any sign of infection. He was clean. Finally, he pulsed the creeper packet, firing it outside his defenses where the Chinese snatched it up.

Maung moved quickly. He coded the Karin semi-aware to begin an entire systems shutdown, anything with even a remote possibility of acting as an electromagnetic receiver, and then retreated back to the control room where he sat up and gasped for air. His head pounded. Only a few seconds passed before he calculated that his attacker still hadn't broken into the cage, so the attack continued on his defenses, the only part of this system he couldn't shut off as long as a beamed threat existed.

"Nam!" he said.

"You're alive! We thought they were killing you, with the way you were screaming, Pa."

Maung couldn't move. His arms and leg muscles locked with spasms and the pain made him grit his teeth so that he had to speak through them. "I need to get somewhere that's EM-shielded. I think the Sommen attack area. You have to carry me there."

"But, Pa," Than said, "what about the Chinese?"

"*Now!*" Maung shouted. "I'm under attack and I can't shut my systems down."

By the time Nam and Than got their helmets on, and then Maung's, his head threatened to split apart.

The deeper they went, the more relief came, little by little. Maung had no idea how the Dream Warrior continued to reach him with coms waves, and guessed that Chinese forces had planted repeaters everywhere but he couldn't risk using the energy to detect them in case it broke his concentration. He told Nam. Maung could barely form words and worried his voice was so hoarse that Nam couldn't understand, but then the old man screamed over the net for the Sunny Side guards to start scanning—to destroy any active transmitters.

"Are you OK, Pa?" Than asked.

Maung couldn't respond. The Chinese had been planning this for weeks, he figured, and just at the moment he repelled one attack method three more popped up, pre-scripted and written, an automatic invasion where each subsequent wave was more intense and in depth than the last; not only did the Chinese not lose their tiny gains, they consolidated them to creep forward through his defenses.

Suddenly it stopped. Maung inhaled and relaxed his jaw, not sure if it was a trick—part of the strategy, to get him to stand down. After a few seconds he relaxed further. Then he examined the packets that stayed in his system, the last signs of his attacker that bounced around in his wetware, waiting to be destroyed.

"We found three transmitters; they're gone now, Pa," Nam said.

Maung's voice was barely audible. "Thanks, Nam."

"What happened?"

"They almost got me. The Chinese launched hundreds of missiles at Karin's external coms blisters and then hit me with a direct attack on my wetware; they pulsed me with a broad spectrum EM attack and I nearly broke."

"That's not good," Than said. "What now, Pa? Now that you're not linked in, are we dead?"

Maung tried to laugh, but then coughed; it took a moment to get his voice back. "No. I trapped a fragment of the creeper when we were down at the Sommen attack site that first time. I managed to put it in a cage and feed it to the Chinese Dream Warrior. Based on the last packets I got from him, it's in the process of eating his mind and I doubt he'll bother us again—at least for a while. If I could handle it, he can handle it too. But with any luck, it will jump from him to the Chinese Fleet."

"You let that into your mind?" Nam asked.

"Yeah. And I found out one more thing; the Chinese encountered it too, when they took all the bodies from the Sommen attack site. The creeper was why they were so nervous about us and so unsure; since we attacked them with the rifle and prevented them from getting any Sommen tech, they assumed that we had figured *everything* out—even how to use the creeper as a weapon."

"Which you did," Than said.

"Barely." Maung checked his chronometer. Less than a minute had passed since the attack stopped but the destroyers were still out there, and if they hadn't been affected by the creeper then there could be another wave of incoming missiles. Maung's cramps had vanished. But now he couldn't move because of the exhaustion and he sagged in Than's arms.

"Get me back to the control room; I think we have incoming missiles."

When they were halfway there, the first missiles hit. To Maung it felt as though the access-way pipes broke free and slammed into his back, cracking against his helmet and causing a cloud of sparks to shower around his head when the heads-up system failed. It happened again a few seconds later. Than dragged them forward as best he could but when the attack continued for what seemed like hours, Maung worried they wouldn't make it. Finally Nang's voice crackled over his headset to announce that the wave was over, and that Karin's missile batteries were gone.

Maung wanted to scream at her for betraying him. Instead he forced himself to focus. "Get me to the control room, Than."

"I'm going as fast as I can."

"It's not fast enough," said Maung. "They're getting desperate."

Nang waited for them in the control room. She launched herself at Maung and wrapped him in her arms, but when he didn't respond she moved away.

"What's wrong?" Nang asked.

Maung slid past her; the pain in his joints made him wince, but a rage increased with every millisecond as his wetware analyzed the data, dug into every conversation he'd ever had with Nang, and it soon overshadowed the muscle pain; Maung had to stop himself from telling her everything. Part of the anger he directed at himself: *How could I have been so blind?*

"Later," he said. Maung tucked into his chair and pulled at the cable. "Right now I have to see if there's something I can do about those destroyers."

Nam grabbed his arm. "Maung, you were almost destroyed. That Chinese Dream Warrior is *still out there.*"

"I know. But without the repeaters, he'll be less powerful."

Maung slammed the connector in. Within a second he linked back to Sunny Side and churned through status reports and radar data, trying to organize everything in a way that made sense. All of the Karin defensive missile batteries were gone. Secondary magazine explosions had caused so much damage that the entire structure— including tunnels and prisoner cells—had depressurized, and the number of dead shocked Maung; every Sunny Side prisoner had died in the attack. He set the observation aside and waited for the radar data to sweep through, expecting another wave of missiles to hit at any moment.

But there was nothing. Only one radar still worked and Maung ran a diagnostic to make sure before using it to sweep a wide arc where the destroyers should be; all four were there. A wave of missiles launched from two of them but instead of heading for Karin, they blinked in a pattern that traced toward their neighboring ships, and Maung had to imagine the particle beams that cut through space and ripped armor panels open, venting the craft and ejecting its occupants into a cold vacuum. His wetware had the answer before he asked for it: *Communications between the two firing ships suggests that the creeper has jumped the link between the enemy Dream Warrior and two Chinese ships, which the creeper now controls. The other two ships are panicking. The Chinese super-aware is dead.*

Eventually the firing stopped. Maung had no way to know if the creeper accomplished its mission to take over all the Chinese systems, but to be safe he shut down Karin's communications so the thing couldn't jump back to them. On radar, the ships continued on their path. All four, two of which looked like they'd broken into pieces, headed toward Karin and within an hour, the two intact ships would impact the asteroid. Without warning, more targets appeared. Before Maung disconnected, the tactical semi-aware identified them as drop ships.

Maung jerked the cable from his head. "The creeper killed at least two destroyers. Less Chinese will be able to attack us. That's the good news."

There was a small group of Myanmar guards in the control room, and they cheered, first hugging each other and then Maung, their happiness crackling over the radio since even Dark Side was starting to depressurize as a result of the Chinese missile impacts. His head still hurt from the last one.

"What's the bad news?" Nam asked.

"Two Chinese ships are on a collision course with Karin. Their combined mass and velocities will do far more damage than their missiles could, and several drop ships have disengaged with one of their ships. They likely contain Chinese troops trying to escape the destroyers, and whether or not they're infected with the creeper is unknown. They'll land here *after* the destroyers hit—to attempt consolidation and take-over."

"We have to get off Karin," Nang said.

Maung's anger at her spilled into his voice. "How? Do you know of any ships that are docked at Karin or if any survived the missile attacks? There is no way to get off here, *Nang*."

"I don't know what's wrong, Maung," she said. Maung heard her voice crack with sadness. "I don't know what I did for you to be mad at me, but I told you a long time ago that there's a ship. A small one. The warden keeps a survey ship in a deep crater so that it's almost impossible to detect unless you're right on top of it. The ship has stealth tech."

"How many can a survey ship hold?" Than asked.

Nang paused before answering. "Only ten."

"This kind of decision," Maung said, "must be easy for you. We escape, leaving all my jungle idiot friends to die."

Nang looked at him, her mouth wide open.

They were free-falling in the prisoners' elevator shaft when the destroyers impacted. All of the guards followed Maung—Dark and Sunny Side—in a long line of environment-suited figures, streaming down in darkness toward Karin's core, and he looked back at the same moment the walls jumped to one side. The rock slapped Maung. He blacked out for a second and the taste of blood filled his mouth from having bitten his tongue. But his suit was intact. Maung didn't recognize that his hearing had gone until the sounds of screaming crackled over his helmet speakers. He looked back again, flicking on infrared. A massive chunk of asteroid had dislodged to block most of the shaft above him, but someone's arm reached through a narrow crack. It groped for something at the same time vapor jetted from a massive gash in the sleeve and someone screamed that they'd been trapped. Maung guessed at least half of the Korean guards were now stuck behind him.

There's nothing you can do, his semi-aware said.

Maung turned off his receiver, not wanting to listen to their screams.

The remaining half of their small band crawled upward. Maung said a prayer of thanks for Than, Nam, and even Nang, and then prayed for those who had gone. He brought up the rear and paused to look back at the same moment his imagination pictured a group of dead guards trying to follow as their suits vented, eventually falling back to disappear in weak gravity. Karin had swallowed their souls, gulping them down its throat. Karin didn't want anyone to escape.

"We have to hurry, Maung," Nang said.

"So you can hand us over to the Allies?" he asked. "So you can finish your spying mission, Tyger Burn?" Maung decided hiding it was a waste of time; a feeling of betrayal had grown strong enough that it eclipsed any other feelings he had for her. He continued the crawl upward, inching toward the Sunny Side shaft exit.

Nang clicked onto a private frequency. "How did you find out about me?"

"*I'm a super-aware!* How did you think you could hide, Nang? You lied. I'd forgotten about the secret ship but now that I review the data, that ship was never for the warden; it's for you, for your operation. I bet nobody else knows about it *except* you. What are your orders? Wait for an opportunity to kill me and then slit my throat?"

"No." She was obviously angry, and her tone saddened Maung. "I wouldn't do that even if it had been ordered, you jungle idiot. Sometimes you don't act like a super-aware, Maung. Do the math. If I'd been sent to kill you, you'd have been dead before you got a chance to activate."

The other guards were waiting. They'd already reached the exit and filled the main tunnel where Maung counted at least fifty, and he said a prayer of thanks that at least this many survived and that no additional Myanmarese had perished. Red lights flashed. Maung knew that the Karin alarms were blaring but the impact had opened the station to space and vacuum.

"So then what?" he asked. "What are your orders?"

"I'm supposed to watch you and report, Maung. That's it. I wasn't even sure you were a super-aware when the mission started."

Maung pushed through the mass of guards as his semi-aware urged him to move—fast. "And to sleep with me."

"That wasn't the plan, *asshole*. I fell in love with you, Maung, and that was *me*—not the plan. But now I'm not sure if I made the right decision."

Maung reeled with confusion. Part of him wanted to hate her out of terror; his semi-aware spit data, warning that the Allies had known his identity and secret for some time. There was a deeper story here and it wasn't consistent with what Maung had always assumed: that the Americans wanted him dead.

This is not the case, his semi-aware said. *I now estimate that there's a seventy-five percent chance they've been trying to capture you for years—not kill you. There's also a significant probability that the Americans did not kill our fellow Dream Warriors at the end of the war. Someone else did.*

Nam cut in. "We have to get to the control room first, Maung. Our Burmese men are fine with waiting here for the Fleet, but first we have to find extra oxygen and a safe place for them to hold out."

"And we don't know where the final Chinese drop ships are landing," Than said. "Or how many they'll face—the ones that can't fit on the ship with us."

Maung nodded. "Are the Sunny Side guards ready to fight too?"

"Most," said Nam. "Some are freaking out, but Nang has already taught one of them how to fire the Sommen rifle. It should help."

Mark your data on who you assess could have killed my wife and the other Dream Warriors, he told his system. *I want it rapidly available any time I need it.*

Agreed.

Maung saw a data port. He pulled his cable out and took a moment to link in, only to find that his helmet port had been crushed; the impact against the shaft wall deformed it so that he couldn't access anything. He tried broadcasting, but there was nothing. The entire Sunny Side was dead except for emergency lighting and making things worse, the impact had broken sections of the tunnels so the group had to squeeze through narrow gaps— some so tiny that Maung widened them by firing the Sommen weapon. Upon firing, he was puzzled again. The rifle gave no sign of having decreased in power, despite all the use it had gotten but there was no time to waste on figuring it out; the group dragged themselves onward through wreckage. Near the command section they encountered the first bodies. A section of the prison had been completely destroyed and prisoners' corpses drifted through the tunnels, contorted in frozen expressions of agony.

What if I stay? he asked his semi-aware. *What if I remain to help with the fight?*

You can escape, Maung. I don't understand.

Maung gripped the rifle so that his knuckles ached. *These are my people. I cannot abandon them to the Chinese, who could have more Dream Warriors.*

At this point, there are no electronics for the Chinese to exploit, Maung, except you. If you stay, you will be the main target. If the Chinese succeed in taking you, then it's highly likely you'd be used to help slaughter your friends.

Maung relaxed a bit once they reached Sunny Side's control room. He handed the rifle to Nam, who handed it to a Burmese guard, and then Maung prayed that everyone could hear his transmission.

"The Chinese have likely already landed. Given their electronic capabilities, they've probably pinpointed our location but we have no idea where they are or how long it will take for them to get here. Use the rifle. Hold out for as long as you can." Maung checked his chronometer. "We can't risk radioing the Fleet since the Chinese are still out there and I can't risk opening ourselves to the creeper. Ten hours. The Fleet will be here in ten hours and all you have to do is defend yourselves until rescued."

An influx of shame prevented Maung from looking up as he finished. "I want to stay but I can't. This is good-bye."

The remaining Myanmar guards saluted him and before he could stop it his semi-aware calculated how many would die in the coming attack, even with the Sommen rifle. Maybe all. His eyes welled with tears and he walked forward, hugging each man.

"I'm sorry, brothers."

One of them nudged Maung gently toward Nam and Than. "Pa-Maung, *go*. If you wait here they might get you and you at least must survive."

Maung sobbed, suddenly overwhelmed by the thought of being responsible for more death, and Nam took his arm, helping him bounce toward the door.

"Show us where to go, Nang," Maung said.

Nam sounded nervous. "You have to radio the Fleet and warn them about the creeper; what if it attacks *them* over radio?"

The four reached the hidden dock and drifted across empty space toward a ship's access hatch, where the Chinese attacks had broken its port locks; otherwise it was intact. Maung marveled at the sleekness of the craft, which even looked fast, a long, slender needle that cut through both space and atmosphere, with a massive engine pod at the rear. A few moments later they were in. Maung and the others strapped into acceleration couches while Nang and Nam powered up the craft.

"I already warned them," Maung finally said. "As soon as the Chinese semi-aware swallowed the packet, I sent a quick, coded, burst transmission toward Fleet and instructed them to shut down all electronics."

"Do you think they did?" Than asked.

Maung let tiredness take over. It was the first time he'd rested in what seemed like weeks and already his eyelids were shutting. "I don't care," he said. "They're Allied scum."

"We still going to Phobos?" Nam asked.

"Yeah. Mars. We've got to figure out what's going on—with the Sommen and Chinese; I'm convinced they're connected. I'm glad you came with me because I can't do this alone."

Nam shrugged. "So Phobos is where you'll find answers."

"Phobos," said Maung. "Avoid the Fleet if you can; make sure to activate every stealth feature this thing has." He was on the verge of falling asleep when he remembered one more thing. "And watch out for Nang, Nam. She's working with the Allies and has been spying on me this whole time. She has to fly this thing, but don't let her make any transmissions."

"How am I supposed to navigate without access to coms?" Nang asked.

"Nam," said Maung, yawning. "Can you and Than fix my data port? It got damaged during the missile strikes." He looked at Nang. "Even if I'm asleep, I've set up several thousand navigation solutions depending on our speed, departure time, and whatever else. We're not letting you talk to your Allied friends, Nang."

"You know . . . we're not the bad guys, Maung. *I'm* not the enemy."

But Maung was already asleep.

BOOK THREE

CHAPTER EIGHTEEN

Maung stared as long as he could at the expanse of red and brown, an infinite plain of volcanic rock and soil that stretched to the horizon, peppered with large and small boulders. Something moved in his periphery. Maung whipped his head to focus but it was too late; they and the Phobos-Mars shuttle—that had just landed them on a pristine concrete pad—now descended under the Martian surface. The Americans had dug their main surface port deeply under the red soil and Maung sighed. *Why did everything have to be underground?*

"Did you see anything out there?" he asked Than. "Anything that moved?"

"I didn't see anything except rock. Why?"

"Never mind."

The weight of gravity descended on Maung, pushing him downward into the cushion so he was glad he sat, but a minute later they stood to exit; he and the others nearly collapsed under the weight of their new bodies. The drugs given to them had maintained their bone density, but not having used their muscles in gravity had taken its toll, and the atrophy was acute, to the point where Nam lowered himself to his hands and knees. They shuffled out of the shuttle and into a receiving area, where a security guard met them, laughing.

Maung noticed how tall and slim the man looked; he wore a gray jumpsuit, a kind of semienvironment rig with a neck ring for locking on a helmet.

"It's OK. You'll get used to gravity again. Eventually."

"I think I'm dying," Than said, then repeated it in English.

"Just be glad this isn't Earth," said the guard. "Acclimatization there is supposed to be worse. A lot worse."

Maung gasped for air, sweating. "I don't think anything could be worse than this."

An alarm sounded. At first Maung froze and Nam and Than dropped to their stomachs, covering their heads in anticipation, but then the guard laughed again and waved them forward.

"Relax. It's just a drill. After what happened on Karin and now that we're at war, we have them all the time."

"What happened on Karin?" Nang asked. "What war?"

"You didn't hear?"

Maung wanted to strangle him for not spitting it out. "No. What?"

"The Chinese nuked it. The rock is still there, partially melted."

"What happened to the prison guards?"

The American lowered his head and sighed. "Nobody made it out. The Chinese landed a few drop ships and unloaded nukes. They waited for the first groups of Allied Marines to land and get close before they set all of them off. The Fleet is fine. But nobody made it off Karin."

Maung dropped to the floor. He couldn't get the guards' faces out of his mind and when Nang put her hand on his shoulder he barely noticed, forgetting for a moment that she had become an enemy; Maung was back on the asteroid, inside Karin.

"Listen," the guard continued, "anyone transferring from zero-g or micro-g assignments, gets a couple of days to acclimate; when you guys are ready to see your quarters and get your assignments, let me know. Take your time. I'm really sorry if you lost people."

Maung sensed wetness on his cheek. He almost laughed when he understood that he was crying and nothing his wetware did could relieve him from the pain of his thoughts—that he killed all those men by not coming up with a better plan.

"Maung," Nang said, quietly so only he could hear it. "I'm sorry I spied on you. Please let me back in. There was *nothing* else you could have done."

More than a few days passed. Maung marveled at the space they were given compared to Karin; all four had their own small room in a suite that met in a common area with a small kitchen and adjoining bathroom and shower, with water conservation timing like Karin's. The similar features made Maung relax a bit. They'd landed someplace safe and almost familiar and so slowly, the showers, sleeping in gravity, and a young American who guided them through hours of exercise each "day" combined to nurse him back. Maung tried to silence memories of Karin. The thoughts were still there, waiting to ambush him, but he distracted himself by marveling at the fact that he'd become so accustomed to living underground—with solid rock on all sides. And he and Nang were talking; it was a start, Maung thought.

One day, someone pounded on their access hatch, startling them all, and a man in an environment suit shoved his way in. He was older than the other Americans on Mars. The man's suit was a faded orange that showed so much wear Maung was surprised it still functioned, and its lower legs and boots were covered with the dark red dust of Mars itself. He cradled a helmet in one hand. The other hand rested on a pistol, the metal of which looked worn, its once blued edges now bright from having been drawn and fired, over and over again.

The man glared. "I don't know how this happened."

"What?" Maung asked.

"You. Four Laotians. On Mars. My posting asked specifically for native born Americans."

"That's me," Nang said. "I'm American."

The man gave her a look that made Maung want to punch him, but this wasn't someone he was used to—not since the war; this, he figured, was someone whose life *was* war and who no longer remembered how to live. His face was muddy red, creased with the wrinkles of having seen too much sun, from having lived outside for decades.

"Someone must have messed up," the man continued. "But I have to assign you somewhere and I may as well give you the most dangerous job. No training required since you all have military backgrounds."

"Who *are* you?" Nam asked.

He ran a hand through short gray hair, and Maung wondered if the man's thick beard, also almost completely gray, was against regulations. "Colonel Gibson. Head of security and someone who spent years in your stinking jungles. Follow me; there's an empty slot in the outposts and you four will work just fine."

"We're *Laotian*," Than pleaded. "Not Burmese; they weren't our jungles." The colonel moved out the hatch and waited for the group to join him in the hallway and Than's voice cracked. "We're not the ones you fought!"

"I wish you were; Burmese are tough sons of bitches who'd be perfect for this assignment. You're going to need new suits for topside duty. And weapons."

"Under there is what you have to be careful of," said Colonel Gibson. "They'll wait for you to screw up." He pointed to the expanse of red dirt, littered with black rocks of all sizes, some of them looking so sharp that Maung made sure not to snag on them for fear of ripping his suit. "There are things underground that will rip your guts out if you're not careful. Do everything I tell you."

The view made Maung queasy. Almost every direction provided an unobstructed line of site to the horizon and a slight breeze whistled in his helmet pickups, an environment that once more reminded him of ghosts and demons so that he silently prayed while they walked. Phobos set on the horizon. Not too far from it, the sun rose, turning the sky a deep blue that faded to red. It was all wrong. His semi-aware had to remind him that the sky colors on Mars were different from earth, but the information failed to settle a feeling that everything had gone surreal.

"I feel sick," Maung said.

Than responded, "Me too."

"Take a damn tab!" the colonel said. "They're right by your mouth on the left side, the pink ones. Anti-nausea. For newcomers. You'll get used to this in a day or two."

The last thing he wanted to do was swallow anything, but Maung forced himself to tongue the pill, letting it dissolve into nothing. A moment later the nausea vanished.

"I didn't expect to feel so sick," he said.

The colonel grunted. "A lot of newcomers get it; Mars is more disorienting than people think, especially if you're accustomed to being underground or on a space station."

"What were you talking about earlier?" Nang asked. "I don't see *anything*. What's in the dirt that we have to watch out for?"

"You *know* they're there," the colonel said. "Waiting for you to mess up, to pull you down; I'll explain it soon, but for now just keep moving. And walk behind me, following the exact path that I take."

"How long you been on Mars?" Maung asked.

"Too long. I've forgotten what green looks like. And now I have to deal with you jungle idiots, as if serving on this hole isn't punishment enough, as if taking antiradiation meds and regular cancer treatments isn't worse than a death sentence, now they give me you."

Maung wanted to scream at the guy, tell him how much he deserved to be here, cooked and forgotten—but he couldn't. Even though his face was invisible behind a reflective gold faceplate, the colonel still looked dangerous. *A hunter.* Maung imagined that the colonel was an adopted child of the planet, a local, whose motions and gestures showed a level of comfort that screamed *I am part of these rocks—just as sharp and ugly.*

"*What the hell!*" Nam yelled, jumping to the side.

The dirt rippled near Maung's feet and he stepped back; without warning the colonel snatched at his suit sleeve, almost yanking him off his feet, shouting for the others to keep up when he jogged toward the sun.

"How far are we going?" Maung asked. Already he was out of breath. The brightening sun darkened his faceplate automatically, to the point where he almost couldn't see.

Than sounded winded too. "And where are we going?"

"Not far," the colonel said. "We're heading for your assigned outpost and we're almost there, but draw your pistols—just in case things get sporty. Apparently they've detected our movements."

"*What* detected our movement?" Maung asked.

But the colonel only laughed.

Maung was almost exhausted when he saw it on the horizon: a small square hut—jet black as if formed from carbon or graphite. At first Maung thought it sat on the Martian surface but as they got closer he soon recognized it was on a perch, that the hut sat on a massive column rising from the red dust and into the sky, so high that Maung hesitated at the idea of climbing it. The colonel told them *this* was their outpost, their new home: a carbon nanotube column bonded to bedrock and atop which rested their post. The early rays of the sun washed the sides of it in light, light that it immediately absorbed and devoured, not reflecting anything.

The colonel stopped about a hundred meters from the column base, and motioned for them to remain still.

"What's wrong?" Maung asked.

"The lift." The man knelt and removed his pack, pulling a series of tubes from it; soon he'd assembled a small grenade launcher, which he used to point at the column's base. "This post has been unmanned for months. But look at the lift entrance."

Maung squinted at a tiny door at the base. It was open, a dark square, slightly blacker than the tower itself.

"It's open but I don't see anything," he said.

"It should be shut. The door doesn't open for anyone except me or personnel assigned to the specific outpost. Get your pistols out and shoot anything that moves."

Maung drew his pistol. He wished for the vacuum of space, which prevented any kind of sounds from traveling, when he heard a kind of loud chattering from the open lift doorway. Something else responded, chattering in the distance behind them. Maung crept forward behind the colonel.

"Why not just use the damn grenade launcher?" he asked. "Something is obviously inside there."

"You stupid? You guys have to live there until I can get rid of you and grenades could damage the power conduits—render the outpost uninhabitable. I'm saving the grenades, in case things get bad out here or behind us. Move, but stay close."

As soon as they got within ten meters of the tower base, a loud warbling rose from inside, almost making Maung open fire, and he watched as the colonel reached for one of three small cylinders on his belt. He flicked a button. The colonel threw the cylinder and it clanked against the far wall of the shaft. Maung instinctively moved back a step when screaming figures fell past the open doorway from somewhere above, inside the carbon tube.

"What the hell are those?" he asked.

"X-75A," said the colonel. "The things you're here to watch, to make sure they don't break the perimeter. This isn't really a prison. Mars is a weapons proving ground, a laboratory, and a factory all in one. They're combat units—genetically engineered for use in a variety of planetary atmospheres."

"This is all wrong," Than said. "They're some kind of monster?"

The colonel laughed. "You don't know the half of it; that's all I can tell you. If you knew *why* we're making them, you'd sit down and let them eat you. But I'll be dead by the time we need these things, so to hell with it. And the scientists worked in a fail-safe for us, so we can handle them until they're deployed for combat missions."

"That thing you threw into the shaft," said Maung.

"Yeah, a UV flare." The colonel moved toward the doorway, motioning for them to follow. "For now they can't survive in sunlight or UV. It burns them. Stay loose though, sometimes one or two of them resist and stick around." He stopped at the doorway and peered in. "They've been digging again; broke in through the door at night and are trying to get down to bedrock. They do a lot of tunneling, so we call them *gophers*."

Maung leaned inside. It took a second for his eyes to adjust to the dim light, but where there should have been a concrete base, it looked as though someone had taken a jackhammer to it, leaving a rough, maw-like hole that descended into darkness. It was so black that it hypnotized him. Maung flinched when the colonel dropped another UV flare, this time into the hole, and from far below they heard loud shrieking, as if from thousands of the creatures. His wetware heated up to process everything. This was another data point, another clue added to the mysteries of the Sommen on Karin and why the drifters wanted to come here.

"What do they eat?" Nang asked. Maung heard the fear in her voice.

"*We* feed them but that won't be one of your jobs. Come on." The colonel reached for the rungs of a ladder affixed to the tube side. "It looks like the elevator is out. I'll have someone come out here for repairs but until then you'll have to take care of yourselves. You'll have plenty of UV flares, though."

Maung followed him upward and within a minute his arms screamed with the effort of lifting himself in gravity and he despaired that it would take forever to get his strength back. He willed himself to keep going. Soon, near-total blackness enveloped them except for the narrow cones of helmet lamps, and he stopped himself from looking down, not wanting any idea of how far away the ground was. When it hit home that they'd be living this high up, he wondered: How far underground did carbon tube go, and how safe *was* this thing?

"This tube," the colonel explained as if reading his mind, "goes hundreds of meters down. A network of smaller tubes filled with UV light surrounds these outposts, to keep the gophers inside their perimeter. The secondary tube network goes down, also all the way to bedrock. There's really no way for them to escape. But every once in a while they test our safeguards and we have to send a construction crew to fill *their* tunnels with reinforced concrete and push them back. This is the first time they've tried getting into an outpost, though. That's not good. It shows that they're getting smart, learning. You're going to have an interesting night; construction won't get here until tomorrow to patch the hole and fix the elevator."

"What are we supposed to do out here?" Maung asked.

"I'll go over everything when we get to the post. But basically you'll be responsible for patrolling the surrounding area, and for making crawl inspections through the perimeter tubes—once a week to keep these things from penetrating and to replace burned-out UV lights. There's an access bunker close by."

Than broke in. "But what if we meet one of those things? Underground?"

"Kill it. And do your best not to die."

CHAPTER NINETEEN

Maung looked out the post's main viewport and over the surface of Mars toward a series of jagged peaks, fascinated by thousands of shades of red. It would be sunset soon. Already the lower parts of the sky turned blue and in the lengthening shadows there was movement. At first Maung thought his eyes played tricks—the result of exhaustion, from hiking such a long distance and then climbing—but soon it was clear that the creatures gathered, waiting for night. They poured out of camouflaged holes. Maung couldn't get a good look, even if he put his helmet on and zoomed in; the things were too far away, and the dim light caused static. But before the sun set, Maung got a better view of the perimeter, a vast area enclosed by electrified fence and UV lightposts, inside of which stood towers like the one they now sat atop. Maung lased the closest one with his range finder.

"How far is it?" Than asked.

"Ten klicks. Far enough. We don't even know if it's manned." Maung smelled smoke and lowered the grenade launcher that the American left with them, looking over to see Than take a drag on a cigarette.

"Real cigarette?" he asked.

"Real. I traded part of my first month's salary with one of those tall guys back at the main facility. This is a weird duty assignment and normal regulations don't apply. Smoking allowed."

Maung stared until Than snorted. "No way, Pa. I'm not sharing. I only have one and this weenie cost me a fortune; get your own."

"Weenie?" Maung tried to inhale as much of the secondary smoke as he could, moving closer to Than, but it did nothing.

"That's what they call cigarettes here. Those funny-looking, tall Americans."

Maung watched as the cigarette slowly disappeared. "I hate you, Than," he said.

Nam broke in and pointed at the elevator airlock. "Sorry to interrupt you girls, but it's getting dark and I don't have confidence in the colonel's fix to our problem. What if we lose power?"

The sun would be gone in minutes. Before he left, the colonel helped the group set up emergency UV lamps to shine down into the broken elevator shaft, to keep the "gophers" from crawling up and into their quarters. Maung flicked them on. The lights were inside the shaft, on the other side of an airlocked entryway, so he couldn't see them but prayed that they worked.

"We'll be OK," he said, at the same time arranging a pile of UV flares, just in case.

"She was crying this morning," Than said.

"Who?"

"Who? *Right*." Than pointed to Nang, who disappeared into one of the small bedrooms off the main living area where he and Than sat, their backs to the viewport. "The only girl for a hundred miles, Pa."

"So?"

"So nothing. I just thought you'd want to know. She's not like the rest of the Allies, Maung. She doesn't hate me and Nam."

Maung stared at her shut door for a few seconds. He sighed and shook his head. "I know. But right now I have to risk linking up with the local network. We came here to figure things out and I have more questions now than I ever did."

When Maung disconnected from the data port, the sound of screaming met him; he jumped up, sore, and drew his pistol. The airlock doors were still shut and everyone was awake, sitting across from the airlock and staring at it with weapons drawn, including Nang.

"What's going on?" he asked.

"They're screaming," said Nam. "We think they're way below us but the metal elevator cables are carrying the noise. The way sound travels on this rock is freaking me out."

Than asked, "What did you find out from your linkup?"

"Nothing. They must have all the high-level classified stuff on an air-gapped system. I say we try and get some sleep; they won't get through and if they do, we're dead anyway. We can go exploring tomorrow."

"Out there?" asked Than.

"Where else?"

"Screw that," he said. "I'd rather deal with drifters and Chinese. Gophers *my ass*." Than glanced at Nam, who looked away, and then back at Maung. "We made a mistake coming here, Pa; this place is not for our people."

It was early when Maung rose. Nang already moved in the common area, and he watched as she made breakfast; her ponytail shone in the little sunlight that filtered through a narrow window in the kitchen, and the smell of coffee wafted toward Maung making him realize that there were so many things he'd missed. Before long he sank so deeply into his thoughts that his family appeared again and Maung almost heard them.

Nang jumped when she noticed him. "I thought you were one of those things."

"I don't hear them anymore," Maung said.

"They stopped screaming about an hour ago."

"Hopefully the Americans will fix the elevator today and we can sleep better tonight."

Nang nodded. She moved past Maung but then stopped with her back to him, and at first she said nothing. Her shoulders slumped. Maung saw that she wanted to talk and he struggled to think of something to say but even with the help of his semi-aware he couldn't see through the confusion—of everything that had happened. She smelled like flowers and Maung wanted to bring her in close, never letting go.

"Everything's really messed up," he said. "Between me and you."

Nang turned and looked at the floor. "I'm sorry I spied on you, Maung. But if you'd read the data I did, you'd understand."

"Tell me."

"I can't. It's all classified and I'd go to jail. But you have to understand something: The Americans aren't your enemy and they didn't kill all the Dream Warriors; they *didn't* murder your wife. You have it wrong."

Maung slid an image of his wife from wetware storage. A Myanmar sunset backlit her as she stood before jagged purple mountains, and her training uniform was the deep Chinese green they'd both been so proud to wear. He wanted to reach for her.

I remember that day, his semi-aware commented.

Stop, Maung thought. *So do I.*

Maung moved into the kitchen and poured a cup of coffee, listening to Nang's footsteps as she returned to her room; when she was gone he threw the coffee away.

Sweat streamed from Maung's forehead. The four of them had been hiking across the red terrain for almost an hour, and the sun crept upward over mountains in the distance. They'd already had to rest twice. It took Maung a while to get used to the way sound barely traveled and the suits had a hard time processing it, sometimes relaying comments through helmet speakers, other times through the radio headset. With such a thin atmosphere, sound couldn't make up its mind. They took a break again, sitting on a wide flat piece of basalt when Nam pointed at a patch of red dirt.

"Look there."

"What?" Nang asked.

"We've been seeing those things' footprints everywhere. Like they swarm the entire surface at night." Nam stood and pointed with his pistol at the dirt. "This section is perfectly flat and clean. No sign of gophers at all."

"Careful," said Maung. "The colonel warned us that they dig traps for the guards. We're supposed to stay on rock when we can."

The patch was about ten feet across and formed a perfect circle. Maung picked up a large rock. He tossed it into the circle's center and they stepped back when the ground cracked open and the rock passed through a one-inch layer of salt, revealing a perfectly cylindrical shaft that descended into darkness. Maung put one hand on his pistol. He shivered at the thought of having to be careful with every step they took, and worried Nam might have been right; maybe coming to Mars had been a mistake.

"Come on," he said. "Let's keep going."

For the next hour they walked in silence. One by one, each of them took a turn at the front of their small column, and Maung tried to pick the best route, heading toward the mountains and what he thought must have been the center of the prison perimeter. Than mentioned more than once that they needed to turn back before midday if they wanted to reach the perch before sunset, but Maung shrugged off the reminder. His wetware had already calculated it. They could keep going for one more hour before he'd turn them, long before midday, in case one of them got injured. Plus, they were still out of shape; Maung didn't want to risk pushing too hard only to have someone sprain or break an ankle.

Fifteen minutes later they reached a low set of hills. Maung moved to the front and led the column up a slope of loose scree, doing his best to stay on sections that consisted more of solid rock than of dirt. At the top of the hill was a notch between two huge boulders. It went strangely quiet. The whisper of wind across his helmet pickups stopped as soon as he passed between the rocks, and when Maung reached the other side, the notch opened into a huge bowl, the sides of which consisted of smooth volcanic glass that glinted black. Maung punched at his faceplate controls to deactivate filters and nearly shouted with the pain of brightness. He snapped them back into place. What looked like smears of blood covered portions of the bowl, and bleached human bones rested along its edges, near the lip.

Nam nudged one near his foot as the others gathered, panting. "Human skull."

"What the hell *is* this place?" Than asked.

Nang whistled. She knelt and ran a gloved hand along the volcanic glass. "Whatever it is, this bowl is slick. Don't step on it; you'll fall straight down. And be careful of the edges, they're razor sharp."

Maung looked down. The bowl narrowed gradually to form a huge funnel, the "hole" of which was about a hundred meters down, and he thought he saw movement. Something vanished when he blinked.

"There have to be gophers down there," he said. He scanned the ridgeline in the distance and then looked downward again. "We should get going back soon. This place will get a lot of shadows and we don't know if they can move in shadow."

Nam clicked in. "Ghosts here too, Pa. You remember that major typhoon once, during the war, that killed so many people that bodies washed up in Yangon for months? Look at all these bones. Lots of men died here, violently, and you know like I do: where men die like that . . . always ghosts."

"We shouldn't even be near this planet," Than said.

Maung's wetware completed its analysis. It reviewed the morphology of the visible bones and body parts, and had drawn data from sensors integral to the Mars station environment suits, and Maung wasn't surprised at the results.

"They're feeding the drifters to these creatures," he said.

Than shook his head. "That's impossible!"

"It's not just possible," Maung said, "it's probable. I can see leftover tubes, and there are tiny holes in all these skulls, in the same places you'd expect for a drifter."

"But how—" Nang said.

Maung cut her off and grabbed at her arm. He pulled Nang at the same time he gestured for the others to follow, leading them back into the notch between the boulders. Nam started to say something over the radio but Maung gestured for him to be quiet. A moment later they rested in the shadows when Maung pointed out toward the bowl and over it, in the direction of the sky. At first there was only a pinpoint of light—a spacecraft. The craft reflected sunlight and made it impossible to identify until it got closer and slowly descended over the bowl, where its engines roared in hover mode. It was a cargo shuttle, Maung realized. Long objects fell from a rear hatch, objects that Maung's wetware identified as corpses, more and more of which cascaded out of the craft to form a stream of dead. The naked corpses reminded Maung of grisly rain, a downpour of flesh and limbs whose open eyes stared as if surprised.

When the craft left, Than asked, "Why? Why feed them drifters and not regular food?"

"I have a guess," Maung responded. "But I need more data. I think there's a food shortage, but it's also possible that this way is cheaper; cheaper for Karin, cheaper for Mars."

"We better go, Pa," said Nam.

They made it back before sunset. This time the tube door was shut, and when Maung punched the access code to open it he saw that fresh concrete had been poured into the hole and chem cured to near total hardness; they stomped on it to make sure. A series of UV lights had also been fixed to the wall, probably, Maung thought, to keep the creatures off it until the material *fully* cured. Above him the elevator hummed. A few moments later it scraped downward, knocking the UV lights off the walls in a shower of sparks and glass, until it squealed to a stop, its door sliding open. Nang shook her head.

"That's great engineering. Someone really thought this one through."

"Typical military work," said Maung. He turned to Than. "Next time we come down, fully inspect that pour job to make sure it's still good. And keep doing it every day until we trust it."

Than holstered his pistol. "Sure. Give the Myanmarese the crap jobs."

When they reached the top, they cycled through the airlock and Maung yanked his helmet off, closing his eyes and letting cool air from a vent blow on his face. His wetware spun up. A moment later it sent him a list of probable scenarios they might face, one of which was that the gophers would eventually deactivate life support.

"We have to go back out there," he said. "Now that we know where to look we can move faster and get there earlier."

"Why?" Nam asked.

"Because I want to go down. I want to see what's at the bottom of that volcanic hole and see if there's anything explaining this place. We can't figure this out via computer, Nam. I tried and there are too many air gaps."

"When do we go?"

Maung thought for a second. "Tomorrow. We should do it tomorrow."

"I'm not going down into that damn hole, Pa," said Than. "You can go by yourself. I want off this freaking rock."

"I'm not asking you to. *I'll* go with plenty of flares to keep them at bay."

"No," said Nang. "Not tomorrow."

"Why?" asked Maung.

"Because I just got a copy of our schedule, courtesy of the colonel;

check the rest of your messages. Tomorrow we have to crawl ten klicks of underground UV conduit networks to change light bulbs."

Maung wanted to protest; Nang must have seen something on his face because before he could say anything she held her hands up. "No. We *have* to follow orders or they'll get suspicious."

"I thought you *wanted* us caught," Nam said.

Nang spun and headed to her room, slamming the door behind her and then shouting through it. "*Screw you. All of you!*"

"Maung," Nam said, rubbing his head. "Don't take this the wrong way, but this is getting too confusing; will you please either get over the fact that she's a spy, or kill her? Than and I would like some peace and quiet."

The next day it took an hour to find the access bunker—a one-meter-square chunk of concrete with a single steel hatch—even with instructions from the colonel; red dirt covered it with an almost perfect camouflage. Maung clipped into a harness. Than and Nam handed him his equipment, which he lowered off a line attached to his belt until it dangled in the darkness of the access shaft. Nobody said anything. A hint of fear nibbled at the edges of Maung's consciousness and he allowed his wetware to kick in, prodding his glands to produce a cocktail of hormones in an effort to prevent fear from growing into full-blown terror. He gave Nang the thumbs up. She pressed a button in a small access box, and a motor embedded in a triangular frame hummed, lowering Maung into the hole.

"I feel like bait," he said.

"You have plenty of flares," said Nang. "Use them if you need to. We also have a separate line so if you need more flares or ammo we can attach them and lower it down."

Maung grunted, watching his slow progress on the suit's heads up, a tiny green dot moving downward. The tunnels mapped out on his faceplate in blue lines that extended in two directions—a grid that resembled a massive fly swatter with millions of tiny squares, and where the lines represented UV shafts like the one into which he descended.

"Whoever designed this system was an ass," he said.

"The good news is that you don't have to go down all the way. Just to a main junction where the controls for robotic maintenance are located."

"Why does he have to go down here at all?" Than asked. "Why can't they do this from a central control room?"

Maung felt cut off, unable to see anything except solid black rock. But he was glad for the conversation; hearing their voices made him feel better and gave him something to distract his thoughts from the realization that he was in their territory now—underground, where those *things* lived.

"It must have something to do with security," he said. "I think these things are so smart and lethal they want humans in the loop— no matter how dangerous it is—to keep a constant watch. Guys in control rooms get lazy." A moment later, a faint glow appeared on the rock near his face. "I must be close to the control panel; start slowing me down."

"Are you monitoring UV on your heads-up?" Nam asked.

Maung's neck hair stood up, chilled by the tone of Nam's voice. "No. Why?"

"The wall-mounted UV strips were active on your way down. They just went out."

Maung flicked his faceplate controls, activating UV, and his heart pounded; everything was dark. He reached for a flare. They were attached to his belt and in the tight space were hard to reach, so he fumbled, cursing quietly inside his helmet. Finally he ripped a flare off. At the same moment he ignited it, something seized his foot and ripped at him, pulling him taught against the safety line until Maung slid the flare down as far as he could. He couldn't see whatever it was that had grabbed him. There wasn't enough room in the vertical tunnel for him to lean over and look down, but the flare must have done the job because he heard the sound of wailing, faint in the thin atmosphere, and the thing let go of his foot.

"What's wrong, Pa?" Nam asked.

"Nothing. Those things are down here and tried getting me but I've got a flare lit." Maung paused to attach the flare to a thin line, which he then looped from his belt, carefully letting it down between his stomach and the rock so that once he'd finished it hung underneath him, preventing anything from approaching from below. "I'm at the control panel now, Nam. Stop and hold me here."

"You need to get out of there," Nang said.

"I can't. If I do, they'll just send us back down here again. Someone has to do this; we may as well get it over with."

"Then *hurry*," said Than.

"Can you link up directly and do it that way?" Nam asked.

"I'd just as soon not, not with those things running around below me. Quiet and let me concentrate."

Maung tapped at the console, which ran off a secondary power line, and finally succeeded in activating it; he went down the checklist on his heads-up. Once it was ready and its main power restored, Maung slammed his fist against the rock at all the caution messages, a kaleidoscope of blinking icons that he had to attend to one at a time before doing anything else. The creatures must have somehow gotten into the primary power conduits, he figured, and Maung brought up a schematic to see where the worst damage was. It took him a minute to trace the lines. But when he did he nearly shouted with the shock of having discovered something and he was about to tell the others over the open radio before reminding himself of the danger. It only took a few minutes to get the robotic repair menu up, and a few more to fill it with repair job instructions, starting with the power conduits.

When he finished he said a silent prayer of thanks. "OK, it's done. Pull me up; we can come back and check the bots' progress tomorrow. I found something else, though."

"What?" Nang asked.

"I'll tell you at the outpost."

"They have a lab and manufacturing complex where they breed these things. It isn't far from here—maybe a day and a half on foot. The maintenance database had a full schematic of power conduits and where they traced."

"So what?" Nang asked. "We can't spend the night out *there*, Maung."

"We don't have to. When the gophers went after the main power line, it triggered an emergency access protocol for repairs; I got to see more than I would have under normal circumstances. Access conduits run from a fusion cluster at the production site and out to all the UV access shafts on the perimeter. Like spokes in a wheel. All we have to do is access one of these conduits and we can crawl to the wheel's center in relative safety."

"Over twenty klicks. Crawling on our hands and knees?"

Than pointed at Maung and wagged his finger. "And what will we find there, Pa? Why do we have to keep risking our lives for this?"

Maung looked at Nam, who looked away; Than wouldn't look at him either. "What?" he asked. "What's going on?"

Nam's voice was almost a whisper. "We're done with this, Pa. We appreciate all you did for us at Karin, but this is too much. We don't want to die on this planet and we're thinking of telling the colonel that we don't belong here; it's time to go home, to Earth, or to prison; I don't care anymore. Those things out there aren't right. Everyone has a point where they can't go on, and Than and I just reached ours; we've been talking about this ever since we left Karin."

"But what about the war?"

"What about it?" Than asked. "We're in just as much danger here as on Earth, Maung. More. And every time you want to go mess around with those underground things I'm not sure if we're coming back."

For a while, nobody spoke. Maung watched Than play with a zipper on his environment suit and he heard the faint chittering of the creatures outside, glad for the moment that Mars' atmosphere carried sound differently; on Earth, the noise would be unbearable. Still, a deep booming came from the tower base where the gophers pounded on the elevator door all night, trying to break through.

"They had it planned," he said.

Than shrugged. "Who had what planned?"

"The gophers. They're smart. They *learned* that technicians come to the control ports and they cut the UV power lines at the same time I went underground. So they had it timed and planned how to execute. They just weren't fast enough."

"That's not going to change our mind," Nam said. "In fact, just the opposite."

Maung shook his head. "You're not getting it. Why? All this time I've thought maybe the Americans weren't as bad as the Chinese. I used to spend all the time I had awake in Charleston trying to figure out how to get my kid American citizenship, to make him part of the one place that was worth living in because they were *nothing* like the

Chinese and there was so much opportunity. The truth? I don't like either country. But it was always clear that the Chinese were evil, the Americans good." Maung paused and then lowered his head in exhaustion. "Now I don't know if that's true."

"Why would you say that?" Nang asked.

"Because they kill prisoners and use them as food. They had a Dream Warrior program, just like the Chinese. And now they're creating monsters and playing god at the same time—just like the Chinese. I want to find out why."

"Not me," Than said. "I'm with Nam. I don't care about your *why*."

Nam nodded. "Sorry, Maung. We're turning ourselves in."

"OK," said Maung. "But can you wait until tomorrow morning? As soon as the sun rises, I'll head out for one of the access conduits, and once I'm gone you two can turn yourselves in. At least that will give me some time."

"*Us*," Nang said. "I'm going with you, Maung. The Americans *aren't* evil and I want to be there when you figure it out. They must be doing all this for a good reason."

Nam looked at both of them, Maung and Nang, shaking his head as if convinced the two were insane.

"OK," he said.

A wind blew as they moved along the same path they used earlier, the one that had brought them to the volcanic glass bowl the first time. Not strong enough to push them, the breeze nevertheless picked up dust to form a red wall that Maung turned to watch as it approached them from behind, heading toward the mountains.

"We've got to get to the bowl fast," he said.

Nang breathed hard enough that it triggered her mic before she answered. "I'm tired, Maung. Why do we have to go back to the bowl? I thought we'd head for the control shaft again."

"The schematics showed the conduit running right through here." Maung plucked a copy of them off his wetware and mentally scanned it for a hundredth time. "The conduit damage came from a spot just below the bowl; we can get to the conduit faster if we risk it."

"I don't know if we can outrun the storm."

Maung stopped and clipped a safety line from his belt to Nang's. "I'll help pull you along. We *have* to make it."

"Why? Can't we just navigate via HUD?"

"No. We'll never be able to see any traps if we try to do it that way, and the dust may block enough UV light to let those things get to us above ground."

Once they reached the notch, Maung slumped against one of the rocks to rest and Nang slid to the ground beside him, still breathing hard in Maung's ears. They had plenty of oxygen. Maung went down the safety checklist again and breathed a sigh of relief when his systems concluded that despite the coming storm, there was still an abundance of UV light, even between the boulders. It was midday. Somewhere overhead was the sun but Maung soon gave up trying to find it through a thick blanket of red clouds and dirt that now sent a pattering rain of debris over his helmet.

"How smart do you think these things are?" Nang asked.

"Too smart. Your American friends have gone mad, Nang."

Nang sat up straight and turned her back on him. "These aren't my *friends*, Maung. I had no idea this place even existed, just like you. But there must be a good reason if the Americans went this far."

"Humanity is disappearing, Nang. And the Allies seem to want to help it. You say that the Allies didn't kill my wife and the other Dream Warriors. Fine. Let's pretend that's true."

"It *is* true."

Maung continued. "I would have rather that the Americans and their allies *were* trying to kill me. At least that would give me some hope that they didn't want to be like the Chinese."

"I don't know how to respond to that, Maung."

"Why were you assigned to me?" he asked. "What were you supposed to do and why?"

Nang turned back to him and picked up a small rock, throwing it against the boulder opposite them.

"To monitor. If I saw evidence that you were a Dream Warrior I was to report it via secure coms. I can't tell you why, Maung. I don't know why."

"Did you report me?"

Nang's voice was barely audible. "Yes. That's why they sent the first fleet. To take you in."

The storm showed no sign of letting up. Already, an inch of dust had covered the ground and Maung thought he heard the chittering of those things so he lifted his pistol to aim in the direction of the bowl. There was nothing. But the light dimmed when the dust thickened, and Maung checked his heads up before cursing at the UV indicator. He stood, dragging Nang to her feet.

"Aren't we going to wait out the storm?" she asked.

"It's getting worse; in a few minutes there won't be enough UV light reaching the surface to contain them and they'll come out."

Maung moved closer to the bowl and yanked a satchel from his shoulder, dropping it to the ground near the rim. He pulled out a bundle of thin cable. It was getting hard to see and he told Nang to help him wrap the cable around a narrow part of one of the boulders; once it was secure, Maung climbed into a harness. When he was ready, he helped Nang into hers.

"I'm tossing some UV flares down and then going first. Don't waste any time. As soon as I radio, clip in and follow me down."

"I can't see a damn thing."

Maung snapped two flares and dropped them on the ground on either side of her, then tossed two more into the hole. "Those should keep them away—at least until I hit the bottom."

His harness servos whined, controlling his descent. Soon the bowl walls steepened. Maung's form reflected off the volcanic glass, even in the dim light and through the dust, and his wetware told him that this was once a vent where Mars lava flowed from the planet's interior and spilled over its face. The walls went vertical. Now the light was almost gone and Maung snapped one more flare, this one for himself; he lowered it from his belt to dangle less than a meter below his feet.

A moment later his boots crunched on touching down; Maung stood, unclipped, and panted. "Your turn," he radioed. "And hurry."

"Clipping in now. I'm hearing things up here, Maung. I think they're pretty close by."

Maung watched the line flick back and forth with Nang's descent; when red dust filtered down from above, he breathed deeply, willing himself to stay calm and to survey his surroundings.

All your components are optimal, Maung, his system said.

He was at the bottom of a volcanic shaft. Above him the sky formed a circle of dim red and Maung arranged the lit flares around him to make sure that nothing got close; then he amplified his helmet pickups to the greatest extent he could—in the hope he'd hear the things if they approached. Three dark tunnels led out from the vent. The tunnels were small holes at about waist height and already Maung's back and knees ached from just the thought of how much crawling lay ahead of them. His boots crunched again, and Maung finally took the time to examine his footing, looking down and regretting the decision; he stood on a bone pile, so thick it blocked any view of volcanic rock underneath.

A minute later, Nang landed beside him and unclipped. "They're up there. I counted two heading for the line when I was halfway"— before she finished, the line whipped down from above, severed by something that had to have been razor sharp and as hard as steel— "down. Maung, what are you doing? We have to get going, *they're right up there.*"

Maung knelt to get a closer look at some of the bones when he noticed something black and perfectly square. He picked it up between two fingers.

"What is it?" asked Nang.

"Tracking chip." He took several more from the pile, shoving them into a belt pouch. "They embed them in drifters so they can be tracked. They used to anyway, when Karin was still around."

"Those are just chips," said Nang. "I don't know what you're planning but you won't be able to change anything, Maung. They can come up with any story they want. Besides, we don't know why this is all happening. For all we know it *is* legal."

"Yeah, I heard you the first time; the Americans have a good reason."

Nang drew her pistol and made sure it was loaded. "Sure. Why not?"

Maung caught a glimpse of movement at one of the tunnels. He squeezed off a shot. The pistol fired chemically propelled rounds, tungsten penetrators that blazed from the barrel in gouts of orange flame and it had been long enough since he'd fired anything like it that the weapon bucked in his hand, almost breaking free and hurting his wrist. The slug chipped the tunnel wall. Other than that, there was no sign that his shot hit anything.

"They're here. Watching." He wrenched another flare from his belt and held it in one hand, his pistol in the other, while moving toward one of the tunnels, one that seemed to head in the direction of the power conduit. "Come on, Nang. Light a flare and stay close."

She started to move when Nang froze and pointed. "*Maung, stop!*"

He saw it too late. A fiber rope ran from the tunnel and ended in a loop, partially covered with bones and dust, and as soon as Maung stepped into it, the line went taut and yanked on his ankle to rip his foot out from under him so he fell on his back. Maung panicked. He dropped his flare and pistol, and scrambled to find a handhold as the things dragged him through the bones toward darkness.

"*Throw me a flare!*" Maung shouted; he screamed it in Myanmarese, too terrified to think.

Now he couldn't see Nang. The suit's computer switched on his headlamp automatically in the darkness and Maung told himself to stop panicking, the wetware screaming that he needed to reach down and get another flare—he had ten more on his belt—and Maung cursed for forgetting. He finally grabbed one, ripping it off its retainer loop, but before he could light it one of the things shrieked. Its claws wrapped around Maung's lower leg. When the tips penetrated his suit and sank into his flesh, they pierced all the way to the bone and Maung screamed again.

Time slowed and part of his mind noticed that Mars had a smell to it, but it was hard to separate that smell from the stench of rotting corpses since so many humans had been sent here as food. *You shouldn't be able to smell the decomposition,* his system warned. *Your suit is venting.* Maung wondered which would kill him first—these things or a lack of air. He finally raised his head to look. The monster shrieked again staring back at Maung and yet not staring because it had no eyes and resembled a cross between a mole and a human, with hairless white skin that stretched to reveal narrow, triangular, daggerlike teeth when it opened its mouth to bite down on his leg.

"I'm so tired," Maung said. His breathing shallowed and his vision blurred at the same time his mind recognized that a poison had entered his blood, a paralytic that prevented him from doing anything with the flare; he couldn't even drop it.

Fascinating, his system commented. *These creatures' claws excrete a substance similar to tetrodotoxin—a paralytic that doesn't kill, but acts incredibly fast.*

Do something! Maung screamed mentally.

No need. Nang has arrived with a UV flare and the creature fled. Its poison effects should wear off.

Something tugged at Maung's leg; a moment later the air stopped venting and the suit alarms stopped blaring in his ear. Nang leaned over his faceplate. She held a flare up and he saw that Nang was screaming something but Maung couldn't move his lips and even keeping his eyes open tired him. Her face disappeared. From the sensation of pressure on his arm, he guessed that she was accessing his suit systems, trying to figure out what was wrong. Before he passed out, he said a prayer, asking his ancestors to help them.

When Maung woke up he had to tongue a painkiller; his head throbbed but it only took a moment for his wetware to run a systems analysis, letting him know that his injuries had been limited to his lower leg but that the bleeding had stopped and antibodies were taking care of infection. For now, at least. Maung sat up.

"Oh thank God," Nang said. "I thought we'd be here forever. Come on, we have to go, *now.*"

"Where are those things?"

Nang pushed him forward, handing him his pistol and a lit flare. "They're all over—in front and behind. We only have six more flares, Maung. So wherever we're going, you better get us there. *Soon.*"

A kind of wooziness refused to let go. At first Maung moved slowly, because having to crawl while carrying objects in both hands made it difficult to move. The creatures gathered in the distance. They stayed just out of flare range but his helmet lamp reflected off teeth and claws, and Maung shivered at the memory of having one dig into his leg.

The tunnel branched. Maung checked his heads-up and chose one, making sure that Nang kept up; she crawled backward to monitor for anything that might attack from behind.

"It's not much farther," Maung said. "A few hundred meters more."

"If we need flares inside the conduit, we're hosed, Maung."

He nodded, even though she couldn't see it. "I know."

"I'm not kidding."

"I know," he said. "But we won't. The conduit has internal UV lights."

"Which they cut off the last time. Remember?"

Maung began to get frustrated but kept his voice even. "I know, Nang. But it doesn't matter. We're out here and we're not going back; it's too late. So let's not worry about it until we get there."

They reached a sharp bend in the tunnel and Maung nearly collapsed with relief; they'd reached the conduit. The creatures' digging had intersected the metallic tube at exactly the point his wetware had deduced—at a hatch, placed there so that men could dig down from above and gain access in case of emergencies. He brushed dust off it and noted where bots had repaired the damage, welding thick titanium patches over sections of the hatch—corner and edge portions that the gophers had succeeded in bending back and snapping off. It must have taken them forever, Maung thought. Already, he could see new scratch marks.

"They're trying to break into the conduit again," Maung said. "You have to give these things credit for persistence."

"Just open the door, Maung."

"I will; we're lucky it's here."

"What do you mean?" Nang asked.

Maung drew a cord from a pouch and linked his suit computer through an armored port next to the hatch. A moment later it popped open. "We're lucky. I mean, my systems predicted that this is where the things had gained access to the conduit, but there was no guarantee that it was exactly at the access hatch. We might have gotten here only to find that they had dug through the steel wall of the conduit, in which case the bots would have patched the steel and we would have had to dig—for who knows how long—to find the hatch."

Once they were through the hatch, the things made a mad push toward them; Maung fired two rounds, killing one so that it blocked the tunnel. He dropped his flare outside the hatch and slammed it shut, breathing with relief when the servos locked the massive door into place.

"*You asshole!*" Nang screamed. She punched Maung in the stomach so that it almost knocked the wind out of him. "You didn't know for sure? *You could have killed us both!*"

Nang panted. The conduit was large enough that they could stand, stooped over, and Maung wrapped her in his arms. She struggled at first but then relaxed and slumped against him, dragging them both to the floor.

"We're safe now, Nang," he said.

"I thought you were dead. When those things took you I thought it was over. You're such an asshole; don't ever do that to me again."

Maung stumbled. He holstered his pistol so that he could use one hand to grab hold of the steel pipes and racks that filled one side of the conduit, and the flow of power interfered with his heads-up and suit systems. His foot was wet with blood; a red light blinked to alert him that his injury was failing to clot and from the suit repairs that Nang made, he judged the things' claws were huge, leaving gashes about twenty centimeters long that Nang almost wasn't able to seal. His wetware had analyzed the compounds in his blood and alerted him to the fact that there were high concentrations of anticoagulants and bacteria.

"I'm going septic," he said.

They'd been walking for an hour. Nang had his other arm wrapped over her shoulder and she coaxed him forward until they reached a dark section of the tunnel.

Nang leaned him against the pipes. "Stay here. I'll take a look ahead."

"Be careful," Maung said.

Nang snapped a flare before she stepped into the shadows, and tossed it forward, raising her pistol at the same time. Three of them jumped from the darkness. Maung fell to the ground and ripped his pistol out, trying to steady it on the floor at the same time Nang's weapon discharged over and over until it emptied. Two of the things were dead, twitching on the floor. But the third knocked her on her back and bared its teeth so that it could sink them into her neck. Maung fired. He kept firing until the thing's head exploded.

Just before passing out he said, "Those must have been trapped in here when I had the bots repair the hatch. Watch out, Nang. There might be more."

"You can't keep going, Maung."

He was half-awake. Sleepiness clung to him so tightly that Maung couldn't tell if it was a dream, but then his head was on Nang's lap and a light inside his helmet blinked orange, alerting him that he only had an hour of air. "I'm really tired."

"I put a tourniquet on your leg. It's stopped the bleeding for now but if we stay here much longer, I don't know."

"What's that noise?" he asked.

Maung couldn't shake the sensation that the ground vibrated underneath them, and a muffled pounding echoed in the narrow space of the conduit, shaking bits of concrete off the ceiling to land on his faceplate. The sound was all around them. Nang forced him back down onto her lap when he tried to sit up.

"Rest. They're here," she said.

"Who?"

Nang looked away. "Fleet. I tapped into the power lines until my suit computer identified one leading to the main station. I used it to send a message and tell them where we were."

"I'm too beat up to be mad right now," said Maung. "But I will be later."

Maung fell asleep. He dreamed the conduit ceiling collapsed near them letting in clouds of red dirt, and the dust parted to reveal hordes of suited figures that descended on them. Two of the figures lifted him onto a stretcher. He couldn't find Nang then and screamed for her before someone jabbed him with a needle, sliding him back into darkness.

CHAPTER TWENTY

Maung knew as soon as he woke; he was an idiot again. He tried accessing his wetware but something blocked the connection, despite the fact that from its heat he could tell that the system was active. It made no sense. Maung guessed the encounter with the gopher did something to damage his systems, and the thought of being stupid for the rest of his life made him want to scream.

"It's OK," Nang said. She was sitting next to him, and placed a hand on Maung's arm.

"Where are we?"

"With Fleet," she said. "They're trying to save you."

Maung's eyes adjusted to the bright lights; they were in some kind of medical facility but it looked more like a laboratory than a sick bay, where banks of robots and computers sat against one wall in a small forest of technology. He prayed to his ancestors, asking them for protection.

"We're in the production facility, Maung. We made it."

"I dreamed about men. They carried us out of the conduit and into the dust storm."

Nang nodded. Maung recognized they were both out of environment suits and she wore a standard emergency suit; it made her look pretty, with her long hair in a ponytail. He tried to reach out to her when he noticed his arms were strapped to the bed.

"What's going on?" he asked.

"There were men, Maung, men assigned to a capture team that I was supposed to call at the right time. I did. We were going to die in that conduit and I had to do something. I'm sorry."

Maung wasn't angry. He wanted to touch her even more and strained against the restraints. "I'm stupid again, Nang. I can't access my systems. What did they do to me?"

"Wait." Nang tried to smile, but Maung could tell it was strained and that she fought back tears. "This is bigger than I thought, Maung. Admiral Villa is here."

"I don't know who that is."

"Filipino-American. Head of Fleet Operations. Even though he's not on the Joint Chiefs, he's more powerful than any of them. *He doesn't go to space,* Maung, especially not when we're at war with China. And he sure as hell never goes to an outpost like Mars, in the center of a place where things like those creatures are running around. So you must have been more important than I realized."

Maung tried once more to process the information in his wetware; the strain made him break out in sweat. "I can't see the importance, Nang. I don't know what it means."

"It's not just that, Maung. The Old Man is here."

"From Charleston?"

Nang nodded.

"Why would he be here? He's a damn criminal."

She shook her head. "He's not. That's his cover. He's Naval Intelligence, assigned to run operations out of Charleston, and giving him a cover as a black marketeer was the best way to get him plugged in. If both the Old Man and the admiral are here, this is big."

Maung struggled to process it. All he recalled was the slum, the pain of his neighbors, his son who he hadn't seen in forever, and tears welled making it hard to see. "I don't understand how they could trust a guy like the Old Man."

"Maung, America isn't *all* white guys. The Old Man came over to the Allied side early in the war and *he* was the one who helped our forces track down your unit. *He's my boss.*"

"He assigned you to follow me."

Nang nodded again. "Yes."

"Why are you telling me all this? It sounds classified."

"Because." Nang grasped one of his hands and squeezed, so hard that it almost hurt and Maung realized that she was scared of something. "They've given me permission to tell you everything I know. They have some questions for you."

"And then they'll kill me."

"I don't think so, Maung. They've chemically cut your wetware connection, but it's not permanent and I don't know what they have planned, but I don't get the impression that they're here to get rid of you. You have something they want."

Maung lost himself in thought. The air was cool and he wasn't in an environment suit, so that when a breeze hit his bare chest he shivered—both from the cold and from fear. There was no point in trying to figure it out; the little mind he had already ached from his conversation with Nang.

"Well what are they waiting for?" he asked.

"Are you ready?"

Maung nodded. "Let's get this over with." A feeling of terror overwhelmed him with one realization: *This could be the last conversation he had.*

A group filed in. Maung watched what looked like a small army of people, and he tried to categorize them based on uniforms and appearance. There were a few military men and women; they were the most obvious since they wore light combat armor and their boots clomped on ceramic floor tiles, and then there was Old Man Charleston. He wore an environment suit like Nang's, and it looked like there were two people with him—a man and a young white girl in her twenties. Both seemed shady. The girl had tattoos, black intertwined patterns that went all the way up her neck, and the man's eyes reminded Maung of a shark's. Last there was a team of scientists. All of them carried armfuls of tech and their numbers overwhelmed both the military and the Old Man's group; they set up instruments on all sides, getting ready for something.

The Old Man stepped up to the bed. "Hey, Maung. It's been a while."

"I had no idea who you really were. My system never even put it together."

"Yeah." The Old Man laughed and ran a hand through his white hair. "I've had plenty of practice keeping in character. Sometimes I have to remind myself not to get too submerged in the underworld; it's more tempting than you think." His smile disappeared then and he looked away, glancing at Nang. "Listen, Maung. This is more important than either you or Nang realize. First, you have to know, US forces didn't slaughter the Dream Warriors."

"Nang already told me that. Who did?"

"The Chinese. You had a key design flaw they couldn't live with."

Maung looked down. "I activate automatically when probed. I know that already. There's too much data leakage."

"Wrong. You were prototypes and so had test features current Chinese units *don't* have, the most important of which is a complete lack of governor systems. *Freedom.* Today, Chinese units we've monitored have so many rules and limitations hardwired into their systems that they're just souped-up semi-awares. That's why you won all those fights; you're better than they are—more random, more creative, faster. The Chinese had to destroy your kind because they knew that as prototypes you had the freedom to do anything. They couldn't live with the risk that one day you'd turn against your masters."

Maung didn't know what to feel—or believe. Lies and deception had always been the Old Man's currency and his system struggled with the question of who the man really was. What was truth and what was a lie? The memory of his wife and her terror at dying made him furious and sad at the same time, and his hands formed into fists so that the edges of the straps started cutting into them. His anger focused on the Chinese now, the possibility they betrayed his family. If the Old Man was telling the truth, Maung now had another reason to hate them and getting revenge—if he survived this—would need his concentration.

The Old Man kept going. "We've been after you not to kill you, but to learn. When your wife got cut down in the jungle, that was a *Chinese* hunter unit made-up to look American; we were hunting you too, but not to kill you. And you gave us a hell of a chase. We lost you in the jungle and missed it when your family dove into the Charleston slums; it took forever to get a bead on you again. We probably never would have reacquired your trail had it not been for that Sommen warrior at the spaceport."

"You guys keep secrets," said Maung. He still fumed, but focused on the thought that maybe his anger partially resulted from not being able to process data quickly. "Too *many* secrets."

"Ask me anything. Tell me what you want to know, Maung."

"Right. Like *you'll* tell the truth. You're a hundred percent American."

The Old Man smiled and switched to Burmese instead of English. "You won't know unless you try, Pa."

Maung thought. He concentrated and Nang smiled at him, nodding, and his doubts faded when he guessed there was no reason for caution anymore. No matter what happened, he was here, tied up, and soon they'd probe him for information so he may as well try and get some for himself. And there was one thing that had been eating him ever since that day at the Charleston Spaceport.

"Why did the Sommen leave our solar system? What is their connection to all this and why did they leave a warrior in Charleston? Why leave all those bodies on Ganymede? Why attack Karin the way they did and then fail to occupy it? Why not just nuke it? Why—"

The Old Man held up his hand. "One at a time, Maung." He glanced at Admiral Villa, who to Maung looked older than the Old Man; the admiral had no hair and his skin had shriveled with age, but there was no smile on his face and the man peered at him with a kind of hardness. He nodded, giving silent permission.

"OK," the Old Man said. "But you're not going to like this, Maung; none of us do." He turned to Nang. "You can go outside and wait. If you hear what I'm about to say, you'll lose any right to pick your job postings, your career, everything. We can't take any chances."

Nang responded without hesitation. "Screw that. I'm not leaving; I want the same thing Maung does. After all this, I *have* to know."

"Nang," the admiral grunted. His voice sounded gravelly and sturdy, one used to giving orders, and even Maung went rigid with attention. "Think about this. I could use you—you're *country* needs you. We are at war. If you hear this, you'll be confined to a useless ancillary assignment to make sure you're not captured . . ."

"Sir, I realize that. I'm asking you with all respect: let me choose?"

At first the admiral said nothing. Then he stepped forward and hugged Nang, who hugged him back. "You were always so stubborn, even when I first met you during your training. The best. Like a daughter to me and my wife." He let go and stepped back, nodding at the Old Man. "Go ahead. She's earned it."

"Thank you, Admiral," Nang whispered.

The Old Man paused to light a pipe. Thick white smoke rose into the air and Maung smiled at the smell of cherry, an odor that was close enough to thanaka that it reminded him of his son and home—and that he wanted a cigarette more than ever.

"The Sommen left because they want to give us time to build up our defenses and military capabilities. They lifted the system-wide quarantine so we can finally gather resources. Right now, Fleet has thousands of deep-space mining operations in play; there are literally a chain of asteroids lined up for exploitation. And we only have a hundred years to get ready."

"Get ready for what?" Maung asked.

"War. In a hundred years the Sommen are coming back. Do you guys remember all those people who left with the Sommen—how you could once walk up to any Sommen ship on Earth and volunteer for their merchant supply service?"

Maung and Nang both nodded.

"Those people were pressed into some kind of slave supply corps; they moved weapons and ammunition from rear areas to the front of whatever war the Sommen had going on at the time, but then one of them returned a while ago—after serving for decades."

"I remember the rumors," said Nang. "Some Ukrainian guy."

The Old Man nodded. "Lev Sandakchiev. But the Sommen dropped him off in Charleston—not Kiev. From what we can tell, Lev was the first human to complete his supply assignment and the Sommen gave him a choice: stay with them and live a cushy life as a member of a kind of merchant class, or go home to Earth. But they didn't tell him it was a test. When Lev chose to go home, apparently it was a huge deal to the Sommen. Few of the alien races they enslave ever choose that path." The Old Man paused to relight his pipe.

"So what?" Nang asked.

"The test is part of their religion," he continued. "Before he came back, the Sommen gave Lev a database containing all the information and data you could want—weapons tech, tactics, strategy, and even their religion and history. We have a team working on the religion part, which turns out to be the most important section of all. The test they gave Lev was part of their search for worthy races; when Lev chose to come home, it was more than a declaration of war. It was a *compliment* to the Sommen, a sign that their prayers were heard and answered—that we, humans, were their equals in courage.

So they'll give us a chance to wage a fair fight. A hundred years is supposed to be enough time to prepare."

"Why the hell didn't Lev just *stay* with them?" Maung asked. Nang was crying and he strained again to free himself. "I mean, now we're going to be annihilated."

"If Lev had stayed, then the Sommen would have destroyed us and taken our resources for themselves, leaving the solar system an empty shell. Those bodies you found on Ganymede? They're the rest of the humans who volunteered for Sommen service, like Lev. Our experts tell us that by beheading them and leaving them like that, for us to find in the territory of our enemy, the Chinese, it was both an offering to their god and a symbol of high respect. No Chinese had volunteered for service—either that or none were accepted. The Sommen hate the Chinese; we think it has to do with how they've gone so far in merging man and machine."

Maung had trouble remembering everything. Nang stopped crying but her expression was one of horror and Maung wanted more than anything to hold her, and it made him glad that she'd come to listen because already the details slowly drained from his memory. He glared at the Old Man.

"Turn my systems on and unstrap me. I can't process all this, it's too much."

"We can't, Maung." He shook his head. "Not yet."

Nang put a hand on Maung's leg. "What was going on at Karin?" she asked. "On Dark Side. What was that facility and why did the Sommen attack it the way they did—instead of just nuking it or something and moving on?"

The Old Man turned to face at the admiral again, and raised his eyebrows.

"Go ahead," the admiral said. Maung was still surprised at the volume and depth of the man's voice. Then the admiral looked at Maung. "You need to pay attention to this, son. This is the part where we make it clear—why we need criminals like you."

The words sickened Maung. He imagined lying on an operating gurney for the rest of his life, wired to semi-awares and bots, probed and prodded in test after test to help the Americans.

"We think," the Old Man said, "Karin is what attracted the Sommen to Earth in the first place. It was a communications station—the first of its kind. We had research programs, started ages and ages ago in an organization that no longer exists, DARPA, for propulsion and communication systems suitable for supporting deep-space missions. Getting communication with anyone beyond the moon was, and still is, a pain in the ass. Then the old DARPA program, now an Allied program, had a break through."

"Dream Warriors," said Nang.

"That's not what we called them, but yeah. Cybernetic systems. It's how we defeated you guys, but we assigned most of our cybernetic units to Karin. The entire station was one big wormhole engine, a massive power plant connected to hundreds of lasers and particle-beam accelerators. I'm not a physicist. But as I understand it, Allied communications researchers became convinced that they could create a tiny wormhole and—more importantly—keep it open long enough to stream a beam of particles that represented zeros and ones. So we did it; we streamed particles."

"Holy . . ." Nang whispered. "How?"

"The amount of energy we consumed to fire lasers and particle beams could've powered Charleston for years, and that was just to open a tiny hole. Then we figured out how to keep it open for picoseconds—just long enough. That's when we stumbled. We had worked out the physics to target specific areas but when we tried it we got nothing; the receiver ships we sent into deep space never got the signal, the particles never showed up."

Maung closed his eyes in frustration. "I can't follow."

"You will later—if we reactivate you—for now just listen, Maung. At first we couldn't figure out what was wrong. Then a bright young physicist named Zhelnikov sent a memo that created a debate that went on for almost a year: He argued that we'd only built half the wormhole; we'd punched into an *alternate* universe, but hadn't finished the connection in space-time to ours. So instead of sending particles to our receiver ships, we'd been sending them to God knows where. That's when Zhelnikov ran some experiments, and a few years later he figured out the power configuration needed to complete the bridge."

"We succeeded," the admiral broke in. "That colossal prick, Zhelnikov, figured out how to 'aim' the holes we created so that a multiship receiver array could pick up the particle beams. Tests between Karin and deep space were all successful. We had developed our first deep-space communications platform and the units like Maung, Dream Warriors, were critical in controlling it. We called it Signum, which is Latin for signal."

The Old Man pulled on his pipe and stared at the floor before speaking. "A year later the Sommen attacked, hitting Karin first. Then they landed a major force at Sommen Lake in Sweden, which is how those pricks got their name in the first place."

"You're no different than the Chinese," Maung said. "Or the Myanmarese. You invented me—people like me."

"*That's a load of crap!*" the admiral barked.

"Wait—why?" Nang asked. "Why would Karin have attracted the Sommen?"

The Old Man nodded. "The Sommen have something in their religion against using machines to augment the body, and interstellar communications conducted the way we did it was especially offensive. Unforgivable. But even worse—to them—was when we accidentally punched into the alternate universe; they picked it up somehow and there's something in these places that even they fear."

"It explains why the Sommen went after *me* when I activated in Charleston," said Maung.

"Now we get to *you*," the Old Man said. His face looked grim. Maung trembled at the thought of what might come next but he couldn't shut his ears and there was no way for him to escape.

"No Allied personnel will ever trust you Maung; we stole Chinese records and know exactly what you did. We know how many people you killed and how many children you scavenged for DNA and organs. Some in our command structure wanted us to execute you as soon as you were captured. But we need you. After the Sommen took Karin, they systematically tracked down every site involved with Signum and killed troops associated with it. We saved a couple of our cybernetic units to use in the war against you, but even they're dead now and aren't of any use to what Zhelnikov needs: a living specimen. All our records were on Karin, in systems the Sommen fried. We've been working for years to figure out how to insert into that section of Karin and exfiltrate any remaining data because we feared if the Sommen detected us, they'd strike. You almost screwed things up for everyone when you broke into the Signum area and activated your system."

"I still don't get it; *why* would working on that kind of program bring a Sommen attack?" Nang asked.

"Because," said the admiral, stepping forward, "their truce terms are clear: We are not permitted to fuse man and machine, and the Chinese have already gotten a warning—that the Sommen are about to wipe them out. If *we* do any cybernetics, they'll strike *us*. So with Maung in that section of Karin, an active Dream Warrior, it could've been interpreted by the Sommen that we're working on Signum again. But we have another idea that follows the damn Sommen rules and Zhelnikov thinks he's the smartest man in the universe— that he's figured out how the Sommen handle interstellar communications. He damn well may have solved the puzzle."

The Old Man nodded. "And that's all we can say. We need your super-aware capability."

"What does that even mean?" Maung asked. "That you *need* me? You'll kill and autopsy me?"

The Old Man laughed. "God, no, Maung. Have you been listening at all?"

"Maung," said Nang, leaning over to look at him. "The Allies didn't kill your wife and friends, Maung. We're not going to kill you now."

Maung cried. It shocked him into hyperawareness. The tears came from nowhere, and streamed off the sides of his temples, their water warm but quickly cooling in the air-conditioned space so they felt like tiny specks of ice, sliding down and dripping onto the gurney. Maung *saw* his son. He was connected over space and time, entering the boy's thoughts and tracing the overwhelming confusion that he faced, alone with only his grandmother. An overwhelming realization that he'd failed his family flooded over Maung, threatening to suffocate him.

As if reading his mind, the Old Man whispered. "We took care of your family, Maung. We have agents on either side of them in the projects. Not the most glamorous assignment. But it's keeping your boy safe. And we shipped your friends, Nam and Than back to Earth; they'll have real jobs waiting for them."

"You want me to become a lab rat," said Maung.

The admiral put his hand on Maung's shoulder. "Not exactly. Mars was a weapons development center and proving ground. These creatures, the ones who've given you all this trouble, are just one project—a genetically engineered force that we can insert and use to infest Sommen systems. They can survive via photosynthesis, or ingestion of millions of different nutrient sources, and can breathe ten different kinds of atmospheres."

"We have a hundred complexes like this all over Mars," the Old Man added. "There's one for communications R and D. You'd be assigned there, Maung, with Nang if she wants it."

"Forever," he said.

"Unfortunately . . . yes. We can't risk this getting out. Almost nobody on Earth has any idea that in a hundred years we could be annihilated. Plus you're still a Burmese soldier, Maung, and worse, a war criminal—you'll never shake that. It's a label you'll carry to your grave."

Nang asked, "What about seeing his son?"

The admiral looked down. "We can't let you go, Maung—not to see your son, not for anything. Even if you refuse to help us, you're stuck here. But if you agree to these terms we guarantee that your son will get the finest life Fleet can give him. We'll move him and your mother to DC, give them both citizenship and a nice home in an upscale neighborhood, and he'll get the best schooling there is. Period. As an American. He may never stand in a jobs line."

"*That's not fair,*" Nang said. "You can't keep him from his child." She glared at the Old Man, who looked down at the floor.

"This is about our *survival,* Nang. Your concerns and Maung's are nothing. I'd kill you both right now if it would give us a better chance, *and I wouldn't lose any sleep.*"

"Nang," said Maung, "they're right. It's OK."

She shook her head; her face went red but Maung couldn't tell if it was from anger, sadness, or both. "They're *not* right, Maung. To take your son from you . . ."

"I've always wanted him to have a chance. You don't get it, you never did. You're American. I'll never forget that I'm Myanmarese and neither will my son, but look at our world, Nang. Where else is there anything bright and shiny? Not in Laos, Cambodia or even the Philippines. *Everyone* wants American. America has existed only for three or four centuries but it's the only place where all things become possible—where you aren't doomed from birth. You can't understand that because you grew up in it. I don't trust Americans and I may never. But my son does. And Nam and Than are safe now."

Maung looked at the admiral. "I'm in. Do what you want."

"*Maung!*" said Nang.

The admiral waved for two guards; they moved in, taking Nang by the shoulders and leading her toward the door.

"Fleet took a pounding a few days ago when they hit Europa and had to regroup here. They're preparing for a Chinese counterattack and we're putting you on the flagship. We have to keep the Mars proving ground safe at all costs."

Nang shouted across the room. "*I'm going too!*"

"Nang!" the Old Man said. "You're staying here. We can't risk having both of you out there, two people who can spill all of our secrets if captured." He paused to empty his pipe in a trash can, shouting before the guards escorted her out the door.

"*And you're pregnant; sending you to space is against regulations.*"

CHAPTER TWENTY-ONE

A team of scientists rolled him through Mars' tunnels, firing questions—"How old are you"; "Where were you born"; "Do you have any allergies"; "What do you remember about the Chinese installation procedures"—and Maung did his best to answer. But he spoke without thinking. The fact that Nang was pregnant and that it must be *his* kid overwhelmed his mind to the point where he wanted to strangle all of them. Maybe the young monk was right; maybe he would have a son *and* a daughter. He strained to find the Old Man, but the straps kept him from sitting up.

"I want to see Nang!" he yelled.

The Old Man's voice came from behind, where Maung couldn't see. "You can't. There's no time. The Chinese Fleet is heading straight for us and we need you on the *Langley*. Right now we can't let you power up but soon, Maung. We'll make sure Nang is safe."

"Do your bowels function normally when semi-aware systems are deactivated?" one of the techs asked.

Before loading him into a shuttle they unstrapped him, but Maung stayed motionless for fear of the soldiers; ten of them levelled weapons at his head.

"Trust is earned, Maung," the Old Man said. "It won't be like this forever; we just can't risk having you attack us right now."

"Three quarters of my mind is dead, Old Man. I can't remember how to tie my shoes. What are you afraid of?"

The Old Man nodded. He waved to a group of techs pushing a

cart stacked with crates. "Get him set. Full environment suit with all the safeguards."

"What safeguards?" Maung asked.

The techs pulled gear from the crates while one undressed Maung and handed him an undersuit. Maung's face went red. All of them took notes and one holo-vidded everything, so that he imagined he was an animal in a zoo. The humiliation made Maung want to reach out and grab the camera so he could smash it over the technician's head.

"We can't afford to have the ship's crew know who you are," the Old Man said. "So the faceplate will be completely frosted. You won't be able to see. But we're sending two assistants who will act as your guards and will make sure you get everything you need. You will have full control of Fleet assets until you die or succeed in turning the Chinese back to Europa."

Maung sneered. "Great but what are these safeguards?" he asked. "If I find out there's something you're not telling me, I'll get very, very angry."

"We have to wire your suit with explosives. In the event that your ship is crippled or destroyed, we can't have you captured, Maung. I'm sorry."

Stunned, Maung searched for something to say. The techs helped him pull on a bulky, lightly armored environment suit, the kind that naval personnel wore, but there was more to it—an oddity that Maung had trouble processing. Strips of thick white material were sewn into the fabric. Maung guessed that the strips contained the explosive, and the thought of being wrapped in it made him cringe.

"I won't *get* captured," he said.

The Old Man snickered. "I know you're more powerful than they are, Maung. But we can't take the chance."

"You haven't seen me fight, Old Man. I doubt there's much you can do to blow this suit once my systems are active. It's the first thing I'll *de*activate."

"We already thought of that." The Old Man lifted the suit's helmet and tossed it to one of the techs. "And if there are any signs of you trying to tamper with the system, it blows automatically. A word of advice: don't screw with it. *And hurry up.*"

Maung panicked. The helmet trapped him and its blank white

faceplate limited his sight to only the heads-up display at the same time it reflected the sound of his breathing, suffocating him with claustrophobia; his inhalations went so ragged that the suit alarm activated, bleeding carbon dioxide to prevent hyperventilation. Two men rested on either side. He heard them strap into acceleration couches after they secured Maung into his. Neither man said anything and the silence pounded in his head to the point where Maung jumped when the shuttle pilot clicked into his speakers to announce the countdown.

Once acceleration violently rammed Maung into his couch, and the engines roared so that he couldn't hear anything except the sound of machinery and fire, he settled down. Soon, he thought. Soon they'd activate him and he could infiltrate all their systems, where he'd at least gain some form of sight—some form of control.

Maung felt sick when the two men helped him out of the shuttle and through what he guessed was an airlock and onto the *Langley*; the sensation of blind weightlessness nauseated him. He did his best not to vomit. Voices surrounded him and Maung's helmet speakers caught the shock in *Langley* crew members who asked what was going on, only to be answered by silence from his escorts. Maung bumped into a bulkhead. One of the men apologized and guided him lower, explaining that they'd arrived at Maung's station and that once he strapped in, the ship's captain would pay them a visit.

"Then we've been authorized to activate your systems," the man finished.

"Anything I should know about the captain?" Maung asked.

The man cleared his throat. "Take it easy when you talk to him; don't say anything to piss him off, because he's probably already going to *be* pissed off since you're taking his ship, sir. Plus, he knows who and *what* you are."

Once the man arrived, Maung went tense. At first there was silence, but then the captain spoke, his voice so soft that Maung had to amplify his helmet pickups to catch the words.

"This is the one?" he asked. Maung assumed that one of his handlers must have nodded because the captain continued. "You're taking my ship from me, son."

"I know," Maung said.

"I can't stop it. This is an order from Fleet. Please don't put any of my men in harm's way unnecessarily; don't get us all killed."

The words stunned Maung; the captain's voice conveyed a concern so genuine that it filled Maung with guilt because he couldn't promise anything; there were no guarantees.

"I'll do my best," he said.

"Good."

Maung felt a prick in his arm—the antidote for the chemicals keeping him from linking with his wetware. In less than a second the connection returned, and Maung broadcast to test for local nets when one of the guards handed him a cable.

"The other end is already linked with the ship's semi-aware cluster," he said.

"As soon as I take over your ship the Chinese will know, Captain."

The other guard laughed. "He's gone, sir. I guess he didn't want to be around when you stole his ship."

Maung reached with one hand for a port at the back of his helmet and when he found it, slipped the connector in, triggering the internal helmet mechanism that slid a thin tube into Maung's neck connection. He *lived* again. Now Maung's awareness expanded beyond his body and he noted that the ship's semi-awares reacted with shock at his presence, that they activated defensive algorithms only to find that Maung had all the proper passcodes. They couldn't *do* anything—except follow. He put them in standby mode so that he could have time to examine and learn, to probe every available system and document the experiences so he'd already be familiar once the battle commenced.

The ship was a massive carrier, within the depths of which were a second fleet of tiny drone missile pods—flying fuel tanks capped with semi-awares and strapped with ten missiles each. Maung linked with each of them to get an idea of their mission planning parameters. He recorded everything. In addition to the fighters, the *Langley* had battery after battery of defensive plasma hardpoints, used to destroy incoming missiles before they detonated close enough to damage the ship. There were some particle-cannon turrets, but not many; the ship wasn't intended to get close enough to enemy craft to use them, and Maung noted that the cannons were slated to be dismantled during the next upgrade. All its weapons were automated. The ship was a virtual city of semi-awares and Maung marveled at the fact that there were any humans onboard since they were really unnecessary and, in some cases, could get in the way.

Maung reviewed the decision-making protocol and scrapped it in less than a second, taking the crew out of the loop and locking out changes. *They are panicking,* his semi-aware warned. Some of the crew tried to hack into the system and Maung dedicated the particle-cannon controllers to fight the intrusion—to keep them out, so he could concentrate on other things.

One of the ship's semi-awares nudged Maung's consciousness, asking for permission to interrupt. As soon as he granted access, the captain's voice rang in Maung's head.

"What the hell are you doing with my ship?"

Maung hated the slowness. The captain's words took seconds to annunciate, time which to him stretched out like years, and he had to vocalize a response that took just as long.

"Getting ready. The Chinese will be in attack range within eight hours. I have to merge with every semi-aware and share my experiences with them so we can come up with something."

"I *need* access," the captain said. "My people need access. You can't cut us out of the loop."

Maung located the orders that the captain had been given. He shot a copy to the terminal the man was using and then highlighted the important parts.

"It's right there, Captain. I'm to be given total control of fleet. I'll need your people to handle repairs and emergencies once the fighting starts and we take damage. Until then, you're of no use."

Silence. The terminal shut off and Maung told the communications semi-awares to broadcast a message to the fleet, instructing them to assemble near Phobos and to have their crews take battle stations. Even this far away, the Chinese could reach him. They had plenty of Dream Warriors, creatures like the one at Karin, who now stroked his communication streams, making stealthy attempts at insertion. These were just probes. Maung examined one stream closely and assessed that the Chinese were just gathering data, not yet interested in taking over any Fleet ships.

His body sensed movement. The *Langley* broke Mars orbit and Maung imagined that it was a blue whale, slowly turning in the water to head deeper out to sea.

By the time they reached the Phobos rally point, Maung had finished studying all the ship's records on Fleet tactics, and its semi-awares ran him through a billion simulations. Now Maung guided them. He fed what he had on the Chinese Dream Warriors into their database and the Fleet semi-awares locked together, joining their collective processing capability to factor the data. The answer was what Maung expected: With so many potential Chinese Dream Warriors, a defense-focused strategy would doom the Fleet. They— even with Maung's help—couldn't fend off multiple Dream Warriors long enough for the ships to engage and destroy their enemy. The Chinese had superior numbers.

Maung was going to have to attack, take over as many enemy systems as he could, and pray he could do it before the Chinese Fleet closed within range to vaporize the *Langley*. A cake walk, Maung told himself.

That is not correct, his semi-aware stated. *Your odds of success are extremely low.*

Maung laughed. He worked the slow process of linking all the fleet communications antennae, forming what eventually would be a massive array, and once it was finished he'd make his first move.

Maung reached out through space, sending infinite tendrils of data in the form of microwaves, a tight beam that he meant to be "bait" as he swept it slowly. Within microseconds he got a pulse. It was gentle. Maung's array picked up a radio frequency that at first looked like that of a pulsar—a narrow beam that hit intermittently— and he ignored it, but as the seconds ticked by the pulsing transformed into a steady scan, tripping the semi-awares' alarms when it tested *Langley* access codes. Maung cursed himself for missing it. He analyzed the data and was amazed to find thousands upon thousands of layers of encryption, eating up precious seconds with each layer he had to crack. It was his second mistake.

Maung was still trying to crack the last layer when one of the Fleet ships, the *Teller,* deviated from its position and set a collision course for the *Langley*. Maung reacted instantly. He activated the particle-beam turrets at the same time he set an evasion course, and the *Teller* barely missed when the *Langley* changed z at the last minute, passing underneath the *Teller* and raking its engine area with beams; the stream of particles was invisible in space. But through the ships' video feeds, Maung tracked gas venting from the rear of the craft, and then secondary explosions when the beams ripped through its fuel compartments. The *Teller* tumbled, heading out into the black of space.

The captain was furious; he pinged Maung from a terminal on the bridge. "You're going to kill us all."

"I can't talk right now," Maung said. "The battle has begun."

"You try that one more time and I'll head to your compartment and rip your heart out—"

Maung disconnected the terminal. But the captain was right. The probe had been a diversion and the real target had been the *Teller*; Maung had been stupid for not seeing such an obvious ploy and promised not to fall for it again, returning his focus to scan the rest of the ships, catching at least a hundred other infiltration attempts that he managed to turn back or blunt. Finally, the Chinese gave up. There was silence in space now, with no radio waves that shouldn't be there and Maung paused to analyze the Chinese data packets he stored during the attack. He was sure: There were between four and six Dream Warriors broadcasting from three different ships—special craft in the center of the Chinese formation.

Maung pinged one of the drone semi-awares and sent it coordinates for an area between the *Langley* and the Chinese fleet. *Can you act as a communications relay?*

It took the drone less than a second to respond, *Yes, but there is a nonzero probability that I will be detected as the Chinese get closer. Also, at that range, there will be no chance for me to return under my own power.*

Maung loaded it with programs and told it to launch. Then he sent out a thousand more drones, each to different coordinates on the Chinese approach route, watching the craft on radar and losing them only after they traveled hundreds of kilometers from the ship. *First phase of the plan is complete,* his semi-aware sent. Maung nodded, reoriented his makeshift coms array, and settled back to wait.

※　　※　　※

Nang is pregnant. Maung could only do so much while waiting and he lost himself in thought, doing his best to still keep part of his attention on his duty while thinking of her. For now she and his child were safe on Mars, and he saw the monk again, his orange robes blowing in a warm afternoon wind. "Your children are going to save us," he said, "while trying to destroy each other."

Each ship was full of people who had no idea what was happening and Maung grew annoyed as some tried to regain control; they reminded him of gnats. The crew buzzed at the edges of his awareness and the ship's semi-awares swatted them back when any got close to breaking in. At a deeper, human level, he sympathized; it must've looked like Maung was leading the fleet into suicide as the Chinese approached headlong in the opposite direction.

Maung perked up. A burst transmission from a section of Mars' defensive network, a series of passive collectors scattered throughout the planet's orbit, cut through his defenses and gave a precise description of the enemy route; before the Chinese could vaporize the collector it provided location, speed and bearing. Maung calmed himself. He let his wetware stimulate the production of more neurotransmitters, sensing his body relax, which was important for what was coming; there was no telling how long the battle would last, only that it could arrive sooner than anyone had anticipated.

Activating the drones, his semi-aware announced.

The activation signal was like turning on a flashlight, visible to the Chinese, and space filled with electromagnetic waves so Maung now had to sift through a fog of energy and a barrage of Chinese assaults. He almost failed to adjust the array. Hundreds of access attempts flooded his fleet's semi-awares and they tugged at Maung, begging for help in fending off the enemy so that he had to dedicate a portion of his mind to countercoding, setting up numerical sandbags to at least slow Chinese infiltration. Finally he moved the array. One by one, he sent the signal to the other drones that immediately acted, running through the scripted programs loaded into their data stores and racked in order of priority.

For minutes there was no change. Then the Chinese emissions shifted frequencies for a fraction of a second, so brief that Maung judged they'd detected incoming attacks and immediately calculated that going after so many drones would slow them too much. Instead the Chinese increased speed; now they'd be within weapons range in less than an hour. Maung analyzed the new changes and his semi-aware concluded that the Chinese planned to rely on numbers rather than novel strategy. Why not? he thought. *There are so few of us, they could lose a good portion of their fleet and still win.* But Maung smiled; he had one last trick for them and had counted on—and hoped for—the Chinese to do exactly as they did: barrel forward, headlong toward the center of the Allied battle group.

Maung's mind counted down. He had three more drones to activate, all at the same location and closest to the Chinese approach, and when the window looked optimal he sent the command. He would get no immediate indication of success or failure. These drones weren't loaded with any of his programs since they had the simplest orders of all, to concentrate all their missiles on the Chinese flagship and then ram its command centers.

The electromagnetic fog changed and in the compartment Maung's face grinned; it was a distress call. Maung gathered unshielded transmissions, the first the Chinese had sent, and relayed them to the crews of all his ships where they were met with cheers. It was a small victory, but to Maung it was a shot of hope; one of the drones had gotten through. It fired all its missiles and heavily damaged the Chinese flagship's engine compartments before slamming into its bridge, crippling the vessel so that it now drifted through space. He scanned for any surviving drones. There was one left, barely within range and Maung breathed deeply in an attempt to prepare for something that was sure to expose himself to Chinese attack. Hopefully he could do it quickly so they wouldn't have time to react. Maung showed the ship's semi-awares his plan; it was the same one he'd used when stationed on the *Singapore Sun*, and the systems churned over the data and numbers.

One of the semi-awares broke in. *We advise against this*, it sent. *There is a recognized Chinese slowness in adapting defenses to new tactics. It's an artifact of their penchant for hard coding on chips. So the defenses on the batteries are likely the same as when you first infiltrated while on your way to Karin.*

So what's the problem? asked Maung.

Multiple Chinese super-awares are monitoring and may expect this move. Your tactic could expose you to them.

Maung ignored the warning. Instead he projected his consciousness in a tight-beam microwave transmission, bouncing off the last drone and scanning the Chinese flagship for any openings in their communications. There had to be one. If the ship broadcast a distress call then it had to unmask at least a portion of its network and Maung soon found the gap, inserting as fast as he could and taking a chance by not setting up any defensive programs; every microsecond counted.

It was the *Nan Yang*, he realized—the ship's name—a massive destroyer that to Maung seemed more like a carrier. Maung streaked through its networks until he reached weapons control and within a few seconds overpowered the Chinese semi-aware. Then he coded. Maung set up multiple programs that grew and strangled the Chinese defenses, branching out until they controlled all the surviving weapons systems, which began firing until their magazines emptied.

Maung backed out. The drone relay he'd counted on disappeared in the path of a Chinese particle beam but by then he'd already vanished, sensing the safety of his Fleet envelop him when his consciousness remerged, and the semi-awares were as close to happy as he'd ever seen; they were glad he made it back.

The *Langley* erupted in more cheers. Maung picked it up over ship's intercoms in every compartment and then the captain himself broke in to give Maung the news. He disconnected from the network. Back in his suit Maung gasped for air when he couldn't see, the helmet frosted so that at first he thought he'd gone blind—until he remembered where he was. The captain clicked into his helmet speakers, practically shouting with joy as Maung fell asleep, exhausted from what he'd just experienced.

"They're turning around!" the captain said. "Whatever you did, one of their ships began firing on its own fleet, destroying and crippling three of their heavy destroyers. The rest of their fleet is heading back to Europa. We've sent salvage vessels now to capture what remains of the ones you destroyed and when we finish, Command wants us to hit Europa again with—"

Maung broke in, barely awake. "Captain, you have to let me go with one of the salvage teams."

"Why?"

"The flagship had two of their Dream Warriors and I need to see them up close for myself. Also, they may still be alive, in which case your crews will be in danger."

The captain paused before answering. "Fine, son; your funeral."

"But first," Maung said, yawning, "I need some sleep."

"It will take time to get the fleet turned and oriented for a boarding trajectory; you have three hours for rack time, but that's all I can give you."

Maung shut the connection and closed his eyes. Without warning, a single realization played in his thoughts and refused to leave.

I'll never see my son again.

CHAPTER TWENTY-TWO

Maung reached out to the guard on his right until he found the man's shoulder; he grabbed it. "Just activate your helmet cam; I can take it over and use it to see."

"There's got to be a better way," he said.

"Sure. Give me a normal helmet with a clear faceplate."

Both guards chuckled. Maung now had vision but seeing from a different perspective confused him and he bumped his helmet on the bulkhead on their way into the main ship. It took a while to work things out. The three of them floated through the *Langley*'s corridor and Maung soon learned that if he stayed directly behind the guard providing him with the camera, latching onto his belt, it was easier to maintain a normal perspective.

They arrived at the main shuttle launch bay, where the captain waited with a team of Marines and engineers. The Marines were at attention. Maung marveled at the way they controlled themselves in zero g until he realized they had special magnetic boots that latched to the floor. All of them wore heavy armor, reminding him of turtles with thick, shell-covered limbs.

The captain clicked in. "Maung. Stay behind on the shuttle when we board. Let my Marines clear the ship of threats and when we're done you can enter."

"But—"

"If we run into a Chinese threat that we can't handle," the captain continued, "we'll call for assistance."

With that they moved into the shuttle. It took Maung a few

minutes to strap in and then a few seconds more to decide that military ships were even uglier than the *Singapore Sun*. The shuttle was all business. The group barely fit in its passenger compartment and Maung looked with concern at two boxlike massive slabs that sandwiched his chair; both had been labeled *Aft Missile Magazine— No Access Without Grounding*. He was glad when the guard looked away, changing his view.

Maung was listening to the Marines' communications after they boarded the Chinese vessel when the Chinese attacked; there were few Marine survivors. The Chinese tried to repulse the boarding party and at first the men considered pulling back to the shuttle; three of them burst through the airlock, where a medic strapped two to a bulkhead so he could crack their suits and begin treatment. Droplets of blood soon filled the shuttle. Maung couldn't stand to see much more and he disconnected from the guard's camera, glad for the first time that he had an excuse not to watch.

Several hours passed before the captain called them over and when he reconnected to the guard's camera, Maung saw that only two Marines were still mobile. Their corpsman was sobbing. Maung wished there was something he could do and helplessness clawed at his chest to the point where one of the guards had to push him into the airlock, reminding Maung that there wasn't much time, before they drifted over and into the Chinese vessel.

Water, oil, blood and a number of other fluids mingled in droplets that floated through the narrow spaces, growing each time one droplet merged with another, and Maung's guard paused every few seconds to wipe his camera lens. If he thought the shuttle was bad, Maung decided, this was a nightmare. Because the Chinese warriors were manufactured—semihuman machines specifically bred for shipboard roles—the corridors weren't meant for human passage and parts of them had been blown open. Maung figured this was what cost the Marines so dearly, since they didn't just have to fight their way through the ship; they had to fight the ship *itself* and widen passageways that prevented them from moving freely in bulky suits. The captain guided them forward over the radio, urging them to hurry since they had a tight schedule.

When they arrived, the captain was waiting outside a massive steel door striped with yellow and black; red Chinese characters marked the upper right portion.

"The bridge," he said.

Maung nodded, making sure they were on a restricted channel before he responded. "I read Chinese, Captain."

"My men have already secured the area but I'm not going in there again. Whatever you're going to do, you need to do it fast. My orders are to space these freakin' things and then see if I can get the ship ready to fly again."

"Fly again?" Maung asked. "Why?"

"Command wants to know if you can control it—use it in the next phase of the battle plan."

"*Whose* battle plan?"

The captain pushed off, heading down the tunnellike corridor and squeezing past Maung; there was barely room for him to pass.

"Just do what you have to. I'm dumping these freakin' things into space in ten minutes."

Maung entered the bridge behind his guard; they moved in single file, squeezing through a narrow set of pipes and conduits with sharp edges that could rip their unarmored suits to shreds, and once through Maung gripped his guard's shoulder even more tightly. The entire section of the bridge that should have been overhead, armored and protecting its crew from the vacuum of space, was gone—ripped off from the explosion that resulted when the drone impacted. Overhead was empty space. Millions of stars filled the void in a view that reminded Maung just how vast and cruel the universe was and Maung wished that the man would focus down at the ship so he didn't have to keep looking at such emptiness. To take his mind off it, Maung performed a quick calculation. Within a second he decided there was no way that, even with a full fuel tank, the drone he sent to ram the Chinese vessel could have caused this much damage and concluded it must have done it with one missile still locked onto a hardpoint.

"What the hell did all this?" his guard asked.

"A drone from the *Langley*. It rammed the ship and still had a missile, which detonated at the moment of impact."

"I don't get it." The other guard pressed in behind them and latched onto a metal pipe—obviously scared of slipping and winding up in space. "Where are the crew members the captain was talking about? I don't see anyone here; they all got sucked out or something."

Maung told his guard to pan his camera around the bridge. He watched the scene creep through his mind and slowed it further as he recorded, so that it slipped by, frame by frame, until he spotted something pale and out of place among the black metal and ceramic of the Chinese wreckage. It was only visible briefly. Water vapor spurt from a burst pipe to create a kind of ice mist that floated off at a constant rate, but it obscured part of the bridge until air in the line created a break. Maung guided the guard toward it. Once they moved past the cloud, he almost threw up.

"That's not right," the guard said. "Are you seeing this?"

Maung nodded. "Yes."

"She can't be more than fifteen. Neither of them. I can't tell if the other one is a boy *or* a girl."

Maung asked him to zoom in for a closer look. When the guard did, he picked up the girl's figure more clearly. Unlike the other Chinese he encountered on Karin, her body was normal and whole from the neck down and dressed in a loose environmental suit. And her face was pale—probably once-flawless skin that had tiny red splotches from rapid decompression. But from the forehead up, she was a nightmare. Her head fused into a bank of cables and wires so that very little of her original gray matter existed, and Maung wondered why they didn't just use semi-awares like the Americans, and forget linking to human tissue. His semi-aware inserted itself, letting Maung know that a human brain injected a randomness difficult to replicate synthetically; *perhaps,* it finished, *the Chinese concluded that this degree of imperfection was critical.*

Next to her, another girl lay strapped into a similar acceleration couch. At least Maung *thought* it was a girl; he couldn't be sure. A section of the ship crushed the Dream Warrior and hid most of her features under frozen blood and steel, so only long hair came from where her head should be, motionless in the empty vacuum.

"We should get going," the guard said.

Maung handed him the end of a cable, pointing to a data port next to the girls. "Plug it in there."

"What for? The bridge is hosed up. Nothing works."

"Just do it. The sooner we try, the sooner I can leave."

Maung plugged the other end into his helmet and waited. By the time the guard finished, Maung had already set up his defenses, ready for anything that might have tried to leap over the connection and into his mind, and he opened the stream. At first there was nothing. Maung projected his way in, the exertion draining him of strength since there was no power to draw from the ship, and he thought he'd have to back out before finding anything useful. Then he found a weak signal. It was like a heartbeat and part of Maung recalled that he'd analyzed something like it before, pulses of packets that rode on such a weak signal that he almost missed them. He ran the data through his system. At first he thought that he'd identified the signal's purpose, but close to the finish his system flashed a warning signal. Maung backed out.

When he unplugged, the guard asked, "Did you find anything?"

"Just a second." Maung sipped on a hose inside his suit, almost draining his entire bladder of nutrient formula even though he hated the taste. His blood sugar was dangerously low; Maung continued swallowing, waiting until the dizziness left and his systems indicated that power levels were returning to normal.

Maung was about to answer the guard when his wetware finished its analysis. "Back to the shuttle!" he shouted.

"What?" the guard asked.

"There are explosives under their couches for self-destruct. They'll go off in less than a minute."

One guard pushed Maung off of the bridge, the other pulling him back into the maze of Chinese corridors. Maung watched the countdown on his heads-up, and when it reached five seconds he told the guards to stop. In the end, he was embarrassed. The explosives barely caused a vibration in the ship's metal, and in the absence of an atmosphere there was little need to move so far away from the bridge because now that he bothered to run the numbers Maung understood what the explosives were intended for.

"Sorry for causing a panic," he said.

The guard behind him clicked in. "What do you mean?"

"It was only meant to liquefy the girls' heads and melt the semi-aware components. Not damage the ship."

"I'd rather we weren't around to see that anyway. I say we get back to the shuttle and let the Marines finish here."

Maung felt alone. The captain gave permission for him to activate a camera on his own suit so that he didn't have to rely on his guards, but he was still forbidden from moving outside his quarters without escort. Left to only his thoughts, he'd go crazy. Maung kept his helmet off as much as possible but the room air soon went stale as they sat, strapped and motionless, with nothing to do while Fleet maintenance struggled with the Chinese flagship. Maung reinserted into the *Langley*'s system, sometimes for companionship with the semi-awares, and sometimes just to pass ideas back and forth about new tactics and to receive news from Earth. The semi-awares refused to give him control. But whoever instructed them never told them to *completely* shut him out of the system after the Chinese attack, and Maung imagined that they liked his company now; he almost thought they had personalities. It was his first time spending so much time with Allied, combat semi-awares, and they kept him occupied with war planning. Maung guessed that the Old Man was allowing it. Whatever the reason, the ship's systems assured him that they valued his input for the coming engagement.

What coming engagement? Maung asked.

We're going to Europa, one said. *Decoded Chinese intercepts indicate their ships will regroup there and make one final attack on Mars. We have no choice; Fleet has ordered Mars to be protected at all costs, even if we are all lost or captured. Additionally, Earth satellites have been monitoring a massive construction project at China's space elevator for years. It could be a new kind of ship. Whatever it is, we assess it is near completion and if we succeed at Europa our orders are to attack the new Chinese ship on Earth before it can launch.*

Another one broke in to finish. *We are to take Europa and Ganymede—expel the Chinese from the outer solar system and then return to Earth. To finish them.*

There was a time, Maung thought, when such a decision would have chilled him and made him think twice—the extermination of an entire race. But now he thought of his wife. A new war had begun and the first battlefield was in his mind. On the one side emerged a part of him he hadn't appreciated even existed, one happy to get rid of China once and for all. The other was the part weary of destruction.

Maung almost couldn't stand the sight of Nang when she sent a holo-message; it hurt to be so far away. Nang looked perfect on the holo, her face bright in the Martian facility's white lighting so Maung thought she was more beautiful than he remembered—more beautiful, maybe, than even his wife. *The Chinese will pay.* Maung's thoughts drifted while he watched Nang speak, and his hearing faded when he focused on the thought of his first wife and her loss, the fact that she died simply because he and the rest of them had become a risk. Maung had to restart the message, forcing himself to pay attention this time.

"We got the Chinese engines running," said the captain, "but she's still in bad shape." He smoked an electric pipe, blowing water vapor into the air. Maung wanted nicotine so badly that the pipe made his skin tingle and he almost asked for a pull—until it was clear from his mannerisms that it was a bad idea; the captain wouldn't get near Maung, floating instead near the entrance, and he barely looked him in the eye.

"How bad?" Maung asked.

"Only one engine works. But it's a large one and we won't be slowed down too much. Plus, if we can use it to get codes and shut down Europa's defenses . . ."

"That'll be useless. They've changed all their codes already, I'm sure."

The captain shrugged. "Well . . . anyway. Get some rack time. We're heading to Europa in twelve hours after our reload of drones arrives. Maung, the admiral wants you to link up with the *Langley* semi-aware systems an hour before that—to decide on a strategy and acclimate yourself with controlling the Chinese ship. It looks like it still has some functional weapons systems. We—"

"Captain," he said, interrupting. "I know how to fly the ship. I don't need you."

Maung worried he'd gone too far but it was too late to take it back. The captain's lips curled in a sneer and he opened his mouth to say something, instead pushing off the bulkhead to close the distance.

"I hope nothing happens to you," he said. "While you're working."

Maung glared back at the man. "This won't be Phobos or Karin or even Mars. This is *Europa*—the key to Jupiter and all the hydrogen we'd ever need, without having to pay the Chinese. It's like nothing you've ever faced. It probably has underground labyrinths stocked with additional ships, Dream Warriors, and all the ammunition they'll ever need; you *know* this. I reviewed the data fed to me by your own semi-awares."

"What's your point?"

Maung closed his eyes, suddenly tired. "That once this starts, you'll probably be dead along with the rest of us. But we have no choice. Because if we don't attack the Chinese, they'll attack us and either way, we die."

Maung's guards shook him awake and he almost couldn't open his eyes; the prior day's battle exhausted him more than he realized and Maung had spent most of the past eleven hours searching his wetware for strategies he hadn't yet tried, modeling them with the number of ships left in his fleet plus the Chinese vessel. None worked. In most cases the Fleet lasted less than an hour against deep, layered Chinese defenses, and only in one did it survive: in the case where the Allies ran away. Maung was about to contact the admiral himself when he got an idea.

He sat up straight and gestured for one of the guards to hand him the cable; it floated near the corner.

"You're linking up already?" he asked. "There's time to eat if you want, Maung."

Maung shook his head, grabbing at the cable when the guard extended it toward him. "No there's not. I have to link with the *Langley* now to see if something else might work. An idea I had. Do you read old science fiction?"

The guard nodded. "I love science fiction."

"Have you ever read a really old book called *The Forever War*?" When the guard nodded, he continued. "Then you're going to love this."

"So there's hope?"

"There's always hope," said Maung, smiling. "Just not certainty. Everything is a matter of chance and probability, except for when it's not."

Maung heard the guards laugh. But the sound disappeared as soon as he slipped the cable into his helmet, linking himself with the *Langley* and shifting his consciousness into the speed of light, bounding through the ship's conduits until he fused with the command semi-awares. As soon as he fed them his idea, they stopped processing. Maung could tell they were intrigued and that they'd judged this was important enough so they put on hold all the other functions they'd been ordered to perform in preparation for the attack; new options automatically had high priority. One by one they came to their own judgments—each of them the same. Maung's calculations were correct. If his plan worked it should deal a serious enough blow that the Allied Fleet could win its fight against the Chinese vessels, *and* avoid the need for ground invasion. *Maybe.*

Maung ordered the semi-awares to look at additional possibilities for using the Allied Fleet, including vessels that should be sacrificed in order to maximize the probability of victory. One of the semi-awares detected that Maung was fading out and asked him, *Where are you going?*

Maung paused. *It's time I got the Chinese ship moving. It's never too early to start.* He pulled out of the command center and rerouted his efforts to the *Langley*'s communications system, linking up with the *Nan Yang.* All of its super-awares were gone. Destroying the ship's autonomous capabilities had been a priority for the Marines so that when Maung navigated its conduits he imagined he traversed empty fibers and nodes, with dark tunnels appearing on both sides whenever he passed through the remains of an important junction. But its guidance system was alive. The captain's techs had finished installing a simple network only twenty-four hours ago, which Maung found active, waiting for him; it was also linked to a temporary network that could allow Maung to activate the ship's remaining weaponry.

It's not a semi-aware, he thought. *But then it doesn't need to be a semi-aware. In fact, what the* Nan Yang *is about to become doesn't require intelligence or awareness whatsoever. Only the laws of physics.*

When he returned to the command center, the other semi-awares flooded him with options and strategies now that they'd decided on a course of action. Maung stacked them for review. He waited for a moment before presenting them with their next challenge—to ignore orders—and the response was what he expected.

The admiral and Command were clear about timetables, one pointed out. *We cannot deviate from those orders.*

Maung knew this was true, and struggled to find a way around a set of specific orders: He couldn't override Allied Command. Maung almost laughed at the fact that figuring out a way around Allied regulations might be more difficult than finding a strategy to defeat the enemy and he churned on the problem for seconds that stretched into minutes before giving up in frustration. Maybe, Maung thought, he should contact the admiral. But to do that would've revealed his plan over radio or microwave, the same as handing his strategy to Chinese intercepts and spies.

Give me access to the original messages from Command, Maung said.

They are sealed with a new set of codes. It will take a moment to access.

That's OK, Maung assured. *Just give me the new codes and I'll handle it. I'll need decryption capabilities when we move out anyway. I'll send you my favorites of the options you gave me and then all of you need to continue refining our strategy because we don't have much time. The* Nan Yang *is moving out now.*

When Allied Command found out what Maung planned, he'd be in trouble. Already the captain pinged him; he was furious that the *Nan Yang* was underway without the rest of the Fleet, not to mention that it was heading in the wrong direction, away from Europa. Maung anticipated they'd soon attempt to override his access to Fleet systems, and so it was not enough to just forge a new set of orders and insert them into the constantly shifting stack of incoming transmissions for decoding and reading. He had to make sure the new orders fit with everything else that was incoming—to give him as much time as possible. It only took a moment to craft them. But Maung spent almost half an hour reviewing every message the ship had received in the last day, making sure that his new creation wouldn't attract too much attention; if it did, someone might contact Command, destroying the entire effort.

Maung ignored his small inner voice, which asked, *What if your plan fails?*

❊   ❊   ❊

At this rate, one of the semi-awares sent, *we shall arrive at Europa one day before the* Nan Yang.

Maung had seen this already, but the fact that others watched the same calculations and helped with decisions made him feel better. *We can't move any slower without increasing our exposure and making them suspicious that there's more to our approach than meets the eye.* He asked, *Can we survive one day against them?* Maung had his own numbers but wanted confirmation.

The odds are against it.

Maung disconnected from the system. He stayed still so the guards didn't notice he'd returned, and so he could have private time to pray and meditate, sending thoughts to his ancestors and asking for their protection. *One day.* They only had to last twenty-four hours Earth time, but in battle that length of time may as well be twenty-four years since there were so many enemy ships arrayed against them. Even if they won, Maung had estimated, most of the Allies would die.

And it would be his fault.

The captain shook him awake. "You're going to slaughter my entire fleet."

"It's not your fleet," Maung said. He rubbed his eyes and checked the time, cursing himself for falling asleep.

"The hell it's not, you little shit."

The captain reached for his fléchette pistol. Maung heard rustling behind him and before the pistol cleared its holster, both his guards screamed past and impacted against the captain simultaneously, one knocking his head against the compartment hatch with a loud crack. The captain went limp. Blood flowed from a huge cut on the man's head and one guard hit the coms panel, yelling for a medic, while the second one snatched a spare undersuit from storage, pressing the fabric against the captain's head in an effort to stop the bleeding.

"Thanks," Maung said.

"The guy was an asshat," one of them said.

The one trying to stop the bleeding asked, "What was this about, Maung? Why is he so pissed?"

"I'm changing the attack timetables. Command gave me the freedom to decide on a strategy but not on the timing for our attack.

I sent the *Nan Yang* on a separate course from ours, and we're moving toward Europa at about quarter speed." When he finished, Maung marveled at how insane it must sound to someone without knowledge of the full plan.

"That's crazy," the guard said.

Maung nodded. "Of course it is. The Chinese will never expect crazy; they'll expect exactly the same tactics and strategy that their semi-awares and Dream Warriors would develop, the ones that make the most sense. So our only hope is in insanity."

The other guard looked shocked. "Had I known *that*, I might have let this guy shoot you."

Maung smiled. The chronograph blinked one minute closer to the start of hostilities and his smile disappeared with the realization that it was almost time. In less than an hour they'd be within range of the remaining Chinese Dream Warriors, and soon after that, long-range missile batteries would fire from Europa. He clamped his helmet on and strapped back into his couch before the medics arrived.

Maung spoke to the guards through his helmet speakers. "Suit up and strap in. Everything is about to start."

Maung's view of the battle was a kaleidoscope pattern of motion, some painted in passive ultraviolet and infrared, but most of it in radar from a sensor ship that he and the semi-awares sacrificed for the task. The ship had no defenses. Maung tweaked its function so the vessel's radar scanned the space ahead at high power, painting anything that had sharp corners, anything made of a hard material. But it also marked the ship itself as a clear target. The rest of the fleet used only passive sensors and Maung sent the sensor ship ahead, burning as fast as it could, so that it provided them with an advance view of the Chinese defenses.

It didn't take long. Maung's alarms tripped at the approach of several Chinese attackers when they overwhelmed the sensor ship's electronic countermeasures; to prevent them from using the ship against him, he touched off one of its own weapons, aiming a missile battery at the sensor ship's fuel-storage area. The explosion blossomed on infrared. Maung wondered if the Allied ship had been there during the previous attack, and part of him hoped that its crew hadn't felt anything when they died in the blast. He and the semi-awares ignored any calculus that assigned value to human life. They only counted victory or defeat. And hundreds of Allied personnel just winked out of existence, a necessary tactical sacrifice.

We are processing the radar data now, unit Maung.

Maung thought the name "unit" was funny. He learned more about the Allied semi-awares every day, and now they couldn't conceive of him as an entity separate from the ship, only that he came and went, as if someone had switched off his power to take him off the network until needed. They had a vague sense of humanity. But to them Maung was different. Maung communed with the command semi-awares and therefore demonstrated a higher order of thought than human crews and *unit* Maung was a compliment.

What does it show? he asked.

One of the semi-awares sent him the data file, which opened in his consciousness, spreading throughout his mind in a field of three dimensions, most of it empty. But he saw tiny dots. The specks formed bright white patterns that Maung had to concentrate on and zoom into, so that they expanded into the outlines of Chinese vessels, some of them huge—even bigger than the *Langley*—while others looked the size of a fighter drone. The semi-awares assembled hundreds of images in sequence. Soon Maung played the radar returns in a kind of movie, showing the larger vessels lumbering movement with respect to each other as the tiny fighters zipped around, practicing maneuvers.

What are the large vessels? Maung asked.

Chinese carriers. We count three. There could be others out of sensor range, however.

Maung struggled to digest the information. Until then, they hadn't seen any sign of enemy carriers, and *three* of such vessels could change the game. Not only did his Fleet only have two, but the enemy carriers were much larger. To Maung, it looked like a cloud of gnats surrounded the vessels, wheeling and turning in tight patterns that indicated high-gees—gees only a semi-aware or a fully-altered human could withstand.

Should we notify the captain? one of them asked.

No, Maung sent. *The captain was injured and needs his rest. We'll continue with the plan. No changes. Three carriers reduces our odds of success but I see no other way forward.*

⚹ ⚹ ⚹

Maung missed the transition—the point at which the Fleet moved from silent anticipation to shouts of horror and missile fire—because he was so entranced by his own efforts to keep systems free from Chinese control. The Allied ships avoided full engagement. Maung and the *Langley*'s semi-awares dedicated some ships to probing attacks to break up the Chinese defensive formations, to draw the enemy out of Europa's gravity well and lead them into drone traps but none took the bait.

At the same time, the main body of the Allied Fleet maneuvered again and again to keep as much distance between its ships and the Chinese carriers, as well as the moon's gravity well. Gravity could ruin Maung's plans. The closer his ships got, the slower they moved and the more fuel they expended and since they were already close to Jupiter now, the rate at which they consumed fuel alarmed Maung; they had to slow down or they wouldn't last until the *Nan Yang* arrived.

A flashing alarm yanked him from his thoughts.

How many? he asked.

Three full squadrons. They took a circuitous route that avoided our main sensors and must be at the limits of their fuel tanks.

Will they get within missile range?

It took a moment for the semi-awares to do their equivalent of huddling before responding, *Yes. We estimate they will have launch capability in thirty minutes. Our scans indicate that these are nuclear tipped, unit Maung. Plasma defenses won't matter. This is because—*

Because they can detonate them outside the range of our plasma cannons, Maung finished. *And the detonation will radiate the hell out of the ships' interiors.*

Affirmative. We estimate thirty percent casualties in the first few hours, with up to ninety percent at the end of seventy-two from acute radiation poisoning.

Maung thought for a minute and got excited. *They don't know I'm controlling the Fleet, do they?*

Why would they know that? one semi-aware asked; it seemed confused. *Our enemy likely surmises that you're handling cyber engagements—since you are—but this is likely the extent of their understanding. Is something wrong?*

Maung didn't answer. He was on the move again, reaching out to the communications center where he broadcast an uncoded emergency message to the Fleet with instructions for each ship to take immediate action. It played out on radar. Miniscule dots appeared alongside the larger dots that represented ships of the Fleet, and the small ones drifted away in a cloud that he hoped wouldn't get drawn into the gravity of nearby moons—or into Jupiter itself. Then the large vessels slowly turned. Maung watched with satisfaction as the entire fleet slowed and pivoted, a maneuver that chewed up twenty of their thirty minutes, and now he mentally urged them to accelerate again, to move toward the enemy drones as quickly as they could. Maung decided against calculating how much fuel the maneuver consumed because he didn't *want* to know; instead he reconnected with the command center.

You provided a shield for them, one of the semi-awares said.

The lifeboats can keep Allied humans alive for at least twenty hours, Maung sent. *But yeah. We'll make sure every missile detonates on us, and this should put them out of range for the worst of the gamma radiation since most will have to pass through us anyway.*

What about you?

Maung chuckled but was confused. *What about me?*

Although your synthetic parts are adequately shielded, aren't you partly organic? Won't this harm that part of you? I can't pretend to understand this design decision, unit Maung. It seems like—

Take over for me, Maung interrupted. *I have to disconnect and do something urgent. Continue with the plan and sound an alarm if you need me to handle a cyber security emergency. I'll be back in twenty minutes.*

Maung unplugged. He ripped his helmet off to find the compartment empty, which was what he expected since he told everyone to abandon ship. But he'd hoped the guards—at least one of them—had stayed. He hated being on the ship alone. Automated voices filled the empty spaces to announce different threats and observations, important words that populated an empty ship with the voices of ghosts and phantoms. Maung said a prayer. Then he unstrapped and kicked away from the couch, heading out the door and into the main ship's corridor, grateful at least to finally be able to move freely.

"*Six minutes to detonation,*" the ship announced.

Maung moved faster. He screamed through passages near the rear of the *Langley*, where his body flew in vast spaces designed to accommodate heavy equipment and machinery, and headed to a computer terminal, tapping at it so frantically that he had to pause and grab onto the wall to keep from spinning away. He found it. Maung memorized the map to the reactor maintenance section and then flew off the wall, not caring that at this speed he could break an arm.

When he reached the maintenance area, less than a minute remained. Maung found what he was looking for and said a silent prayer of thanks to his ancestors—that there was no gravity in space. He lifted several large slabs of lead shielding and leaned them against each other at the same time he squirted adhesive, then placed several more slabs so that a tiny lead box encased him on all six sides. Maung couldn't worry about the tiny gaps that remained; time had run out. Already a semi-aware counted down from ten and Maung shut his eyes, praying out loud after he clamped his helmet on.

When the countdown reached zero there was nothing. At first Maung thought he'd avoided danger but then the temperature inside his makeshift box rose and his semi-aware listed the effects of gamma and x-rays, which interacted with solids to raise their temperature. But it was only a few degrees. At the same instant Maung flinched when loud alarms rang through the ship, announcing elevated radiation levels on all levels and electronics failures. He reached out wirelessly, hoping to link up with the semi-awares, but Maung couldn't find a signal and realized that for the time being he was stuck there—until radiation levels fell.

His plan was in the hands of the semi-awares.

By the time he made it back to his compartment Maung was out of breath from dragging a medical bot. Even though the thing weighed nothing, it was awkward. Several times between sick bay and his couch he had to pause and unsnag its dangling, spiderlike arms from pipes and hatches, and he doubted the thing would work at all—now that it took such a pounding in transit. He shut the hatch and cycled the air. Maung's readings showed there was some radiation still but it wasn't bad, and he released his helmet with a hiss, holding his breath for a moment before exhaling. He forced himself to inhale.

Maung set the bot on the floor and strapped it down so it stood beside his couch, looking down on him. He activated it. The bot sprang to life and expertly unzipped the access ports on the suit so it could make injections and take samples, after which it paused for a few moments before announcing that Maung had radiation poisoning. It injected him with microbots, then announced a ninety percent chance of survival.

When he put his helmet back on to relink with the semi-awares, they seem startled. *We thought you were gone for good,* one sent, and Maung thought to himself, *So did I.*

How is the fight going? he asked.

In the six hours you've been absent, we've lost forty percent of the Fleet and our sister carrier, the LeGuerre, *lost one main engine; she won't be able to keep up with us, unit Maung. Chinese losses are negligible.*

When will the Nan Yang *arrive?*

All of the semi-awares answered at the same time. *One more hour. It's almost to the point where the Chinese would not be able to counter the* Nan Yang's *attack, even if they spotted it.*

Maung hesitated before giving the next order. That he'd made it this far stunned him, making him wonder if any of it was real, like maybe he'd had a bad nightmare; soon he'd wake up next to Nang so he could lean against her stomach and listen for the first sign of their baby. But it *was* real. And with one hour to go, the next phase would have to be carried out soon or the enemy could lose focus on the *Langley,* not caring anymore and returning to a more general defensive posture. Maung couldn't let that happen; if he did, the *Nan Yang* would be spotted.

Pull LeGuerre *out of formation,* he sent. *Move her slowly toward Phobos so it looks like she's retreating.*

What for? one asked.

Just trust me.

Once the *LeGuerre* pulled out of formation, the Chinese made their move and the decision tore Maung's soul in two. He rejoiced when the enemy took the bait, but it would kill thousands of Allied crew members in a crossfire; the *LeGuerre's* move put the Fleet lifeboats between it and the Chinese. He conferred one last time with the semi-awares. A minute later they turned the main Fleet to meet the enemy, launching all their remaining attack drones; the *LeGuerre* then launched her fighters, but they stayed in defensive formation, circling around the mother ship.

Unit Maung, we suggest arranging our cruisers and destroyers in a more efficient pattern, a semi-aware sent.

Maung took a moment to compartmentalize his processes so he could communicate without pausing the offensive. *Why?*

We analyzed their tactical movements; they intend to focus primarily on us, with only a secondary concentration on LeGuerre.

Do it. Maung gave the order before he could think and crunch the numbers; he wanted to move quickly and avoid any possibility that the semi-awares might announce the lifeboats were in danger. Most of all, Maung wanted to avoid reports of how many personnel had died.

We predict that LeGuerre *will succeed in diverting one Chinese carrier group; it improves the* Langley's *chance of survival significantly, unit Maung.*

But Maung couldn't decide if he *wanted* to survive. He noticed the swarm of radar returns that appeared from the enemy carriers, a set of dots that represented an oncoming storm of missiles and fighter drones. The *Langley* had crossed into enemy range. Maung resisted the urge to give orders because the semi-awares had already gamed this scenario a thousand times, and he instead watched with concern as the *Langley* and its surrounding vessels launched their own attacks, sending what to Maung seemed like a countless number of missiles toward the enemy. The Fleet concentrated its fire on one carrier—the one that held the Chinese Dream Warrior.

Maung marveled at the fact that, for now, the battle had been sterile; the two clouds of missiles passed each other, but some blinked out because they hit Chinese fighters who positioned themselves in sacrifice. Others disappeared when Chinese fighters fired their own missiles to intercept. His sensors showed that space had filled with hundreds of silent explosions, the kind that only occurred in a cold vacuum, sending hot sparks that looked like clouds of glitter until metal particles cooled to invisible dust.

Are the incoming missiles nuclear tipped? Maung asked.

Negative. We surmise that once they saw the crews evacuate, the enemy decided kinetic strikes would be more effective. None of them scan positive for nuclear payloads. While you were gone during the nuclear attack, our shielding was largely effective in countering the system-generated electromagnetic pulse. Some repairs were necessary, but nothing major.

Well, thought Maung, *at least that's one thing that worked in our favor.*

Time was still the enemy, he realized. It was also a torture device. He watched the countdown for the incoming missiles and it seemed to slow with each second, giving him time to think and estimate the damage about to occur. And when the second Chinese group got within range to launch its missiles and fighters against *LeGuerre,* it slowed even more. Maung wanted it to end. By the time the missiles struck the *Langley*'s escorts, he smiled because now Maung wouldn't have to anticipate the results and could begin assessing the damage to determine if they'd survive or not. He was so immersed in this thought that he almost missed it.

Messages arrived to alert them of damage to various vessels, and at first it was a trickle. Within moments the trickle became a torrent. Three cruisers split into pieces when their magazines exploded and then touched off the fuel tanks in a series of sympathetic detonations. Maung was amazed that all three fired a last volley; it looked like everything they had. Then his body sent him a dim sensation, one that indicated the *Langley* shook, again and again, with warheads that penetrated the fighter hangars and detonated, ripping broken fighters to shreds and opening the hull to vacuum. All the *Langley*'s compartments depressurized. Maung took a moment to return to his body and make sure his suit was sealed and that he had plenty of oxygen for the second round.

When he returned, the semi-awares gave him the news. Three quarters of the Fleet ships weren't just knocked out; they had disintegrated into small metal chunks, but Maung reminded himself: *It's OK; this is part of the overall plan, and so far it's working.*

How much longer until the Nan Yang? Maung asked.
It will pass the point of Chinese intervention in ten seconds.

Maung judged he was about to make what could be his last decision. Once they followed his order, they couldn't turn back and it was all up to inertia; there was never any chance of them destroying the Chinese Fleet. But if the damage from the *Nan Yang* was as bad—or worse—than their estimates, Maung had also judged there was a good chance the Chinese would flee.

What about their carrier—the one we targeted?

Its engines are gone, the semi-aware sent. *The ship is almost without power and we get no communication indications from it.*

Maung made his decision. *Turn the fleet,* he sent. *Now. Fire everything we have left, all vessels, and order the remaining fighters to fire their missiles and then ram the remaining Chinese carrier. Target all missiles on the final undamaged carrier in this group and we'll deal with the one going after* LeGuerre *later.*

The deceleration ripped into Maung, who knew that his body was being subjected to an incredible force, so strong that when he returned he'd feel the pain and soreness. But slowly the Fleet shifted. His screen lit with thousands of radar returns so that he had to dedicate a significant portion of his wetware to figure it all out, to trace the missiles and fighters, friendly and hostile. A status report arrived from *LeGuerre.* All its engines were offline and its remaining semi-awares survived on one remaining fusion reactor. There were no more fighters. Its attack damaged the incoming Chinese vessels but did not stop them, and almost a quarter of the Fleet's lifeboats were now offline, destroyed by enemy particle cannons when the Chinese had passed through. *So many of Fleet's crews,* he thought, unable to fathom it. *Gone.*

Unit Maung!

Maung snapped to, still in mild shock from figures describing the dead and damaged. *So many are gone,* he sent.

Unit Maung, the enemy fleet has disengaged.

What do you mean, "disengaged"?

The semi-aware sounded like it was about to laugh, barely able to form its next message for being so happy. *They are breaking off their pursuit of us and* LeGuerre, *and all remaining fighters are heading for their carriers. The enemy is not returning to Europa, unit Maung. It looks like the entire fleet is turning for a new heading—toward Earth.*

They've detected the Nan Yang, Maung sent.

Affirmative. Our missiles and drones will likely damage the remaining Chinese carrier so that it will not make it, but we just lost LeGuerre. She is totally destroyed. And we are now out of missiles and drones.

Maung was about to respond when the final volley of Chinese missiles streaked in. He saw it on radar. One by one remaining Fleet ships blinked out and the weapons-control semi-awares went into a frenzy that Maung had never seen, a kind of berserk mode where they were incapable of receiving commands or giving messages as all their processing capacity was taken up by point-defense operations. Some spewed plasma into space. Others fired particle cannons in wild patterns designed to maximize their chance of hitting the last incoming missiles. Maung wanted to hug them. Only three missiles made it through, striking the crew decks and vibrating the ship around him so violently that the semi-awares reported systems failures throughout the vessel.

Maung screamed in pain. His emergency procedures kicked in to force him out of the ships' systems and when he remerged with his body, Maung looked down to see a bloody hole in his suit leg, where his thigh had been shredded by shrapnel and where a long jagged piece of the *Langley*'s hull protruded from his bone; it took a moment for him to realize: He couldn't breathe.

Maung grabbed the medbot's input tablet and tapped. Soon his vision blurred. He was unsure if he entered the right commands before he passed out, but he dreamed that the bot came to life and had a human face, Nang's face, smiling down at him and whispering everything was going to be fine. This was a hallucination, he thought. In a vacuum there was no way to hear a whisper. And Nang was back on Mars, anyway. *Safe.*

CHAPTER TWENTY-THREE

Maung thought he was hallucinating. It looked like he was in a sick bay and both his guards were back, grinning down at him. At first they were blurry and Maung screamed, thinking they were Chinese—that he'd been captured.

"You're not captured," one said.

The other one laughed. "You scream like a girl."

"Where am I?"

"In sick bay. You got a nasty leg wound from one of the missile attacks but a medbot took care of it and sealed your suit. It was almost too late. By the time it injected three series of bone, skin, and blood vessel repair microbots and sealed your suit, you had gone without air for two minutes. It had to resuscitate you twice."

Now Maung remembered. He tried to sit up but they pushed him back down. "The *Nan Yang* and the Chinese fleet," he said.

"The Chinese fleet is gone, minus two carriers you destroyed. And the *Nan Yang* hit Europa hours ago, just before the remaining Fleet ships began collecting us from the lifeboats."

The other guard anticipated Maung's question, speaking before he could even ask. "There are only three ships left, Maung, and they're all heavily damaged. The *Langley* and two destroyers. We lost almost all the Fleet. Half of all personnel are dead because the Chinese made sure they nailed any lifeboat that came within particle-cannon range."

Maung drifted toward the verge of passing out. Their figures blurred again and Maung fought, blinking his eyes rapidly in an effort to shake off the dizziness if only for a few more seconds. There were so many questions. He was active for most of the fight but his injury took him out at the end and circumstances had robbed him of experiences and memories that should have been his.

"What about Europa; how badly did the *Nan Yang* damage it?"

One guard smiled and then let go of the bed, floating slowly away. He motioned for the other one to follow. "We have to go, but you need to see for yourself, Maung. The semi-awares recorded it. There's a tablet under your pillow and it's loaded with vid of the impact."

Maung looked for the handset and slid it out from under the pillow. He turned it on. *You won't see much*, his semi-aware stated and Maung nodded; the ship had been moving fast. They'd sent the *Nan Yang* at constant, maximum acceleration for a slingshot maneuver around Jupiter, boosted so that by the time it reached Europa it was traveling at hundreds of thousands of kilometers per hour relative to Europa's orbit.

At first there was nothing. Then the moon's surface erupted in what looked like a massive explosion of ice and water vapor that sent a visible ripple around the entire surface. To Maung it looked like a tidal wave. The ice rose in massive swaths that left huge cracks behind, cracks which then filled with liquid water that froze almost instantly to heal the wound, until another wave followed behind—this one smaller, but still large enough to crack the surface a second time.

Maung grinned. There was no way the Chinese surface installation—or its occupants—survived. If there was any chance of *that*, their fleet would have never abandoned Jupiter's moons to the Allies, who now owned the system.

The war, he concluded, was going very badly for the Chinese.

Within a few hours, Maung felt like he was going crazy and asked to leave but the head physician refused to let him; the sick bay had filled with injured. Wounded crew members filed in, carried by nurses and doctors wearing magnetic boots, and the medics strapped them into cots. Most were unconscious—drugged to kill their pain. Maung couldn't stand seeing the ones who were missing limbs and he shut his eyes, not wanting to witness the results of his decisions and not wanting more memories of war superimposed on the ones he already carried. Sometimes the wounded woke up. It took a minute or so for the attending bot to float over and administer more painkiller, a minute or so of screaming and groaning that Maung knew was his fault.

His guards finally got Maung out of sick bay when they notified the admiral that the doctors had placed him in the main treatment room where any number of people could see him. Back in his compartment, Maung sighed. The hum of machinery drowned out any other noise and the red stains on the floor and walls suggested that he'd lost more blood than he realized. A massive four meter by four meter patch had been welded to the wall, covering the hole punched by the portion of the enemy missile that had penetrated.

"You're lucky the semi-awares dumped the air out of here," one of the guards said. "They created a vacuum just before the missiles hit."

Maung looked at him with a blank face. "Overpressure?"

"Yeah. I've seen missile strikes on ships before and if you're not wearing Marine armor, the overpressure inside compartments liquefies your internal organs."

"That's a really pleasant topic," the other guard said.

"I'm just stating a fact. I didn't mean anything by it."

"It's OK," Maung said. "I knew that already anyway."

Maung tried to plug in, thinking that maybe linking with the semi-awares again would distract him with news of the Fleet or of Earth. But he couldn't access. Every time he tried to link a signal pinged, indicating that he wasn't authorized.

"They're blocking me," Maung said. "Do you guys know why?"

"Fleet locked everything down for an internal investigation. Everything is frozen. We can't even get coms to Mars right now."

The other one nodded. "Only the captain knows what's going on. We have to just wait for him to come back."

"Where is he?" asked Maung.

"Europa. With the surviving Marines and a refill crew. All three remaining ships are overloaded with people and have almost no fuel or air left so he took them to Europa to melt ice and process it for hydrogen and oxygen."

"Any chance of another Chinese attack?"

The guard shook his head. "I doubt it. They're all halfway to Earth by now and it looks like the Chinese are bugging out."

Maung shrugged. "You mean they *bugged* out."

"No, I mean *from Earth*. Their command—the elites and a large military force—are leaving Earth, abandoning the rest of the Chinese people to rot in underground cities planetside. We just got reports that the thing they're building at their elevator is some kind of deep-space vessel."

Maung processed the data. It made sense for the Chinese to run now, because the Sommen were going to slaughter them anyway. Plus they'd just lost a major battle, one that would cut them off from the rest of the solar system and revoke their access to the biggest supply of fuel off Earth. Maung factored in a million different variables. A full statistical analysis took a few minutes but at the end of it he had his answer: The Chinese had likely been planning a departure since the Sommen first arrived, long before they'd been warned against continuing with their man-machine creations.

"Maung?" the guard asked.

"What?"

"Any idea why the Chinese would leave Earth?"

Maung shook his head. "No clue," he lied.

The refueling operation took more than twenty-four hours, and by the end of it Maung almost couldn't sit still. Nang was on Mars. And he never got a chance to send a message to his son, on Earth— one he had prepared when he first took control of the Fleet—so when after ten hours his leg improved, Maung began harassing the captain and asking for access to the *Langley*'s network. The captain never responded.

Maung was asleep when a coded message came in, and one of the guards jiggled him awake, handing him the cable link. He jacked it in. Maung was still half-asleep when the semi-awares guided him through the coms link and before he could ready himself, the Old Man stared at him.

"Is everything OK with Nang?" Maung asked.

The Old Man nodded. "It's fine. We just got something puzzling and wondered if you and the *Langley* command semi-awares could give a shot at analyzing it. We have an idea down here, but we need a second opinion."

"Sure," said Maung. "Send it over."

As soon as the transmission played, Maung recognized it, without running it through a formal analysis. He couldn't decipher the language. But the spectrum was identical to what he observed in Charleston and there was no mistaking the guttural sounds mixed with hisses and clicks.

"It's Sommen," said Maung.

It took a second for the transmission to reach the Old Man, and a second for his response; he looked shocked. "You sure? You've only had it for a few seconds."

"I'm sure. It's exactly like the emissions I recorded from the one at the Charleston spaceport. Where did you get this?"

"It originated from the Kuiper belt. Near Karin. An automated reconnaissance platform picked it up and it sat in the Mars storage banks for a while waiting to be analyzed; we're lucky to have intercepted it. It was tight beam and they sent it right after you found the bodies on Ganymede."

Maung shivered. He couldn't see the empty space around the ship and now the blindness made him feel vulnerable, and he imagined that every moon, asteroid, and planet could hide unknown numbers of Sommen. *They were there.*

"They're watching us," Maung said.

"Yeah." The Old Man paused to whisper something off camera then turned back to Maung. "One of our fast scout ships should be arriving at Fleet in the next hour. It's there for you. We need you back on Mars now so we can get to work; who knows how long it will take for the remaining Fleet ships to move out of Europa's orbit; we can't wait that long."

Maung sighed, relieved. He agreed with the Old Man, pulled out the cord, and slammed his helmet on. One of the guards asked what was up. After he told them, the men took his arms and guided Maung into the corridor.

"Thank God we're getting out of here," one of them said. "The *Langley* is a freakin' missile magnet. You should have seen this ship get hit from the perspective of the lifeboats."

Maung slept for most of the trip back. But whenever awake, he couldn't stop thinking about his family and his thoughts spun out of control, flicking back and forth between his mother and son, and then Nang and his unborn child. *I will never see Charleston again*, he realized. It was too late now; he'd made the deal with the Old Man, but he had to convince them to let him send the message to his son— one last contact. But then maybe it *wasn't* a good idea; Maung knew how he would feel if his father had disappeared voluntarily and at the top of his list of likely emotions the move would evoke were hatred, betrayal, and terror. When sleep finally came, it was a welcome vacation from worry.

Nang melted into his arms. When she kissed him, Maung felt her tongue against his and they ignored the embarrassed looks from the other guards and scientists, continuing to kiss until the Old Man finally cleared his throat.

"I thought you'd get killed," Nang whispered.

He buried his nose in her hair. "I had to make it back to you guys."

The Old Man interrupted. "Listen. We have to get working."

"Working on what?" Maung asked. "We nailed the Chinese, and they're about to leave Earth for good."

"They *already* left—while you were in transit. Now we have to figure out what to do with all the ones remaining on Earth."

Maung looked at the Old Man and cocked his head. "Where will the elite go—the ones on the ship?"

"Far away," Nang said. She wouldn't let go of Maung. "We think they're headed for a wormhole near the Lupan system, but it will take forever for them to get there unless the rumors are true—that they developed a new drive."

Maung was still confused. He glanced at the Old Man and then back at Nang, and the Old Man must have figured out what was bothering him. He put a hand on Maung's shoulder and squeezed.

"We already notified your son and mother, Maung. They've been moved to a neighborhood in the Virginia suburbs of DC. You should see their house; it's huge. And we forwarded your message—the one you stored on the *Langley*."

Maung blinked against tears, and Nang squeezed him tightly. "Is he OK?" he asked.

"He's sad," the Old Man said, looking away. "But you're making the same decision I would. Someday, when he's older and maybe